The Wonderland Effect

by Robert Arrington

The Wonderland Effect

By Robert Arrington

Cover Design: Diane Gronas

https://dianegronas.com/

Published July 2015 by Robert Arrington

Copyright © 2015 by Robert Arrington

ISBN: 978-0-9861765-1-7

Table of Contents

CHAPTER ONE

A Very Un-merry Birthday

July, 2005

The cake was beautiful. The frosting was pale lavender, serving as a canvas for a depiction of Mulan and Mushu the dragon sitting beneath a cherry tree. The delicate limbs, rendered in piped brown icing, were covered with hundreds of pale cherry blossoms. It had taken Alice's mother hours to create.

Alice hated it.

Not that Alice disliked Mulan, but her mother had simply selected the theme for Alice's ninth birthday party based on the chance discovery of some closeout merchandise on a web site. She had shown Alice the cups and plates when she got home from school the day they arrived.

"Look, Alice, your party settings came today. Who do you want to invite?"

Alice had been speechless. Mom knew what she wanted, and this wasn't it. "Mulan?" she finally wailed after several seconds. "But I wanted..."

"I know what you wanted," Mom interrupted. "But I refuse to indulge you in this Wonderland mania any longer. It's time to move on. You and your normal friends will still have plenty of fun, you'll see."

Alice stomped her foot. "No, we won't. It's not fair."

1

"That's enough, Alice. You're lucky to be getting a party at all, what with your other friends popping in unannounced and unwanted all the time."

"They would fit in at a Wonderland party," Alice dared to suggest.

"A six-foot housecat doesn't fit in anywhere. And don't even get me started on the rabbits. It's only because your father promised to be here that we're doing this at all. Now, what's it going to be? Mulan, or a nice quiet day at home? Alone."

Alice visibly wilted. "Mulan," she mumbled miserably. Any excuse to have people over was a good thing. At least it meant Mom and Dad wouldn't be shouting at each other for a few hours.

To Alice, it seemed like they had disagreed about almost everything for as long as she could remember. There was a brief time after she accidentally poisoned herself on her eighth birthday when their mutual concern over her had brought about a truce.

But then Alice had started displaying a number of paranormal powers. In a short time, she found herself experiencing many of the same effects that the storybook Alice had encountered. Plus, the characters from Carroll's books became frequent visitors in the Littleton household. Alice felt special and loved exploring her new abilities.

Her parents reacted very differently. Her father was worried someone would take her away to study like a lab rat. Her mother just seemed frightened they would all be labeled freaks. Both agreed that she should keep her abilities a secret and made her promise not to use her powers where outsiders could see. She did her best, but sometimes her special friends popped up at the worst possible time. Ches, especially, seemed to delight in pushing the bounds of safety by appearing behind people, only to disappear when they looked his way. So far, no one had gotten a clear look at her companions, or connected her with any of the unusual things that sometimes happened, but the tension level at home

2

was almost unbearable. Mom, especially, hated the whole mixed-up package of Alice's powers, and tended to snap at her over the least little display.

Sometimes, Alice almost wished someone would discover her secret. It couldn't be worse than the stress of constantly trying to hide what she could do.

Once Mom had attained victory in dictating the party theme, she seemed content to let Alice figure out what she wanted to do during the event. She promised to take care of food and the cake, but then simply told Alice to get approval for any money she wanted to spend on games and activities.

Over the next couple of weeks, life in the Littleton home proceeded as normal. This meant Dad split his time almost equally between the university and his study, Mom spent hours prowling the malls without finding anything that pleased her, and Alice tried to come up with party games that didn't seem too lame.

Alice quickly enlisted her best friend, Miranda Sullivan, to help plan the party. Miranda had been present when Alice's first ability had activated, so she was in on the family secret. Together with Ches, Hatter, and Marchie, the girls took refuge in Alice's bedroom after school, tossing out ideas while watching the movie on DVD.

Miranda sucked thoughtfully on the end of a lock of her coppery hair as the movie started playing through for the second time. "Maybe we could build a Great Wall out of cardboard boxes in the backyard," she suggested.

"Where would we get them?" Alice asked after some thought. "There would have to be a lot of them. Then we'd have to get rid of them after."

Miranda grimaced. "Yeah, sounds like a lot of work."

Marchie plucked a cube from his ever-present sugar bowl and threw it at Miranda. However, the hare's large floppy ears fell forward over his eyes as he released it, so it simply glanced off the dresser beside her head.

"No good," he exclaimed, though whether he was referring to Miranda's idea or his aim was unclear.

"Marchie, stop that at once, or it's back to Wonderland with you!" Alice chided.

Marchie pouted until he got hit in the face with Alice's stuffed monkey, Barrello, which Miranda had used to return fire. He immediately became immersed in grooming the toy, picking imaginary parasites from its head and flicking them away while muttering, "Flee, foolish fleas" over and over.

"I wish I could run away," Alice sighed from where she slouched in the one chair her room offered. "We've watched the whole movie and still haven't come up with anything good."

"We could still do Pin the Tail on Mushu," Miranda suggested half-heartedly.

"How exciting," Ches chimed in. "Perhaps we should have medics standing by in case someone needs oxygen."

"Sourpuss," Miranda accused, sticking her tongue out at the huge cat stretched out on Alice's bed. Ches merely closed his eyes and purred contentedly.

Hatter paced in the small area by the bedroom door. Deep in thought, he twirled his pocket watch on its chain around his index finger, reversing its direction each time the chain became completely wrapped up. "Perhaps we should get advice from a professional," he said.

"We can't afford that," Miranda replied. "Those people have had so much training, they charge way too much for their time."

4

Mom snorted in irritation as she set the hot dogs on the table and glanced at her preparations. "Well don't do that once your other guests start arriving," she said. "I've got to set out the chips and the condiments for the hot dogs." With that, she disappeared back into the kitchen.

"Well, it's a good thing Wonderland isn't known for its crickets," said a cultured voice from the living room. "It would be rude of you to ignore your friends."

The girls rushed over to the doorway stared through it at Ches. The six-foot long, gray and black feline was stretched out on the couch like it was a throne.

"What are you doing here?" she said in a frightened whisper. "I told you that you weren't invited. If Mom sees you, she'll completely wig out."

The Cheshire Cat cocked his head to one side as he regarded Alice. "Do you really think she'd start throwing hairpieces out the window? That would be something to see."

"That's not what I meant and you know it."

Ches let that pass. "Your mother is the one who doesn't want me here. Even queens can't command cats, so why would she expect me to listen to her? Anyway, what sort of friends would we be if we missed your party?"

"The kind of friends who don't want to see me grounded for a month."

"Tish tosh, you've a whole world open to you whenever you like, and there's not a thing she can do to keep you from it," he replied.

"I can't stay there forever, and she can do anything she wants to make me miserable once I get home," Alice countered. "Please, you've got to go before she sees you."

"As ever, your wish is my command," Ches replied sarcastically as he began to fade from view. "But remember, you've been saying for weeks that you want this party to be memorable."

"That's not quite what I said," Alice exclaimed, but it was too late. Ches was gone.

Miranda stared at the spot the feline had just vacated. "That doesn't sound good."

Alice nodded in agreement. "You've got to help me. If any more of them show up, we've got to keep them out of sight."

"I'll try, but that lot's not going to be easy to hide," Miranda said with a grimace. "At least Ches fades in gradually most of the time. How are we going to explain it if Hatter suddenly crashes the party in front of everyone?"

Alice was prevented from answering by the doorbell. Over the course of the next several minutes, the remainder of her guests arrived. After her mother served everyone hot dogs and drinks, they moved into the living room with their plates, where everything was quickly consumed.

As she was finishing her own food, Alice heard a new voice from the hall leading towards her father's study. "Well, this lot is lazy, make no mistake about it. Probably wouldn't last ten minutes in the pool of tears," it muttered.

Alice scrambled to her feet and signaled Miranda with a quick wave. As her friend drew everyone's attention back towards the dining room with the call "Let's play a game!" Alice quietly entered the hallway to confront the Dodo.

"Cheerio," the bird said as he removed his pipe from his beak. Somehow, his wing managed to secure a grasp on the object. "You and your friends look like you need a bit of exercise, eh? What would you say to a rousing caucus race? Just the thing to get the blood pumping."

"I'd say 'Not today', that's what," Alice responded crossly. "You've got to go."

"Hrumph! Well, I guess I know when I'm not wanted. I stopped by to say 'Happy Birthday', and here's the thanks I get."

"I'm sorry. Thanks, but please, you've got to go before someone else sees you."

"Oh, very well. But mind you, be nicer to the others." A moment later, the Dodo disappeared, leaving behind only a puff of smoke from his pipe.

Alice returned to the living room. Miranda's suggestion for a game had floundered, since she hadn't been able to come up with a suggestion the other girls liked. However, the distraction had worked, and that's what Alice considered important.

In the lull that followed, Alice's mother stepped into the room. She was wearing a thrown-together costume that still managed to evoke a sense of a Chinese officer's tunic and leggings. A thin mustache with tightly curled ends drawn with an eyebrow pencil completed the effect. Alice's father had planned to play the part of the officer. Although her mother had agreed to step in when he found he couldn't be there, Alice sensed that Mom didn't have to try very hard to act condescending and put upon as she addressed the recruits.

"All right, conscripts, enough gabbing! Form a line!" The girls readily lined up facing Alice's mother as she paced before them with a scowl on her face.

"What a pathetic bunch this is," she sighed. "We have a war to fight, and this is what I'm given to work with. Well, I'll whip you into the best shape I can in the time we have. Maybe some of you will survive. Now follow me, single file."

The girls dutifully marched after her as she led them out into the back yard, where Alice and Miranda had set up a sort of obstacle course, beginning with an archery station. Two cardboard targets with cutout circles stood about 10 feet away from a firing line where two toy archery sets lay waiting.

Alice's mother continued her spiel. "You're definitely not ready to take on the Mongol horde in hand-to-hand combat, so let's see how you do with a bow. I think your best shot at surviving this war is to make sure the enemy never gets close to you. We'll start with you, conscript," she said, pointing to Alice. "What's your name?"

"Alice," she replied without thinking. She was too busy looking around for party crashers.

"Isn't that a girl's name?" her mother snarled, eyes narrowing.

Alice blushed as the other girls giggled. "Um, sorry. My name is Alvin."

"All right, Alvin, you take position here." She pointed at Miranda, who was next in line. "What's your name, conscript?"

"Randy, sir."

"OK, Randy, you take the other station. You've each got three arrows. Put as many as you can through the holes in the target, then retrieve your arrows for the next shooters. Got that? Good. Proceed."

Alice and Miranda picked up their bows, nocked an arrow apiece, and addressed the targets. Miranda put two of her arrows through the holes, but Alice's first two shots went well off to the side before she managed to send the final arrow through her target. The girls ran to retrieve their arrows.

"Alice, what's going on? You weren't even trying," Miranda accused as she knelt next to her to pick up one of the arrows.

10

"Didn't you see it? There was a rocking-horse-fly hovering beside the target. I was trying to shoo it away before anyone else noticed."

"Oh, well, I guess it worked, because I don't see it now."

They hurried back to the firing line and handed off the arrows to Lisa and Kyra. Once they were done, Heather and Cathy took their turns. Cathy and Kyra were declared the joint winners of the competition, both having achieved perfect scores.

"All right, listen up, recruits. There's more to survival than being good with a bow. You're going to need to know how to move through terrain without being spotted. That will require strength and discipline." Alice's mother held up two paper strips with those words written on them. She gestured towards a large inflatable play area erected near the archery range. It consisted of a flat bouncing area with several posts projecting up from it in staggered rows. Additional slips of paper were scattered throughout the bounce area. On the far side, a ladder built into the side of the play area lead to the top of a 20-foot slide.

"You will enter the forest in order of your performance on the archery range. Once you have proven your worth there," and Mom shook the paper slips she held suggestively, "You will proceed over the mountain to our next camp. No doubt you'll be hungry by then. Unfortunately, the Huns raided our supply caravan. That means you'll have to catch fish to eat, or you'll just go hungry."

She stepped over to a plastic wading pool filled with water and scooped up short tube made of thin rubber, slightly thicker than a balloon. The tube was shaped like a cylinder with a hole through it lengthwise where the rubber wrapped around to form a sort of elongated donut. It was filled with water, which made the tube hard to hold onto even when it was dry. Wet, it was nearly impossible to grip. The one Alice's mother had picked up squirted out of her grasp to splash back

11

into the pool. "As you can see, they're slippery devils. Nevertheless, I expect each of you to catch three."

"Next, we'll be going on a nice cross-country run to build up endurance. When we get to the river, you'll need to hop across the pilings. If you end up in the river, you'll be swept back to the starting line by the current and you'll have to start again." As she explained this task, Alice's mother paced alongside a course marked out on the ground by yellow string stung between wooden stakes. The pilings were just cardboard circles spaced far enough apart to pose a bit of a challenge to the recruits' jumping skills. The river was marked out with blue string and more stakes.

"Finally, when I judge you are ready, we will take the battle to the enemy." The last station was beneath a tree, where a piñata resembling a hulking barbarian hung, awaiting the young soldiers' wrath.

Once she was sure everyone understood the course, Alice's mother started Cathy and Kyra off, making each subsequent group after the first wait thirty seconds before they followed the group ahead of them. Alice entered the forest last, and alone.

By this time, she was frantic with worry. It was only a matter of time before another of her companions barged in unannounced. Hatter wouldn't be so bad; he could always be passed off as an eccentric relative. But too many of Wonderland's creatures were humanized animals or other things that could not be explained away as elaborate costumes. Their features were too expressive for that to be believable. Alice hadn't considered that when she was holding out for the Wonderland theme, but now she realized that her mother was right. If they appeared before her schoolmates, they would frighten most of them.

Alice had found three "discipline" slips and discarded two of them before she finally found one that said "strength" and headed towards the ladder. Then she had a sudden flash of inspiration. If she went into the house, pretending to need to visit the bathroom, she could go to her room and summon her companions one by one. If she let them have their way and wish her a happy birthday, maybe they'd stay away long enough to let her finish the party and send her guests home. She started up the ladder intent on carrying out her plan.

However, she never got the chance to put it to the test. As she clambered onto the slide, she heard two excited voices by the tree where the piñata was hung.

"Let the ruffian have it!" called the first.

"Give him what for!" answered the second.

A quick glance confirmed Alice's fears. The Tweedles, two rotund, short boys in school uniforms, were dancing around the paper-mâché Mongol, whacking him with their crude wooden swords for all they were worth. Everyone was already aware of them, thanks to the racket they were making, so there was no chance of getting rid of them without some sort of explanation. Fortunately, they looked human and Alice had almost a year's worth of experience in explaining away her unexpected visitors.

Alice dove down the slide and hurried over to the tree, arriving about the same time as everyone else.

"Boys, stop," Alice demanded, but it was too late. Ghengis Khan gave up the fight and candy spilled on the ground.

"What are they doing here?" Mom said through clenched teeth, her face flushed.

"We're defending the realm," Tweedledee exclaimed gleefully.

"You should thank us," Tweedledum crowed.

"But you're not supposed to be here!" Alice's mother shouted.

"It was his idea," Tweedledum said, pointing at his brother.

13

"No how," countered the other. "I followed him."

"Who are you?" Heather asked. "I don't recognize either of you."

"They're our neighbors, uh, from down the street." Alice said.

"They go to a private school," Miranda added.

"Mom's right. You were not invited. I promised you I'd save you each a piece of cake, but you can forget about that now. Look at what you've done; our game is ruined!"

"Get out of here at once," Mom said, her voice shaking in anger. Alice winced, knowing very well who was going to be the target of all that emotion once the party was over. Maybe if she did a good job of covering up, she'd only be stuck at home for three weeks.

"Who wants cake?" Alice asked the other girls brightly. "No sense in letting this ruin the whole party. Boys, you just let yourselves out the side gate, and don't think your mother won't hear about this."

Alice, her mother, and Miranda started gently prodding the girls back towards the house. After a few steps, Lisa looked back and gasped.

"Where did they go? Those boys just disappeared," she exclaimed.

"Don't be silly. They just ducked through the side gate, like Alice told them to," Miranda said.

"How could they have got there so quickly? We only just turned away from them."

"They know they're in trouble," Alice said. "Nothing like guilt to make someone move quickly."

14

Thankfully, Lisa just shrugged and continued back towards the house. Mom grabbed Alice by the shoulder, holding her back as the others started filing through the door.

"I told you to keep your friends away. Do you have any idea what will happen if anyone sees something we can't explain away?"

"I'm sorry. You know they don't always listen to me. I'm doing my best."

"Well, do better. Let's wrap this party up as quickly as we can, before you broadcast our secret to the entire neighborhood."

Alice considered asking her mother for a few minutes to summon her friends in private, but the look on her mother's face made her decide against it. She simply nodded and followed her mother inside.

When Alice walked into the dining room, she noticed that the cricket she had spoken to earlier had roused the rest into a mob and was leading them in a chant.

"What do we want?"

"FREEDOM!"

"When do we want it?"

"NOW!"

Miranda picked up on the peculiar rhythmic quality to the chirping and glanced at Alice with questioning eyes, but Alice gave her a quick shake of her head. She'd fill her friend in on the revolt later. Right now, there were more important things to do.

Mom wasted no time. "Gather round the table, girls. We'll sing "Happy Birthday" as soon as I light the candles.

She quickly removed a match from a box beside the cake and struck it on the side of the box. But it never got near the candles. As the

15

match flared to life, a sugar cube came flying through the air and dashed the match out of her fingers, instantly snuffing it out.

"Oh, no," said Alice.

She turned towards the living room doorway, as did everyone else. The only difference was that Alice, her mother, and Miranda already knew what they would see. To the rest of the group, the rather scruffy-looking hare standing just inside the room was a complete shock. He stood about four feet tall from the crown of his head to his oversized feet. His ears, which were very long, only added a few inches to his overall height, however, because they drooped down in front of him, framing a face that wore an anxious, yet angry expression. He wore patched clothing reminiscent of an earlier era, and in his left hand, he held his large, multicolored sugar bowl.

"Wishes should be honored," he whispered tensely, but his eyes seemed unfocused, almost as if he were talking to himself.

Kyra stared at the impossible creature for a moment longer. Then, unable to reconcile what she was seeing with her sense of reality, she screamed and backed up rapidly. As she did, her foot caught on the area rug and she stumbled into the sideboard. The party favor bags and cricket cages fell to the floor. The impact caused the bamboo to flex and the doors to the cages popped open.

"Freedom! Scatter and find a way outside," cried the cricket Alice had spoken to earlier. The hopping insects startled several of the other girls, who gave out yelps and exclamations as they tried to dodge them. Alice moved quickly to calm Marchie, who didn't tend to respond well to sudden noise and activity. Sure enough, his eyes wide with sudden fear, the hare began hurling sugar cubes at random as quickly as he could. One bounced off Alice's forehead just before she reached him.

Lisa made a break for the front door, but ended up crashing into Hatter, who suddenly appeared in front of her. The two fell in a tangle of arms, legs, and tea things. Meanwhile, Kyra regained her

16

balance and turned for the kitchen, only to pull up short as a woman with an oversized head and carrying a large peppermill stepped through the swinging door. The Duchess's cook took one look at the cake and offered her expert opinion.

"It needs pepper," she declared, and swung her mill, dispensing a huge cloud of the spice over the cake, and filling the air in the immediate area. Alice's mother, Heather, and Kyra were quickly overcome by fits of sneezing and coughing. Miranda, who had been rushing forward to try to usher the cook back into the kitchen was also engulfed.

"Marchie, it's all right," Alice said in the most soothing voice she could manage under the circumstances. She finally managed to catch hold of the hare's right hand. "Calm down. I'm here; you'll be all right."

For just a moment, Marchie seemed to focus on her and she thought he would settle. But then the Dormouse surfaced in the punch bowl and looked around sleepily, yawning hugely. Cathy reacted as though she thought the Dormouse was trying to attack. She screamed and dove under the table, bumping the leg as she went. This caused the Dormouse to overbalance and he fell sideways, upsetting the punch bowl. A miniature flood was released across the tabletop, pooling where the tablecloth had bunched up.

Marchie stilled for just a moment and then screeched "No!" He hurled the entire sugar bowl, whether at Kim or the Dormouse Alice couldn't tell. It landed squarely on the cake, sending blobs of icing arcing outwards.

♠ ♣ ♥ ♦

Alice sat on the floor by the sideboard with her knees drawn up to her forehead. Her recollections of what had happened after the cake was destroyed were kind of fuzzy. A few images stood out in her mind, but for the most part she couldn't put them in order. She remembered several card soldiers marching through the room, their pasteboard bodies severely overbalanced by their long spears. A chess bishop had been lecturing Lisa on proper movement, insisting that she move a single floor tile at a time like a proper young pawn. The thing that finally broke the logjam at the doors was when Ches appeared and started stalking one of the crickets. The guests had found the strength to push all of the Wonderland creatures aside at that, and the room had emptied almost instantaneously.

Miranda had offered to stay, but there really wasn't much she could do. Alice guided her out the door, telling her she would see her at school on Monday. Then she had gone back to the dining room to face her mother's anger.

By the time she got there, all of her Wonderland companions had disappeared. Her mother was simply staring at the room. Most of the balloons were popped and several of the rice sacks had broken open, scattering their contents across the floor. Her presents were all on the floor, partially crushed with rips in the wrapping paper. In the relative silence, the chirping crickets sounded deafening.

"Mom, I'm so sor..." she began, but cut off mid-word at the look her mother gave her. It was a look she usually reserved for homeless people she encountered on the street. She didn't say a word, but simply walked out of the room and up the stairs. Soon, the sounds of dresser drawers and closet doors being forcefully opened and closed drifted downstairs. Alice trembled and sank to the floor, tears streaming down her face as she began to guess what those sounds meant.

She was still there, arms wrapped around her knees, when she heard her father's car pulling into the driveway. A minute later, he opened the door and stepped into the entry hall, where he stopped short in stunned disbelief at the scene laid out before him. Then he moved forward as quickly as his cane and injured leg allowed, and bent down to grasp Alice's shoulder.

"Sweetheart, what's happened? Are you hurt?"

Alice looked up, shaking her head slightly. "Oh, Daddy, I'm so sorry. I couldn't control them. I tried to keep them away, but they just kept coming. And now Mom..." She broke down in fresh sobs, unable to look her father in the face any longer.

He patted her on the back ineffectually. "Now don't get worked up over nothing. I'll go talk to her and we'll sort this all out. You'll see."

Alice knew better, but said nothing as her father straightened up and turned towards the stairs. He stopped as he reached the base and saw his wife coming down, wrestling an over-stuffed suitcase step by step with one hand while her other arm was clutching a jewelry box that had bits and ends of several necklaces hanging out of the partially closed lid.

"Meredith, what..." was all he managed to say before she unleashed her anger on him.

"Don't you dare, Arthur!" she shouted. "I've had it. You just had to go off to your precious meeting and leave me here to deal with your daughter and her sprites or demons or whatever. Well, I'm not hanging around to deal with the fallout. You two can figure out what you want to tell everyone to try and explain away this fiasco, but I won't stay here another minute!"

He looked dazed. "But where will you go?"

"I'm moving in with Alan."

"Dr. Casey?"

"Oh, don't act so surprised. You can't possibly be that clueless. On the other hand, you're so lost in your work, maybe you are. Anyway, my lawyer will be in touch."

Alice's father trailed after her mother as she stormed out of the house. The sounds of their argument faded to unintelligibility as they moved away from the front door.

Left alone in the room, Alice looked around. She couldn't bear to face her father when he returned. She considered jumping to Wonderland, but the idea seemed too cowardly. It would be like turning her back on her responsibility for what had just happened. But there was another option.

Alice picked up a paper cup from the floor. It was empty, but as she reached for the table to pull herself upright, the tablecloth shifted, releasing a quantity of punch that had pooled in its folds. She caught a bit of it in her cup as it trickled down the surface towards the floor. Then she quickly drank the contents.

Action and intent brought about the desired result as Alice and her clothes began to shrink. In seconds, she was three inches tall, small enough to crawl under the decorative cutout at the base of the sideboard. She moved all the way to the back edge and slumped in a corner, noting only then that she was not alone.

"Whoa! You look wrung out," the cricket chirped. "Did they have you locked in a cage, too? You look kinda familiar."

Alice sighed and turned her back on the insect, who took the hint and left her alone. When her father came back inside, calling for her, she did not respond. She stayed beneath the sideboard all night, consumed by her guilt and serenaded by occasional chirps from her companion.

CHAPTER TWO

A Shocking Discovery

October, 2012

FBI Agent Gerald Hightower had seen just about everything in 12 years on the job. He had seen people abused, abducted, and murdered for every conceivable motive. Money and power were often at the root of it, of course; sometimes it was even something that masqueraded in the perp's mind as love. He had faced it all unflinchingly, secure in the knowledge that he had the fortitude to face down the worst humanity could dish up, expose the truth, and do his part to serve up justice. He was confident and proud.

Tonight, he was scared.

He ran through the deserted pre-dawn streets as a steady rain did its best to wash the grit from the streets of this small California town. The Bureau maintained a safe house nearby, and Agent Hightower prayed he would be able to reach it. He paused for a moment in the deepest shadows of a storefront's doorway to check behind him for signs of pursuit. Nothing stirred.

Without further hesitation, Hightower resumed his run for safety. He reached the front door of the safe house without incident and let himself in. After turning on a table lamp he conducted a quick search of the premises to make sure he was alone. Finally, he allowed himself to collapse into an armchair.

He took out a hip flask and took a hard pull on the contents. Ordinarily, he would feel guilty about drinking on the job, but this was a

21

special occasion. He needed to report back to his boss in the San Francisco field office, but he wasn't sure how he could without sounding like a raving lunatic. He needed time to think.

Twenty minutes later, he was no closer to finding a solution to his problem, and a combination of the whiskey and post-adrenaline-rush crash were close to putting him to sleep where he sat. But he instantly jerked back to full consciousness as a knock sounded at the front door.

Hightower drew his gun in a smooth, practiced action and thumbed the safety off, thankful that even in his current state he hadn't allowed himself to hit the flask too heavily. Easing over to the window, he cautiously twitched the edge of the curtain aside to get a look at the doorstep. There was definitely someone there, but he hadn't turned on the porch light, so what illumination reached the figure from a nearby street light only served to cast his face in deeper shadow. He soft-stepped to put the wall to the right of the door to his back before calling out, "Who's there?"

"Hightower, is that you?" came the reply. "It's me, Oglethorpe."

Hightower exhaled in relief. Oglethorpe was a fellow FBI agent out of the Sacramento office. Strictly speaking, he was out of his territory, which was why he and Hightower had agreed to work together when the path of their respective investigations crossed in the field. Maybe Oglethorpe had discovered something that would help him make sense of this mess. He eased open the door, confirmed that Oglethorpe was alone, and only then reset the safety and put his gun away.

Oglethorpe pushed through the door, giving Hightower an appraising look as he passed him on his way to the living room. He was a short, pudgy man wearing a rumpled black suit and tie with a plain white dress shirt. All of the clothes looked about two sizes too big on him, and the shirt and tie bore traces of his last several meals. He sported a two-day growth of beard. "You look like hell warmed over," he noted.

"If you'd seen what I've seen, you wouldn't look this good."

"Tell me about your day. I've hit nothing but dead ends."

Hightower considered the agent on the sofa. He was going to have to try to explain what he had discovered to someone, sooner or later. Practicing on an agent he probably wouldn't have to work with again seemed as good an opening as he was likely to get.

"Okay, but I'll tell you now, you're not going to believe me. I almost don't believe it myself. We've stumbled onto something bigger than either of us guessed.

"After we compared notes this afternoon, I decided to follow up on a lead I had turned up in relation to our human trafficking gang. In that type of business, there's always a need to get rid of witnesses, or victims who are no longer useful to the cartel. I'd heard about some suspicious activities near a warehouse on the edge of town. I decided to poke around and see if I could turn up any signs of anything unusual."

Oglethorpe frowned at him. "Why didn't you tell me about this?"

"I considered it weak; it could have anything. You had your own leads, so I didn't mention it. Now I wish I had."

"Hrmph. So what did you find? Not a body or you'd still be there processing the scene."

"Actually, you're not far off. I walked in on an execution."

"You're kidding me."

"No, seriously. I was parked down the street, staking the place out and trying to decide on the best way in if I needed it, when I saw a limo pull out of a side street and approach. The door went up and the limo pulled in, There was a van already there, and as the warehouse

23

door closed, I thought I got a glimpse of some poor slob being pulled out of the van with his hands tied."

"So naturally you called for backup."

"Yeah, I called it in. But I figured the prisoner was a goner if I waited, so I entered by myself through a side door."

"Picked the lock, I assume?"

"Actually, I didn't have to. It was already unlocked."

"Hrmph, pretty sloppy."

"Yeah, God bless the criminal mindset. Anyway, as soon as I got inside I heard voices and went to investigate. Sure enough, there was some tall, heavyset guy in a black suit questioning the victim I'd spotted. He was tied to a chair. I started working my way around the perimeter, using the racks in the warehouse for cover, trying to get a good look at the interrogator."

"What was he asking the prisoner about?"

"I couldn't catch most of it. The guy in the suit was talking in a threatening whisper. Playing for psychological advantage, I guess. But I caught something like 'your son' at one point. Could have been threatening to hurt or kidnap the prisoner's son if he didn't cooperate. Maybe he had already kidnapped the kid and was dealing with a failed rescue attempt."

"That's all you got?"

"No, just wait; I'm getting to the unbelievable part. I had only gotten about halfway to the position I had picked out for myself, when Mr. Suit says 'Okay, cut him loose.' At first I thought I must have heard him wrong, but sure enough the hired help cut the guy's ropes and let him up off the chair. He seemed pretty surprised, I'll tell you."

"They just let him go? That is unbelievable."

24

Hightower shook his head. "I didn't say they let him go."

"So what happened?"

Hightower closed his eyes, seeing the sequence of events all over again in his mind. "Mr. Suit just pointed at the guy and kind of flicked his wrist to point up, and the prisoner vanished."

There was a long moment of silence before Oglethorpe said, "Come again?"

"He vanished. As in there one moment, not there the next. I can't explain it, and believe me, I've tried to figure this out since it happened. The floor of the warehouse was poured concrete; they didn't drop him through a trap door or anything like that. I think...I think Mr. Suit disintegrated him."

"That's crazy talk."

"God, I know what it sounds like. That's the only reason I haven't reported in yet. I keep trying to come up with some explanation that makes sense so I don't come off like a nutcase."

"What happened to the backup you called in?"

"I don't know. I was so surprised by what I saw I dropped my gun. It sounded like a truck dumping a load of scrap metal in that empty warehouse, and they were after me in a moment. I knew I didn't want whatever happened to the prisoner to happen to me, so I scooped up my gun and ran. I made it to my car and managed to get in and get it started before Mr. Suit and his henchmen came running out the side door after me."

"I didn't see your car outside," Oglethorpe noted.

Hightower nodded. "I didn't get very far in it. I was facing towards the group from the warehouse, so I had to spin it around. I had just gotten pointed in the right direction when I caught a glow from behind me in the rear view. I looked up into the mirror and Mr. Suit had a hand extended in front of him; it had electricity crackling all around it. And then he threw a friggin' lightning bolt at me."

Oglethorpe blinked slowly. "A lightning bolt?"

"Yeah, a lightning bolt." Hightower's voice somehow managed to convey both weariness and a challenge. "It hit the back of the car and lifted it up off the ground. It damn near flipped it over. The bolt or the impact from hitting the ground again ruptured the gas tank. I barely managed to get out of the car before Mr. Suit ignited the pool of gasoline with another bolt. Kind of lucky, actually. They couldn't follow me immediately with all that flame between us, otherwise I'm not sure I would have got away."

Oglethorpe rubbed his jaw as he considered the agent's tale. "Okay, I'll accept that you ran into something unusual. You were shaken up pretty bad, maybe even hit your head during the crash. Maybe your mind's playing tricks with some of the details. Given time, you'll probably remember things more clearly."

Hightower opened his mouth to argue the point, but stopped before he said anything. Oglethorpe was willing to accept that something weird had happened, and realistically that was the best response he had any right to expect from the story he'd just told. If they partnered up and went back to investigate, maybe they'd figure it out in time for him to give his boss a more realistic account of events. Maybe the other agent was right and his mind was playing tricks with his memories. A part of him hoped that was the case, because the alternative was too frightening to consider.

And if that other possibility – that some gangster was running around displaying powers that defied rational explanation – turned out to be true, maybe he'd at least be able to return to the office with another credible witness to back up his report.

Oglethorpe broke into his thoughts. "By the way, did you mention me to your boss or any other agents out of your office?"

Hightower shook his head, a bit confused by the sudden switch in topic. "No, I haven't spoken to anyone since we went our separate ways earlier today. Why?" Some thought was prodding at the back of his mind, demanding attention, but Oglethorpe continued before he could coax it into clarity.

Oglethorpe waved the question away as inconsequential. "Just wondering how much of my own investigation I was going to have to explain when we check in. What about Mr. Suit? Did you get a good look at his face?"

Hightower shook his head. "No, he was facing away from me in the warehouse, and the glare from the lightning bolts washed out everything when I caught sight of him in the mirror." He stared morosely at the carpet, noticing as he did that he had tracked mud all over the place. Oglethorpe's footprints trailed his own from the door.

Hightower frowned. Something about that thought had almost brought the troublesome thought from a moment ago into focus. Then he had it. He drew his gun again and leveled it at his counterpart. His hands felt sweaty, and he felt a strong urge to put something solid at his back.

"How did you know where to find me?" he demanded. "This is an FBI safe house maintained by the San Franciso office. An agent out of Sacramento shouldn't have any knowledge of it."

Oglethorpe regarded him calmly for a moment, then sighed. "Finally put it all together, did you? Well, why not? That's why they pay you the big bucks."

Oglethorpe's right hand began to glow with a blue-white light, which quickly brightened as small arcs of electricity arced between his fingers.

Hightower fired. The whiskey and fear threw his aim off; but as close as he was he still managed to hit Oglethorpe just below the

27

jawline. But the furrow the bullet left along the side Oglethorpe's neck stopped bleeding and healed over almost instantaneously. He fired three more times, hitting the imposter in a tight grouping in the center of his chest. Hightower saw the bullet holes appear over his opponent's heart, but for all the effect they had, he might as well have been using a squirt gun. Oglethorpe merely grimaced in annoyance and flicked his hand towards Hightower, catching him with a searing bolt that slammed him against the wall before he dropped to the floor, burned and paralyzed but still alive.

Oglethorpe rose from his seat and walked towards the fallen agent, the fingers of his hand still arcing and crackling angrily. "You're right, of course. I trailed you from the warehouse. It was child's play, seeing as I could teleport from rooftop to rooftop to keep you in sight without revealing myself. I had hoped I might be able to use you to misdirect the investigation that will undoubtedly follow after you called down the troops on the warehouse, but that's not to be. So, time to tie up loose ends instead."

Oglethorpe gestured and lightning arced to the wall by the window looking out on the front yard, setting the curtains on fire. The flames quickly rose and ignited the ceiling, spreading across the room. Soon, the whole structure would be involved.

"Well, that should do it," he said to Hightower, who was desperately trying to regain control of his body. Noting the other's feeble movements, Oglethorpe shook his head. "Sorry, can't risk you making it out of here now; you know too much."

He sent another blast of energy into the prone figure, which bucked wildly for a moment before collapsing back into a motionless heap. Oglethorpe nodded to himself and took one more look around to confirm that the fire was spreading to his satisfaction.

A moment later, there was nothing but the flames and the corpse.

CHAPTER THREE
A Call to Action

Alice turned her bike onto Devonshire Drive and coasted into the Sullivans' driveway. As she came to a stop, a white-crowned sparrow glided down from a nearby treetop and perched on the handlebars.

"Good morning, Hopwing," Alice said. She had named the bird after his tendency to flap his wings even when he was just making a short jump along the ground to get to another seed or crumb. "What are you still doing here? Wasn't your flock ready to move further south a couple of days ago?"

The bird cocked its head to the side to look at Alice and bobbed its head. "We were, before Twigbeak begged for a delay. He claims one of his wings is too sore for such a long flight."

"That's a shame," Alice said as Miranda came out the front door and collected her own bike. "If he's still not up for the trip in a couple of days, bring him by my house. I'll take care of him until he's ready to go. Maybe he can join another flock moving down from farther north."

Hopwing gave a trill that served as his laugh. "You're too kind-hearted for your own good. Don't you worry, the truth is he could go today if we really needed to be out of here. Twigbeak's just stalling."

"Why would he do that?"

"He's got his eye on a fat worm he's spotted in Mrs. Johnson's flower bed. He's been after it for almost a week now, but it keeps burrowing in just before he can get to it. It's driving him crazy. Well, I felt sorry for him, so I backed him up when he asked for more time. As long as Mrs. Willis keeps her feeder stocked, we can afford to hang around a bit longer. Until some of those other flocks arrive from the north, at any rate. It's nothing to concern yourself about."

Alice giggled in spite of herself. "Now who's too kind-hearted? I'll miss you when you go. Say good-bye to Pertfeather for me if I don't get a chance to see her before you go."

"I will," the bird replied, winging back to the trees.

Miranda wheeled her bike over to join her friend. In the years since Alice's mother had left, Miranda's coppery hair tones had deepened to a shade of red that complimented her green eyes very well. "What was that all about?" she asked.

Alice shrugged. "Politics. You see, Twigbeak..."

Miranda rolled her eyes. "Forget I asked. There's more important things to talk about. Like, when is your dad getting you a car? You've had your license two whole weeks now."

Alice shrugged and flipped her long blonde hair over her shoulder. "I don't know. He's been so busy lately. I mean, it took two months after my birthday just to get me to the DMV for my test. And now car shopping? I'll be lucky if I'm driving before you!" Alice pushed off and started down the street as Miranda fell easily into position beside her.

Miranda made a face. "Don't even joke about that. I mean, today's nice and all, but it's going to start getting cold soon, not to mention the rainy season's nearly here. We're sophomores! We're too old to be dropped off at school in Mom's van!"

"I'll try to work on him tonight. Maybe there'll be time this weekend."

"Good luck. Hey, did you check your email last night?"

Alice shook her head. "No, why?"

"He made the jump yesterday."

"Jump? Oh, that Bombgard guy?"

"Baumgartner," Miranda corrected. "Felix Baumgartner. He set a free fall parachute record from about 24 miles up and broke the sound barrier. You know Mr. Allen is going to want to talk about it in physics today. I sent you a link so you could watch the video online."

"Oh." Alice felt bad. Mr. Allen was one of her favorite teachers, and she hated to show up for his class unprepared, even though physics wasn't one of her better subjects. "Well, quick, fill me in. What do I need to know?"

"You need to know to concentrate on your school work. I can't always be there to feed you the answers."

"Okay, I promise to be good. Just give me a couple of details so I won't look like a fool."

"All right. Uhm, let's see. The balloon took just under three hours to reach jump altitude, but his descent, including time in free fall and then with his chute deployed, was a less than 10 minutes. At his fastest, he was going around 830 miles per hour, well over the speed of sound. He broke all of Kittinger's records, with the exception of the one for the longest time in freefall, which he missed by about 17 seconds."

"Kittinger. That's the Air Force guy Mr. Allen told us about?"

"Yeah. He jumped from about 19 miles up in 1960."

"How could Felix fall five miles further and spend less time in free fall? That doesn't make sense."

"Yes it does. That just shows how much faster he was traveling. Kittinger never broke the sound barrier. I think the reporters covering the jump mentioned that over 99% of the atmosphere was below the level where Felix jumped from, so there was virtually no

31

friction slowing him down until he got into denser air later in the jump. The denser air actually slowed him down to subsonic speeds before his chute deployed."

"Okay, got it. I think."

The conversation was suddenly interrupted by a klaxon sounding from Alice's pocket. She immediately braked and pulled her phone from her jeans.

Miranda frowned at her as Alice checked the screen. "Really? A Federation red alert? What kind of ring tone is that?"

Alice shook her head. "It isn't a ring tone. It goes off when there's a new Amber alert. I'm subscribed to their Twitter feed."

Miranda crossed her arms as she looked at her friend. "Tell me you're not doing what I think you're doing."

Alice looked up from her phone and shook her head. "I would, but you're too good a friend to lie to like that."

"Not the Wonderland Effect again; you've been obsessing about it for a year now. How many times do I have to tell you that's all in your mind? You are not a focus for weird events."

"How can you say that after last fall? Being held hostage by a gang of bank robbers is a bit unusual, don't you agree?"

"News flash: everyone in our class had that experience. It was a school field trip, after all."

"Yeah, but if I hadn't been there, those guys never would have wound up at the museum like that. Just think how many things had to go wrong with their escape plan to leave them stranded there, of all places."

"It was a strange chain of events," Miranda allowed, "but you can't know it wouldn't have happened the same way if you'd been home sick or something."

"But I wasn't, and because I wasn't a lot of people who might have gotten hurt, or worse, went home safe."

Miranda sighed. "But..."

Alice interrupted. "And that's not the only time I've been in a situation where my powers helped out. You know it isn't."

Miranda shook her head. "That's not the point. You've got these powers, and your special friends, and you treat the whole package like a hammer."

Alice cocked her head to the side, momentarily confused. "Huh?"

"If you only have a hammer in your toolbox, every problem looks like a nail. Although in your case, it's more a matter of ignoring anything that isn't a nail. It's not healthy."

"So what am I ignoring?"

"Life! When are you going to go on a date? Or at least show up at a school dance or football game?"

Alice shrugged. "I'm doing well enough to keep the companions in check during school hours. What would happen if one turned up at the movies while I'm with, uh, some guy?" She returned her attention to the screen on her phone.

"David Beaumont. It's okay to say his name, you know."

Alice blushed as she continued to fiddle with her phone. "Why bother? He's got a girlfriend, plus five or six wannabes just waiting for things to get rocky between them. He hardly even knows I exist."

"Well whose fault is that? You hardly talk to anyone but me. You do know you're a hottie, right? You've rejected so many advances the school's male population has withdrawn to lick their wounded pride, but with a little effort, there's no boy who could resist you, David included."

"You really think so?"

"I know so," Miranda affirmed.

"Well, I'll think about it. But right now I've got something else to do."

"Now? School's about to start!"

Alice held up the phone so Miranda could see the latest alert. "Look, I followed the link from their tweet. Billy Williams was abducted from Nelson Park yesterday evening. There's no mention of a parent or anyone they suspect of taking him. When strangers take a kid, he's almost certain to be in a lot of danger."

"I'm sure the police are doing everything they can to find him. It's not your problem. If you don't focus on your school work, repeating tenth grade could be."

"The police don't have access to the channels of information I do," Alice countered. "I'm just going to swing by the park and see what I can turn up. It won't take long." Alice put her phone away and got her bike moving again, leaving Miranda little choice but to follow.

Miranda caught up and rode in silence until they got close to the school. "Are you sure this is a good idea?" she asked.

"Billy's just six years old. And he didn't go missing halfway across the country; he was snatched right here in Vacaville. If his body turned up later and I hadn't at least tried to help, I'd never forgive myself."

Miranda thought about that for a moment. "Okay, let's go then."

"I appreciate the offer, but there's no sense in both of us getting in trouble. Dad will be mad at me, but he'll understand if I skip

34

school to help someone. But your parents will just think you're turning into a delinquent. Go on to class."

Miranda hesitated, then reluctantly nodded. "Be careful. Powers or no, you're not bulletproof."

"I will." The girls pulled up at the side street that lead to the school, and Alice gave her friend a quick hug, made slightly awkward by the fact they were still astride their bikes. Then she continued down Marshall Road towards Nelson Park while Miranda turned towards the school entrance.

♠ ♣ ♥ ♦

Gary was bored. That was something he hadn't banked on when he signed on to work for a paranormal. The discovery that there were people with actual super powers was exciting, and Oglethorpe paid his operatives well. So Gary hadn't hesitated when he was offered a slot in the organization, his mind full of super-powered battles like those he read in his comic books.

Of course, lacking any powers of his own was a drawback, but there was always hope, right? Tony Stark didn't have anything but brains and money once he took off his armored suit. Gary kept hoping he'd be given a suit, or at least a fancy blaster pistol, sooner or later. The fact that he'd never seen any evidence of any such hardware up to this point didn't worry him. If there were people who could throw lightning bolts around, there must be others who built super tech. Just stood to reason.

But for now, he was paying his dues. Which meant he was stuck here in front of Will C Wood High School, keeping watch for unusual activity from inside Oglethorpe's tricked-out van. He didn't know why his boss thought there was a paranormal lurking somewhere among the students or teachers, or even what sort of powers he should be looking for. After months of fruitless observation, all he was sure of was that he was ready for a change. His own high school days, with all the attendant make-work, weren't that far behind him, and staying this close stirred up unpleasant feelings. At least there were good tunes on the radio.

Gary scanned the stream of kids moving towards the school. First period would be starting soon, which meant he would have time to head to the store and look for some new CDs; he was bored with his old ones. Or maybe he would just stay put and browse for a new game for his iPad. Both options were equally unappealing.

His eyes came to rest on two cute girls on bikes who had stopped at the corner where a road branched off from Marshall to the school entrance. After a brief exchange, the redhead went on towards the school, but the blonde was taking off down the main road. What was she up to?

Gary weighed his options. A kid cutting class was nothing new, but if she was planning on cutting, why bother to come all the way to school before taking off for greener pastures? In the end, simple curiosity was all that prompted him to start the engine and follow.

He let the girl get a good head start before he pulled out. He'd overtake her in the van pretty quickly, and his interest would be pretty obvious if he had to keep pulling over or circling a block to keep her ahead of him too many times. But luck was with him. She wasn't going very far, and a red light allowed him to stop once without attracting attention while still keeping her in sight. So he was able to pull to the side of the road and remain unnoticed as the girl got off her bike near a playground at the park.

At the moment, the park was deserted. Gary watched his target, but did not notice anything significant for a minute. He was on the point of starting the van again and heading for the music store when it occurred to him that the girl was not behaving like a typical slacker. She didn't head for the swings or sprawl on the grass, but seemed to be moving with a purpose. He reached for a control console set between the driver's and passenger's seats and flipped a couple of switches.

A video display set in the dash came to life, showing a view straight ahead of the van. But as Gary turned a dial in the control panel, the parabolic microphone and spy camera mounted on a rotator plate on the roof of the van responded. The whole assembly had a very low profile, and a luggage rack on the roof helped hide it from casual observation. The view panned to the left until it was centered on the girl. Another switch zoomed the image in closer.

The blonde had removed a ziplock baggie from her pocket and was approaching a squirrel that was exploring a grassy area near a tree. She flicked something towards the squirrel while speaking in a light, clear voice. "Hey there, little fella, you hungry? I've got some peanuts here."

Gary grunted in disgust. There was nothing of interest here. He was reaching for the controls to switch off the surveillance equipment when her next words caused him to stop dead.

"They're all yours if you can give me a little information."

♠ ♣ ♥ ♦

The first three squirrels Alice questioned were not able to help. She left each a few peanuts by way of thanking them. She was beginning to think she was wasting her time when her luck took a turn for the better.

Skitter was a bold young male. "I think I saw the boy you described," he said. "His mother gave him some food made of hard, sweet oats."

"A granola bar?"

"I guess. Anyway, he was dropping big chunks of it all over the place, and just kind of wandering around with it while his mother

37

talked with another woman. I followed the boy to gather up all the food that was going to waste."

Alice nodded. "Great, did you see what happened to him?"

"Yeah. There was another human, a man, by the sidewalk over there. He had a puppy on a leash and was playing with it. The boy wandered over to see it. The man put the puppy in the back of his car, and the boy walked right up to it. Suddenly, the man grabbed him, pushed him in the car, and slammed the door. Then he jumped in and drove away."

"What did the car look like?"

"Light colored, but with a bumpy darker patch by one of the rear wheels. It had a high center with lower parts in front and back."

"Hmm, sounds like a light-colored sedan with a sloppy epoxy patch. Did it look something like this?" Alice drew a rough sketch on the ground with a stick.

Skitter looked at the sketch. "The patch had a rougher shape, it bulged out more on this side, and it was closer to the back of the car." He used one paw to trace the outline of the patch.

"Was it on the side the driver got in?"

"Yes."

"Thanks, you've been a great help." Alice emptied the bag of peanuts on the ground near Skitter's burrow and thought about what she had discovered. She considered calling the police with a description of the car, but she didn't know how much use it would be. Maybe there was a way to continue her investigation herself.

♠   ♣   ♥   ♦

Gary was fairly bouncing in his seat in excitement. Finally, the breakthrough he had been looking for! He would be richly rewarded when he reported this to Oglethorpe. Maybe he would even be in line for the mechanized suit at last!

While the girl interviewed squirrels in the park, he pulled out a copy of the high school's yearbook from the previous year. A few moments of flipping through the book rewarded him with the information he needed. The girl was Alice Littleton, now in the tenth grade. He returned his attention to the monitor and listened as Alice completed her conversation with Skitter. It was a one-sided conversation from his perspective, but Alice seemed to be getting the information she wanted. The squirrel was behaving in a most unsquirrel-like manner as well, apparently sketching out something in the dirt with his paws.

A couple of minutes later, Alice was back on her bike, taking off down a major cross street. Gary let her get well ahead of him and then pulled out after her. He couldn't continue following her this way, he knew. Sooner or later, she would have to notice the van with darkened windows tailing her. It was time to make other arrangements.

A short time later, Alice turned in at a gas station with a convenience store and dashed inside, leaving her bike laying on the ground near the door. Perfect.

Gary pulled up to the pumps and got out of the van. Ignoring the pumps for the moment, he reached into his pocket as he walked towards the entrance, dropping a handful of change on the ground next to the bike. He stooped to retrieve the coins, and swiftly secreted a tracking device in the hollow underside of the seat. Mission accomplished, he sauntered into the store and grabbed some chips and a coke. By the time he got to the counter, Alice was paying for her own selections - a large bag of sunflower kernels, beef jerky, M&Ms, and a bottle of water.

Alice hurried out, got on her bike, and started back the way she had just come. Gary let her go, secure in the knowledge that he could find her again and trace her movements without further risk of exposure. Just to play it safe, he topped up his gas tank before he left the gas station.

♠ ♣ ♥ ♦

Alice rode back to Miranda's house as quickly as she could. Vacaville was a good-sized city, and she knew her chances of locating the kidnapper were slim if she relied solely on her own ability to cover ground. Fortunately, she wouldn't have to do that. It was time to activate the air corps.

Alice stopped several houses short of Miranda's when she spied Mrs. Sullivan's van in the driveway. Mrs. Sullivan wrote advertising copy for a living, and often worked from a laptop on her dining room table. Alice didn't want to advertise her truancy to her best friend's mom.

It took a couple of minutes to attract Hopwing's attention, calling out as loudly as she dared while still hoping to avoid detection by parental units. As Alice had anticipated, Hopwing was sympathetic to Billy's plight once she explained the situation.

"Hopwing, I need your help. You and your entire flock. Can you gather them all and meet me in my back yard as quickly as possible?"

"Of course," the sparrow replied. "Fledglings must be protected at all costs. We'll be there as soon as I can gather them."

"Thank you. Tell them there's a reward for their help."

Once Hopwing had departed, Alice headed for home, selecting a route that avoided a direct view from the Sullivans' living room window. She let herself in, stopped by her room to pick up an art pad and pencil, and then went out the back door. She settled herself on a chair on the patio and began to draw a rough sketch of the kidnapper's car, paying particular attention to the epoxy patch. She doubted her helpers would be able to distinguish a Lincoln from a Chevy, but recognizing a distinctive shape like the patch should be within their grasp.

As Alice worked, the sparrows started to arrive. Shortly after she finished her sketch, Hopwing arrived at the head of a vast horde of sparrows of several different types, as well as other species: larks, goldfinches, wrens, and others Alice could not identify. All told, there were a thousand or more birds blanketing the yard, perched along the fence, and sheltering in the trees. Alice smiled at Hopwing as he landed on her shoulder.

"I see you brought in all the troops."

"Well, some others overheard me spreading the word to the flock, and they wanted to help out. Most of them didn't know where to come, though, so they just followed me."

"Great work. We're going to need all the help we can get."

Alice addressed the entire group. "May I please have your attention? I have an emergency, and I need your help." In a few moments, the multitude fell silent, or nearly so, and Alice continued in a slightly softer voice.

"As you have heard, a human fledgling, a boy, was taken from his mother last night. I need your help to locate him. The man who took him was driving a car that looked something like this," she said, holding up her sketch. "Make particular note of this dark patch on the rear fender. If we can locate this car, we should be very close to saving the boy. Please spread out and look for this vehicle. Hopefully, it's still somewhere in the city, or at least nearby. If you find it, come back and tell me right away. I'll need you to lead me to it."

"What about the reward? Hopwing said there was a reward," one of the larks called from a tree.

Alice nodded. "I got a better response to my call than I'd dared hope for, so I'm a little short at the moment." She pulled out the bag of sunflower kernels she had bought earlier. "Consider these a down payment. If we locate the car, I'll set out fifty pounds of bird seed in the empty lot beyond that fence. Anyone who helped search will be free to collect as much as he wants."

Alice could barely hear herself think for several seconds as the birds gave voice to their approval of this pronouncement. The cacophony finally settled down enough for Alice to make herself heard once more. "There's not a moment to waste! Make sure you have the shapes of the dark patch and the car firmly in mind, then spread out and search the city. We must bring Billy home!"

It took several minutes for the back yard to empty of avians, as many wanted a closer look at Alice's sketch after helping themselves to a few of the sunflower seeds she scattered in the grass. Finally she was alone with time to think. The description of the car was vague at best, but the police might still be able to make something of it. Alice pulled out her cell and called the anonymous tip line. When the operator came on the line, she told him she had seen a sedan pull out of the parking lot at Nelson Park with a boy matching Billy's description in the back seat.

Alice hung up and sighed, uncertain what to do with herself. She probably had hours before she could expect results from her net of avian spies. So she went inside, made herself a snack, grabbed some magazines, and then returned to the back yard where she could be found easily. All she could do now was wait.

CHAPTER FOUR

A Mathematical Interlude

"*Merde*! *Szar*! *Mut*!" Esme Iovan cursed as she checked her carefully calculated answer against the solution in the back of her algebra textbook. She was correct except for one detail, the same detail that had been plaguing her all along.

The librarian cleared his throat suggestively from his desk near the back of the reading area as he looked at her significantly. Esme glanced up at him and smiled apologetically. "Zorry, Mr. Head. I vill try to keep it down."

The librarian nodded, satisfied, and returned to whatever had been monopolizing his attention on the computer before her outburst. Though why he should really care how much noise she made was beyond her. Prometheus Academy had a ridiculously small student body. The private school had just opened and served a mere thirteen students, only two of which were even in the library at the moment.

Andrew Young was looking at her curiously from where he had been browsing the shelves for some book or other. She had only met the *ganje* briefly last night during the student and staff mixer held to welcome the kids to their new home away from home. He struck her as a bit of a nerd. And now he was coming over.

When he reached the table, he bowed with a ridiculous flourish thrown in that left his right hand extended with the fingers pointing up and the palm facing him, like he was a waiter offering her a menu at some fancy restaurant. Suddenly, his fingers twitched and his formerly empty hand presented her with a gold-tone coin held lightly between his index and middle fingers.

"A dollar for your thoughts," he said.

Esme quirked an eyebrow at him. "Perhaps I have learned ze idiom incorrectly? I zought it vas 'a penny for your zoughts'."

"Put it down to inflation."

Esme heaved a mental sigh. She had suspected where he was going with the gambit as soon as he spoke; it was too much to hope for that he could come up with something original. She nodded at the coin. "Zat vould be really impressive if I didn't know your power vas creating illusions."

Andrew looked hurt. "My illusions are purely light-based; my actual power is light wave manipulation. And while I could use it that way, I wouldn't degrade my craft in such a fashion." He spun the coin on the table, where it wobbled and then settled, creating a rattling sound all the while.

Esme applauded politely. "Vell zen, I guess I am impressed."

Andrew grinned. "Thanks. So what got you so upset?"

She sighed. "Algebra. I mean, who cares if ze answer is fifty or negative fifty, as long as I vorked the problem right?"

"Yeah, well, if you were running a business, it would be the difference between owing $50 and being owed $50. It's kind of an important distinction."

"Okay, you are right. Vat is really frustrating is zat I can never get a straight answer from a teacher. Zey won't explain why a negative times a negative is supposed to give a positive result; ve are just supposed to take it on faith. But it just does not make sense to me."

"Oh, is that all? I can help with that."

44

"Seriously?" Esme said skeptically.

Andrew walked around the table and sat down next to her. "Sure. Let me demonstrate."

He gestured and two groupings of three black dots appeared in the air, each group slowly spinning as if mounted on invisible wheels spinning in opposite directions. "Multiplication is just shorthand for adding up things in equal sets. Two times three, for example, is just a way of saying 'add two sets of three', which gives us six." As he finished, the two groupings looped together, forming one group rotating together around a common center.

Esme folded her arms across her chest. "Do you have to start with ze absolute basics? I learned zis when I vas seven."

"Patience, this won't take long. Now, the concept is the same with negative numbers. Two times negative three is how we say 'add two sets of negative three', giving us negative six." As Andrew spoke, the dots went through the same sequence as before, except this time they were red.

Esme nodded. "OK, so how does zis help me?"

"Well, now comes the wrinkle. What do you think we mean by negative two times negative three?"

Esme opened her mouth to blurt out a reply, but said nothing when she realized she didn't know the answer. So instead, she closed her mouth and gave the question some serious thought. "I suppose ve mean take avay two sets of negative zree," she finally hazarded.

"Great, you've got it!"

"But how can you show zat vit your floating dots? Vat are you taking ze two sets avay from? You have to start vit something, right?"

45

"Yep, and what we have to start with is zero. But we have to represent zero in a special way." Now one black and one red dot appeared where all the other dots had been before. "A positive one and a negative one cancel each other out, leaving zero" The two dots drifted together and both winked out of existence as they met.

"Like matter and antimatter?"

"You could think of it that way. So would you agree that as long as we represent a positive one and a negative one in pairs, we can have as many pairs as we want and the sum is still zero?"

"Uhm, sure."

"Okay, then we represent negative two times negative three this way." Two grouping of dots appeared, each rotating around their respective centers as before, but now each grouping consisted of three pairs of black and red dots.

Esme gasped. "I see it! Now ve can take avay two groups of negative zree, vich leaves behind a positive six!" Andrew manipulated his illusion in time with Esme's speech, causing the three red dots in each rotating group to leave their black partners and slowly fade away. Then the black dots looped around to rotate as a single group around a common center.

"You've got it."

Esme gave Andrew a brief, impulsive hug. "Zank you. Zat makes so much more sense now. Maybe now I vill be able to keep it straight in my calculations since it does not seem like such a trivial detail anymore."

Andrew smiled. "You're welcome. I guess I'll see you later at the student meeting with Mrs. Kilkarni."

"I guess so."

Andrew got up and walked out of the library, leaving Esme in a thoughtful frame of mind. Quite apart from the mathematical insight he had provided, his illusion show had sparked another idea in her mind. Andrew might just be the answer to another pressing problem she faced. It would require her to get close to him, but that was a price she just might be willing to pay. She'd have to see how things went during team selection.

CHAPTER FIVE

To the Rescue

"I found it, I found it, I found it!"

Alice looked up from her magazine. She realized she had been staring at the same advertisement for several minutes now. Her mind refused to focus on the page, drifting back again and again to Billy's predicament. Waiting was the worst.

But now it appeared that the waiting was at an end. She didn't recognize the voice, and she eagerly scanned the area looking for its source. The call had been faint, but it was rapidly approaching.

"I found it, I found it, I found it!" A young goldfinch banked sharply around a tree, dipped momentarily below the level of the fence, then zipped over it and landed on the end of the chaise lounge Alice was lying upon. Once there, it hardly seemed to move any slower, hopping about excitedly while keeping up its triumphant trill.

Alice sat up and the magazine slipped unnoticed to the ground. Holding a finger before him as a perch, she spoke calmly to the bird, though her own pulse was racing with anticipation. "Calm down, easy fella. I need details. What have you found?"

The bird hopped up on the offered perch, all the while exclaiming happily, "The car, the car! I've found the car! I know where the human fledgling is!"

"Great job. What's your name?"

"Triller, I'm Triller. Come see, come see! The mark! It's there!"

"And you saw the boy?"

"Yes, Yes! In the house! Come see, come see!"

"I will," said Alice. "I'm going to follow you on my bike, Triller. You'll have to fly a little way and then wait for me to catch up. And you'll need to stick to streets so I can follow. Can you do that for me?"

"Of course, of course. Come see, come see!"

Alice went back through the house with Triller perched on her finger. She quickly locked up and then went to her bike. She clipped her water bottle to the frame and confirmed she had the rest of her purchases from the convenience store in the pouch belted around her waist before signaling Triller to set out.

The bird led her across town, past Nelson Park and into another residential neighborhood. About twenty minutes after leaving the Littleton home, the bird landed on a mailbox in front of a nondescript single story house with a chimney. A privacy fence enclosed the back and side yards.

"Here it is, here it is," he cried.

Alice, who had not yet caught up to her guide, stopped several houses up the street from the dwelling the bird was indicating and gestured for Triller to come back to her. He did so, perching on her handlebars.

Alice scanned the street. It was approaching lunchtime, but luck was with her and no one was in sight at the moment. "Are you sure that's the right house? I don't see the car."

"It's in the back, it's in the back! Under the tree! I saw the mark when I stopped to rest. Come see!"

"And the boy?"

"I saw him through a window. It's in the back, too!"

"Okay." Alice got off her bike and leaned it against a tree, then unclipped the water bottle. "Let's go have a look."

♠　♣　♥　♦

Gary finished watching "Big Trouble in Little China" on his iPad for about the hundredth time. He had returned to his apartment and dispatched a preliminary report to Oglethorpe on the new paranormal he had identified. Talking to animals wasn't the coolest power imaginable, but his boss would probably be able to think of some way to utilize her. He wasn't expecting a quick response to his email, so he was just following his standard orders in this type of situation and keeping track of his target.

In this case, he was relying on the tracer he had hidden on her bike to track her movements. Except that there hadn't been any movement for quite some time. His software showed the bike was parked at an address on the west side of town that he had confirmed was her home through the simple expedient of checking the phone directory. After a while, he got bored and switched to the movie.

Now, with the final credits rolling, he jumped back to the tracking software, custom made by someone in Oglethorpe's organization, and checked on Alice's whereabouts.

"Interesting," he muttered, "Something got our girl motivated; she's all the way across town now."

A glance at the log showed she had not been at her new location long, only a few minutes. It was another residential area. Ordinarily, it would be a safe assumption that she had just biked over to a friend's house, but the little drama he had witnessed in the park earlier suggested she had other things on her mind today. Maybe it would be worth the time to drive over and see what had attracted her attention.

♠ ♣ ♥ ♦

Alice approached the house, moving along the sidewalk as if she were simply passing by on her way someplace else, and tried to study it without being too obvious. The drapes were pulled closed on the front windows, which were all covered by decorative yet functional security grates. Taking advantage of the fact that whoever was in the house probably wasn't observing her, Alice hurried over to the privacy fence where limbs of a big tree growing in the side yard hung over the barrier. Triller flitted to the top of the fence nearby.

"The car is under this tree. Come see, come see!"

The top of the fence was about a foot over Alice's head and was formed into blunted spikes. She reached up and grasped the top of one of the slats, then took a drink from the water bottle. Immediately, she began to shrink, stopping when she reached a height of three inches. Since she had maintained her grip, she was now hanging from the top of the fence and it was relatively easy for her to pull herself between two slats where they had been formed into the points. Soon, she was standing on the support brace that ran along the back of the fence near the top.

The car was parked on the far side of the tree from the fence. Backed into position as it was, the patch would be concealed from most airborne observation. Even if a police helicopter did spot it, there was nothing to make it stand out. In short, the police were not likely to connect it with Alice's anonymous tip without further help.

The back yard was not very deep, running only 10 yards or so from the back of the house. The privacy fence ran along an alley behind the row of houses, broken only by a high, solid gate big enough to let the car in and out of the yard. A tool shed stood near a back corner of the lot. Otherwise, the yard was empty. It was time to locate Billy.

Alice moved along the support beam towards the side of the house. Once she reached it, she leaned forward into a shallow dive. She did not plummet to the ground, but gently glided away from the fence

52

and along the side of the building with her body parallel to the ground, slowly losing altitude. Not true flight, this was a legacy of the fictional Alice's slow-motion tumble down the rabbit hole. When Alice's powers had manifested, she had discovered that she could slow her descent when she fell, and even control her direction of travel, much like a hang glider pilot.

Alice calculated that at her current rate of descent, she would not be more than waist high to a normal adult when she reached the corner of the house, and she wanted to get a look in the windows along the back. She drifted from side to side and finally located an updraft where the sun's warmth caused the air near the wall to rise. She utilized this lift to spiral upwards, rising above the eaves by several feet before the lift played out, then cut across the corner of the roof and out above the back yard before swinging back to get a look in the windows. Unfortunately, the curtains on all of them were drawn as well. Alice glided to a landing on the top crossbar of one of the security grills. A moment later, Triller landed beside her.

"Not here, not here! The next window! He peeked out between the curtains."

Alice noted the position of the room and started casting about for a way into the house. A pet door would have served, but the back door didn't have one. After a moment, Alice concluded there was only one option.

"Triller, do you think you can lift me?"

The goldfinch cocked his head, assessing her new size, then bobbed his head. "Yes! Where to, where to?"

Alice pointed above the roof. "There."

Triller grasped Alice gently by her shoulders and lifted her into the air, heading for the chimney. At her direction, he flew several feet above the top before letting her go. Alice glided into position , centering herself on the opening. She made sure there was no draft of hot air to indicate the fireplace was in use, and then allowed herself to drop straight down the chimney in a gentle descent that kept her clear of the sides. Her one fear was that the flue might be closed, but it had been cool the night before and the fireplace had been used. She glided between the slats of the barrier and landed towards the front of the fireplace to minimize the amount of ash she would have to walk through.

The fireplace was closed off by a wire mesh curtain. From Alice's perspective, this was perfect, giving her an opportunity to examine the room beyond without much likelihood of being seen. The room was empty save for some rather shabby furnishings, just a couch and a couple of upholstered chairs facing a television, currently off, at the far end of the room.

Taking advantage of the quiet, Alice pulled back one side of the mesh curtain where it met the other and pushed her way past it into the room. An entrance to a hallway leading to the rest of the house was to her left at the far end of the room. Faintly, she could hear the sound of another television tuned to a children's show drifting down the corridor. The room Triller had seen Billy in would be down that hallway. Alice headed in that direction.

While the living room was adequately lit by lamps set in the corners, the hallway was dim and gloomy. Alice moved towards the far end, where she expected to find Billy's room.

Before she had advanced very far down the corridor, a small head emerged from a doorway to the right at the far end. A low growl issued from the golden retriever puppy as it spied her, though Alice thought it sounded more confused or curious than angry. Then the puppy bounded forward, yipping excitedly.

"Master, master, come see! A bug! Does it want to play?"

54

Alice held up her hands and called out softly but urgently as the animal approached, towering over her. "Hush! You must not wake, uh, Master. It's very important."

The puppy halted, peering curiously at her, amazed to understand her so clearly. "Why not? It's master's house." He sniffed her, then jumped back with an excited yip. "You smell odd. Maybe Master squish you like other bugs."

"Look, uh, what's your name?" Alice asked. She wanted to divert the dog's mind from squishing.

"Master calls me Carrot."

Alice imagined a carrot set in a trap to draw in an unsuspecting rabbit, but decided there was no point in explaining this to the dog. "Master brought a boy here last night, didn't he? He shouldn't have done that. I'm here to take the boy back where he belongs."

Carrot growled and crouched, prepared to spring at her. "He belongs here now."

"Is the boy happy here?" Alice asked insistently. "Did he come here willingly?"

Carrot backed up a step, clearly troubled. "He cries a lot. But I did, too, when I first came here. He will like it here soon."

"No, he won't. People are not like dogs. We need to be with our mothers and fathers much longer. Besides, Master will hurt the boy, if he hasn't already. What Master has done is wrong, Carrot. I'm here to fix it."

The puppy whined in confusion and looked back down the hall. "But, he is Master."

Alice pulled the package of jerky from her pouch, along with the bag of M&M's. She opened both, taking several pieces of the dried meat and a single candy. "Here," she said, laying the meat on the floor between them. "Have a snack while I get the boy. I promise I won't hurt Master, if I can help it. But he must give up the boy." Then she ate the piece of candy, focusing on the jerky as she did so. The jerky expanded to its regular size, freed from the influence of her shrinking power.

Carrot hesitated, torn between his loyalty to Master, the possibility Master was doing bad things, and his desire for the treat.

"Has the boy seemed happy at all since Master brought him here?" Alice prompted.

The puppy's head dropped as he acknowledged her point. Carrot settled to the floor and started in on the first piece of meat. Alice gave him an affectionate scratch behind one ear and then continued down the hallway.

When she got to the far end, she found a closed door to her left with light spilling into the hallway from the gap beneath it. She could see a hasp had been attached to the door and frame, and a padlock secured the door against entry. Even though she could probably squeeze under the door, given her current size, getting her in would do nothing about getting Billy out. For that, she would need to find the key.

A deep, gravelly snort from the room Carrot had appeared from startled Alice and she spun around to face the doorway. Even given the relative gloom of the hallway, the room beyond was dark and reminded Alice of a cave. She crept cautiously forward, inching her way into the darkness and then pausing to give her eyes time to adjust.

A few moments later, she was able to make out a form lying beneath a heavy blanket on a rumpled bed. The figure rolled over, and a man's forearm dangled over the side. Alice swallowed nervously. Judging by the thickness of the arm, the bed's occupant was very strong. She held her breath, waiting to see if he was waking up, but after a full minute without further movement she exhaled softly and glanced around the rest of the room. She decided she couldn't stomach calling the bed's occupant 'Master', even in the privacy of her own thoughts. She settled on 'Raptor', for the man's mindless, remorseless appetites.

A nightstand next to the bed supported a lamp and a whiskey bottle. From her viewpoint near the floor, Alice couldn't see any liquid in the bottle; perhaps that explained why Raptor hadn't been roused by Carrot's excited barks and yips. It was also impossible to tell if there was anything else on the surface. The same went for the dresser across from the bed. Chances were the keys were on one or the other. Once she had gotten inside the house, she had elected to stay small in case she needed to hide quickly while she tried to get to Billy. Now her size was no longer an advantage.

She carefully removed another M&M from the baggie she had retained in her hand and slipped it into her mouth. A few seconds later, she was back to her normal size and was able to see the keys lying on the dresser. Moving silently, she crossed the room and carefully picked up the bundle of keys, trying not to let them rattle against each other too much. Raptor never stirred.

Emboldened by the thought that the man was unlikely to awaken soon, Alice returned to the hallway and started trying to locate the correct key to remove the padlock. While she tried the fourth key in the lock, the red alert sounded.

Startled, Alice dropped the keys as a surprised exclamation from behind her let her know that Raptor was awake. Alice bolted back down the hall, slapping at her pocket.

"Hey, what the hell are you doing in my house?"

"Hatter, I could use some help here," Alice whispered urgently as she made it back to the living room, belatedly silencing her iPhone.

Her companion appeared by the fireplace, holding a teacup and saucer. He looked at her with mild interest.

"You called?" he asked before taking a sip of tea.

Alice pointed back towards the hallway. "Bad man, slow him down," she pleaded as she darted towards the kitchen.

Just then Raptor rounded the corner. Carrot was dancing around his feet, yipping excitedly. The man was wearing a T-shirt and a pair of workout shorts, and he was carrying a pistol. He saw Alice first and pointed the weapon at her, but noticed Hatter before he fired. He apparently saw Hatter as a greater threat, because he tried to redirect his aim at him. As a result, his first two shots split the air between the intruders in his home, while the third shattered the teacup in the Hatter's hand.

The sound of the gunshots frightened Carrot, who dashed back down the hallway. Alice screamed, certain her friend was about to die. But Hatter surprised her, dodging towards her so that the next shot missed him to the other side. Before the befuddled man could stop tracking his arm to reverse his aim, Hatter swiftly reached up, plucked the advertisement card from his hat band between his index and middle fingers, and hurled it edgewise at the gunman. The impromptu missile struck him in the back of the hand holding the weapon, and the corner embedded itself in the flesh between two bones. The man cried out in pain and rage, dropping the gun.

"You are so dead, you freak," he shouted at Hatter, and rushed at him.

But Hatter was far from done, for Alice's request had been quite literal. Even as he threw the card, Hatter had been drawing his watch from his pocket. Now he held it out towards Raptor and said, "Slow."

Instantly, the man's progress was reduced to half of its former pace. A look of confusion slowly spread across his face; from his perspective, Hatter and everything else suddenly seemed to be moving twice as fast. In the tight confines of the house, it still took some effort

58

for Hatter to avoid him, but he was able to elude Raptor's clumsy attempts to punch or grab him. The man's mouth opened and a low-pitched rumble, completely unintelligible to anyone not slowed to the same time frame, filled the air. Alice decided it was just as well she couldn't understand him; he was probably cursing up a blue streak and threatening to kill both of them.

Alice had to keep moving to stay out of the kidnapper's way as well. He was mostly focused on Hatter, but he tried to grab her if she strayed too near. She had to find a way to neutralize him before he got lucky. After a minute or so of dodging around the room, she saw an opportunity.

"Hatter, when I give the signal, give him a dose of hyper time," she called.

"Are you sure? He looks pretty strong. I wouldn't want to give him any advantage," Hatter said.

"Just do it...Now!" Alice replied.

Raptor had just turned towards her, making a slow-motion lunge in an attempt to capture her in a bear hug. As Alice shouted "Now", she was already crouching and covering her head with her arms.

Hatter brandished his watch again, and the kidnapper suddenly shot forward at four times his previous rate of speed. Caught unprepared for the sudden shift, he struck Alice and sailed over her, continuing headfirst into the curtains covering the front window. Even through the pain Alice felt from the impact, she clearly heard the window breaking.

A moment later she was able to confirm her plan had worked. Raptor was out cold. He had smashed into the security bars after shattering the window and taken down half the drapes as well.

"Keep an eye on him and tell me if he moves," she called to Hatter as she pulled out her phone and called 911. She quickly gave the operator the address and told her she had heard several gunshots from inside the house while passing by on her bike.

♠   ♣   ♥   ♦

Gary cruised by Alice's bike and parked his van on the side of the road a few houses further down the street. The girl was nowhere in sight, but she'd have to come out sooner or later. Gary switched on the camera and panned over to the front of the house where the bike was parked. The flip of a few switches converted the parabolic microphone to laser mode, which allowed him to hear what was going on in the home based on the way sounds from inside the house deflected the glass in one of the front windows. but all he could make out were the sounds of a vacuum cleaner and a television tuned to a talk show.

Gary was about to try redirecting the laser to a different window to see if anything more interesting was happening in another room when the sound of gunshots drew his attention to the house directly across the street.

For a couple of minutes, nothing more happened and Gary cursed his luck. If that girl had managed to get herself killed, he was going to lose his bonus. But then the front window fell away in a shower of shards as a heavily-muscled man flew through the glass, smashed into the security grate, and then fell back onto the floor inside.

Gary quickly reoriented the rooftop camera and enabled the low-light mode in an effort to make out some details within the gloomy interior. Unfortunately, the sunlight washed everything out, but the parabolic microphone brought him the sound of Alice's voice, reporting gunshots to a 911 operator. After that, the girl withdrew deeper into the house and his feed fell silent.

When he heard the sound of sirens approaching, Gary quickly started the engine and pulled out from the curb, leaving the neighborhood at a leisurely pace. He had learned enough for now and he had a new report to file.

The girl had super strength! How else could she have sent such a big foe through a window like that?

♠ ♣ ♥ ♦

Alice swiftly returned to the hallway. Carrot was nowhere in sight. Alice figured he was probably cowering under Raptor's bed. She hoped he would find a good home full of happy children once this mess was straightened out. Returning to the padlocked door, she picked up the keys, and removed the lock. She opened the door and looked inside.

The room was haphazardly decorated for a young boy; there were posters on the wall of trains and robots, and the bedspread had a pattern of planets, rockets and stars printed on it. The television was still tuned to a cartoon, but Alice didn't see anyone.

"Billy, are you here? My name is Alice, and I'm here to help you. It's time to go home."

The closet door moved slightly. Alice approached the door and crouched down, speaking as gently and encouragingly as she knew how. "Billy, it's all right. The bad man can't hurt you anymore. I'm going to get you out of here, all right?"

Slowly, the door opened and a young boy looked out at her. Tears were streaming down his face, which bore a large purple bruise beneath the left eye. He looked around the room to confirm his captor was nowhere in sight before focusing on Alice. "Really and true? You'll take me home?"

Alice hesitated, then said, "I've called some very nice people who are going to take you home. When they get here, just tell them who you are. Can you do that for me?"

Billy nodded, then broke down sobbing. Alice gathered him in her arms and rocked him for a minute, murmuring vague reassurances in his ear. She only released him as the sounds of sirens approached.

"Wait here a second, Okay, Billy?"

Billy had regained a bit of his composure and nodded as Alice stood and stuck her head out the door. "Hatter, time to scram. The authorities can take things from here."

Without waiting for a reply, Alice gently pulled Billy to the door. "Those nice people I told you about are here; just go down the hall and when they come in, be sure to tell them your full name. Are you ready?"

"Aren't you coming with me?"

Alice shook her head as she heard the front door being forced. "I can't let them see me. It's our little secret, Okay? Go on now, hurry!"

Billy started down the hallway, and Alice wasted no time in summoning her looking-glass. As soon as the mirror appeared, Alice stepped through it. But before she completed the transition, she heard a gasp behind her and caught sight of Billy's reflection from where he stood in the doorway, eyes wide. But it was too late to stop, and a moment later Alice emerged fully into Wonderland.

She was standing in a forest, with nothing but the sounds of nature around her. When she had first come here, years ago, and met Ches for the first time, she had naturally named the place Wonderland. But as time went on she slowly realized the truth. This was an alternate Earth, one unpopulated by humans. It was a blank canvas on which she had superimposed her fantasies, before she learned how lonely a place it really was. She seldom came here anymore.

Alice glanced back at the looking glass, which blinked out of existence a second or two after she fully separated from it. She hoped Billy hadn't been too traumatized by what he had just seen; he'd been through so much already. But as there was nothing she could do about it either way, she took a deep breath and summoned the looking-glass again. This time, she emerged in an alleyway downtown. In Alice's experience, dimension-hopping was not a precise mode of travel. Her two transitions, mere steps apart from her perspective, had moved her several miles and she faced quite a hike to get home. Plus, she'd have to retrieve her bike sooner or later. She hadn't thought her plan through before she entered the kidnapper's house, and so hadn't anticipated leaving by the route she'd chosen. And next time, she'd need to be sure to silence her phone.

Curiosity aroused, Alice pulled her phone out again and checked to see what had set off the alarm. As she read the latest Amber Alert, she grinned in spite of herself, and then started laughing out loud. She had tripped herself up – the alert notified searchers for Billy Williams to be on the lookout for a light colored sedan with a rough epoxy patch on the rear driver's side fender.

CHAPTER SIX

School Assignments

Esme eased into the auditorium. She was not the last to arrive, she noted, nor was Mrs. Kilkarni anywhere in evidence. Good, she had some time before the assembly began.

She walked down the center aisle towards the front of the room. The facility was too big for the school, with seating for five hundred. The entire population of the academy, support staff included wasn't even a sixth of that. Esme supposed it was a sign of Mrs. Kilkarni's ambition, though how she was ever going to find enough students with paranormal abilities to fill this room and keep the teachers and staff busy was a mystery.

The early arrivals were scattered out and isolated in the vast space. Besides the students, spread out in pairs or small groups, a dozen teachers, none of them paranormals, were seated together in the front two rows to the right of the stage. Esme had been surprised to find non-powered people working at the academy, but on reflection she realized she shouldn't have been. Paranormals were vanishingly rare, so much so that most people were unaware of them.

Houston Lane, Coach Lane to the students, was one of the two empowered individuals among the staff. He sat at the edge of the group of teachers, seeming to merely tolerate the animated conversation of Mr. Honeycutt, who taught history. The coach had the physique of a world-class body builder; at first Esme had assumed his power was super strength. But she had learned during the mixer that he was actually a teleporter, able to not only move himself from one location to another, but also other people or objects.

The other paranormal, LaRonda Teresi, sat on Houston's other side, her face hidden by her mass of long dreadlocks. She was oblivious to everything going on around her as she fiddled with something in her lap that Esme couldn't see, although she had no doubt it was some sort of electronic gadget. Esme's impression from their brief meeting during the mixer was that Ms. Teresi was completely absorbed in her research. Her manner towards students and faculty alike had been terse to the point of rudeness, and she had left the event at the first opportunity. Esme figured that her attitude could be a good thing or a bad thing. Either she was going to neglect her duties as science teacher, in which case homework might be considered optional, or she was going to hold them all to impossible standards. Esme hoped for the former.

Andrew sat next to the Korean kid in the front row of the middle section of seats, deep in some geeky conversation. She slipped into the row behind them and rested a hand on his shoulder when she got close. Andrew's companion fell silent as he looked up at her, and Andrew's mouth actually fell open when he turned to see who was behind him.

Esme smiled inwardly at his reaction. She had gone through a good deal of effort to play up her Romani heritage today. Her long, dark hair fell in tight curls past her shoulders, held back from her face with a colorful scarf. She wore a lightweight top with short sleeves pulled down to leave her shoulders bare, and there was just a bit of midriff on display above her tight jeans. Another scarf was threaded through the belt loops and tied at her hip, and large gold hoop earrings completed the outfit.

"Uh, hi, Esme. What's up?"

Esme smiled invitingly at Andrew. "I vas zinking ve should get out of here after ze assembly is over. Ve can go explore the town together, no?"

"Cool," Andrew's friend said enthusiastically. "I'll bet everyone will be up for that."

Esme frowned at the dark-haired boy. "I vas speaking to Andrew; JUST to Andrew," she said frostily.

"Oh, sorry."

Esme watched Andrew's face light up in a goofy grin as the realization sank in. One of the most exotic girls in school was taking an interest in him! True, there were only six girls in this school, and none were unattractive, but Esme figured he was more than half convinced he'd find himself waking up in his bed in two minutes, trying desperately to hold onto this dream. Perfect.

"Uh, I'll catch up with you later, Min Ki. Maybe we can hang out tomorrow afternoon."

Esme lifted one eyebrow.

"Uh, or not," Andrew said.

Esme smiled and led him away.

♠　♣　♥　♦

Min Ki Moon watched Andrew and Esme move to an empty area several rows behind the teachers. A chuckle from behind him diverted his attention. Turning in his seat he spied a boy with Hispanic features sitting a few rows back. He bent over a sketch pad in his lap, and switched back and forth between a selection of colored pencils and ink pens too rapidly for any normal human. Min Ki had seen him at the mixer, but the other boy had kept to himself, sulking in the shadows, and Min Ki had never gotten around to talking to him.

"Don't worry. She'll be done with your friend by the end of the week," the boy said without shifting his attention from whatever he was drawing.

"Who are you?"

"Julio, Julio Zarzosa."

"Why do you think they'll break up so soon?"

The boy snorted and shot a look at Esme, who was leaning towards Andrew, engrossed in their conversation. "Take a look at her. Even given the slim pickings around here, why would someone who looks like that go after the geek right off the bat? She wants something from him, probably help with her homework. Once she's got it, she'll dump him."

Min Ki thought about it, and decided that Julio was probably right. None of the students here knew each other well yet, though Min Ki and Andrew had been getting along well enough after discovering a common interest in comic books and action movies. In other words, neither was the type to attract the kind of attention Esme was bestowing on Andrew. Still, it wasn't Min Ki's business. Hopefully Andrew was self-aware enough to realize what was up and enjoy the ride while it lasted.

"What are you drawing?" Min Ki asked, looking for a way to change the subject. A quick look around the auditorium failed to turn up any likely subjects, and Julio wasn't looking up at anything in particular as he worked anyway.

"Tattoo samples," Julio replied.

Intrigued, Min Ki got up to take a look at the pad. It was too far to walk all the way around the section of seats and back several rows. so Min Ki decided to suit up. A moment's concentration caused a translucent, semitransparent suit of psychic armor to manifest around him, styled like that of a Korean warrior from around the 13th century.

A moment later, the armor's legs started to lengthen until Min Ki was ten feet off the ground. A few steps later, he was standing in the row behind Julio, and the legs quickly retracted before his armor disappeared.

The sketchbook page was rapidly filling up with pictures of tropical flowers, singly or in groups. Min Ki was impressed. The images were very realistic, given that Julio was apparently working from memory, and the colors were vibrant. Julio obviously had talent, and Min Ki could easily recall seeing many people sporting actual tattoos that didn't look half as good.

"Wow. Those are great. But why flowers?"

"I do all sorts of designs. Gotta give the public what they want, man. Flowers are the theme for this page of my book. Besides, the chicas love 'em."

"And you do actual tattoos?" Min Ki asked doubtfully.

"Nah, too young to be licensed, or even sign on as an apprentice. But I'm going to open my own parlor someday. For now, I make some cash doing face painting and body art at street fairs. It still gets me close to the ladies. The prettier they are, the slower I work, know what I mean?"

Before Min Ki could respond, a new voice cut into the conversation. "Such a shame. I thought for a moment we had a real artist in our midst, but now I see you're just an opportunist."

Julio and Min Ki looked to the left, where the speaker stood in the aisle, just a few seats away. The boy wore pressed slacks, a dress shirt, red tie and a dark blazer. He looked like he was expecting to intern with IBM.

"You're the senator's kid, right?" Julio asked.

"Yes, that's right. Regis Adair."

"Well, Regis," Julio said, his voice dripping venom as he pronounced the name, "I don't expect a brat born with a silver spoon up his butt to get it, but out here in the real world, we do whatever we have to do to pay the bills. My art is going to do that for me and the company of beautiful girls is a nice perk. Ain't nothin' wrong with that."

"I see. I just thought art was supposed to mean something. You know, provide commentary on our society, cry out against injustice, that sort of thing."

"It means I won't ever have to sleep on the streets. You want more than that, try the museum."

"I think his designs are pretty."

This came from an attractive girl standing next to Regis. She was dressed stylishly but more appropriately for an informal school assembly, if you ignored the profusion of jewelry. Her left wrist was snuggly encircled by a bracelet set with an emerald, and a ring on the middle finger of her left hand displayed an amethyst. On the opposite hand, she wore a large ring on her index finger, on which three star sapphires surrounded a sparkling diamond. Surprisingly, she also wore a fine gold chain that emerged from beneath her wavy brown hair to support a pendant bearing a teardrop shaped sapphire crystal in the center of her forehead. All of the jewelry was gold, and none of the stones were less than a carat. Min Ki wondered if the pendant had some sort of religious significance. He couldn't think of another reason for such an unusual placement.

"Yes, well, if he can't produce anything of substance, I guess 'pretty' will have to do," Regis sighed. "Let's go find a seat. Mrs. Kilkarni will be starting soon."

Sure enough, the administrator was walking down the far aisle towards the stage. Elaine Kilkarni was in her late fifties. Her brown hair was shot through with gray and gathered up in a bun at the back of her neck. She wore a tan business suit, pumps with a low heel, and carried a clipboard with a thin sheaf of papers in the crook of her left arm. She did not greet anyone as she marched to towards the stage, but her eyes surveyed the room closely, noting everything.

Min Ki looked back to Regis and the girl, who were settling into seats in the second row. "That dude is bad news," he said.

Julio grinned in spite of himself as he returned his attention to an orchid. "What was your first clue?"

♠ ♣ ♥ ♦

Kasie sat down next to Regis and snuck a glance back at the boy with the sketch pad. "What was that all about?" she asked. "You practically picked a fight with that guy for no good reason."

A self-satisfied smile settled on Regis's features. He looked towards the stage, where Mrs. Kilkarni was just setting her clipboard down on the lectern. "You're only partly right. I did pick a fight, but I had my reasons."

"Really? Why'd you do it then?"

"My father taught me that a leader is defined by his enemies. The surest way to gain influence with students and teachers here is to take a stand against the bad elements. That's Julio, and anyone who hangs around with him."

Kasie mulled this over for a moment. "How do you know they're the bad elements? Did you have a run-in with them at the mixer or something?"

"No. Julio's the bad element because I've designated him to be, and his friends by association. The rest is simple PR. Just wait; in a few days, they'll be social pariahs."

Kasie sat back in her chair. She had gravitated to Regis during the mixer because he was confident and charismatic. She was honest enough to admit the aura of wealth that clung to him like a heady cologne was part of the attraction. She had sensed there was something more, however, and now she was convinced her instincts were trustworthy. As she gave her attention to Mrs. Kilkarni, she leaned in towards Regis and threaded her arm through his, laying her head against his shoulder, and her smile matched his.

♠ ♣ ♥ ♦

Julio continued his work as Elaine Kilkarni set her clipboard on the lectern and looked out over the auditorium. She did not say a word, nor did she clear her throat. Such props were unnecessary. Her simple presence and the force of her attention was enough to draw everyone's awareness; the room became silent in a matter of seconds as the stragglers quickly found seats.

"Mr Zarzosa, if you please?"

Julio sighed and quickly put away his implements, but then put his feet up on the seat in front of him and crossed his arms, looking bored.

"Thank you. Welcome, students and faculty, to the official opening day of Prometheus Academy. Most of you students have had a day or two to explore the grounds and settle into your dorm rooms. Our faculty, of course, have been here a bit longer, preparing for the year ahead of us. Tomorrow morning, the regular schedule of classes will commence."

Julio snorted. Kilkarni could talk this place up all she wanted, but he could still see it for what it was: a prison. Julio's parents had sentenced him to three years of this crap, the better to be rid of a troublesome son they couldn't relate to.

"Before we get to that, however, I wanted to take this time to address the students as a group," Elaine continued. "You are exceptional individuals, each and every one of you. For good or ill, you possess powers and abilities that are inexplicable using natural scientific laws, at least as mankind currently understands them. You have all endured the stress of hiding those powers, seeking to fit in among normal humans while looking for answers to the questions those powers naturally engender. 'Am I alone?' 'Why am I like this?' and, perhaps most intriguingly, 'What could I achieve if I could fully explore these powers?'

"Prometheus Academy was built to aid you in your search for answers. You already know now that you are not alone. As to why humanity has started developing paranormal abilities, your guess is as good as mine. Perhaps future investigations will reveal the genesis of this sea change in humanity's gene pool. Or it may remain a mystery all of our lives. All that appears certain at this point is that the phenomena is becoming more emergent. A generation ago, a place like Prometheus Academy could not have existed, because it would have been nearly impossible to assemble even such a small group of paranormals as this. My hope is that future generations will come to fill this hall, and others like it around the world.

"Which leaves us with that tantalizing question, 'What is possible?' Left to your own devices in the outside world, that question would likely be doomed to remain unanswered. Uncertainty about how normal humans might react to blatant displays of your powers has lead all of you to hide your lights under a bushel, to use a Biblical phrase. Such an environment is not conducive to testing the limits of mankind's newest frontier. And so I established this school.

"As I assured you and your families before you accepted your scholarships, it is not my intention to thrust you into the limelight of public scrutiny. My purpose is to provide you with an environment in which you may use and explore your powers openly, as long as you show proper respect for others. Everyone around you is in on the secret.

"Even though most of your teachers are not gifted in the paranormal sense, they have all demonstrated an unswerving dedication to excellence in their profession. They are here to provide academic guidance, as well as more general wisdom and counsel to help prepare you for whatever comes after graduation."

They're here, Julio thought, *to collect big fat paychecks in exchange for a ridiculously light work load.*

"For the time is coming when our secret will be exposed," Mrs. Kilkarni continued. "The growth of the paranormal population virtually guarantees it. My hope is that when that day arrives, Prometheus Academy, with its staff, students, and alumni, will shine like a beacon in the darkness to show the rest of the human race that paranormals need not be universally feared; that the empowered can and have worked to aid the greater good.

"Sadly, some of you already have personal experience that not all of those with powers have chosen this path."

Julio was surprised to notice several grim-faced nods in response to this pronouncement. He had convinced himself that the stories he had heard since arriving at the school were nothing more than a complex bogeyman conjured by Elaine to entice families to send their gifted children here. Maybe there was more to the tales than he had believed.

Elaine paused for a moment, and Julio found himself drawn in despite himself. His arms uncrossed and his feet came down. He gripped the arms of his chair tightly.

"We know a man named Oglethorpe and his organization are recruiting others gifted with powers," she finally continued. "In some cases, they have resorted to kidnapping and brainwashing to bolster their ranks. Oglethorpe's ultimate objective remains unclear, but we can say with certainty he is not opposed to thievery, intimidation, and even murder in pursuit of it. I am greatly concerned by the potential his organization's activities have for turning humanity against paranormals.

"Lacking any powers of my own, I cannot offer much in the way of protection if Oglethorpe ever learns of our presence here. Some might even question the wisdom of gathering so many potential recruits in one place. But experience has taught me that his resources are everywhere, and his methods are effective, as much as I might wish they were not.

"So, in memory of my dearly departed husband, whose own power established the fortune that has allowed me to fund this endeavor, I have created Prometheus Academy as a refuge. Here, we will gather as many of the gifted as possible to hide them from Oglethorpe's greedy gaze. Here, we will nurture a more positive vision of the future of humanity, where might will not be the determinant of what is right. Here, we will preserve an example to show society that conflict between the gifted and the rest of humanity is not a foregone conclusion."

Julio shook his head, trying to clear suddenly muddled thoughts. Even if Oglethorpe and his goons really existed, why should he care? He had his own plans, and they didn't include any stupid struggles against wannabe overlords. Julio would look out for himself, and he could outrun any trouble that might try to find him.

Elaine had paused for effect, but now continued her address, unaware of Julio's distress. "It is my intent to offer you as close to a normal high school experience as circumstances allow. You will be taught the core curriculum mandated by the laws of the state of Nevada. And you need not fear that you'll miss out on social events like school dances, which will be open to any of your peers from the local community you may care to invite. However, we will not be fielding sports teams, for what I trust are obvious reasons.

"Remember, secrecy is our primary shield, and the building and grounds are intended as a safe zone for the use of powers, generally speaking. But we do not wish to appear too closed off from the community, and the normal functioning of any school requires some presence of non-school personnel on the grounds from time to time. If

75

you wish to invite a friend from town onto our campus, you may do so, as long as he or she checks in at the front office. Whenever anyone not privy to the knowledge of paranormals is present, the receptionist will make a general announcement over the school intercom, using a code phrase that will change periodically. Be sure to stay up to date on the code phrase so you'll know when we have visitors; use of powers during such times is forbidden, for the good of us all. Is that clear?"

She received nods from all of the students.

"Excellent. Now, in addition to the normal high school experience, you will all be expected to participate as members of teams that will be given special tasks throughout the year. The purpose of the teams will be to aid you in learning to utilize your abilities, and as such, team assignments may strike you as unusual. With such a wide range of paranormal gifts represented here, I don't know how they could be anything else."

This was greeted with a few nervous chuckles and giggles from the audience.

"I am now going to assign you to your teams. As I call your names, please come to the stage and gather in your respective zones."

At this cue, the curtains at the back of the stage parted, revealing free-standing wall sections colored yellow, red, blue and green.

Elaine glanced at the clipboard, then called out, "Team Yellow: Autumn Glassford, Kip Tarrin, and Levi Drafton, please come forward."

Autumn was one of the younger students, and had the well-toned physique of a gymnast. She had dark skin and wide, full lips framing perfect white teeth. She wore her wiry hair in a short, bushy mass kept back from her face by a yellow bandanna that crossed the top of her head, looped behind her ears, and was tied off at the nape of her neck.

Kip Tarrin also had an athletic appearance, but in the mold of a football player. Given time and a growth spurt or two, he would probably rival Mr. Lane in terms of bulk. His sandy brown hair was in a state of disarray, as if he had been in a strong windstorm. He bounced up out of his seat as soon as his name was called, full of energy and enthusiasm.

By contrast, Levi Drafton, a tall, skinny black kid with hair trimmed close to his skull, seemed almost sickly. He moved with a loose-limbed gait that covered ground slowly, and the assembly had to wait almost a minute after the others reached the space in front of the yellow wall section for him to join them.

Elaine faced the group. "Team Yellow consists of our elementals, representing the ability to control water, weather, and fire." She gestured to each in the order she had called them as she identified their elements. "These are strong forces, and we often hear of their potential for destruction on the news. I am tasking the three of you to find ways to use your powers for the betterment of the local community, without revealing yourselves. Report your activities back to me in one week, and I'll select a team leader based on your performance. Understood?"

After receiving assent from the members of the team, Elaine returned her attention to the remaining students. "Team Red: Min Ki Moon, Julio Zarzosa, and Constance Crutchfield, please join us."

The two boys made their way to the stage, where they were joined by a girl with dark hair that almost looked black until the light hit it just right, revealing red highlights. She wore it in a short bob cut. Despite her purely occidental features, she chose to dress in clothes with a marked Asian style. She wore simple leggings that reached to her calves, and a long sleeved, loose-fit tunic, belted at the waist, with

77

square cut panels that hung down to just above her knees in front and back. The entire outfit was an off white, made of a lightweight cotton material.

Elaine faced the team. "I will admit to some misgivings regarding this team. Given sufficient imagination and initiative, I'm sure you could all find other ways to employ your powers, but in the end, I have to admit that they are most readily adapted to combat."

"Yahoo! Danger Room, here we come!" Min Ki exclaimed.

Elaine shook her head with a rueful smile. "No, I'm afraid our facilities do not include mechanized traps and obstacles, nor would I add them if I could. Now I realize that forming a combat team right after I've spoken about my desire for peace may seem contradictory. But I also spoke of allowing you all room to fully develop your capabilities, and I do not want to channel your efforts into unprofitable areas just because I'm a bit squeamish about them. Also, I wouldn't want to live with the knowledge that I denied you scope to learn to defend yourselves in the event that you're ever attacked. So I have asked Coach Lane to work with you. In one week, you will have a mock combat on the school grounds, and the winner will become team leader. Agreed?"

"Oh, yeah! I'm going to lead the world's first super team! I was born for this," Min Ki said, pumping a fist. Julio rolled his eyes at the other's enthusiasm, and realized he didn't really have a choice in the matter. He crossed his arms and nodded. Constance gave Elaine a curt nod with a sort of half bow.

"Okay, next up, Team Blue: Regis Adair, Sarah Thompson, and Andrew Young."

Sarah was a slim fourteen-year-old with long, straight black hair tied back in a simple ponytail. She approached the rest of her team warily, as if she were trying to decide if she fit in with them.

"I formed this team based less on your powers, and more on your overall characteristics. Developing your abilities needn't focus exclusively on paranormal abilities, though I shall endeavor to set you tasks that will allow you some scope for their use. Regis has supernatural luck, Andrew manipulates light and creates illusions, and then we have Sarah."

Elaine approached Sarah and took her hands in her own, giving her fingers and encouraging squeeze. "I don't know if you can properly classify a photographic memory as a paranormal ability, but it is certainly useful, and rare in the general population to boot. Besides, in light of your family's recent tragedy, I couldn't very well turn you away after accepting your brother. I never want you to doubt you have a place here. There's no reason to think you cannot excel here as much as anyone else.

"Regis, you seem to have a certain knack with people," Elaine continued, while Julio and Min Ki shared an incredulous look. "Andrew, you've got a good, agile mind. Therefore, I'm giving your team one of those unusual tasks I mentioned earlier."

"When I was searching for a location for the academy, Boulder City offered certain economic incentives to bring the school here. Later, as the opening date approached, I received an application for Mayor Karlin's son. Naturally, I was forced to turn down the application to preserve our secret. Now, the mayor is spearheading an effort, as head of the city council, to revoke those incentives on the grounds that we have not accepted any local students into the academy."

Elaine shrugged and spread her hands. "The incentives are actually rather trivial; I only accepted them because it would have raised questions to refuse them. I don't want any of you to worry; if the mayor succeeds in his initiative, we'll simply pay the increased taxes and proceed as if nothing has happened. However, the issue appears to have divided the council rather evenly, so I have decided to turn the lemons into lemonade. Or, rather, to have you do it.

"I want each of you to make a study of the mayor and the other council members. Read up on their past decisions, see what charities they support, what cars they drive. In short, use any information you can get access to and get inside their heads. The person who can give me the most accurate prediction of which way the vote goes and who votes on which side of the issue will be declared your team leader. Mr. Head will have some resources in the library to help get you started. Clear?"

Regis raised his hand. "Mrs. Kilkarni, when is the council due to vote on the issue?"

"An excellent question. They are holding a special, closed-door session a week from tomorrow evening. I'll need your predictions no later than noon the day of the meeting. Anything else?"

No one said anything more, so Elaine turned back to the auditorium. "Team Green: Kasie Hardine, Julianna Vasari, and Esme Iovan, take your places, please." Then, to Scott Thompson, who was waving his hand for her attention, she said, "I haven't forgotten you, Scott, dear. Stand by. I have something special in mind for you."

Julio watched as seven girls responded to this summons. Esme, of course, he already knew by sight. The girl with the jewelry seemed to be Kasie, or at least she had stood up when Elaine called that name. The remainder of the group looked like quintuplets, and they converged on the stage from widely scattered parts of the room. One had been seated nearby while he was working on his samples, but he had been too busy to notice at the time. As they drew close, the girls simply walked into each other and merged like so many soap bubbles, though the final figure was no larger than any of the individuals.

Julianna was pretty, if more conventionally so than Esme, and didn't seem to require bling to reassure herself of the fact like Kasie. She was trim enough that she probably worked out a couple times a week, but also displayed ample curves, and had long blond hair that tumbled past her shoulders in big waves and swirls. Julio decided he could do a lot worse than to get lost in there for a couple of hours. Maybe she'd like a free sample of body art?

As Julianna reached the others on stage, Elaine addressed the last team, breaking into Julio's reverie. "Team Green, your task will piggyback on Team Blue's. In order to properly assess their reports, I'll need a transcript of the closed-door session next Tuesday night. It will be your job to procure it and get it to me as quickly as possible."

There was a moment of silence. "Mrs. Kilkarni," Julianna finally hazarded, "Are you telling us to break the law? Trespassing, breaking and entering, stealing?"

Elaine gazed thoughtfully at the ceiling. "I was wondering if any of you would bring that up. I'm glad you did, because it raises an important point regarding your abilities." She paused a moment, looking each of her students in the eye briefly as she scanned the entire group. "With great power comes great temptation. Once you leave Prometheus behind you, there will be few who will be able to deny you anything if you want it badly enough. So your education here will involve more than just written tests, and many of your assignments won't be subject to traditional grading. Even a simple pass or fail judgment may be difficult to assign with certainty. We will be discussing moral implications of the ways in which you use your powers, whether they are used in pursuit of team goals, or your own explorations, at dinner every Wednesday night. Who gets hurt, and in what ways? What do you gain? How do your choices shape you? So be prepared to give an account in the event someone challenges your actions or decisions.

"So, I'm not going to answer your question, Julianna. I'll leave it to you to determine how much you want the leadership position, and what means you deem permissible to achieve it. In the end, you may decide that there isn't an acceptable way to achieve this objective. If so, that's fine. Just be prepared to defend your choice."

81

♠ ♣ ♥ ♦

As the assembly broke up, Elaine approached Scott Thompson, Sarah's older brother. He was a thin, lanky lad with short-cropped red hair and scattering of freckles.

"Why didn't I get assigned to a team, Mrs. Kilkarni?"

"You're a special case, Scott. You're the oldest student here, and the only one who will be graduating at the end of the year. I don't want to disrupt the other teams through attrition just yet."

"So where does that leave me?"

"With a special assignment. Follow me."

She led Scott to the seats where the faculty had been sitting. Most of the teachers had already left, but Houston Lane and LaRonda Teresi were still in their seats. Houston looked smug, LaRonda defiant. As Elaine approached, she stood up angrily.

"What's the meaning of this? Your pet goon here won't let me return to my lab. Every time I start to walk away, he teleports me back to my seat."

"Calmly, my dear, calmly. I asked him to make sure you didn't disappear on us too soon. I want to introduce you to your new assistant."

LaRonda's milk chocolate complexion flushed several shades deeper. "I didn't ask for no assistant. What the hell do you think he can do for me anyway?" she said scathingly as she looked at Scott.

"Get you to class on time, for one thing. I'm sure you'll find other ways for him to be helpful."

LaRonda glared at Scott, who looked at the device in her hands nervously. It didn't look like a weapon, not exactly. But then again, there was no telling for sure. He got ready to dodge, just in case.

"LaRonda, remember that I placed certain conditions on your employment here, and access to that playground you call a lab. Teaching the science courses was one, and taking on Scott here as your assistant is another. Give him access to the lab and your schedule so he can make sure you don't get too lost in your projects. And I would take it as a personal favor if you kept him up to date on the status of your efforts. Sometimes your reports are indecipherable."

LaRonda slumped, defeated. She waved Scott ahead of her, motioning towards the exit at the top of the aisle. "All right, boy, you heard the lady. Let's get the nickel tour done so I can get back to work."

CHAPTER SEVEN

An Unexpected Visitor

"Are you crazy?"

Alice attempted to keep up a calm demeanor in the face of Miranda's outburst. It was after school the day following Billy's rescue and she had been filling her friend in on the details. She had only gotten as far as her entry through the chimney before Miranda offered her assessment of her mental condition.

"I had to be sure Billy was there, didn't I?"

"No, you didn't. You promised me you were going to be careful. What if that maniac had a gun?"

Alice guiltily glanced down at the chicken she was prepping for the oven. "Uhm, actually, he did." Seeing Miranda's look of horror, she quickly added "It was all right; Hatter disarmed him. He threw that card from his hat brim like a shuriken. I never knew he could do that. Then he slowed time for the perp; after that there was no way he was going to catch me or anything."

Miranda turned her attention to Hatter, who was sitting across from her at the kitchen table. "Thanks for protecting her. Even if she was stupid to put herself in that position to begin with."

"Hey!" Alice objected.

Hatter wagged a finger at Alice. "It was rather reckless, you know. He got off several shots before I tagged his hand, and if he hadn't been trying to reorient on me... Well it doesn't bear thinking about, does it?"

Alice grimaced at him. "You're not helping. Why don't you have some tea?"

At this, Marchie perked up. He had been sitting rather morosely in the corner, perched on the kitchen stool, staring into his sugar bowl.

"Tea?" he exclaimed. "Lumps all around!"

A moment later, he was flinging sugar cubes at everyone in sight. Alice dodged those sent in her direction easily as she swept up a kitchen towel to wipe her hands. Long hours of experience allowed her to anticipate his dispersal pattern. Hatter picked up a vase of flowers off the table next to him and used it to deflect two sugar cubes the hare hurled at him. Miranda was less fortunate, suffering direct hits on her forehead and left shoulder. Ches, who was stretched out on the floor nearby, got hit on his rear hip. Flicking his tail in annoyance, he teleported around the kitchen several times in such a quick sequence that he almost appeared to be in two or three places at once before he came to rest on the table between Miranda and Hatter. Marchie hopped up and down gleefully.

"Gotcha!" he cried. "Lump it and lose it!"

Alice quickly snagged a piece of bread from an open bag on the counter, spread a bit of butter on it, and rushed over to the hare. "Here, Marchie, trade with me," she coaxed. "It's the best butter, you know. That's it."

After a bit of initial hesitation, Marchie willingly swapped his sugar bowl for the bread and butter. He sank onto his haunches, sniffing his snack appreciatively and muttering "Lump it and lose it" to himself over and over. Alice sighed in relief and set the bowl on the counter by the stove. She looked over to Hatter, picking up the conversation as if nothing had happened.

"So, was that 'yes' to tea?"

Hatter plucked the flowers from the vase and tipped some of the water into his cup. "I think I'm in the mood for something with a stronger bouquet," he said.

"Suit yourself. Miranda?"

Miranda rubbed at her forehead ruefully. "Pass. Did that leave a mark?"

"Not much of one, and it's already fading. He can't throw those things with much force."

"Compared to what? It still stings." Miranda shrugged dismissively. "But never mind, we were discussing your suicidal tendencies. Once Hatter had disarmed him and hit him with the slow-mo, how did you take the kidnapper down? I heard he was thrown through a window."

Alice, who had just resumed sprinkling lemon pepper seasoning on the chicken, was prevented from answering by the doorbell. Quickly finishing her task, she transferred the chicken to the oven as quickly as she could. In spite of her haste, the doorbell rang a second time just as she finished.

"Bother! I'll have to go see who that is. Hatter, would you mind hurrying the chicken along? Dad wants to eat early tonight."

Hatter finished off his cup of vase water, smacked his lips appreciatively, and pulled his watch from his pocket. "No problem."

Alice was already out of the kitchen and moving towards the front door. Checking the peephole, she spied an overweight, middle-aged man wearing a black suit and tie with a rumpled white shirt.

"Salesman or evangelist?" she muttered to herself. Well, there was only one way to find out.

"Hi," Alice said as she opened the door a few inches. "Look, I don't mean to be rude, but I'm in the middle of fixing dinner, so we're really not interested in buying anything today, okay?"

The man gave her a sour look. He shook his head as he reached beneath his coat to produce a small leather case that he flipped open to reveal a badge and ID card. "Special Agent Oglethorpe, FBI. May I come in? I need to speak to Dr. Littleton."

"Oh! Uhm, sure, I guess." Alice stepped back, allowing the door to open fully. She led the agent into the living room as her heart hammered wildly in her chest. The FBI! This couldn't be a coincidence this soon after the business with Billy. "Dad's, uh, he's in his study. Wait here and I'll get him for you."

Oglethorpe waved a hand dismissively, his attention devoted to examining the room. His eyes took in the worn furniture, but focused primarily on the pictures on the wall and the DVDs and books on the shelves. Shrugging, Alice left him to it and walked down the hallway to the study door. She knocked firmly, then opened the door and poked her head in.

"Hey, Dad."

Arthur Littleton looked up from his computer screen in surprise. "Is dinner done already? Hatter must be giving you more help than usual."

"No, but it will be ready soon. In the meantime, we have a visitor."

Arthur reached for his pipe and a pouch of tobacco. "From your tone, I assume you're not talking about Miranda. She's here so often I'm thinking of setting aside a room for her."

"It's an FBI agent."

Arthur stopped in the middle of loading the tobacco in the bowl. "Good heavens, really? What does he want?"

"He didn't say anything except that he wanted to talk to you."

"Well, I guess I'd better not keep him waiting. Under the circumstances, maybe it would be best to ask Miranda to go home. Whatever this is about might be confidential."

Alice nodded and followed her father back to the living room. Special Agent Oglethorpe was waiting patiently.

"Well, here he is, sir," Alice said to their guest. "I'll just get back to work on dinner."

"Actually, I'd like you to stay. What I have to discuss with your father concerns you as well."

"Me?"

"Alice?" Dr. Littleton exclaimed. "What is this all about, Mr...?"

"Special Agent Oglethorpe," he filled in, proffering his badge and card again. "I'm just here to add in a few details I need to wrap up a case. Shall we sit down?"

Alice edged nervously towards the kitchen as her father looked questioningly at her. "Uhm, why don't I get us something to drink before we begin. Could I offer you a cup of tea, sir?"

Oglethorpe shrugged and sat down heavily in an upholstered armchair by the coffee table. "If it makes you feel better, why not?"

Alice fled to the kitchen, her mind a swirling jumble of thoughts. This had to have something to do with Billy, but why would the FBI have any interest in her? How had they even made a connection between the kidnapping and her?

89

Miranda frowned as she noted Alice's agitation upon her return. "What's up?" she asked.

Alice moved about the room, assembling a tea tray as quickly as she could. "There's an FBI agent in the living room. He wants to talk to me and Dad, and he says it concerns me!"

"What?"

"Miranda, you'll have to go home. I'll let you know what's happening as soon as the agent leaves. You'd probably better leave by the back door. I don't want to drag you into anything, especially since you didn't do anything wrong."

"Neither did you!"

"I know. This doesn't make any sense! But until we know more, better safe than sorry, right?"

"I guess." Miranda rose and gave Alice a quick hug. "It's going to be all right, you'll see. Call me as soon as you can."

Alice smiled her agreement and then turned to the others as Miranda let herself out. "The rest of you need to go, too. I think I'm probably going to have enough trouble answering questions as it is. Oglethorpe will never understand you."

Hatter tipped his hat to Alice before winking out of existence, while Marchie simply vanished, taking the remainder of his snack with him. Ches faded out gradually, starting with his tail. "We won't be far if you need us," his mouth said just before it, too, slipped from sight.

Alice picked up the tray, squared her shoulders, and forced her way through the swinging door. Her father and the agent were sitting silently as she set the tray down and settled on the couch next to Dr. Littleton. She quickly poured a cup of tea for Oglethorpe, barely able to keep her hands from shaking enough to avoid spilling it.

"Cream or sugar?" she asked.

"Sugar. One lump is fine."

Alice added a sugar cube to the cup and set it before their guest, who ignored it. She started to pour another cup for herself, but then decided she wasn't in the mood. Her father declined a cup as well.

"Well, now that we're settled, what can I do for you, Agent Oglethorpe?" Alice's father asked.

"I'm wrapping up some loose ends related to the Williams kidnapping case."

Arthur frowned. "What has that got to do with me?"

"Do you know how the boy was located?"

"The news says someone phoned in an anonymous tip."

"Exactly. What the reporters failed to mention, because they didn't know, is that phone records show the geophysical location of the call in question was inside the kidnapper's house."

Alice suddenly felt cold. "Why would you be looking at those records, though? Isn't the whole point of an anonymous tip line supposed to be that callers remain anonymous?" she asked, striving to keep her tone casual.

Arthur looked at her, and she could see him making connections in his mind. She hadn't made a big deal of it, but her bike was still on the street a few doors down from Billy's erstwhile prison, and her father had noticed its absence. She studiously avoided making eye contact, focusing instead on Oglethorpe.

"Ordinarily, you'd be right," the agent replied. "However, there were some irregularities in this situation that warranted further digging. For one thing, someone had already subdued Mr. Player before the authorities arrived on the scene. He was clearly thrown through a window from inside the house. That was enough to suggest that he might have had a falling out with an accomplice."

"That still doesn't explain what you're doing in my living room," Dr. Littleton said. "The activities of a pedophile across town have nothing to do with me."

"That may be. But the interesting fact remains that the phone that called in the anonymous tip is on your wireless account. How do you explain that?"

"It was mine," Alice blurted out, instantly gaining both men's full attention. "I meant to tell you, Dad, but I kept forgetting. I lost my phone last week. At first I thought it was just somewhere in my room, but after it didn't turn up for several days, I figured I must have left it someplace."

Dr. Littleton suppressed an approving smile, instead forcing his features into an annoyed scowl. "And naturally you still haven't put a lock code on it like I keep telling you?"

Alice bit her lip in mock embarrassment. "I did, but it was just 1234. I guess whoever found it figured it out."

"Great. Whoever it is has probably run up a huge bill by now. We'll have to get that phone deactivated right away." He turned to Agent Oglethorpe. "Well, I guess that clears that up, at least insofar as we can help you. Is there anything else?"

"Well, now that you mention it, there is one more item. Alice, I wonder if you might explain this to me."

He reached back under his coat, pulled out a manila envelope and passed it across the coffee table to her. Alice opened it and teased out the contents. It was a series of 8x10 photos of her in the park, talking with Skitter the squirrel. Her hands involuntarily tensed, crumpling the photos slightly. Without a word, she passed them to her father.

"I have an audio recording that goes along with these images," Oglethorpe volunteered. "I'd play it for you, but I'm afraid most of us would find the conversation hopelessly one sided. Right, Alice?"

"So I played hooky and pretended to talk to a squirrel. Like you never did anything pointless and irresponsible when you were a teenager?"

Their visitor laughed dismissively. "Surely you can do better than that, Miss Littleton. As I recall, you mentioned the kidnap victim by name, and 'pretended' to learn that the kidnapper drove a light-colored sedan with an epoxy patch. Not to mention, your bike was parked on the street while Mr. Player was subdued, which was before the authorities arrived."

Dr. Littleton threw down the photos and glared at his visitor. "This has gone on long enough! Who are you, and why have you been spying on my daughter? You're no FBI agent, I'm certain of that!"

"I agree," Alice said. "Most people would be shocked by that recording, but you're not, are you? You're acting like this was expected."

Oglethorpe smiled and picked up his tea before settling back comfortably in his chair. "Don't worry. Your secret is safe with me."

"For a price, isn't that what you mean?" Dr. Littleton asked. "Well, sorry to disappoint you, but my salary doesn't leave much for paying blackmail."

"Relax," Oglethorpe replied, taking a sip of his tea. "I'm not..."

Before he could finish the thought, however, he suddenly stiffened in the chair as electricity visibly arced and crawled across his body, creating a fantastic light show and filling the air with the scent of ozone and burnt cloth. The Littletons watched with open mouths until the display subsided several seconds later, leaving the *faux* agent wide-eyed with faint whiffs of smoke rising from his clothing. Then, amazingly, he began to laugh uproariously.

"Wow, I didn't see that one coming. What did you put in that tea?" he asked breathlessly.

93

"The tea? Nothing but some sugar," Alice replied, glancing at the bowl. Now she noted that in her haste in the kitchen, she had scooped up Marchie's sugar bowl instead of the one that was actually a part of the tea set. She had been too distracted earlier to notice. But why should that have produced such an effect?

"That's it, I've had enough. I don't know who you are, but impersonating an FBI agent is a serious charge. I'm calling the police," Dr. Littleton said, levering himself off the couch with his cane.

"Wait, wait! Please! You're right, I obtained entrance to your home under false pretenses, but I assure you my intentions are not dishonorable. You've already forced me to reveal a part of my secret." He held up a hand and allowed electricity to arc across his spread fingers. "If you'll indulge me for just a few minutes, I'll come clean. I promise you, my story is worth hearing."

Arthur paused, obviously torn between outrage and curiosity.

"Dad, let's hear him out. I think there's something going on here that we need to know about."

After a brief pause, Arthur resumed his seat. "All right then. Get to it and make it snappy."

Oglethorpe nodded and cleared his throat. "Right. Well, as you have figured out, I share certain characteristics with your daughter. In fact, I represent a group of empowered individuals."

"A vigilante group?" Arthur asked.

"Oh, no, nothing of the sort, I assure you. We are merely a loose association of gifted individuals seeking out others like us. We strive to maintain the secret that powers exist at all, just as you and Alice appear to have been doing. Vigilantism would only serve to endanger that secret. In fact, it was Alice's own venture into that arena that prompted me to approach you as I did. I trust you've concluded by now that Alice was in Mr. Player's house? Anyway, I needed a plausible cutout in case I determined that Alice was too much of a threat to our secrecy to be informed of our association's existence."

"Hrmph. Well, I can assure you that I will be having a long discussion with Alice about her recent activities. I think this interview might serve as an object lesson on the sorts of attention such public uses of her powers can bring." He looked at Alice sternly, and she quickly nodded. "So if you're not catching criminals, what does your association do?"

"Associate. With one another. Surely you have felt curious about why Alice has developed the abilities she has. But it's not the sort of thing one can talk about with just anyone, is it? Our primary function is just to provide our members with a community of others like themselves that they can communicate with freely and openly. A lot of that goes on in online chat rooms hosted on our own secure servers, but we also host social events several times a year so our members can meet each other in person."

"That's great!" Alice exclaimed. "How many members do you have? What are they like? Please, I want to know all about you."

"Hold on," Dr. Littleton interjected. "That all sounds well and good, but so far all I have is the word of someone who's already lied to me once today. Even if you are telling us the truth now, this all sounds very expensive. Like I said earlier, I'm not rich. The chat rooms are one thing, but we can't afford to go flying all across the country to get to these meetings."

"I would be happy to show you the chat rooms once Alice has been properly vetted. As for cost, we are blessed to have a wealthy benefactor who believes that gifted individuals are so rare that none should be excluded from our activities merely on the basis of finances. If Alice is accepted, she will receive all benefits at no cost to you."

"I see. And what other activities does your association engage in? You've indicated your primary agenda is social, but that implies there's more to it than that."

Oglethorpe smiled and nodded agreement. "Indeed, that's quite perceptive of you. We also engage in research into the origins and the science of powers."

"I hope you're not expecting to use Alice as a lab rat. That's just the sort of thing we've tried to avoid by keeping her powers a secret."

"Naturally, and we're entirely sympathetic to that desire. But consider what will happen once word of the gifted gets out. It will, you know, sooner or later."

"I've considered the possibilities for myself, of course," Alice said. "But until now I've more or less assumed I'm unique. Now that I know there are others, it changes the picture."

"Correct. If humanity is suddenly confronted with a whole community of empowered individuals, it's going to raise all sorts of questions in people's minds. And people feel threatened by what they don't understand. Therefore, we intend to be prepared with as much information as possible when that day arrives."

"And you compile that information by..." Arthur prompted.

"Yes, yes, we experiment a bit on ourselves. How else can we proceed? But we do so with a unique perspective, since we know that we'll all be examined sooner or later. We're talking about using scientific instruments to detect potentially unseen interactions between our powers and the environment, and scans to detect what portions of the brain are involved in their expression. We don't use drugs or anything more invasive than I've just mentioned. No one is about to forget that your daughter is an exceptional young woman. As a member of our community, she will be treated as such."

"I see." Arthur turned to Alice. "What do you think?"

"You need to ask? I'd have a chance to meet others like me, compare notes, exchange experiences. I'm in!"

Oglethorpe cleared his throat. "Uhm, yes, well, that remains to be seen, doesn't it?"

Alice looked at him in alarm. "Oh, you can't shut me out now! Why would you want to be so cruel?"

"It's not that I want to, but I have to ascertain you're a proper candidate. Merely possessing powers is not sufficient. We have to know that your beliefs and goals parallel our own. We have turned others away, although admittedly they never actually learned of our existence. May I ask you a few questions?"

Alice glanced to her father, who nodded after a brief hesitation. "Yeah, go ahead," she said.

"Excellent. Now, how old were you when you had your first paranormal experience?"

"I was eight."

Oglethorpe raised his eyebrows in surprise. "So young! If I may ask, did this follow an extremely traumatic event, either mentally or physically?"

"Yes," Arthur replied. "She accidentally poisoned herself on her eighth birthday. I was just back from a trip to South America, and she found a small vial of concentrated extract from a new plant species I had discovered. She was trying to act out the 'drink me' scene from *Alice in Wonderland*. We came close to losing her. How did you know?"

"Well, I didn't know details, of course, but it usually takes something life-threatening, or something that threatens a child's sense of safety or identity, to bring out powers at such an early age. It's far more common for them to emerge at puberty, or shortly thereafter. But there are certain benefits to the early onset scenario."

"Such as?" Arthur prompted.

"Powers that manifest at an early age tend to be more powerfully expressed, or express themselves in a wide range of unrelated spheres. Tell me, Alice, are you capable of more than talking to animals?"

"Yes. I can make myself grow or shrink, and I can shrink inanimate objects. I also have a limited flight ability, similar to a hang glider. And then there are my companions, of course."

"Companions?"

Arthur chuckled. "Alice's powers all have parallels in the Alice books. Characters from Lewis Carroll's writings are frequent visitors in this house."

"Ches, come on out and say hello to our guest," Alice called.

Ches faded in just behind and to one side of Oglethorpe's chair. "Well, this is a pleasant change of pace. They usually want me to stay out of sight. Whatever you've done to change their minds, I heartily approve."

"Amazing," Oglethorpe said as he half-turned in his chair to greet the feline. "And there are others?"

"Just about anyone or anything from the books has turned up at one time or another, but Ches is my most frequent companion. Hatter and Marchie, that's the March Hare, are also regulars."

"I see. I take it you read the books before your poisoning episode?"

"Several times, as well as some of Carroll's other pieces, like *The Hunting of the Snark*. I just picked up the first Alice book because it had my name in the title, but before long I was absolutely fixated on his stuff."

"Yes, that fits. Powers often express themselves in ways that reflect the person's interests or psychology."

"When you found my powers emerged early, you mentioned that they often express themselves in a variety of spheres," Alice said. "What are powers like for those that emerge in puberty?"

Oglethorpe paused before answering the question, but finally said, "I think the best analogy I can come up with is language. Do you know what would happen if you took a newborn from America and gave it to a family in Africa to raise?"

"It would grow up speaking the adoptive family's language rather than English." Alice answered.

"Exactly. There is no genetic predisposition for a child to learn one language over another; it's entirely dependent on the environment the child experiences. Every baby is capable of learning the clicks and whistles that are a part of certain languages, for example, but if his environment is lacking those particular vocalizations, the corresponding pathways in his brain will not develop; other vocalization patterns that are present are reinforced instead."

"How does that relate to powers?" Dr. Littleton asked.

"Well, it's probably not correct to say that a baby with the potential to become empowered is capable of expressing every power possible, but evidence from early emergence scenarios suggests that a wider range of powers is possible early on. Whatever mechanisms determine what powers the child will express have not settled into a definite matrix at eight. In terms of our analogy, the child could still easily learn any of several different languages."

"So when I was poisoned at eight, I gained powers that allowed me to control my size, speak to animals, glide, and summon my companions."

"Right. Those abilities are entirely unrelated to one another in terms of the ways in which they affect the world around you. The only thing that ties them together is your love of Lewis Carroll's stories. Your psychology worked to select abilities that fit the mold of your interests. If you had liked Roald Dahl's books, you probably would have powers that related to candy and giant fruit in some way. But if your powers had emerged at the usual age along with your love of Wonderland, you might have only gained the ability to control your size."

"So the other empowered only have one ability?" Alice asked.

"Not quite. It's more like they only learned one language. So they might have just as many abilities as you, or close enough, but they would all be related to one focus, like fire."

"Or electricity," Dr. Littleton said, indicating their guest.

"Exactly," Oglethorpe agreed. "Just out of curiosity, Alice, which of your powers manifested first?"

"That would be my looking-glass. That's how I get to Wonderland."

"Wonder-. Are you telling me you have access to another world? What's it like?"

"Kind of boring, to tell the truth. As near as I can figure, it's a parallel Earth where people never evolved. But it's where I first met Ches, so what else was I going to call it? I went there a lot when I was younger, but I can't take anyone else with me, and there's no one to talk to aside from the animals, so now I hardly ever bother."

"When you say looking-glass, do you mean that you turn a reflective surface into this portal?"

100

"No, I summon a mirror whenever I want to use it."

"Could you demonstrate?"

"Uh, sure, I guess." Alice looked to an open area beyond the coffee table and the mirror and its stand appeared instantly.

Oglethorpe got up and crossed over to stand in front of the mirror. He reached out to touch it, but his hand simply passed through it like a hologram. "Could I see you use it?" he asked.

"I'd really rather not."

Oglethorpe glanced back over his shoulder. "Is it painful?"

"No, but a transition to Wonderland and back can put me anywhere from the next room to a couple of miles away. I'm not too keen on a long hike at the moment."

"I see," he said. He glanced back at the mirror, catching Alice's gaze in the reflection. "Even so, I'm afraid I must insist."

Without breaking eye contact, Oglethorpe extended his right hand back towards Alice. She felt a force like an unseen hand grip the front of her dress, and she was suddenly pulled through the air, right over the coffee table, to Oglethorpe's side. Before Arthur could get to his feet, her supposed benefactor put his hand in the middle of her back and pushed her roughly into the mirror.

As Alice's hands intersected the plane of the glass, the mirror seemed to shatter. Large, jagged shards fell noiselessly towards the floor, vanishing along the way. The missing glass revealed a swirling white vortex beneath, with motes in all the colors of the rainbow merging and flowing towards its center. She screamed as the pain hit her, and she saw her arms stretching out and distorting impossibly into long, thin streamers before her. They vanished into the pearly wash of astral forces. Suction unlike anything she had ever felt grabbed her, forcing her deeper into the center, the pain escalating each moment. As her head crossed the threshold, the sensation spiked, and her vision blurred, then quickly faded to darkness.

CHAPTER EIGHT

A Place Called Boulder on the Wild Colorado

"Mr. Lane, Mr. Lane, I need help!"

It was late Tuesday afternoon. Autumn Glassford burst into the gymnasium and pulled up short, realizing that she had just interrupted, well, something. Constance, Min Ki and Julio were grouped around the PE teacher, who was holding up what looked like a laser tag harness. He was turning towards the entrance with an annoyed look on his face.

"Oh, I'm sorry, I didn't realize..."

"Never mind, out with it. What's so urgent?"

"Oh yeah. Well, you remember the assignment Mrs. Kilkarni gave us? Team Yellow, I mean?"

Mr. Lane nodded, twirling his hand impatiently, conveying 'Get on with it' without words.

"Right, well, I've been monitoring the Nevada Division of Wildlife radio frequency, and there's a boat that's signaled it's in trouble after a collision somewhere north of Sentinel Island. If I can get there quickly enough, I figured I could help out until rescue craft arrive."

"Is that all? Well, off you go then," he said sardonically. "Bippity boppity boo."

With a casual gesture from Houston, the gym and its occupants vanished from Autumn's vision.

♠ ♣ ♥ ♦

Autumn appeared about five feet above the surface of the water and plummeted into Lake Mead. At first she was angry with Coach Lane. She had expected him to send her to the shore of the lake, where she could strip down to the one-piece swimsuit she always wore beneath her clothes. She spent at least a part of each day in the water, so it was easiest just to be prepared.

However, on reflection, she decided the coach was right. Lives were at stake, and though she could move through the water extremely fast, time was of the essence. She quickly discarded her shirt and jeans, letting them sink into the depths, and letting her lungs fill with water as she did so. In less than a minute she was adapted to her new environment and ready to begin her search.

She could make out the bulk of Sentinel Island to the south, so she put it at her back, sank to a depth of about 30 feet, and screeched into the emptiness before her. She hung in the water, arms and legs spread wide to catch the returning echoes from the sound waves she had created. She mentally marked the locations of objects on the surface, counted to thirty, then sent out another wave of energy. As the echoes returned, she quickly discounted the objects that had moved significantly from their previous positions. There were only a couple of objects that had remained stationary, and she headed for the closest.

Autumn had practically grown up on the ocean, 'home' schooled by her oceanographer parents on the Trident III, a research ship that spent the better part of each year at sea. Before her powers developed, she had been content to learn how to man a radio, work a winch, and do sundry other things needed to help keep the ship functioning and its wealth of equipment in peak operational condition. Afterward, she spent as much time as possible in the water outracing dolphins when she wasn't doing schoolwork.

Luck was with her, and when she reached the object her sonar had identified, she found it was the boat that had radioed for help. Autumn figured it had been about five minutes since the initial broadcast, and the situation had obviously deteriorated significantly in that time. From her position below the water, she could see that the vessel, a thirty-foot motor craft, had struck a small sailboat, and was taking on water through a hole in the bow. The hole was not huge, but given time it could sink the craft.

The more immediate concern was the sailboat, however. The craft's lone occupant appeared to be unconscious. He was tangled in the rigging, and as Autumn approached, he was pulled under the surface in spite of his life vest as the hull began its final plunge to the lake bed.

Autumn quickly closed the distance and paced the man's descent. She had to free him. A quick glance at the mass of cloth and rope was sufficient to convince her that it would take too long to free him without cutting him free. She aimed an index finger at the rope about six inches below where it was wrapped around the victim's leg and directed a powerful burst of water in a very focused, narrow jet across its width.

The force of the water, concentrated in such a narrow cross section, could cut concrete in open air. Construction companies used a device called a water saw for just that purpose in situations where it was important to avoid the sparks caused by more conventional techniques. Underwater, Autumn found the cutting power dulled somewhat by the surrounding fluid, but it was still sufficient to meet her current need. With a couple of additional swipes, she finished freeing the man and watched his body reverse course and shoot towards the surface.

Autumn followed. She would have to surface and clear the water from her lungs before she could resuscitate the man, and doing so would run the risk of revealing herself. But she was not about to let him die at this point. Fortunately, someone on the larger craft noticed the disturbance as he surfaced. Within moments, a woman was in the water beside him and, with help from someone on the deck, the sailboat's pilot was hauled aboard.

Autumn noted a disturbance on the surface to one side of the motor boat. A stream of water was arcing from a hose draped over the side; the owner had started a pump. Maybe she could make sure it had a chance to get ahead of the water pouring in through the hole. Autumn concentrated for a moment, and the water nearby responded to her will. A column of water pushed up against the underside of the bow, lifting the gash above the waterline. Satisfied that she was doing as much as needed to be done, she settled in to wait for the rescue craft to arrive.

♠   ♣   ♥   ♦

"What can I do to help?" Scott asked, looking at the strange device.

Ms. Teresi was leaning into an open hatch on the side of a three-foot metal sphere sitting on a support scaffold in the middle of the laboratory's floor. The device, whatever it was, had a fairly simple-looking control panel on the side, consisting of a single button and a couple of knobs, though nothing was labeled. A power cable was attached to the bottom of the sphere and snaked off around a shelving unit containing bins of mismatched electronic components.

"You could go away," LaRonda suggested hopefully.

Scott shook his head. "You've got an evening class in an hour, and I'm supposed to make sure you get there. In the meantime, there must be something I can do to help you finish...whatever this is."

"No, there really isn't. So if you're staying, go sit in the corner and shut up."

"Come on, Ms. Teresi. Look how big this thing is. I'm pretty good with a soldering iron, Just show me what you need done, and I can work on a section that's well away from where you're working."

"No. You'd ruin it."

106

"That's not fair. You're not even giving me a chance. Let me show you what I can do."

LaRonda sighed and pulled herself out of the device to look at Scott for the first time since he had entered the lab. "It's not a matter of what you can do, it's a matter of what you can't do."

"Then teach me. I'm a quick learner."

"I can't. This depends on more than knowledge and skill."

"Huh?"

"It's my power, dunderhead. Look, if I tell you to run a cable from point A to point B, when you're done, I'll have a length of standard copper cable connecting two components, right?"

"Yeah," Scott said. "What's wrong with that? It'll be connected properly."

"Even if it is, it won't do the job I need it to do. I alter the basic properties of the materials I work with as I add them to my devices. So if I need that length of wire to act as a superconductor, even at high temperatures, it will. Now do you get it? All my devices are custom built by me, because they have to be."

"Oh," Scott said, crestfallen. He had been hoping he could learn how to build weird science devices like Ms. Teresi, but it looked like that wasn't going to happen. Still, this was the assignment Mrs. Kilkarni had given him, and he was determined to make some sort of contribution. "But there must be something I can do besides sit in a corner and act as your alarm clock."

Ms. Teresi scowled at him, considering. Finally, she threw up her hands. "Fine, I'll never get anything done with you yammerin' at me all the time. Why don't you try to sort out the components in those bins over there?"

Scott looked at the bins. It would probably take him all quarter to sort through all those tiny bits and pieces. Well, he had asked for a job, and now he had one. He sighed and walked over to look at the nearest shelf. "What are you working on, anyway?"

"A force field generator. Now let me work."

Ms. Teresi walked over to a radio sitting in the middle of the clutter on her work bench and switched it on. Hard rock music blasted out of the unit, rendering further discussion all but impossible. She returned to the hatch in the sphere, and Scott pulled out the first bin of components.

After a couple of minutes, Scott decided he needed to empty the bin and sort the pieces into piles. He got a plastic sheet from the workbench and brought it back over to the shelf. The workbenches were all too cluttered; it would be easier to work on the floor. He spread the sheet out and dumped the first bin. He figured if he was lucky, he'd get these components sorted by the time he had to hustle Ms. Teresi off to her first class.

He had been working for about ten minutes when the music suddenly cut off. Coach Lane's voice immediately filled the void, however.

"LaRonda, get out of there. I've been trying to get your attention for over a minute."

"Damn it, I'm working here. I know it isn't time for class yet, so stop interrupting me."

"Get out here now. This won't take long, but I want to be sure you're paying attention. Mrs. Kilkarni's got a job for us."

Scott's ears pricked up at this. He was hidden from Coach Lane's sight by the shelving unit. What sort of job would the principal have for her two paranormal teachers? He sat absolutely still and listened intently.

108

Ms. Teresi extricated herself from the sphere, not without some grumbling, and faced Coach Lane with arms crossed and an exasperated look on her face. She didn't say anything more, but waited for him to speak his piece.

"Elaine has located another potential student. She's afraid Oglethorpe may be closing in as well, so we're being tasked with making contact. Meet me in the garage right after dinner tomorrow night; we're taking a road trip."

"Damn, does it have to be tomorrow? Why can't we just get it done?"

Coach Lane frowned. "A young girl's life may be at stake; that takes priority over any little project you may be working on. As to the timing, Elaine feels the need to prepare our approach so that we don't frighten the girl or her father."

Ms. Teresi slumped in defeat. "OK, I'll be there."

"Good. Be sure to wear your party outfit. It could be a rough outing."

♠　♣　♥　♦

"Andrew, would you do me a favor?"

"Huh?" Andrew responded, still engrossed in the movie he and Esme were watching in the students' common room. She had waited for what she thought was a lull in the action, but apparently a scene where the heroes verbally sniped at each other while the camera did some sort of barrel roll around a spear passed for high drama in Andrew's world. Esme sighed; perhaps she'd have more luck when the movie was over.

But Andrew surprised her. He tore his gaze from the screen, hit the pause button, and gave her his full attention. "Sorry, you needed something?"

Esme smiled at him. "Yes. You know the photographer's coming tomorrow to take pictures for the student IDs and yearbook?"

"Sure."

"Well, I want your help to look my best."

"You look great, Esme. What could I possibly do?"

"Just a little creative editing. I have a mole on my neck that makes me very self-conscious."

"You do?"

"Yes, see, right here?" Esme leaned in close to Andrew, drawing his attention to a small but dark dot. "When I look at my yearbook, I don't want to be reminded of it."

"So why not have it removed?"

"I'm going to, but I can't have it done in time for the pictures tomorrow. So would you use your illusion to hide it?"

"Sure, if it'll make you happy."

"Thanks," Esme said, rewarding him with a light kiss on the cheek. "But promise me something else?"

"Um, sure, what?" Andrew asked.

"I don't want to take a chance on the illusion not blending in properly. So don't just hide the mole. Make an illusion that covers all of me. Just make it look like me without the mole."

"Isn't that a little extreme? Honest, I can just cover the mole and no one will ever know. It's..."

Esme gave Andrew a longer, more forceful kiss. As she finally ended it, she ran her fingers through his hair and tickled the back of his neck. "I want you to cover all of me," she said with a warm smile. "Please?"

110

"Um, sure, whatever you say, Esme."

Esme snuggled close to Andrew, and closed her eyes with a self-satisfied smile. "Thank you."

CHAPTER NINE

A Moment in Wonderland

Something was tickling Alice's nose.

That was a vast improvement over the pain she had been feeling. The intense agony had settled down to a dull, whole body ache, something she could almost choose to ignore. In fact, she felt like ignoring just about everything at the moment in order to just rest and bask in the sheer absence of sensation. So the tickle was really annoying.

Reluctantly, Alice opened her eyes. Late afternoon sunlight assaulted her eyes. It took her a moment to confirm that she was outside, and not lying on her living room floor near a window. She was on the ground, and a tuft of grass vibrated against her nose with every exhalation of breath. Groaning, Alice rolled over onto her back and stared up at the sky. She was in a glade in the middle of a forest. She closed her eyes again and listened. She could hear water tumbling over stones nearby, but there was absolutely no sound of traffic, planes, or anything else she could identify as man-made. She guessed she had made it to Wonderland.

Something about that bothered her. She examined that thought for a bit and suddenly sat up straight in alarm. "Dad!" she exclaimed. If she was here, her father was alone with Oglethorpe! She had to get back!

Before she could scramble to her feet, a voice drifted to her from the gathering gloom. "I wouldn't worry about your father, if I were you. My people have orders not to move against him - yet."

113

Alice looked toward to voice and was surprised to see Oglethorpe leaning against a tree. He flipped open an old-fashioned lighter and lit a cigarette, completely at ease. Alice felt a flare of anger towards the fake agent. She realized she had no idea who he really was or what he wanted, but she did know he didn't belong here. Wonderland was hers. She had never anticipated seeing another human here, and for him to be the first felt like a violation.

"How did you get here?" she asked hotly.

"I hitched a ride with you, obviously. Anyone ever tell you you're slow?"

"Why? Why would you want to come here?"

Oglethorpe sighed. "Yep, definitely slow. You've had access to this place for, what, seven years, and you've never thought about the potential? You've got the inside track - hell, the only track - to the riches of an entire planet, and you want to know why I wanted to come here? Wake up, girlie! California's gold deposits are near here. Or this world's equivalent. Somewhere over in an alternate Africa, a Hope Diamond is just waiting to be scooped up. I could go on for hours. I'm here to stake a claim!"

"You think I'm going to let you strip mine my world? Guess again."

"Oh, you think you're going to stop me?" Oglethorpe snorted. "You can't. You know why? This is just between you and me. There are no courts here, no authorities to enforce your claim for you. This is a simple case of conquest. As the strongest party here, I'll do what I damn well please."

"Yeah?" Alice replied. "Well, you just forgot one thing. You've just signed up for a permanent camping trip. You're stuck here, because I wouldn't take you back to Earth if I could. So what good are all those resources going to do you?"

Oglethorpe laughed derisively. "What makes you think I'm stuck? I'll let you in on a little secret. My power isn't throwing around lightning bolts. It's duplicating powers. I just have to be in contact with someone when they use one and I then I can use it for myself. See?"

He gestured and a mirror appeared beside him. This one was rectangular rather than oval, like Alice's. The wood of the frame was darker, and in place of ivy and flowers, there were carvings of faces screaming in terror or pain. It could have been the shadows beneath the trees, but Alice thought even the glass looked smoky and dim.

Oglethorpe smirked at her. "I can go home any time I want. What's more, I don't have any psychological baggage against bringing in more people. I can move in work crews, even heavy equipment, at key positions all over the planet. I'll be so rich, Warren Buffet will look like a homeless vagrant. And then comes the best part."

"Which is...?"

"I take over back on Earth. With both wealth and the powers I've collected, no one will be able to stand against me!"

Alice blinked, trying to process this vision. Finally, she burst out laughing. Oglethorpe looked at her in annoyance.

"Wow," Alice said, "I bet your comic book collection is the envy of all the inmates back at the asylum! You really expect to take over the world on the basis of money and some cheap tricks?"

"They're more than just tricks, girlie, and I paid for most of them in blood." Oglethorpe shrugged. "True, most of the blood wasn't mine, but lots of people paid a high price to make me what I am. You've seen only a fraction of what I'm capable of."

Alice shook her head in disbelief. Her life revolved around chaotic personalities and unpredictable events, and she felt like she should be handling this conversation better. But the events that had followed Oglethorpe's appearance on her doorstep didn't fit the usual mold. It was as if the looking-glass had deposited her in the middle of a cheap action heroes movie, and she felt disoriented by the shift in perspective. She found herself saying whatever came into her head, her conscious thoughts hopelessly outpaced by her mouth.

"Okay, well, if you're going to do this, you might as well do it right. What are you going to call yourself? Captain Detructicon? No, wait, I've got a better one. Annihilus! Don't you just love it? Can't you just see yourself with a big scarlet A on your tights? Oh, no, wait, that might give people the wrong idea."

Oglethorpe scowled at Alice. Electricity danced along his forearm and lashed out to strike the ground in front of her. She gave a startled cry as she jumped back, feeling the hairs on her arms standing on end.

"Make no mistake, Alice. This is no game, and I will not tolerate foolishness. As of right now, this world is mine. Your ability to come here is either an asset to me, or an unacceptable security risk. So make your choice."

"Choice?" Alice asked, voice trembling. The sudden attack had shocked her out of her weirdly disjointed sense of the situation. Speech was once again a conscious, rather than automated, activity. While she still didn't believe Oglethorpe could actually pull off a takeover back on Earth, his ability to threaten her here was entirely credible.

"Yes. It would be useful to have an agent capable of checking up on my interests here without having to bring her here myself. Agree to serve me, and you'll find me a generous master. Your duties would necessarily include travel all over the world, both here and back on Earth. A lot of people would consider it a dream job. Of course, if you refuse, you'll never leave this clearing. I can't have you trying to fight some sort of guerrilla campaign against my workers here."

Oglethorpe's tone of voice was chilling. He could have been asking her to choose between two types of pie for dessert. A nugget of anger at Alice's core suddenly transformed into a crystal of pure, diamond-hard resolve. She swore to herself he would never remove a single flake of gold from the smallest stream as long as she had any say in the matter.

The Queen of Hearts popped into existence behind Oglethorpe. "Off with his head!" she shouted.

As Oglethorpe turned towards the the Queen, Alice hastily reached into her pocket for a piece of candy and popped it in her mouth.

"You'll have to do better than that, girlie," Oglethorpe said.

"I intend to," Alice replied, her form swelling until she was fifteen feet tall. She rushed forward, leveling the most powerful punch she could muster at her opponent's head. "Now let's see who's the stronger party."

Oglethorpe swiveled back to her, braced himself, and caught her descending fist in one outstretched hand. He stopped her attack cold. Alice froze in shock. True, even at her current size, she couldn't throw a car at someone. She could easily pick up the heavy couch at home, though. Yet her opponent had countered her as if she were no more than a toddler throwing a tantrum. Oglethorpe grinned nastily and took advantage of her surprise by allowing her fist to move forward several inches as he bent his elbow. Then he pushed forward against her knuckles and Alice flew backwards twenty feet, landing heavily on her back.

"Ow! Okay, I guess that's still you," she muttered to herself.

"It's not too late, girlie. I appreciate a little spunk, but this is your last chance."

I need a distraction, Alice thought. She mentally called for her companions most suited to that task, and ten card soldiers, the nonroyalty of the suite of clubs, appeared in an arc between her and Oglethorpe.

"Company, advance!" Ace bellowed. The others did their best to comply with the order, but their formation was ragged as several overbalanced their lightweight bodies with their heavy halberds and took several seconds to recover.

Oglethorpe cocked back his left arm, suddenly wreathed in flames, and hurled a fireball at Deuce. It burned a hole straight through the center of the soldier, who only had time to say, "Oh, bloody 'ell" before the flames consumed the rest of his body. Oglethorpe started striking out at the card soldiers with alternating lightning and fire attacks, which both produced devastating effects against his pasteboard foes.

While her enemy was occupied, Alice crawled to the stream near the edge of the clearing, swallowed a mouthful of water she hastily scooped up with one hand, and began to shrink. *He's too strong. Being a giant only gives him a target he can't possibly miss. Maybe I can gain an advantage if I can hide.*

Alice wasted no time in making for a clump of bushes. It wasn't the closest cover, but she thought it would offer her the best chance of being able to watch what Oglethorpe was up to while remaining out of sight. But he finished dispatching her contingent of protectors before she reached her goal. "You can't hide for long, Alice," he called, and prepared to throw a fireball at her.

Alice noted the danger as she glanced back over her shoulder at the sound of his voice. Reacting without conscious thought, she summoned the Pudding from the banquet scene in *Through the Looking Glass*, placing it directly between her and Oglethorpe. The fireball impacted on the pudding, which immediately blazed up. "Such impertinence!" it said as it hopped up and down angrily on its platter. "A pudding expects to be set on fire, but still!"

118

The ploy worked well enough to allow Alice to reach the bushes. However, she continued directly through the clump and veered to her left as she came out the other side. Another fireball set the bushes ablaze so quickly, she felt the heat painfully on her back as she pushed her way through grass stalks to get away.

"Oooo, nearly got you that time, girlie," Oglethorpe taunted. "Why not make this easy on yourself? There's no way you're going to take me down with a bunch of storybook characters."

By this time, Alice had taken refuge in a tangle of roots at the base of an oak tree at the edge of the clearing. She hunched down and tried to breathe quietly through her mouth. Her own heartbeat thundered in her ears, fueled by her fear. If Oglethorpe had enhanced hearing, that alone would probably lead him to her. "Think, Alice," she commanded herself quietly. "What have you got to work with?" But her mind refused to focus on any single thought long enough for her to examine it. She was left with nothing more than a confusing blur of images, sense memories, and random phrases surging back and forth like a pool of water in the midst of a storm.

She looked up in desperation, and noticed movement within the canopy of a nearby tree. Focusing on it, she saw a pair of eyes with vertical slits for pupils hovering a couple of feet above a stout branch.

"Ches?" she whispered.

A familiar feline smile spread out beneath the eyes, displaying teeth that suddenly looked longer, sharper, and altogether more dangerous than Alice had ever appreciated before. One of the eyes winked at her. Alice felt a bit of courage swell within her, and she risked a peek over the root to see what Oglethorpe was doing. He was walking along the edge of the clearing, scanning the underbrush as he moved. Alice scrambled around the base of the tree to put the trunk between them. She had to lure him into position.

119

She ate another piece of candy to return to her regular size, put her back to the tree trunk, and called out to him. "I don't suppose that job offer is still open?" She did not have to work at putting a quaver in her voice at all.

Oglethorpe chuckled. "So you're starting to see reason? Or is it just that you've realized how out of your league you are?"

Alice swallowed and risked a look over her shoulder and around the trunk. Oglethorpe had let his electricity and fire die down. He watched her with a confident sneer on his face, hands on his hips. She took the ebb in open hostilities as a good sign and turned to fully face him. "Hey, you're asking me to commit to something big. I had to be sure you were up to it, right? You can't blame me for wanting a little demonstration before I agreed to help out." She cautiously stepped out from behind the tree, fully exposed to his retaliation and ready to dodge or dive for cover if necessary.

He studied her for several seconds, then finally snorted in acceptance. "Well, I have to admit I'm surprised. I've recruited plenty of supers to my organization, but I didn't really think you'd be one to sign up. You don't fit the mold." He approached her suspiciously, but without caution, and reached out to cup her chin in one hand, forcing her to stare into his eyes. "So what's your angle? What do you want?"

Alice thought desperately, and gave him the only answer he was likely to believe. "Money. I want more out of life than what Dad's been able to provide on his measly professor's salary. I mean, look at me! I got my license months ago, and he hasn't even been able to buy me a used junk heap. I still have to ride my bike to school or take the stupid bus! I deserve better!" She stared defiantly into his eyes, willing him to believe the lie.

He finally released her, allowing her to take a step back from him. "Well, looks like this is your lucky day. Give me a minute to put out these fires and we'll be on our -".

120

Oglethorpe's comment was cut off by a loud snarling sound from a branch overhead. Before he could react, Ches landed on his back, claws extended. The sound of ripping cloth and Oglethorpe's startled cry of rage filled the air, but Oglethorpe remained on his feet. He tried to reach back to grab the cat, but he couldn't get a sufficient grip on Ches to pull him off. Ches wasted no time, but sank his teeth into Oglethorpe's neck and shoulder. The man stumbled forward into the underbrush and collapsed. Alice stepped back and watched the wildly moving vegetation, through which she caught occasional glimpses of the combatants. Suddenly, everything became still and silence took the place of the sounds of the fierce struggle.

"Ches?" Alice called hesitantly.

The bushes moved again, slowly this time. The fight was over and the victor was moving back towards the clearing. Finally Ches' head appeared between two tightly spaced plants as he entered the open space, favoring his left forepaw. Alice released a breath she hadn't even realized she was holding as relief washed the tension from her body.

"Ches! Thank goodness! Let me help you."

Alice started towards her friend, but had taken no more than a step when Oglethorpe came hurling through the air. His leap carried him onto Ches' back. Alice had only a moment to take in the ragged wounds on the man's face and neck. Oglethorpe's front was covered in blood, which had obviously flowed and spurted from the slashes and puncture marks Ches had inflicted, but now the wounds barely trickled and Oglethorpe seemed not to be inconvenienced by them in the slightest. He reached down, grabbed the cat's head by both sides, and then looked up at Alice, staring directly into her eyes across the yards that separated them. He twisted Ches' head violently, Alice heard a loud crack, and the feline fell limply to the turf.

"Nooo!" Alice screamed, horrified by the suddenness and brutality of Oglethorpe's attack. The crystalline core of her resolve vaporized, swept away in an white-hot explosion of feeling unlike anything she had known before. She had begun this fight determined to stop her foe from using Wonderland for his own selfish ends. Alice knew intellectually that might require killing, but emotionally she was unprepared for that. She valued life too much to really believe that the confrontation would lead to that end. But loosing Ches changed her in an instant.

Restraint vanished. Alice wanted Oglethorpe *gone*, something she had never truly wished for about anyone previously. And with that fervent desire, something stirred deep within her, answering her call for revenge. As the entity rose up in her consciousness, she knew it instinctively for what it was, and a verse came unbidden to her lips as she willed her newest companion forth.

> *"In the midst of this world you are trying to seize,*
> *In the midst of your laughter and glee,*
> *May you swiftly and violently vanish away,*
> *For my snark IS a Boojum, you see!"*

Oglethorpe stood up straight, tense and wary as something joined them in the clearing. The presence was undeniable, though sight did not serve to reveal it at first. A flicker to one side drew his eyes and Alice's to a spot equally distant from both of them. At first, Alice thought she was seeing the shadows of tree branches moving in response to the breeze. But she quickly corrected that assessment as she noted the shape, seen only in outline as a slight warping of light that was easier to make out as the figure moved. It looked like a large bird similar to an ostrich, but with a thicker neck and a massive, wide beak. It moved like a predator, and the sight of it filled Alice with dread.

"What is that?" Oglethorpe said, showing nerves for the first time since their confrontation began. As he spoke, the shape quickly oriented on him and took two quick steps in his direction.

Alice wanted nothing more than to look away, close her eyes, or run away into the surrounding forest, but she was rooted to the spot. She seemed incapable of even blinking. She shook her head and said, in a small, quiet voice, "Your end."

Oglethorpe had no time to respond. The figure darted forward, closing the remaining distance between them in a second, and latched onto Oglethorpe's wrist with its beak. Oglethorpe screamed and tried to pull away, but even his massive strength could not wrench him free of the entity Alice sent against him. He started to fade. His body became translucent as his voice faded, seeming to come from farther and farther away. Within moments, he and the Boojum had vanished.

In the quiet that followed, Alice shuddered, and then ran to the sprawled form of Ches, still lying near the edge of the clearing. She felt the hot tears spilling down her cheeks as she noted the unnatural angle of his head to his body, and the glassy stare that took in nothing. "Oh, Ches. Don't leave me, Puss. Please don't." She stroked his fur, then stretched out her arms to encircle his still chest in a hug as if she'd never let go. But Ches' remains proved as elusive as he'd ever been in life, and the body vanished, leaving her slumped and sobbing in a world of her own.

CHAPTER TEN
A String of Bad Luck

"The tonfa is a peasant weapon," Constance said. She unzipped her equipment bag and removed one of the pair she carried and offered it to Julio. Her voice echoed slightly within the mostly empty confines of the gymnasium, but Min Ki's exclamations as he went through his own workout routine provided enough background noise to keep the feedback from being too distracting. So far, she had managed to avoid stumbling over her words while talking to her new teammate by restricting herself to short greetings and responses. She figured she should be able to get through a discussion of her weaponry as well. She had delivered this same talk numerous times at martial arts demonstrations.

Her role as instructor was an improvisation. After Coach Lane gave them a quick introduction to the harnesses they would have to wear during the leadership match, he had left to deal with some sort of special project. He teleported away with nothing more than a vague "Get in a good work out" by way of instruction.

Julio took the club and turned it over in his hands. It measured about 18 inches, with a handle sticking straight out about a third of the way along its length. The wood was squared off where the handle attached, but quickly became cylindrical to either side.

Constance pulled the second tonfa from her bag and then continued. "It was supposedly derived from the handles of millstones villagers used for grinding grain. If that story is correct, it made the perfect weapon for the underclass. The red oak construction made it

125

durable, it was available in great numbers, and its use melded well with open handed, or unarmed, fighting styles, which is all the peasants could aspire to."

Julio grasped the first implement by the short handle with the longer section projecting beyond his fist and swung it experimentally. "The grasp seems kind of awkward," he ventured.

Smiling, Constance retrieved the weapon, then stepped back with one in either hand. When she had a clear space around her, she launched into a kata, wielding both with confidence. She paused at times to let Julio see how she employed the weapons.

"The tonfa is versatile. It can be grasped like a regular club, but with the handle it can also be used to block." Constance held one by the short handle with the longer section tight against her forearm, which she raised to counter an imaginary attack. The shorter section projected beyond her fist. "It can also concentrate the force of a blow in a very small area." She thrust underneath her raised arm with the alternate tonfa, held in an identical position to the first. She stopped with the tip inches from Julio's nose. He gave her a nod to signal his understanding of how much damage the blow could have done if it had been delivered in earnest, and Constance continued with her routine. She fell silent as she flowed smoothly from one stance to the next, enjoying the familiarity of the exercise as she fended off and punished a veritable hoard of unseen foes. When she finished, Julio applauded appreciatively.

"That was pretty awesome," he said. "Uhm, can I ask you something?"

Constance bit her lower lip and nodded, feeling a quiver in her stomach. *Maybe he likes me and wants to ask me out.*

"Thanks. Well, I was wondering," Julio began, and Constance felt a small thrill of hope. "I'm a speedster, and Min Ki is, well ..." Julio gestured towards the gymnasium's ceiling.

Min Ki was well into his workout, swinging from one rafter to another as the arms of his psychic armor swiftly extended to allow the gauntlet to grasp the next beam in line. As he released each beam he passed and swooped forward, the extended arm smoothly retracted to keep him well above floor level. This had the added effect of accelerating his forward progress. Min Ki had mapped out a course for himself around the periphery of the space and seemed to shave seconds off his time with each lap.

Constance took in the display and Julio's implication in a couple of seconds and nodded for him to continue.

"So what's your ability? I mean, being a martial artist is cool and all, but it really doesn't stack up against powers. I figure there has to be more."

"Oh," Constance said, forcing a smile in spite of a momentary flash of disappointment. "All you've seen me do are standard exercises and katas any practitioner learns. But you're right, that's not the whole story."

She resumed her starting stance for the kata she had just performed with the tonfas. But in place of beginning the routine immediately, she closed her eyes in concentration. A second later, her hands and weapons were wreathed in eerie blue-white flames. She opened her eyes in time to see Julio take a step back in surprise. She calmly began her kata once more, and the flames swirled and flared behind the clubs as they wove through their intricate dance. As she finished, she flipped one of the weapons to Julio. As it left her hand, the flames instantly winked out of existence. Julio caught it reflexively. He seemed on the verge of dropping it, but quickly relaxed and tightened his grip.

"It's not even warm," he said.

"That's right," Constance replied. "But I can set fire to anything I hit, or at least deal a little extra hurt."

127

"Cool, we've got a human torch on the team," Min Ki called. He had halted his latest circuit of the gym and was now lowering himself to the floor with one slowly elongating arm. "Can you control the fire to make cages and stuff, too?"

"I'm not a human torch. My flames are fueled by my Chi," Constance replied. She pronounced the odd term with a leading "k" and it rhymed with pie.

"What's that?" Julio asked

"The internal energy martial artists channel," Min Ki answered as he retracted his arm. He let his armor wink out of existence as walked over to join his teammates. "Some people equate it with the life force."

"Right," Constance said. "And my power allows me to do a lot more with it than most masters."

"Like what?" Min Ki asked eagerly.

"Well, I always liked watching kung fu movies, especially those that included mystical elements. When I got my powers, I found I could mimic a lot of those stunts. So I can't fly, but I can run or stand on the scantiest support, like the warriors who fought on top of the bamboo forest in *Crouching Tiger, Hidden Dragon*."

"Impressive. What else?" Min Ki prodded.

Constance gave him a crooked smile. "Show up at the leadership match and I'll give you a demonstration."

Min Ki's cheerful expression collapsed in shock. "Huh?"

"You didn't expect me to give up all my surprises, did you?"

Julio chuckled and clapped the other boy on the shoulder. "She's got you dead to rights, man. We may be a team in name right now, but until the match is over, no one should be putting their best moves on display. You haven't, have you?"

Min Ki looked down in embarrassment. "I guess I really hadn't thought about that. I was so excited to be where I could do stuff openly, I've just been cutting loose and having fun."

"Well, that probably isn't a fatal lapse in judgment, in your case," Candace consoled him. "That armor of yours is pretty versatile. We'll have our hands full just dealing with what we've seen so far."

"Really?"

"Oh, yeah, we're totally outclassed," Julio said, giving Constance a hugely theatrical wink he fully intended Min Ki to see. He laughed at the look of consternation that appeared on his teammate's face. "Never mind, Min Ki. Let's grab some dinner. This won't look so bad in the morning."

♠ ♣ ♥ ♦

As Red Team left the gym, Julio lapsed into a reflective mood. He still wasn't happy his parents had dumped him here, but he had to admit Constance and Min Ki were good company. In time, he thought he might even be tempted to call them friends. Given the way his last twenty-four hours had played out, he probably needed some friends in this school.

It had all started with his encounter with Regis Adair before the team assignment assembly had started. Julio and the senator's kid were far too different in their outlooks on life to ever be friends; he had known that as soon as he spotted the twit. Regis smelled of wealth and privilege, and probably had "Young Republican" etched in gold filigree on the stick that was rammed so tightly up his ass. Still, Julio wasn't the type to pick a fight. He would have been more than content to ignore Regis and let him go his own way.

Regis, however, seemed to have other ideas. He had deliberately provoked Julio with his snide comments, for no good reason as far as he could see. Maybe that was just his way. Maybe he habitually tried to enlighten the poor, ignorant savages he came in contact with so they could join him in his budding ideal society. But Julio sensed there was more behind their exchange, and he felt uneasy whenever he reviewed the incident. His gut told him that he and Regis weren't through with each other yet.

Regis was just one person, though. So Julio tried to forget about him and concentrated on getting through his first full day of classes at Prometheus Academy, starting this morning. That proved more difficult than he had counted on.

His day started out wrong before he even got out of bed. His alarm clock didn't go off, so he overslept and missed out on breakfast. He managed to get to his first appointment, Mr. Honeycutt's history class, with a few minutes to spare. So as the other kids were settling into their desks and gossiping, Julio decided to work on a few sketches.

He turned to a fresh page in his portfolio and began drawing cartoonish figures with exaggerated features to represent various vices. He had drawn caricatures of Vanity, Wantonness, and Greed and was halfway through another when he was startled by the sound of a throat clearing right behind him. Mr. Honeycutt was standing there, looking unaccountably angry. After all, class hadn't even started, so why should he care if Julio was wasting time sketching?

"Uhm, good morning, Mr. Honeycutt," Julio ventured.

"I see you haven't wasted any time in stereotyping your classmates, Mr. Zarzosa," he said coolly. "Though as you probably haven't spent more than five minutes getting to know any of them, I find your willingness to openly associate them with such negative character traits the height of arrogance."

"I, uh, what?" Julio was having trouble understanding what had gotten his teacher so worked up. But the exchange had drawn the others' attention, and the students all clustered around his desk to see what he had been drawing.

130

"Aiee! What is the meaning of this?" Kasie Hardine demanded, pointing at one of his drawings with the finger that bore her diamond and star sapphire ring.

"Or zis?" chimed in Esme, indicating another.

Julio looked at the angry girls, then glanced down at his artwork, still completely in the dark. Suddenly, his stomach clenched up as he noted the details. He had been working quickly, even for him, and so he hadn't really stopped to look at each finished sketch before he started on the next. Kasie's finger rested on the drawing of Vanity, which he now saw bore an unmistakable resemblance to her, right down to the profusion of gaudy jewelry. Worse, Esme had apparently served as his inspiration for Wantonness.

"Oh, shi-," he said, hastily censoring himself as he caught sight of Mr. Honeycutt's disapproving frown. "I mean, I'm sorry. I didn't mean-"

"For us to see your poor excuse for jokes at our expense?" suggested Regis. Julio noted with dismay that Greed looked just like his self-appointed rival. "You know, I had begun to think I was too hard on you at the assembly yesterday. Now I can see I had you pegged, right from the start."

"No, please," Julio begged, eyes darting from one angry classmate to another. "I didn't mean to insult anyone. I'll rip these up right away."

Mr. Honeycutt dropped his hand on the middle of the paper, preventing Julio from tearing the page out of his book. "Not so fast, Mr. Zarzosa. I'll need this for evidence of your disrespect for faculty." He indicated the figure for Pompousness. Even half-finished, the jawline and shape of the nose made it clear who Julio had in mind. "Congratulations, young man. You've just set the all-time record for fastest detention earned - ever."

131

Julio quickly decided that discretion was the better part of valor and merely nodded. He allowed the teacher to remove the sheet, which Mr. Honeycutt folded up and put in his desk drawer.

As the history teacher began his lesson, Julio's thoughts were a confused jumble. How had he managed to produce such insulting pieces without being aware of what he was doing? True, he did see traces of each of the vices he had portrayed in his subjects, but he knew better than to openly mock people, especially when most of them had never offered him any harm. His frustration with being at Prometheus Academy at all must have been affecting him more than he realized.

With such a small student body, news of his transgression was common knowledge before second period began. For the rest of the day, everyone he came in contact with gave him the cold shoulder, or glowered at him as they passed in the halls. Only Regis and Constance behaved differently. Regis wouldn't condescend to act like Julio's opinion mattered to him. But instead of glowering at him, Regis just gave him a knowing smile whenever they met. Julio couldn't figure out what he had to be so satisfied about. He actually would have preferred the stock, disapproving frown everyone else favored.

Constance's behavior towards him was, if anything, even more confusing. His schedule included a Red Team meeting just before dinner, and Julio had made his way to the gym dejectedly, convinced he would spend his entire time at school without ever recovering from that morning's misunderstanding. At first he was hopeful, because his female teammate had actually given him a small, encouraging smile. Yet when he had tried to engage her in conversation, he found she would hardly spare him two words together.

"Why are you even bothering to try to make nice with us?" Min Ki had challenged him. "I'm sure you've already got your pictures for us all figured out."

"How many times do I have to say I'm sorry?" Julio exclaimed. "You have no idea what it's like for me."

"What do you mean? What makes you so special?" Min Ki asked.

"I'm a speedster."

"So?"

Julio sought for a way to make the other boy understand. "Look, have you ever said something on the spur of the moment, and immediately regretted it?"

"Well, sure," Min Ki allowed. "Who hasn't? But what's that got to do with this morning?"

"Tell me why you said those things, even though you knew better."

"I don't know. My mouth just got to running faster than my brain. I said it before I really thought about it."

"Exactly. And when I get inspired, my drawing can be just like that. My body responds as quickly as your mouth, and I can draw one picture and be on to the next before I even have time to evaluate it."

"The pictures were still mean-spirited," Min Ki said.

"Yes, they were," Julio admitted. "And when I went back to look at them later on, I would have seen that I had unintentionally modeled the figures after actual people and I would have scrapped them. It was just bad luck that someone else noticed the problem before I did."

Min Ki looked doubtful. "Really?"

"Look, we were getting along before the team assignments, right?" Julio said. "On that basis, can't you just accept that I'm not usually a complete jackass? At least provisionally? I did admit I was wrong, after all."

Min Ki thought about that, then stuck out a hand. "All right. If you can't trust a teammate, who can you trust?"

Julio gratefully shook the other boy's hand, and the tension level dropped by several degrees. Then, after Coach Lane's brief appearance, they had set about directing the remainder of the session themselves. Min Ki had begun swinging from the rafters, while Constance had suggested that she had something to show Julio that might help him be more effective in combat. That had lead to her lecture on the tonfa.

As Red Team entered the cafeteria, Julio felt a slight surge of hope. It looked like he had managed to win over two people, or convinced them to give him another chance, at least. Detention wouldn't be so bad, and maybe he could recover from this morning's disaster after all.

As he approached the service line, he noted that Julianna was at its end, and he hurried over to get close to her. If there was just one more person he could improve his standing with, the beautiful blond would be his choice.

"Hi. Anything look good tonight?" he asked her as he helped himself to an empty tray.

Julianna gave him an unfriendly look and then pointedly turned away. She helped herself to a bottle of fruit juice from a refrigerated cabinet and moved further down the line. Julio grabbed a bottle of water and followed to where she had been stopped by the people ahead of her.

"Come on, don't be like that. I'm not a bad guy. I've been apologizing for this morning all day. You can't stay mad at me forever. Besides, I didn't even draw a vice figure based on you."

Julianna turned to face him at that. "You managed to draw insulting figures of both of my teammates, though. How do I know you

134

wouldn't have come up with something equally nasty for me if Mr. Honeycutt hadn't stopped you?"

"That would never happen," Julio assured her. "Angels have no vices."

Julio thought he saw a slight twitch at the corners of Julianna's mouth at that, as if she was trying hard not to smile in spite of herself. She looked away and took another couple of steps along the serving counter, where she pointed at her main dish selection for the attendant to serve up. As Julio stepped up next to her, she stood on the toes of her feet as she reached up to take the plate off the shelf above the glass partition.

Before he could say anything to try to charm Julianna further, Julio heard an involuntary cry of surprise from behind him. Glancing over his shoulder, he saw that Kip Tarrin had approached the line, deep in conversation with Levi Drafton. Kip was using broad, sweeping gestures to emphasize his point, and had just bumped Constance's shoulder. Her tray, with an uncapped cup of soda, was about to fall. His speed-enhanced senses had allowed him to take this in instantly, and he reacted without thought, lunging towards the impending spill to catch the cup before it could hit the floor.

As he moved, he felt a tug on his foot, and then heard an outraged scream and the crash of falling dinnerware, followed immediately by more angry shouts. He turned back towards Julianna, but she was no longer standing in line. Julio found her at the center of the commotion, where she was picking herself up off the floor by an overturned table. The faculty who had been eating there were splattered with the remains of their dinner, but looked clean compared to Julianna, who seemed to have pulled everything down on top of her.

Julio just stood there, staring at this spectacle, completely unable to explain how it had come to pass. Julianna finally regained her feet and stalked over to him.

"You idiot! What did you do that for? And to think I almost fell for your 'poor misunderstood artist' act. You stay away from me, you hear?" She grabbed the soda from Julio's unresisting hand and threw it in his face before stomping away. "And I'm sending you the cleaning bill, you freak!"

Julio just shook his head in dismay as Min Ki walked up next to him. "What happened?" he asked.

Min Ki grinned at him. "You did. Your shoe's untied."

"Huh?"

Min Ki pointed at his foot. "Your shoe's untied," he repeated. "When you stepped up next to her, your shoelace flopped under her foot while she was getting her plate. And you've got the end of the lace knotted where it's gotten frayed, see? When you moved to catch Constance's cup, you swept her leg out from under her with so much force, you threw her back into the table. Man, that was something. You've got to figure out a way to use that in a fight."

Julio sighed in defeat. "Yeah, I'll work on that."

CHAPTER ELEVEN
Aftermath

Alice stepped through the mirror and looked around. Night had fallen and she was in back of some sort of commercial building, but did not recognize it immediately. She walked to the corner and looked out on a familiar scene. Sighing, she pulled out her phone and punched up a number from her fast dial list. Then she crouched down, her back sliding along the wall until she was sitting on the pavement, hidden by the shadows at the back of the store. Her mind was still back in a lonely forest clearing.

Her father picked up almost immediately. "Alice? Where are you? Are you okay?"

"I'm...not hurt. Can you pick me up at the Starbucks on Peabody Road?"

"Of course. You don't sound too good. What did Oglethorpe do to you?"

"I'll tell you about it later. Don't worry, he won't be back."

"How can you be sure?"

"Dad, please, just come get me." Alice could feel new tears on her cheeks, and her voice was on the verge of cracking.

"Sorry, I'm on my way. Thank God you're safe."

Alice took a bit to compose herself after she hung up, then hauled herself to her feet and moved around the corner toward the front of the building. She had appeared behind a 7-11. She could have asked her father to pick her up here, but she felt a need to move. The Starbucks was just over a block away, so she had plenty of time to get there.

As she walked across the parking lot, a new thought suddenly occurred to her, and she stopped short. The driver of a car pulling in to get some gas had to brake hard to keep from hitting her and blew his horn angrily. Alice quickly moved to the sidewalk as she reached for her phone again.

After several rings, Miranda finally picked up. "Hey, what's up?"

"Are you okay?" Alice asked.

"Uh, yeah. Why wouldn't I be?"

"The FBI agent turned out to be a fake. He's had people watching me. He attacked me."

"Ohmigod. Seriously? Are you hurt?"

"No, but..."

"Alice? What happened?" Miranda prompted when she stopped.

"He...He killed Ches," she finally said past the lump in her throat.

"What? How? How did you get away?"

Alice shook her head. "I can't talk about it now. I'll fill you in later. The important thing is he may have people watching you. We're together so much, he can't have found me without noticing you. I don't know if his people will want to talk to you or anything, but be careful. If you even think someone is following you or anything, tell the police or your parents or someone."

"Tell them what? My best friend is a superhero and I'm being stalked by her arch nemesis?"

"Just tell them someone is following you and it's creeping you out. That should be enough."

"Yeah, I guess so."

"Miranda, you know how we always wondered if I was the only super? Well Oglethorpe, the fake agent, had powers, too. He was wicked powerful, and he hinted he had friends. I don't know how much of what he told me was BS, but don't take any chances. Assume anyone tailing you has powers, but won't want to use them in public. You're probably safest where there are lots of witnesses. Got it?"

"What about Oglethorpe? I don't even know what he looks like."

"He's not a problem anymore."

"How do you figure?"

"I killed him." Even as she said it, Alice could hardly believe it. Shouldn't she be feeling...something?

"No way! How?" Miranda sounded excited by this news, and Alice felt a spike of resentment flare up.

"I don't want to talk about it," she replied sharply. "But his friends will be pissed when they find out. Just be careful. I've got to go."

"Yeah, okay," Miranda replied in a quiet, hurt tone. "I'm so sorry about Ches. See you tomorrow."

Alice hung up and started again towards Starbucks. So much had happened in the past couple of hours that she was having trouble processing it all. Her mind kept jumping from one image to another. There was Oglethorpe, confident in his power and toying with her pathetic attempts to fight him. Ches stretched out limply on the ground. Lastly, there was the fearsome not-presence of the Boojum. This new

139

companion or power frightened Alice more than anything else she had just experienced, and she mentally shied away from examining her memories of it whenever her thoughts brought her back to it.

A few minutes after she reached her destination, her father's car pulled into the parking lot. He nearly got clipped by a car traveling the opposite direction when he made the left turn without quite enough time, scraping the undercarriage on the driveway in his haste to get to her. He braked hard, with the car coming to rest at a bit of an angle across the handicapped space. He left the motor running as he struggled from the car and Alice rushed to him. They embraced, and Alice felt the tension she had been carrying lessen slightly as she breathed in the too-sweet scent of his pipe tobacco.

Her father finally broke the hug. "Let's go," he said. "You can tell me all about it in the car."

Alice got in the car and curled up into a ball on her seat, resting her forehead on her knees. Dr. Littleton took a bit longer to get into the car and set his cane where he could easily grasp it when he was ready to get out again. "You look like you need a good night's sleep. I'll warm you up some milk when we get home."

Alice lifted her head in alarm. "No! We can't go home."

Dr. Littleton paused in the act of putting the car in gear. "Come again?"

"Oglethorpe has friends. He said they had orders not to move against you yet, but they're bound to do something once he fails to make contact with them again."

"I see. And what exactly happened once you two disappeared?"

"Well, we wound up in Wonderland, obviously," Alice said quietly. "His ability was to copy powers. He said he could use his own looking-glass after the jump, and summoned it just to prove his point.

He was going to strip Wonderland of its resources and use them to fund a coup here on Earth. Then he told me to join him, or else."

"He threatened to kill you?" her father prompted, an undertone of anger in his voice.

"Yeah. We fought, and I couldn't do anything to him. Then Ches attacked him and I thought he had killed him. But a few seconds later Oglethorpe leaped out of the bushes, and I could see his wounds closing up even as he moved." She let her head rest on her knees again and closed her eyes,letting fresh tears flow without bothering to wipe them away. "He caught Ches and broke his neck."

Dr. Littleton frowned. "But you seem convinced he's gone for good. What did you do?"

"I got really angry. I've never felt anything like it before. It, I don't know, woke something up? Inside me. The Boojum got him."

"The Boojum? Is that one of your companions? I don't recall that character from the books."

"It's not from the Alice stories. Carroll wrote a poem called 'The Hunting of the Snark' about a bunch of bumbling adventurers out to capture a half-mythic bird. On the surface, it's all his typical nonsense. But if you look at it closely, it's really all about death. If you met a snark that was a boojum, you'd 'never be met with again', which is exactly what happens to the main character."

"And you called up this Boojum?" her father asked.

Alice nodded, staring straight ahead without seeing the coffee house before them. "There wasn't even a body left. It was like I unmade him or something. I've turned into a monster."

"No!" Dr. Littleton said, reaching over to grab her hand. "Listen to me, you didn't choose this fight. Oglethorpe, or whoever he really was, backed you into a corner and threatened you. He's got no complaint coming just because you came out on top. And you're worth a thousand of him, so you don't need to feel bad about ridding the world of him."

"I know, and I don't feel bad that he's gone. I'm just scared." Alice turned her head to look her father in the eyes. "It was too easy. A flash of anger, and suddenly this absolutely unstoppable force just ended him, despite everything he could do. Now that it's been set free, what if it starts appearing when I get irritated now? Or just starts randomly popping up like my other companions? What if the next victim is innocent?"

He reached across the seat gap, pulled her to him, and kissed her forehead. "I don't believe that could happen. You may allow your companions to get up to a little mischief now and then, but they've never been malicious. You have more control than you realize."

Alice swallowed and tried to let his words reassure her. "Thanks. I hope you're right."

"All right. Now, it looks like we need some time to figure out our next move, so give me a minute," her father said as he pulled out his own cell phone. He called his teaching assistant and told him he would need to substitute for him in his classes for the next few days. He said only that a family emergency had come up and he would be in touch when he had more information.

"There, that's one thing taken care of," her father said as he put the car in gear and backed out. "Now, where shall we go?"

CHAPTER TWELVE
A Hot Night in Town

Levi was sweating, and not from the heat. True, there was plenty of heat inside the burning house, but flame was his element and it did not hurt him. So when he had entered the house on his self-appointed rescue mission several minutes ago, he had been supremely confident of his ability to get people out.

However, he had failed to take other factors into consideration. For example, a partial collapse of the ceiling had rendered one hallway impassible. The flaming support beam that had fallen across it wouldn't burn him, but he lacked the strength to move it and he feared that incinerating it to ash on the spot would trigger a further collapse. So he had to find another way around to the trapped kids upstairs. That took time.

Once he had reached his initial goal and picked up the smallest child, a little girl who looked to be about four, he had dared to think the job was as good as done. He got the two older boys to grab onto his shirt so they could follow him out, and he used his power to control the flames enough to open a pathway for them. Not an obvious one; it wouldn't do to give away his abilities. But with just a bit of courage and encouragement, he was able to get the boys moving.

The problem was the smoke. It had started to fill the air, and even Levi was having trouble breathing. To make matters worse, he was disoriented and lost. He turned to the older of the two boys, who was about eight.

"Where are w-," Levi broke off, overcome by a fit of smoke-induced coughing. He fell to one knee, but managed to retain his grip on the girl, who was crying or screaming whenever she wasn't coughing. "Where are we? Which way is the front door?" he managed once the fit had passed.

The boy looked quickly around the room at furniture that was almost completely ablaze, and pointed almost directly back the way they had just come. Levi mentally cursed his bad luck; he had missed the doorway in the haze.

The group headed in the new direction, but the going was difficult. Levi's feet felt like they were weighted down, and the boys, lacking his heat endurance, hampered him even further. The door finally came into view, but then Levi was inexplicably on the floor with no memory of falling.

His position on the floor allowed him a breath of fresher air and he revived a bit, just enough to look back and note the boys were down and not moving. He looked back toward the door, but it seemed too far. He struggled to rise anyway, but another coughing fit overwhelmed him, and blackness closed in.

♠   ♣   ♥   ♦

John and Ted, volunteers in the Boulder City Fire Department, entered the building wearing their protective gear and oxygen tanks. Within ten feet of the door, they discovered four unconscious bodies of children and brought them out. Leaving them with the attendants at the ambulance, they returned to the building and conducted a sweep. They did not discover any more occupants.

Back outside, they found the children reviving. Three of them, a young girl and two boys who looked to be about a year apart, were definitely of Asian descent. The oldest boy, though, was an African American in his mid teens.

An Asian woman came running up the street, screaming at the sight of the house in flames. John intercepted her. "Ma'am, calm down. I think we got everybody out. Three kids plus the babysitter. Is that everyone?"

"Where? Let me see them!"

He indicated the ambulance and the woman rushed over. She wept in relief once she saw all of her children were safe.

"Ma'am, we would like to contact the baby sitter's parents and let them know he's all right," Ted said. "Can you tell us how to get in contact with them?"

The woman looked at Levi in confusion. "There was no baby sitter. I just walked to the store to buy food for breakfast tomorrow after putting the children to bed. I've never seen that boy before in my life."

♠   ♣   ♥   ♦

Officer Jay Carpenter was feeling satisfied with his night. He was on his way back to the Boulder City Police Department with a burglary suspect he had apprehended after a tricky chase through one of the nicer neighborhoods. The incident would make for a nice accomplishment on his record, and by the time he finished processing his prisoner, it would be time for his dinner break.

As he approached the department parking lot, he was startled to see a nude figure run into his field of view from behind the HQ building. The young girl swiftly crossed Arizona Street about fifty yards ahead of him. Jay couldn't believe it. Hadn't streaking gone out with the 70's? And why run past the police station? She was practically asking to get caught.

All of this flashed through Jay's mind in a moment. By the time he lost sight of the girl, he had pulled over and grabbed his radio mike. "Dispatch, this is Carpenter. I'd like to report a 314 in progress.

145

The suspect, a teenage female with black hair, just crossed Arizona Street headed towards City Hall. Do you copy?"

"Carpenter, this is Sergeant McGregor. I'm on Colorado approaching Bicentennial Park. Do you need assistance?"

That was a bit of luck. Colorado Street bordered the park on the north, and city hall was at its southern edge. The park wasn't very big; with help there was virtually no chance the streaker would get away. "Roger that, McGregor. I have a suspect in the car and cannot pursue on foot. Search the park. I'll try to cut her off on the east side."

"Roger, Carpenter."

"Carpenter, this is Dispatch. Since the suspect is so close to HQ, we're detailing a couple of uniforms to take the west side, just in case she doubles back."

"Roger, Dispatch. Thanks."

Jay flipped the car around and turned on the spotlight as he came even with the back of City Hall. He quickly swept the area, but saw no movement. Continuing a bit further, he turned north onto the south-bound section of Avenue G, a rather pompous name for what really amounted to a parking lot. At this time of night, there was no traffic and very few parked cars. He stopped at the north end of the lot and panned the spotlight around the new area, but again failed to locate the streaker.

Frowning, Jay got back on the radio. "McGregor, I've got nothing over here. You see anything?"

"Negative. Shall we check the buildings?"

"This time of night? Everything should be locked up tight."

"I guess she got away, then."

"But how? There's no place for her to go."

"You sure of what you saw?"

"Roger that," Jay replied. "Well, I've got a suspect to book, so I guess the kid's going to have a good story to share with her friends."

As Jay signed off, he thought about his last comment. Maybe there was something there. After all, what was the point of streaking if you weren't going to brag about it?

CHAPTER THIRTEEN
Wonderland Reprise

"I think we should go public," Alice said.

Her father's hands gripped the steering wheel harder, but he refrained from objecting immediately. They had been driving for several hours now, with no clear goal in mind. They had discussed several possible destinations, but without knowing how long Oglethorpe's organization had been watching, it was hard to guess how well the shadowy group could anticipate their choices. They had agreed between themselves that they should try to get somewhere they had never gone before, but they hadn't been able to settle on a safe place. A brooding silence had settled over the car's interior as they both considered their options.

Finally, Dr. Littleton heaved a sigh and glanced over at her. "Okay, tell me why you think that's a good idea."

"Mainly, because it's the last thing Oglethorpe's group would want us to do. Based on my own experience, it looks like he approached the newly empowered and either recruited them or copied their powers and eliminated them. Keeping powers a secret will allow the rest of them to continue preying on the newbies while they work towards whatever their ultimate goal is. The empowered they haven't discovered yet deserve to be know about the danger, and the authorities ought to know there is a threat."

Her father thought for several seconds before responding. "I can't argue against your logic, but have you considered what life will be like for you after? Assuming the government doesn't just try to sweep you up and lock you away somewhere, you'll loose any semblance of privacy. Everyone will want a piece of you. Those who don't want to kill you, at any rate."

"Why would anyone want to kill me?"

"Could be any number of reasons. I'm sure there's at least one religious fanatic out there who would see powers as a sign you're trying to usurp God's authority, or Allah's. The point is, it only takes one crazy person willing to take action to hurt you, or worse."

Alice bit her lip, then shook her head. "I don't see how trading the certainty of someone being out to get me for the possibility of the same has a down side."

Dr. Littleton shrugged. "Who says it's a trade? There's no reason to think the ones chasing us now won't continue despite you being out in plain sight. It even makes their job easier in some ways. Besides, it's not just you that's going to be affected if we do break this news. The public is going to be interested in everyone close to you. I don't mind the disruption to my life, necessarily, not if it's in your best interests. But Miranda might not like it, and I know your mother won't."

Alice's eyes grew wide as she followed that thought to its logical conclusion. "And Samantha," she finished, referring to her half-sister. Alice's mother had re-married as soon as her divorce was finalized, and she and Dr. Casey had a little girl within the year. Sam was only six, and totally unprepared to be thrust into the light of public scrutiny.

"And Sam," her father agreed. "We may have to consider that option sooner or later, but let's think about it before we take an irreversible step, okay?"

150

Alice hesitated. She was tired, and emotionally wrung out after Ches' death. Maybe it was a bad idea. "Then what should we do?" she asked.

"I don't know, Honey. I think we need to get some rest before we make any firm decisions, but for now I just want to put some distance between us and anyone trying to find us. Why don't you try to catch a nap?"

Alice didn't think she was likely to get any sleep, but there was no point in trying to discuss matters further at the moment. So she just nodded, eased her seat back a bit, and made a makeshift pillow out of her jacket. Her father tuned in a public radio station that was playing classical music, keeping the volume low enough that the sound wasn't intrusive. Much to her surprise, Alice soon found her eyelids drooping, and she slipped into a dream.

Alice and Miranda got together for a play date as soon as she was home from the hospital. Unfortunately, shortly after Miranda arrived it started to rain. With the weather conspiring against their plans to have a picnic in Alice's tree house in the back yard, the girls wound up in the attic, half-heartedly poking through old boxes of junk and wishing for something interesting to do. It was Miranda who first noticed the looking-glass sitting in a dim corner.

"Alice, look at this," she exclaimed. "Isn't it pretty? Why would your parents hide this away in the attic?" She started shifting dusty boxes out of the way to get closer to the mirror.

Alice looked at it and instantly decided that Miranda was right. It was obviously an antique, and hiding it away in a cramped attic made no sense at all to her. The glass was suspended in a light-toned wooden frame that was carved into forms of twining ivy and flowers. The frame was held upright by a stand that allowed it to be tilted forwards or backwards. She felt an intense sense of connection to the piece.

"You're right, Miranda. I wonder if I could convince them to let me move it into my room. Wouldn't it look fantastic at the foot of my bed?"

Alice helped her friend, and soon they had cleared a pathway. Miranda, who stood slightly in front of Alice, reached out to adjust the angle of the mirror, and suddenly recoiled in horror.

"Aieee!" she screamed, backing into Alice with such force that the two of them toppled backwards over one of the boxes they had just moved. Alice, caught unawares, had the breath crushed out of her and took a moment to recover as Miranda rolled off of her and scrambled towards the ladder as fast as she could, not bothering to come fully to her feet until she was several feet away.

Alice got up and dusted herself off, looking between the corner and her friend, trying to figure out what had caused Miranda's reaction. Her friend's head was the only part of her visible, poking up through the trap door in the attic floor. Her eyes were wide and frightened.

"Alice, come on! We've got to get out of here!"

"What's wrong, did you see a spider? Don't worry, I'll brush it off." Alice started towards the corner.

"No! There's no spider! It's the mirror! It's a ghost!"

Alice stopped short and looked back at Miranda in surprise. "A ghost? How can a mirror be a ghost? Did you see something in it? It was probably just a shadow, you know."

Miranda shook her head emphatically. "It wasn't a shadow or reflection. I reached out to touch it and my hand went right through the frame! Don't you see? I've read about ghosts, and sometimes they take the form of an object that figured in someone's death. Let's get out of here!"

Alice turned back towards the mirror, her curiosity aroused. It looked solid enough. She approached it and cautiously reached out her hand and pushed against the frame. It swiveled slightly, just as she had expected.

"Look, Miranda, it's all right. You must have stumbled and reached past it or something. It's just a mirror, after all."

Her friend slowly inched her way back into the attic, looking embarrassed. "I – I was sure I saw my hand go right through it, though," she said.

Alice smiled sympathetically. "Your mind must have played a trick on you," she said. "Too bad, because it really would have been exciting to find a ghost." She turned back to the glass, and reached out to wipe some dust off the mirror's face. "Let's see if we can move it. Mom and Dad are less likely to say no if we can get it to my room, don't you..."

Alice stopped in mid-sentence as her hand passed through the surface of the glass. She felt a cool, pleasant sensation, as if her hand had passed though a curtain of mist, and a gentle tug, more mental than physical, urging her onward. The unexpectedness of the situation disengaged her brain, and she stepped forward without thought, passing through the plane of the mirror effortlessly. Miranda's scream of terror jolted her back to her senses, but by then her forward momentum was too great to overcome, and the sound of her friend's distress was cut off instantly as her head emerged on the far side of the looking-glass.

Alice stumbled as she came to a halt in the middle of a wood. She glanced about, and was just in time to see the looking-glass blink out of existence behind her. Once it was gone, she could see nothing but trees stretching off into the distance in every direction. A light rain was falling, and the cool air was full of the rich, loamy smell of earth and decaying leaves. Alice strained to hear anything unusual, but nothing came to her ears save the sound of raindrops on the leaves overhead.

Alice had read Carroll's stories dozens of times. The desire to experience something like her fictitious namesake's adventures had no doubt been what had driven her to drink the contents of her father's laboratory flask and thus poison herself in the first place. But now that she was well and truly through the looking-glass, the thought of having an adventure of her own was starting to lose its appeal. She had no idea where she was or how she was to get home, and spending the night in a cold, wet forest didn't bear thinking about.

However, the mirror was gone, so the only choices she seemed to have were to wait there in hopes that it would return or to try to find her way out of the woods on her own. She considered the problem with as much logic as she could muster. "I've only seen the mirror once in eight years," Alice thought, "so the odds of it appearing here again before suppertime are quite small." She sighed. "I guess I'll just have to walk out."

Suiting actions to words, Alice selected a direction at random and began walking. At first, the going was relatively easy, but she had never been a particularly active child, so she soon began to feel tired. She was so intent on the internal catalog she was forming of the minor discomforts the journey was inflicting on her that she failed to notice the sounds of rustling underbrush and vegetation for some time. She had just reached the crest of a deep gully, where a stream ran through the forest, when a movement to her right broke through her reverie and drew her attention to the far side of the brook.

The animal standing there was huge. The gully before her was perhaps 15 feet deep, yet the beast's eyes were on level with hers as it stood there with one foreleg braced against the bole of a tree. It looked something like an enormous bear, but Alice could see that a massive tail helped it to balance its weight on its haunches. It regarded her with relative indifference, then reached up with one paw, tipped with claws a

154

foot long or more, to hook a branch and pull it down to a comfortable level. A long tongue snaked out to wrap around a clump of leaves and pull it into its mouth. A moment later, it released its hold on the branch, which sprang back to its previous position. The beast continued to stare at her as it methodically chewed.

Alice stared back in astonishment. "It's – it's a..." she stammered.

"A giant ground sloth," a cultured voice from behind her supplied.

Alice spun around, but there was no one behind her.

"You need not fear; they're herbivores. Mostly. Maybe a bit of carrion here and there, I can't quite remember. At any rate, leave it alone and it will probably return the courtesy," the voice continued.

Alice reoriented and finally located the speaker. It was a house cat, lying on a branch overhead. Or at least, what a house cat would be if it were six feet long, not counting the tail.

Alice tipped her head to one side. "And you must be the Cheshire Cat," she ventured.

"Must I? Well, if I've no choice in the matter, I suppose I will be," the feline returned. "But that being the case, what must you be?"

"Stark raving mad, I think."

"Delighted to meet you. May I call you Stark?"

"Um, just call me Alice."

"What an unusual nickname. Does it derive from Stark, or Raving?"

"Neither. I'm just Alice."

"Well, Alice, how did you come to be here?" the cat asked.

"I stepped through a mirror," Alice replied.

"Sounds rather painful. Did you cut yourself?"

"No, you don't understand, I..." Alice began, then snapped her fingers as inspiration struck. "Wait a minute, in the books, Alice was always dreaming! I'm not really here at all!"

The cat looked at her doubtfully. "Do you always talk about yourself in the third person that way? Ordinarily, I'd agree that someone who spoke like that isn't really all there. But you seem to be present."

"That's a different Alice," she replied impatiently. "The point is, I'm dreaming. I probably hit my head on something when Miranda knocked me over – I bet she did get startled by a spider. Everything since has been a dream, including THAT," she gestured at the sloth, "and YOU! I'll probably wake up in the hospital around supper time with a bandage on my head."

The cat shook its head sadly. "So I'm not here either? A pity. I was rather beginning to like it here." He casually stretched out a forepaw and sharpened his claws on the trunk of the tree, leaving several deep gouges in the bark. "Well, at least the tree seems to think I'm here."

Alice shrugged. "And why not? It's not here, either. Well, are you coming, or what?"

"Coming where?"

"To the mad tea party, of course. It's bound to be around here, somewhere. Now let me think. Alice decided to visit the March Hare, so that's where we'll go. Which direction does he live in?"

"I don't know," the Cheshire Cat replied.

"But you must! You were at the party, too."

"I was? You mean the party we're going to now?"

"Exactly!"

"Well, if we were both there, don't you remember the way?"

"I told you, that was a different Alice."

"I'm confused."

"Oh, just pick a direction," Alice directed. "It's only a dream, so we're bound to get there in the end."

"Um, that way?" the cat suggested, gesturing away from the giant sloth.

"Good idea, I don't feel like wading the stream anyway," Alice said approvingly. "Now come on!"

She looked back up to the branch where the Cheshire Cat had been a moment ago, but the tree was now devoid of felines.

"Ready?" the cat asked from beside her.

Alice gave a small jump, but then reached out to stroke the cat's great head with a grin. "I forgot you can do that," she said.

"I had forgotten, too. How curious," the cat replied.

The two of them set off through the woods, enduring the wet and cold. They had walked for no more than a minute or two before they heard a curious call from among the trees to their right and behind them. It was a rather high-pitched and oddly soft sound, more exhalation than vocalization, yet apparently loud enough to be heard from some distance. For no reason Alice could put into a thought, the sound filled her with a sense of growing unease.

"What's wrong?" the Cheshire Cat asked. "You look worried."

"That sound isn't right," Alice replied. "Alice went straight from meeting you to the tea party, and there wasn't anything mentioned about strange sounds in the woods. But there was something..."

The relative quiet was suddenly broken by a strong and fierce roar. Alice caught sight of movement off in the trees, but could not make out what was there, save that it was large. She stopped and stared into the relative gloom until the movement was repeated. Alice suddenly felt a chill that had nothing at all to do with the weather. "What's the name of this forest?" she asked.

"It's your dream," the feline replied. "What do you call it?"

"Um, T-Tulgey Wood?" Alice ventured quietly.

The roar was repeated, and Alice could now see the head from which it came clearly. It was a strange mixture of reptilian and insectoid features which was, nevertheless, too familiar. As suspicion solidified into recognition, the bulging eyes lit up in a bright flash and a bush between Alice and the creature burst into flame.

"Run, Puss! It's the Jabberwock!" Alice cried.

"Quick, hop on my back," The Cheshire Cat suggested.

Alice needed no further urging. Once she had straddled the enormous cat and looped her arms around his neck, he bounded away from the fearsome beast. Alice glanced back and was able to see the Jabberwock fully by the light of the burning bush as it rushed past in pursuit. A very small corner of her mind that wasn't gibbering in terror was perversely pleased to note that it was not wearing the waistcoat Tenniel had rendered in the famous illustration. Her love of nonsense did not extend so far as to being killed by something so silly.

Not that she was in any way keen on the idea of being killed at all. And her glance had served to tell her this was still a very real possibility. The Jabberwock's odd half-flying, half-hopping gait covered the ground quicker that she would have guessed.

The cat cast a quick glance back at Alice as he ran. "Why are we running if this is just a dream?" he asked.

"It's a tradition. We've got to go faster!" she yelled. "It's gaining on us."

"Okay, hang on tight. I'm going to try something," the Cheshire Cat replied.

Alice secured her grip around the cat's neck. The next moment, she saw the feline appear about fifty yards ahead of her, which meant he was no longer supporting her. Alice crashed to the ground, tumbling through mud puddles and drifts of soggy leaves before fetching up against the base of a rather large bush with prickly leaves. A moment later, the cat was beside her again.

"Um, sorry," he said ashamedly. "I thought you'd go with me when I did that."

Alice required a moment to catch her breath before she rolled over and attempted to get back to her feet.

"Well, I didn't. Don't you know how – Ow!"

Alice gasped as her right ankle objected as she tried to put her weight on it. "Drat! I think I've sprained my ankle. Get me out of here!"

The words were no sooner out of her mouth when the Jabberwock's roar sounded again, this time much too close. The bush Alice had landed in burst into flames. She was still crouching beside it, and felt her skin singed as she instinctively lurched away from it. But her ankle refused to bear her weight and she fell into another wet pile of leaves, which at least had the effect of quenching any flame on her clothes before she could get seriously burned.

"Keep moving," the Cheshire Cat cried. I'll try to draw him off and then circle back for you."

Alice looked up in time to see the cat vanish and simultaneously reappear behind the Jabberwock, now only a couple dozen yards away. The feline immediately leaped at the creature's hindquarters, raking them with his huge claws. Alice couldn't tell from her vantage point if the attack caused much damage, but it at least succeeded in getting the dragon-like thing's attention. The head whipped around and snapped at the cat, but he vanished and reappeared on its opposite side, renewing the attack from the Jabberwock's flank. Alice only watched as a third and fourth attack followed, interspersed with more bites from the Jabberwock that never quite seemed to latch onto its foe. Then the cat streaked away, heading back the way they had come with the snarling thing flapping and hopping after it.

"Don't just lie there. Move!" the cat yelled as he ran. Then, as he leaped over a bush, he disappeared a split second before the bush itself immolated under the Jabberwock's dread gaze. The cat continued his run from a couple of yards beyond the flames.

Alice looked around and spotted a forked stick a few yards away from her leaf pile that looked like it might serve as a crutch and crawled towards it as quickly as possible. A minute later she was on her good foot, hobbling away as quickly as she could. Her left arm ached from the seared skin she had received when the bush caught fire.

Of course there's no prince with a vorpal sword about when you need one, she thought bitterly. *Probably can't be bothered for anyone in peril short of a princess, and I haven't made it across the chessboard to become a queen yet.*

Suddenly, Alice was crying. It just wasn't fair. The storybook Alice only had to read about the Jabberwock and got to go to a party. So why was she covered in mud, hurt, and struggling just to survive? Why couldn't her dream be fun, too?

Suddenly, the Cheshire Cat was beside her again. Alice realized the Jabberwock's roars had receded into the distance a bit, but anywhere within hearing distance was too close as far as she was concerned.

"Come on, let's get you home," the cat suggested.

Exhausted and still sobbing, Alice could only nod as she clambered on the cat's back once again, favoring her injured foot as she did so. Once she was settled, the feline started off at a moderate pace, evidently not satisfied that his small passenger was in any shape to hold herself on top of him if she should be bounced about too much. After a couple of minutes, Alice managed to regain enough control to talk again.

"Where are you taking me?"

"Hopefully somewhere away from that monster," he replied. "We've got to move quickly, though. It will find us again before too long. Will you be able to hang on if I speed up a bit?"

"Yes. Do you know any people who can help us?"

"I don't think there are any people here."

"You mean no one lives in these woods? No wonder if the Jabberwock lives here!"

"I mean I don't think anyone lives here anywhere."

"What makes you say that?"

"A little bird told me."

"I'm not in the mood for riddles," Alice complained. "Just tell me why you don't think there are any people around here."

"I'm not being cryptic; a little bird told me. There he is now."

Alice caught a flash of red off to her right. Orienting on it, she saw that a cardinal was flitting from branch to branch, keeping pace with her and the Cheshire Cat. The bird seemed to be looking at her with some curiosity. A second later, the bird flitted over to land on the cat's head.

"I've never seen anything like you, right enough," the cardinal said. "You've only got fur on the top of your head, and what

161

body covering you have," he indicated Alice's dress, "looks flabby, like it could fall off you at any second. Are you ill?"

"No, I'm a girl," Alice replied, accepting a conversation with the cardinal as yet one more odd aspect of her dream. "Have you really never seen people before?"

"I'm pretty sure I'd have remembered. Are there very many of you?"

"A few billion, I believe," Alice replied.

"You must have great camouflage," the cardinal said dubiously. "Present company excluded, of course."

Alice had no opportunity to reply as the Jabberwock's roar sounded behind them again. The cardinal's head jerked towards the sound, and then he launched himself into the air and flew off in the opposite direction. He quickly disappeared among the trees.

"Alice, hang on! We've got to go faster if we don't want it to catch us," the Cheshire Cat cried. She scarcely had time to secure her grip before the cat accelerated to the pace he had used before the disastrous teleport attempt. Alice clenched her teeth against the pain as the motion jarred her injured ankle, but didn't complain.

After a few moments, as the Jabberwock failed to gain on them, Alice concluded the cat's attack must have injured it, at least slightly. However, they were not pulling away from it, and though it was far enough back that she could only catch glimpses of it through the trees when she glanced in its direction, Alice feared the beast's persistence would outlast the Cheshire Cat's endurance.

After a couple of minutes, something else began to intrude on Alice's awareness, despite the fear that was taking up most of her attention. It was a sense that she had noticed something important, or at least should have noticed it. But she just couldn't resolve it into a conscious thought until they crested a rise and approached an area where the trees crowded less closely together.

"Ches, stop!" Alice cried, pulling back with her arms around his throat as she sat up in shock at the scene before her.

"What? Why? We need to keep moving!"

"There, up ahead! That's my tree!"

"Your tree?" The feline veered towards the aspen Alice had indicated. "What's so special about that tree?"

"Dad built my tree house in it."

"But there's nothing in it now," Ches observed.

"I know. But that's definitely my tree. And our house should be right over there! We should be in the middle of a whole bunch of houses right now. I don't understand."

Alice closed her eyes, retracing her wanderings since she had stepped through the mirror. "And that stream where we saw the giant sloth! I know that stream, it's Alamo Creek. Where is everybody? I want to go home!"

And suddenly, the looking-glass was back, sitting incongruously on one of the branches that should have been supporting Alice's tree house, twenty feet above the ground.

"Look, Ches! There! But how can I get to it?"

"Leave that to me. You need to go through it, right?"

"Yes, but..."

"Just hang on tight!"

Ches' change in direction had allowed the Jabberwock an opportunity to gain ground on him, and the monster seemed to sense that its prey had found a possible way to elude it. It gave a cry of rage and its eyes flashed once again. The looking glass proved impervious to its gaze, but the tree's crown burst into flames as Ches drew near and gathered himself for a running leap.

"You might feel a little warm in a second," he yelled as he jumped at the mirror.

Alice scarcely had time to scream before she found herself airborne. A split second later she was hurtling forward by herself; Ches had vanished. But she had no time to react to the realization before she passed through the plane of the mirror.

She landed on her parent's coffee table, sending magazines, television remotes, and assorted other odds and ends to the floor before she rebounded, crashed into the back of the couch, and landed on the cushions.

She was immediately aware of a high-pitched scream. Or was that a pair of screams? Looking up from her untidy sprawl, Alice saw her mirror vanish from the far side of the table before noting Miranda sitting in the recliner to one side of the living room, staring at her as if she was seeing a real ghost. Her father was perched on the arm of the chair, frozen in the midst of his efforts to console Miranda or calm her down. Alice's mother was standing next to the phone stand, its receiver in her hand. Both of her parents were staring at her as if they'd never seen her before.

Her mother was the first to recover. "Never mind, we just found her," she said into the receiver in an absentminded tone. She hung up and rushed to her daughter. "Alice, thank God you're safe! But what's happened to you? Where did you come from? How?"

"Ow!" Alice cried as her mother caught her in a fierce hug. "Take it easy, Mom. You're bruising my bruises."

Meredith reluctantly let her go. Dad was by her side, checking her for injuries. "Alice, what on earth happened to you? Is that a burn on your arm? How..."

"What were you thinking?" Miranda cut in from across the room. She hadn't budged from the chair, and she was glaring at Alice with wild eyes. "You scared me half to death when you disappeared through the mirror. Your Mom and Dad thought I was nuts or having a fit or something! Where did you go?"

"I'm sorry, Miranda. I didn't know what was happening at first, and by the time I did I was, well, somewhere else. It was really weird, but one thing's for sure," Alice said with a wince and a growing sense of wonder as shifting her weight made all of her various injuries flare up in protest, "it wasn't a dream."

CHAPTER FOURTEEN
New Wrinkles

Regis parked his bike outside Taylor's Cleaners. After going over the relevant portions of the material Mr. Head had assembled for Team Blue, Regis had concluded that the vote on the incentives for Prometheus Academy would be very close indeed. By his reckoning, the deciding vote would be cast by Jonathan Taylor, the most recent addition to the Boulder City Council. He was so new, in fact, that Regis felt a need to meet him personally in order to predict which way he'd vote.

He could have driven to this meeting, but the approach he had decided on called for a bit more tact. Rubbing Mr. Taylor's nose in the actual differences in their financial positions by showing up in a fancy sports car might poison him against the academy. Whether the tax incentives were trivial or not, Regis was not about to contribute to the mayor's efforts to revoke them. In fact, he planned to produce exactly the opposite effect.

Regis entered the business to find two customers at the counter. The one at the counter was complaining about a stain that Mr. Taylor hadn't gotten out of his favorite shirt, and the woman next in line had a huge basket of items to drop off. Regis felt a surge of frustration. At this rate, it would take thirty minutes for him to even get to the counter to talk to the owner, and he would have a difficult time engaging him fully if any other patrons came in.

Fortunately, Regis was without equal when it came to creating his own luck. He focused on the woman first. A moment later, she straightened up suddenly and let out a startled gasp. "I'll bring these back tomorrow, Jonathan. I just remembered I left my oven on. Tell Helen I'll come to your house tonight to pick her up for the girl's night out."

As Regis shifted his attention to the man at the counter, he slumped and shook his head. "Well, I guess it's my own fault for wearing it to the all-you-can-eat barbecue buffet in the first place." A minute later he had paid his tab and departed. As the transaction was completed, Regis concentrated on the business itself. Over the next several minutes, anyone planning on entering the establishment would suddenly remember a more urgent appointment that needed to be tended to first, decide to stop off for a quick snack somewhere, or otherwise delay their arrival. The lull in business was just what Regis needed.

Mr. Taylor closed the drawer on his register. "How can I help you, young man?"

"Mr. Taylor?" Regis asked, and continued once the business owner nodded. "Hi, my name is Regis. I was wondering if I could talk to you for a few minutes. It's for a school project."

"Regis? Not Senator Adair's kid?"

"Yes, sir."

"Huh. I had heard you were at the new school. So, what do you want to talk about?"

"I'm taking a political science class this semester, and I need to write a paper on the decision making process for a political body. I was hoping I could interview you."

"I see. So you're trying to get an inside scoop on the incentives issue? I'm afraid I can't talk about that at this time."

"Incentives?" Regis looked puzzled. "Actually, I'm interested in the rezoning discussions to extend the scope of businesses on the west side of town."

"Rezoning? That was last year's business. Why would you want to talk about that?"

"Judging by the local newspaper articles in the library, there were two sides with compelling arguments for their positions, and it took quite a while for the city council to reach a decision. I figured it would make a good assignment if I can get enough details on how the council worked together on the issue."

Mr. Taylor drummed his fingers on the counter, considering the request. Finally, he asked, "Why would you come to me with this? Your father's a senator. That's the kind of access any other student would be green with envy over. Why not choose something from his career?"

Regis looked down and kicked at the floor with the toe of one sneaker, looking as embarrassed as he could. "Dad's world is complex. I can't follow all the special interests' influences. I'm not saying the city council's job is easy or anything. I'm just hoping the process will be more accessible to a political newcomer."

"Even so, I'd expect your father would have more insights to share with you than me."

"Yeah, well, Dad's pretty busy. If I don't get something the first time around, I'm lost because he's already moved on to two more line items. I guess he's just used to answering questions on his terms. So I thought, maybe, if I started small I could finally, I don't know, make some sense out of it all. Stop being a disappointment to him." Regis cut off, bit his lip, and sniffed as if in the grip of powerful emotions. Then he took a deep breath and said, "Look, it was probably a stupid idea. I won't bother you anymore. Sorry I wasted your time."

He turned quickly toward the door, but took no more than two steps before the local politician called out, "Wait!"

Regis allowed himself a very small, satisfied smile. *Gotcha.* He quickly reverted to his previous anguished expression before he turned back to the counter.

"Hey, it's going to be all right. Look, this isn't the best time, but I can meet you for a cup of coffee after I close up, and you can ask me anything you want. Politics isn't really as complicated as you think. Give yourself a little time to absorb the basics, and you'll be in line for the Presidency before you know it."

"Really? Oh, thanks, Mr. Taylor! I really appreciate it. Is eight o'clock at the cafe down the street good for you?" At the older man's nod, Regis backed to the door and gave him a huge smile. "Great! See you then!"

As he retrieved his bike, Regis scoffed at the councilman's assurances. *The Presidency. Why would I want a job where they take away your playthings after eight years, tops? Once I'm a senator, I'll be dictating policy the rest of my life. And my powers guarantee I won't even have to dig up dirt on my rivals; all the sordid details I need will fall right into my lap whenever I need them. I'll go down in history as the luckiest politician the world has ever seen. And the most powerful.*

♠ ♣ ♥ ♦

Fire Chief Ralph Bluman walked through the door of Prometheus Academy's administrative office and looked around. A receptionist sat at a desk behind a chest-high counter, consulting a sheet of paper. As he walked up to the counter, she gave him a friendly smile, held up a finger to indicate she would help him in a moment, and reached for the PA microphone. Clicking the transmit button, she spoke calmly into the pickup. "Billy Batson, please report to the cafeteria for KP duty. Billy Batson to the cafeteria, please."

"Now, how can I help you, sir?"

"I'm Ralph Bluman, from the Boulder City Fire Department." The chief took out a notebook and flipped it open. "May I speak with Mrs. Kilkarni, please?"

"I'm sorry, sir, but she is traveling on business at the moment. Can I help you?"

"Well, it's a delicate matter concerning one of your students."

"I have full discretion to address anything that arises in Ms. Kilkarni's absence. But if it's confidential, perhaps we should move into the back office?"

When the fireman signaled his agreement, the receptionist rose from her desk. She appeared to be in her forties, and her figure was what could charitably be described as hefty. But she carried herself comfortably as she raised a hinged section of counter to allow Chief Bluman beyond the visitor's area and led him to the office door. "I'm Sherry Wisson. Can I get you anything before we start? A cup of coffee?"

"No, thank you. I would prefer to conduct my business as quickly as possible." He looked through the door to a well-appointed room dominated by an institutional metal desk. Two rigid chairs sat in front of the desk. Sherry walked to the desk and sat behind it, and Ralph selected one of the visitor's chairs after shutting the door behind himself.

As soon as they were seated, Ralph leaned forward. "Ma'am, I'll get straight to the point. You know that my men pulled one of your students from a burning house Tuesday night?"

"Yes, Levi Drafton," Sherry confirmed. "We're so grateful. He's a fine young man."

"Hmm. Yes, well, there are some irregularities in his story we need to address."

"Really?"

171

"Yes. Mr. Drafton says he was passing by on his way to the movies when he discovered the fire and took it on himself to attempt to rescue the children he heard crying for help."

"I would agree that that was foolish, but you seem to be implying... Well, I don't really know what you're implying."

"Here's the thing, Ms. Wisson. We know when the children's mother left to go to the store, with a pretty high degree of confidence. She says she put the kids to bed and walked straight to the store. We have the time stamp on her receipt, plus the report of my men on the scene, and comparing the two confirm that she couldn't have been gone more than 20 minutes. Yet in that space of time, fire all but completely engulfed the house. The squad on the scene was hard pressed to keep damage to neighboring homes to a minimum."

"I still don't see where you're going with this," Sherry said.

"What I'm saying is that this fire spread too fast. That's usually a sign of intentional action on someone's part."

"And you think it was Levi? That's a pretty harsh accusation."

"It's less than an accusation at this point, but more than a suggestion. I've seen a lot in my time on the job, Ms. Wisson, and I can tell you that people set fires for a lot of different reasons. Some do it as a sort of wish fulfillment. They try to rescue people they've put at risk through their own actions in order to gain fame and praise as a hero."

"And you think Levi did something so horrible?"

"There's only one piece of the puzzle missing. Fire won't spread that fast without gasoline, or something else to act as an accelerant. But so far, the forensics team hasn't been able to turn up any traces of whatever the person who did this used. As soon as they do find it, we're going to be looking at Mr. Drafton very carefully to see if we can prove he had access to the chemical. If he did, things could get very hot for that young man, very fast."

"Why are you bringing this to us now?" Sherry asked.

"Two reasons," Bluman replied. "First, we need to talk to his parents, and do a little digging into his past. If he has a history of that sort of behavior, it could go a long way toward confirming our suspicions. Second, we want to know that Mr. Drafton is going to remain available to us if we have any questions. I believe your academic year is just starting?"

"Yes, delays in construction caused us to start late. The students won't have a very long summer break before we start up again next year."

"So it's safe to assume Mr. Drafton will remain in town for the next several weeks?"

"Yes. Most of our students' families have expressed their intention to let the children remain here until the Christmas break, including Mrs. Drafton. She's a single mom. I can get you her contact information."

"Thank you. That would be very helpful."

In a residential neighborhood in Vacaville, a cat stretched out on a patio and basked in the warmth of the sunshine and the residual heat coming off the concrete. Suddenly, a mirror in a dark wooden frame appeared on the slab nearby. The cat raised his head, disturbed by this change in its tranquil domain. A moment later, a man in a wrinkled black suit stepped through the glass. The cat rolled to its feet, fur bristling, and hissed at the intruder. The man aimed a kick at the animal, but it dodged and disappeared into the bushes.

Oglethorpe took stock of his surroundings as he pulled out his cell phone. It appeared no one was home, or at least he hadn't been

173

noticed by anyone inclined to object to his presence. Good enough. He planned to be gone soon. Alice had been more resourceful than he had expected, but he would deal with her.

He hit a speed dial, and the phone was answered on the first ring, as expected. "It's me," he said. "What's the status on the target?" He listened to the response. "What the hell do you mean we've lost contact? Never mind. Make a note that we need to place tracking devices on all of a target's vehicles before we make the initial approach in the future."

Oglethorpe paced for a moment as he thought about what he had learned during his interaction with Alice and her father. "OK, I think I have an idea to help us track her down. I'm on my way. I want the team assembled in fifteen minutes so we can get started."

He disconnected without another word, and then teleported away.

CHAPTER FIFTEEN
Running

When Alice woke up from her dream of Wonderland, she discovered her father had pulled up to a bank's ATM. The clock on the dashboard said it was just after eleven. She could see the screen clearly, and watched without speaking as her father withdrew the daily maximum from his account. Shortly afterward, they checked into a motel by the highway for the night.

The next morning, they hit the road early and continued driving East. A few hours later, Dr. Littleton hit another ATM and filled up at a gas station using his credit card. A few miles further down the road, they grabbed something to eat at a drive-thru. Then they turned to the South. Some of the tension seemed to drain out of her father after they had changed direction.

"We don't know what sort of resources Oglethorpe's organization has at its disposal, but I'm working on the assumption that they'll be able to access financial records," he said. "If so, we've laid a trail pointing clearly in one direction, but now we need to become invisible. I've got a little over $600 in cash, and we've got to make it last as long as possible."

"So where are we going?"

"I think it's time we looked in on an old friend from my college days. Hank lives in San Francisco. I don't want to bring our troubles down on his head, so I'm going to take a couple of days to loop around and approach the city from the South. If there's no sign of pursuit by then, I think it will be safe enough to visit him and see what we can come up with for our next move."

Alice shrugged and drew her knees up under her chin again. She was too depressed to try to think about a solution to their current problem. Besides, her Dad seemed to have things covered for another day or two at least. Instead, her mind insisted on dwelling on her dream.

The dream was accurate. Her first trip to Wonderland had been terrifying, but it had also brought Ches into her life. Other companions had started appearing shortly after that, as did her other powers. But Ches had always been the most comforting aspect of the whole business. She recalled afternoons spent in her room, lying on the bed with a good book, Ches a warm, purring presence beside her. She didn't know how she would have coped with her mother's abandonment without him.

But why had her mind dredged up this particular memory now? It could be as simple as returning to the starting point, but that didn't feel right. She sensed that something about it was important, but her conscious mind just couldn't pick the essential detail out of the mix.

Her brooding was interrupted by an alert tone from her phone. She dug the device from her pocket and opened the messaging app.

CoprTop156: Where R U? R U safe?

"Who is it?" her father asked.

"Miranda. She's worried I didn't show up at school, I guess." Alice bit her lower lip in shame as she realized she had given her friend so much cause for panic. "I called her before you picked me up last night and warned her about what happened, in case someone tried to grab her or something."

"Hmm. Probably a good idea. Be careful about what you tell her now, though."

"Dad!"

"It's not that I don't trust Miranda," he replied. "But text messages can be intercepted, or someone might steal her phone. Don't put anything out there she doesn't really need to know."

Alice nodded, seeing the sense of his concerns, and turned her attention back to the phone.

> **TeaTime730:** I'm OK. Dad thought it was time for a road trip.
>
> **CoprTop156:** U could have told me. I've been freaking out all day!
>
> **TeaTime730:** Sorry. Anything suspicious there?
>
> **CoprTop156:** Nothing yet. Where are you going?
>
> **TeaTime730:** Not sure yet. I'll get word to you when I can. May be gone a while.
>
> **CoprTop156:** :(
>
> **TeaTime730:** Do me a favor and delete these messages.
>
> **CoprTop156:** OK. Stay safe.

Alice sighed as she put away her phone. Had it really only been two days ago she had set out to find Billy? That decision had created an earthquake that had rocked her comfortable world to its foundations. She wondered if she would have done things differently if she had known of the consequences. After weighing both sides of the fallout, she concluded she probably would have. Billy was safe, and Oglethorpe was gone; both of those were huge pluses. But her personal losses loomed so large in her mind. But in the end, it didn't matter. The die had been cast.

The afternoon dragged on. They drove, and neither Alice nor her father felt a need to talk very much. Dr. Littleton changed the settings on the radio as stations passed out of range, keeping the compartment filled with classic rock or classical music as chance dictated. Finally, he pulled off the highway to refuel. As he pulled up to the pump, Alice noted a McDonald's a little further along the frontage road, and her stomach rumbled.

"I think it's time for some food. Pick me up down there when you're finished?" Alice asked, pointing at the restaurant.

Dr. Littleton glanced over to see where she was indicating. "I could just drive us over. This won't take long."

"I need to stretch my legs," Alice replied.

Her father nodded, and Alice scrambled from the car. Almost more than the thought of food, the idea of movement suddenly seemed irresistible. She was already walking away as her father released the catch on the gas tank cover.

Before she had taken three steps, Hatter suddenly appeared beside her. "I say, that was a nasty business back in the clearing. How are you holding up?" he asked.

Alice sucked in a breath as tension flooded her body. She glanced around as casually as she could to see if anyone had noticed Hatter's transition. A woman pumping gas near her father was looking directly at them, but after a moment she shook her head and went back to watching the numbers change on the display. Alice had seen it many times before. Most witnesses to something impossible chalked it up to misperception and went on about their business. After all, everyone knew people didn't just suddenly manifest out of thin air, right? Even so, the current stakes were high, so this was no time to chance drawing unwanted attention.

"Are you crazy?" she hissed. Then she sighed and held up a hand before he could reply. "No, don't answer that. Silly question, all things considered. But remember, we're trying to be inconspicuous. So get with the program."

"Really?" Hatter replied, and then shrugged. "Well, as you wish. What's the plan?"

"We're going in here to get something to eat. Dad and I have been driving for hours."

They reached the door just as a grumpy looking family exited the building. Alice and Hatter entered and stopped short when they saw the crowd at the counter. Raucous teenagers were standing four and five deep along its entire length. Alice glanced out the window on the opposite side of the building and saw a school bus parked there. Great. A field trip had arrived five minutes before her.

"Let's go. We'll get our food quicker if Dad drives us somewhere else." Alice turned to where the Hatter had been a moment before, only to find he wasn't there. It took only a second to locate him, however, just sitting down at a table occupied by a mother and a little boy who were almost through with their meal.

"Hey, this table's taken," the woman protested.

"Really? What's holding up your food, then?" Hatter asked, helping himself to a french fry from the pile in front of the boy. He sampled it, grimaced, and spat the half he had bitten off on the floor. "I'm assuming this is food? I don't think even the Dormouse would have anything to do with this."

The boy looked at the Hatter's clothes with open curiosity. "Are you here for a happy meal?" he asked. "Ma wouldn't let me get one today."

"How was yours feeling then? Angry, gloomy, or introspective, perhaps?"

"Intro-what?"

"Really? I haven't felt intro-what in ages," Hatter sighed.

179

Alice reached the table before the woman or boy could respond to that. She often found it hard to keep up with the time manipulator. "Uncle, you promised you would stay with me today," she scolded. Turning to the woman, she put one hand to her chest. "I'm so sorry, but he's in his manic phase today and I'm pretty sure he skipped his meds. I hope he hasn't been too much trouble."

The woman stood up and moved away from Hatter, pulling her son up as well. "It's Okay, we were just about finished anyway."

"But Ma, I'm not done with my fries," the boy said.

"Hush, you've had enough," the woman said, dragging him towards the exit.

Alice returned her attention to Hatter. "I can't take you anywhere," she said. She glanced around the restaurant nervously. There was a short and stocky Hispanic man in blue jeans and a plaid work shirt looking at them, but when he noticed her returning his gaze he looked down at his food. "Don't you know what 'inconspicuous' means?"

"Certainly. 'In' is to be part of a group, and 'conspicuous' means to draw attention. So we're in the group of people who draw attention to themselves."

Alice stared at Hatter is disbelief. "You can't possibly believe that's what I meant. 'In' means-. Oh, never mind. Let's get out of here."

Hatter stood up, carelessly flinging the half-eaten french fry he still held over his shoulder. It bounced off the chest of a bulky, muscular young boy carrying a tray of food into the dining area. "Hey," he protested, changing direction to approach Hatter, "What the hell, man. Aren't you a little old for food fights?"

"Actually, I prefer dances," Hatter replied. "There's nothing like a good lobst-"

"Whatever. Just watch what you're doing, or I'll make you regret it."

The boy had started to turn away, when Hatter noted the green boxes on his tray. "Apple pie?" he said. A moment later, he had snatched one of the boxes, removed the pastry, and taken a huge bite. "Oh, now this is much more like it," he said around a mouthful of the treat.

"All right, that's it!" The boy set his tray down on a nearby table. Alice stepped between the two quickly. "I'm sorry, my uncle has some issues with impulse control," she said placatingly. "Here, I'll pay for the pie."

"Like that's going to make it good?" the boy scowled. "Have you seen that line at the counter?"

"All right, here's a five," Alice winced inwardly at the expense. "You can get one of your friends to buy you another pie with their order. And we'll leave."

For a moment, Alice thought the boy was going to attack Hatter anyway, but he finally took the money and went to a table where one of his friends had already sat down with his own order. He left his tray there and started toward the mob in front of the counter.

"Now let's get out of here," she said, but when she looked at Hatter, his eyes were fixed on the back of the store.

"That was delicious," he said. "We must get some more."

"You're kidding, right? It'll take half an hour to get-"

But Hatter didn't wait for her to finish her objection. He moved quickly to a clear spot at the very end of the counter. As she tracked his progress, Alice noted the tell-tale signs of his time manipulation power in action. He did not run; his body posture was all wrong for that. But his walk nonetheless covered the ground between him and his goal as if he had sprinted. And of course, she was left behind again, managing only two or three steps before he reached the counter, even though she had half expected something like this to happen. All in all, it was rather like being in a waking nightmare where she was completely powerless to accomplish a simple task like leaving the building.

Hatter did not stop at the counter, but hopped up onto its surface, with no more apparent exertion than if he had decided to take a flight of stairs two steps at a time. Then, just as quickly, he hopped down on the other side and started removing apple pies from the holding bin on the back counter.

"Hey, you can't be back here," one of the cashiers said angrily. She was an older woman, and Alice could see in an instant she wasn't the sort to put up with any nonsense. "What do you think you're doing?"

"Uncle, stop that," Alice called as she finally made it to the front of the crowd. "I'm so sorry, ma'am. I'm just now realizing he didn't take his meds this morning, even though he swore to me he did."

The cashier shifted her attention to Alice, apparently having decided that interacting with her would provide a swifter resolution to the disruption. "You'll need to get him out of here," she said. "And I expect you to pay for those pies. I can't sell them now that he's touched them."

"Of course. Umm, I don't suppose that, since you're ringing up the pies anyway-"

"Sorry, sweetie. Pay for the pies and get out. I don't want him here any longer than necessary."

Alice nodded in resignation and handed her some money. As she waited for the change, she heard a loud, thump from the drinks station where the kids from the bus were filling their cups. It was an odd sound, both metallic and distorted, as if it was underwater. As she glanced that way, Alice saw several people stepping back from the area warily. The sound came again, and this time Alice saw the iced tea urn lurch an inch to the left along the counter and tip slightly. Now everyone's attention was focused on the metal cylinder, and the lid jumped and rattled on the top, but then settled once more. Uneasy muttering rose from the crowd, and those nearest to it took several more steps back. Alice shook her head in desperate denial, and moved toward the nearest door as unobtrusively as possible. Then, with one more thump, the lid was flung up and away as a hairy, soggy form pulled itself into view with forepaws hooked over the top edge of the dispenser. The Dormouse yawned hugely as the witnesses fell utterly silent in shock.

A moment later, the tea urn toppled over, spilling tea and the wet rodent, which was the size of a terrier, to the floor. The silence ended in a cacophony of screams and the sounds of feet stampeding towards the exit. Alice was one of the first through the door into the parking lot, and she ran for the access road. Her father pulled up just as she got there, and she wasted no time in opening the door and clambering inside. "Go!" she cried as she slammed the door. She figured her companions had probably already returned to Wonderland under cover of the chaos inside the building.

Dr. Littleton took in the scene of panic in the parking lot as people continued to stream from the restaurant as quickly as possible. Years of living with Alice's powers had produced a certain utility in rolling with the unexpected, and he simply nodded and got the car moving. He didn't speak until they were back on the highway.

"You want to tell me what that was all about?"

Alice closed her eyes and shook her head. "Hatter got a little out of control, but I was dealing with that. But then the Dormouse popped up in the tea urn."

Her father thought for a moment. "That would be alarming, especially if I had been eating food prepared somewhere with that big of a rat problem."

"Yeah. Right now, all that's important is to put some distance between us and that McDonald's as quickly as possible."

There was a brief pause. "Oh, and let's find a KFC or something for dinner tonight. Anything but burgers."

CHAPTER SIXTEEN
Friends and Foes

In the end, they did stop at KFC, but after the McDonald's incident, Alice was too nervous to eat in the store. They pulled into a mostly deserted parking lot a few blocks from the highway to eat their meal. There were no floodlights illuminating the area, which had actually been one factor in favor of choosing the spot. But clouds had rolled in during the day, and the lights from whatever town they were currently in reflected off them and turned the night into an electric dusk.

"Do you really think we can avoid Oglethorpe's friends?" she asked. She had already finished most of her meal, and was nibbling on the last of her wedge fries.

Her father didn't answer immediately. She looked over to see him thoughtfully sipping his soda. He shrugged. "It's impossible to say. We don't have enough data. Why?"

"I've just been thinking. You know, about how far I'd go to stay free of them. I mean, are we going to have to buy fake identities and start new lives? What if I never get to see Miranda again? Or Samantha? What about our house? Or your job?"

"Hey, calm down. We're a long ways off from abandoning all that. This situation could change very fast. It would depend a lot on additional developments, but I think I'd be inclined to go public, to one degree or another, before we try to pull a vanishing act."

"What do you mean 'to one degree or another'?"

"Well, there's a difference between appearing on national TV and going quietly to the FBI, or some other government agency. I'm not really sure who would have jurisdiction in a case like this, but Oglethorpe did try to kidnap you."

"I thought you didn't want the government involved in our lives that way."

Her father sighed. "It's all pretty muddled right now, I admit. On the one hand, I'm nervous about how much control they might try to exert over you. If we go that route, it would probably be wise to keep an ace up your sleeve, like your looking-glass. That way, if they try to lock you up, you could slip away into Wonderland and we could meet up someplace we designated before hand."

"If they haven't locked you up, too. Revealing our secret to just a government agency would make it easy for them to make us disappear if they decided they want to keep a lid on the news."

"Right. But broadcasting the information to everyone could backfire just as easily. If we get to that point, we'll have to weigh our options carefully." He crumpled up the wrapper from his sandwich and dropped it into the empty paper bag on the seat beside him. "But enough of this for now. Let's get rid of this trash and get back on the road. I want to cover some more ground before we find a motel."

Alice gathered up her own garbage and added it to the bag. "Here, let me take it. I'll dump it in that trash can over there and we can go," she said. She pulled the latch on the door and started to push it open. The door only swung out a few inches before it suddenly stopped, as if she had hit a post or something. She looked out the window in confusion. There was nothing there to block the door. Then the door slammed shut, catching her shoulder in the process and pushing her back from the opening. "Ow!" she cried.

"What's wrong?" her father asked.

Alice rubbed her shoulder ruefully. "Something just slammed the door in my face." She looked around the parking lot fearfully, but nothing stirred for a good fifty yards in any direction. "I think someone doesn't want us to get out of the car."

Her father tried his door, but he wasn't able to make it move at all, even after confirming it was unlocked. "Right, time to go," he said grimly.

He started the engine, but before he could put the car in gear, it suddenly lurched upward. The two of them looked out in astonishment as the ground dropped away from them. After they had risen what seemed like several hundred feet in the air, they stopped, and then the car began moving sideways away from the highway.

"They've found us!" Alice said, panic pushing her voice higher than normal. What are we going to do? I don't even know how they're doing this."

"Maybe that fellow can tell us something," a muffled voice said from behind her. They both turned and looked out the rear glass to see Hatter sitting cross-legged on the trunk, sipping a cup of tea and gazing at something above them.

Alice quickly rolled down her window, grateful to find that whatever held the door in place was not preventing this action. She leaned out and looked up, and was able to make out the figure of a man silhouetted against the clouds. She was not able to discern any details, however.

She leaned back inside the passenger compartment and nodded to her father. "Yep, there's a man up there, sure enough. He's flying about twenty feet above us."

Without a word, her father reached across, opened the glove compartment, and pulled out his pistol. Alice pulled back in surprise. She knew he owned a gun. Before the accident that had permanently injured his leg, Dr. Littleton had often traveled to very remote areas all around the world looking for new plant species to study, and a gun was often essential to survival. She just hadn't been aware he had it with him.

"You do realize how far we'll fall if you shoot him now?" she asked.

He gave her a humorless grin. "He's got to put us down sometime," he replied. "If he wanted to kill us he'd have dropped us already. Just sit tight, and don't do anything drastic."

Alice nodded, then turned to look out the rear window again. "Hatter, shift us into hyper time, please." When her father looked over at her, she shrugged. "It's just a little boost to our reaction speed. That's not drastic, is it?"

"I guess not."

A short time later, the car began to descend towards a well lit area. As they came closer, Alice noted it was a construction site. The skeleton of some multistory structure was just beginning to rise from the foundation. There were piles of building materials laid out in neat stacks, as well as a shed with equipment parked around it. A generator hung thirty feet off the ground from the end of a cable attached to a crane in an attempt to keep it out of the reach of thieves. As the car settled into the work area, it barely cleared a tall chain link fence with tarps strung around the inside to hide the site from the view of passing pedestrians. At this time of night, the streets were deserted anyway.

As the car gently touched down, the flyer who had brought them there landed about thirty yards in front of them. Alice realized she had seen him before. The man had not bothered to change his jeans or plaid work shirt, although he had donned a knit ski mask. Since she didn't have a name for him, she decided to call him Lumberjack.

"Uh, Dad, this guy's been following us. He was at the McDonald's a couple of hours ago."

"Not that I thought he snatched us by chance, but good information anyway," he acknowledged. "I wonder why he brought us here?"

Alice thought she had a pretty good idea, but couldn't bring herself to say it out loud. *How many TV shows have I seen where the murderer hid the body in the foundation of a construction sight?*

As soon as the man landed, he removed the ski mask covering his face. *So not a good sign*, Alice thought. *He doesn't care if we can identify him.*

Then, as if the night hadn't been strange enough already, another man stepped out from behind a pile of steel beams to stand beside him. He was a thin, black man with close-cropped hair, apparently in his late twenties. His face was covered in a pattern of small tattoos made of darker circles that gave him a fierce appearance totally at odds with his uniform. *He looks like an extra from South Pacific*, Alice thought. The tan army uniform was immaculate and freshly pressed, despite giving every appearance of being from a time long past.

The first man looked to Soldier Boy, jerked his head impatiently towards the Littleton's car, and started walking towards them. *Gotta admire a man who loves his work*, Alice thought wryly. *He looks like he can't wait to get started.*

"Stay here," her father said. "If they want a fight, they should have brought an army." Dr. Littleton opened the car door and wrested himself to a standing position, relying on the vehicle itself rather than his cane. Thanks to Hatter's temporary enhancement, he still managed it in less time than a normal man would have taken.

"Stop right there," he called out, leveling the gun at Lumberjack. The man kept advancing at the same steady pace, however, so Alice's father pulled the trigger twice. Alice briefly saw some sort of distortion in the air about a foot in front of her father's target, accompanied by the sound of the bullets ricocheting randomly into the work area.

"Uhm, I think they brought an army, Dad. He's the tank." Alice grabbed the bag that contained her last wedge fries, shoved open her own door and got out as quickly as possible. She was in time to see her father shift his aim to the refugee from Broadway and fire again. As quickly as he did, a semi-translucent image of some sort of primitive tribesman surrounded by an otherworldly greenish glow appeared and a bullet wound blossomed in its forehead. But rather than dropping, the tribesman grinned and gave a mocking laugh that sent chills running down Alice's spine. Then he disappeared as quickly as he had come. Alice looked over at her father with wide, stunned eyes. "Please tell me that freaked you out as much as it did me."

Before her father could answer, Lumberjack held out his hand, and her father's gun was pulled from his grip. It flew to the other man, who caught it, set the safety, and tucked it into the waistband at the back of his pants. *Yep. Definitely telekinesis,* she thought. *And powerful, at that. Why do I always have to be outclassed?*

"Wehmahn noerhm," Lumberjack said in a deep, drawn out rumble. Alice shook her head. Communication between people who were not experiencing time at the same rate was almost impossible, and she couldn't afford the time it would require to puzzle out the man's meaning.

Instead, she rummaged in the bag she had been planning to throw away before the carjacking and found one of the wedge fries. A quick bite later she was fifteen feet tall. Stepping quickly to a pile of building material, she picked up a piece of rebar. The thin metal rod had a lot of give, and wavered about as she lifted it. "Mama's got a switch, and she's taking a couple of naughty boys to the woodshed," she called out, even though she knew the supers in front of her could only hear something similar to Charlie Brown's teacher crossed with one of the Chipmunks.

190

She advanced on Lumberjack. Soldier Boy was spooky, but telekinesis was a quantifiable threat she intended to deal with. She lashed out with the rebar, flicking the tip at him three times, as hard as she could. Each time, it rebounded off of the air before him with a loud, sharp crack, but it seemed to her that she was getting a bit closer to him with each strike. After three more attacks, she succeeded in forcing him back a step.

Just as she was gaining confidence, she noticed Soldier Boy gesturing at her out of the corner of her eye. The rebar suddenly felt much lighter in her hand, and much springier. It also wasn't cutting through the air as easily. As her latest strike connected, the rod broke off a foot from her fist, and she saw with surprise that she was holding a bit of bamboo in place of steel. She looked at Soldier Boy with new respect. He shook his head and wagged a finger at her, a babysitter from hell chastising a stubborn toddler. Alice decided she needed someone to keep him occupied.

The Tweedles appeared on either side of him and took a quick look around. Alice pointed at the - what? Wizard? - and said "Get him, boys." Delighted, the schoolboys swung their wooden swords over their heads and let loose with enthusiastic war cries. They ran around him, striking at him without pause. But every attack was met by another apparition of a tribesman, which vanished after preventing the sword from connecting with its intended target. The Tweedles were quickly distracted, forgetting who their true target was in their glee.

"That's six foes I've put down now," Tweedledum called to his brother. "I'm beating you!"

"No how!" Tweedledee objected. "I've got nine already!"

Well, they're certainly not doing any damage, Alice thought, *but I defy him to conjure up any more tricks with that going on around him!*

191

She turned her attention back to her original adversary, but she had given him too much time to regroup. She felt a crushing force grab hold of her, pinning her arms to her sides. Struggle as she might, she could not break free. She looked back to the car. Her father had managed to retrieve his cane. Hatter still sat on the trunk, dunking a scone he had produced from somewhere in his teacup as if he hadn't a care in the world.

"Dad, run for it! He's got me trapped!"

"I'm not leaving you! Call the Boojum, it's our only hope!"

Alice recoiled from the idea. The Boojum meant death, and she didn't want to become some sort of paranormal assassin. "No, there has to be another way."

Soldier Boy stood with his arms crossed, index fingers pointing up past his shoulders. He spoke some sort of invocation, still garbled by the time differential, and brought both fingers to bear on the Tweedles. Both cried out as if in great pain and vanished.

"Alice, we're running out of options. I know it scares you, but you've got to do it! They're not going to show us mercy once they learn what's happened to Oglethorpe."

Alice knew her father was right, and braced herself to call on the dread entity. Just as she started to mentally reach out to it, though, her concentration was broken by an explosion.

The lock and chain that fastened the gate leading to the street beside the construction site burst apart and the gate swung wide. A truck with a canvas covering over the rear cargo area, suitable for transporting troops, roared onto the lot and screeched to a halt. A silver figure was leaning out the passenger side where a door should have been. The right arm was raised and pointing forward. Evidently, this was the source of the blast that had opened the way.

Alice's conjecture was immediately confirmed as a bolt of energy from a muzzle-like projection on the back of the figure's forearm crashed into the barrier around Lumberjack. He stumbled back, unhurt but unbalanced by the force of the attack. Suddenly, Alice was free as he turned his attention to the new threat.

As this happened, the driver vanished from the cab and appeared beside the telekinetic. The driver was a body-builder type, and he wielded a huge Bowie knife. He struck at his opponent's back, but was apparently unable to overcome his formidable defenses.

Before Alice could process the new developments and decide on a course of action, Soldier Boy drew back his arm, and a spear composed of translucent white light appeared in his hand. Though it had every appearance of being about as substantial as mist, he held it easily, and hurled it at the silver figure. The weapon struck the armored combatant in the left calf as he clambered out of the cab. The ghostly missile passed through the armor as if it was mere cloth. The cry of pain as the figure fell sprawling to the ground made Alice revise her assessment. The armored fighter was definitely a woman. The insubstantial spear vanished a couple of seconds later. Soldier Boy conjured another spear and called out to the woman, but made no move to throw it immediately.

Meanwhile, the bodybuilder had given up on his knife and looked around the site. His eyes came to rest on the generator hanging from the crane, and he pointed at it. It vanished, reappeared above Soldier Boy, and started to fall as the teleporter took a couple of hasty steps to the side. Lumberjack, still keeping half an eye on the armored fighter struggling to her knees, could only spare enough attention for a clumsy mental swipe at the falling machinery. It was enough to deflect it away.

And right at Alice, just as the effects of Hatter's time boost gave out, leaving her flat-footed in the middle of a future crater.

193

A short burst of sound, like a band saw tearing through wood, blasted over the work site and the generator's trajectory shifted once again. It was spinning end-over-end as it crashed down on the hood of the Littleton's car and smashed through the windshield. Fortunately, Dr. Littleton had already moved away from the vehicle, though Hatter was tossed off the trunk and landed on the ground behind the car.

The band saw started up again, this time a continuous drone. A teen-aged boy with short cropped red hair flew out of the back of the truck, then turned to hover about twenty feet above the ground. He pointed at Lumberjack, to the accompaniment of a short increase in the howling buzz's volume. Again, Lumberjack was driven backward, but his defense seemed to hold up.

The body builder shouted something at the flying teenager. He was obviously upset, but Alice couldn't hear any of it over the noise the boy was producing. He ignored his grounded companion and sent an invisible bolt of energy at Soldier Boy, which was intercepted by another grinning specter.

Alice scooped up a large wheelbarrow nearby and rushed at Soldier Boy, grasping the implement so she could scoop him up. Maybe his other-worldly protectors wouldn't be able to help him avoid getting trapped, and then everyone could focus on his companion.

Her target had been preparing to launch his spear at the boy hovering overhead, but seeing her charging toward him, he threw the weapon at her instead. Alice reacted instinctively, swinging the wheelbarrow into its path and continuing the movement off to her side. As the spear passed through the metal, she felt a slight tug, confirming her suspicion that the projectile had at least some tendency to interact with solid matter. The motion deflected the weapon enough so that it only grazed her side in passing, rather than impaling her. Nonetheless, the pain was greater than she had ever encountered before. The wheelbarrow tumbled away and her charge faltered as she clutched at the wound. Her side felt warm and sticky with blood.

The boy glowered at Soldier Boy and pointed at him. This time, the sound was a weird ululating whine, almost beyond Alice's hearing. Although a ghostly figure interposed itself, this attack carried through the spirit, and Alice saw Soldier Boy's head snap back in reaction. Immediately, the apparition's laugh was cut short as it vanished and the black man crumpled to the ground.

Lumberjack called out to his partner, but it was lost in the sonic chaos. He ignored everyone else, flew to his companion and scooped him up with his power. Then, with one anguished look at Alice, he lifted into the air and bore his friend away into the night.

CHAPTER SEVENTEEN

Rerouted

Alice sank to her knees and braced one arm against a convenient pile of cinder blocks. The wound in her side hurt badly, but even so she tried to keep the new trio in view. They had certainly saved the Littletons from their kidnappers, but their motives remained unknown.

The boy who had driven them off landed a good ways off from Alice, to the accompaniment of a lot of swirling dust, sand, and even small pebbles. When his power cut out, the band saw sound subsided to a tinny ringing in her ears. As soon as he landed, he moved through the debris cloud toward her. The body builder reached her first, though, appearing beside her like another companion.

"I have some experience treating field wounds," he said gently. "Let me take a look." His voice was thin and distant in her numbed ears, but she nodded and allowed him to move her hand, far bigger than his own at the moment, away from her side. He pulled the ragged edge of fabric away from the site of the wound and grunted. "Well, it probably hurts like a son of a bitch, but you'll live."

The boy reached them, but before he could say anything, the man glared at him and snapped out an order. "There's a first aid kit in the back of the truck. Get it."

He hurried off without a word, looking apprehensive. Alice said, "I could really use something to drink, if it's not too much trouble."

"And bring a bottle of water while you're at it, Thompson," the man called after the retreating youth.

Dr. Littleton limped up on his cane. "Alice, are you all right? What did you think you were doing, rushing into a fight like that?"

"Relax, she'll be fine. She did pretty well, all things considered. I'd say she bought Thompson enough time to find an effective attack."

"And just who are you?" Dr. Littleton asked. "Not that I'm not grateful for your help, but the past few days haven't inclined me to trust anyone like you."

"Empowered, you mean? Well, if Oglethorpe crossed your path, I can't say that I blame you. I'm Houston Lane, and this," he indicated the woman in the silver armor as she limped up to the group with her helmet in her hands, "is LaRonda Teresi. I guess you could say we represent a group that's banded together to keep clear of the folks who've been giving you problems."

Scott trotted back over with a red canvas tote bag bearing a red cross on a white field on the side. He handed a bottle of water to Alice, who took it gratefully, and returned to her normal size after a quick sip.

"That's handy. It'll make dressing this wound easier, for sure. Lean back and let me clean the area," Houston instructed Alice.

"I'd prefer if you let me do that," her father interjected.

Houston glanced at him, then nodded agreeably and backed away from her. "Certainly, Dr. Littleton. I should have assumed a man with your background would want-"

"You know who we are?" Alice's father asked in alarm. "How-"

"Easy now, Dr. Littleton. Surely you didn't think we happened along by chance? We've been looking for you for days, and you don't know how glad I am we managed to get here in time to help out. We'll explain everything later, but for now, I'd really recommend getting that wound cleaned up so we can get you back to our base. You're not safe here in the open."

"And if we don't want to go with you?"

"Are you freakin' crazy?" LaRonda cut in. "I just took a damn spear in my leg for you, and you don't trust us? Maybe we should just leave you to twist in the wind you ungrateful-"

"LaRonda, that's enough," Houston snapped, and the black woman shut up. But she stared at the ground and shook her head angrily, setting her dreadlocks thrashing like a nest or irritated serpents. Houston kept her in his sights a few seconds more to make sure she would stay out of the discussion, then returned his attention to the Littletons. "Look, I understand your caution, but I'll give you two good reasons for coming with us. But if you still don't want to trust us, I won't force you."

"I'm listening," Dr. Littleton said. He found a bottle of hydrogen peroxide in the kit and splashed it liberally over the cut in Alice's side.

"Right, then. First off, we've got a healer back home that can patch your girl up in minute. That will save you days of having to care for that wound."

Dr. Littleton slapped a large gauze patch over the wound and placed Alice's hand over it to get her to hold it in place while he rummaged in the kit again. "A not insignificant advantage, if it's true." He acknowledged. "Your second point?"

"Just that you're not going anywhere in that," Houston said, indicating the wrecked car with the generator still sitting halfway through the windshield, where it wasn't deforming the roof.

199

Alice's father grimaced in spite of himself as he finished taping the gauze in place. "Sad, but true," he said. "Well, Alice, what do you think?"

"A healer sounds good," she replied. "Getting out of here would be a bonus."

"Very well, Mr. Lane, it looks like we're coming with you. How far is home?"

"Miles and miles, but don't worry, we'll be there in less than a minute. First, we'd better clean up, though." He gestured at the Littleton's car, which vanished. The generator was left behind and crashed to the ground. "We'll make alternate arrangements for you later, but right now we don't want to leave any clues behind in case anyone else is following you. Let's get in the truck."

"About damn time," LaRonda said, moving stiffly towards the vehicle.

"Thompson, you're up front with us. I want you where I can keep an eye on you. Dr. Littleton, are you and Alice all right with riding in the back? I promise it won't be for long."

"That's fine. Help me get her up."

Shaking his head, Houston stooped down and gently scooped Alice up and carried her to the back of the truck. Rather than placing her on the edge of the floor, though, he teleported into the truck bed and sat her on one of the benches running the length of the bed on either side. When her father reached the back of the truck, he brought him on board with a quick gesture, rather than allow him to climb up with his weak leg.

"Okay, have a seat, but I wouldn't bother trying to get too comfortable. We'll be home soon." As Houston hopped down and started towards the driver's side door, Alice felt the truck shift as the others climbed into the front seats. She closed her eyes and leaned against her dad's chest as he put his arm around her and the single driver's side doors slammed up front. Nothing more happened for a minute or so, then the door opened again and they heard footsteps coming back along the driver's side.

"Now what?" she heard her father mutter. Alice suddenly realized that the footsteps sounded different. Where there had been the crunchy sound of gravel shifting moments before, now the sound was the sharp sound of boots on concrete. She opened her eyes and sat up as Houston came into view.

"We're here, folks. I told you it wouldn't take long," he said.

Alice looked out and saw that the vehicle was now in some sort of garage, or hanger. The space was huge, and several other cars and trucks of different types were in view, along with work benches, grease pits, and barrels of different fluids. As the Littletons stood up, Houston teleported them down to floor level. With a wider field of view, Alice could see a tunnel leading out of the area's far end. It curved out of sight a hundred yards or more from its starting point.

"I called ahead, but it will probably take a few minutes yet for the healer to get to the infirmary. I can carry you again if you'd like, Alice," Houston offered.

"I think I'd rather walk, as long as we don't have to go too far and we don't have to hurry."

"All right," Houston said as the others joined the rest of the group. "First things first, though. Thompson, get back to your room. Consider yourself on detention for a week."

"What? You should be thanking me! I-"

"Had no business stowing away in the truck?" Houston interrupted. "You're right, you didn't. You're not cleared for field ops; no student is. Consider yourself lucky to be getting off so lightly. Next time, I won't be so lenient."

"But Coach, I helped! You and Ms. Teresi weren't making much headway against those two at the construction site!"

"And what if you had gotten hurt, or killed?" Houston snapped back. "You're all Sarah has left in this world. Did you even think about her?"

That shut the boy up. He looked down in shame, but maintained the tension in his frame that signified his defiance. Houston nodded. "That's what I thought. Now go, and we'll talk about this later."

After a moment of further hesitation, the boy turned and walked away without another word and stepped through a doorway.

Dr. Littleton cleared his throat. "Did you say he was a student? Where are we, exactly?"

Houston grinned. "Yeah, that's right. This is probably the most exclusive boarding school in the world. Welcome to Prometheus Academy!"

♠　♣　♥　♦

The garage had been a temple dedicated to maintaining a fleet of vehicles in a constant state of peak operational capacity. By contrast, the infirmary was a glorified broom cupboard that gave only incidental acknowledgment to the fact that human bodies were prone to disease and damage. The back wall was occupied by a counter and cabinets with glass-fronted doors, through which Alice could see a surprisingly sparse assortment of pill bottles, bandages, and similar supplies. An examination table sat in the middle of the space, and a desk with a computer stood ready to impede the progress of anyone entering the room.

A middle-aged woman with graying brown hair sat in the chair behind the desk. As the group started filing past the desk, she stood up and approached Alice. "Oh, my dear. Come in and have seat here."

She indicated the examination table. "Kasie will be here in just a moment to take a look at you."

"The kid's not the only one who got hurt out there," LaRonda said edgily as she clanked into the room. "Not that anyone seems to care that my leg hurts like a mother-"

"Yes, yes, we'll look to you too, Ms. Teresi," the woman said. "Take my chair for now, and please try not to scuff up the tile with your, ah, extreme footwear." LaRonda seemed inclined to argue, but thought better of it and walked carefully to the offered chair and sat down to the sound of protesting pneumatics.

Meanwhile, Dr. Littleton assisted Alice in getting into position on the examination table. As they got settled, the woman turned to Houston.

"Would you find Sarah and send her here, please? I think she may prove useful." Houston nodded and nearly collided with a girl wearing a short skirt and a tight-fitting designer shirt about Alice's age as he reached the door. Rather than deal with the complexities of getting both of them past the desk, he simply teleported away.

"Is this going to take long, Mrs. Kilkarni? Regis and I were just getting ready to head into town to catch a movie," the new arrival said. The light flashed off a profusion of jewelry as she approached the table.

"This young lady and her father are our guests, Kasie. As a representative of the academy, I expect you to demonstrate a proper sense of hospitality. Is that clear?"

"Yes, Ma'am," Kasie said, displaying at least a bit of deference.

"Excellent. Now, our guest is hurt. Please see what you can do for her, and then Ms. Teresi needs some attention, too."

"Sure thing," Kasie replied. She stepped up next to Alice and looked her over clinically. "What's your name?"

"Alice Littleton."

"I'm Kasie Hardine. Now don't worry, Alice, this won't hurt a bit once I get the dressing off." Kasie carefully removed the tape and eased the top bandage off, leaving only the folded gauze pad that was directly on the wound. It was not quite soaked through, but it had absorbed a considerable amount of blood.

"Good, the bleeding has stopped." Kasie retrieved a container of sterilized water and began applying it carefully to dissolve the congealed blood adhering the gauze to Alice's skin. She had soon discarded the sodden mass and revealed the damaged area. "Now for the easy part," she said.

She held both hands with palms down over Alice's side, and a white glow emanated from them to bathe the injury. A similar glow shone through her T-shirt, centered in her belly. Alice felt only warmth and a pleasant tingling sensation. After about thirty seconds the glow faded, and Alice glanced down to discover that she was completely mended.

"Thank you," she told Kasie. "That's a very handy ability. But why does your belly glow when you use it? Is it some sort of chakra thing?"

Kasie shook her head. "Not exactly." She flipped up the hem of her shirt to show her navel. She had three piercings positioned so that the gemstones on the ends of the metal pins framed her belly button. Alice saw a black jet, a yellow topaz, and a pearl. Kasie pointed to the last of them. "A pearl is the only 'gemstone' that comes from a living source; I draw on it for healing. I get different powers from the others."

"If you're done with show-and-tell time, would you fix my damn leg now?" LaRonda interjected.

Kasie moved swiftly to her and knelt by her side. "Of course. Which leg is hurt, and how do I get the armor off?"

Without a word, LaRonda removed the leg covering. There wasn't as much blood as Alice would have expected. Perhaps the armor fit snugly enough to function as a pressure bandage. Kasie quickly treated LaRonda, who got up and left after gathering up her helmet and the pieces of her armor's leg with nothing more than a grunt of thanks.

Kasie looked tired, but turned to Mrs. Kilkarni. "Is there anything else?"

"If it's not too much trouble, dear, why don't you take a look at Dr. Littleton's leg? It's an old injury, but see if you can do something for it."

Alice's father looked startled. "You think it's possible to repair this? It's been almost ten years since my expedition."

Kasie moved next to him. "I'm not sure. I'm feeling pretty tired after the work I've already done tonight, but let me at least get a feel for the damage." She raised her hands once more, and the glow returned, though somewhat dimmer than it had been before. She took a long time, moving slowly from his hip down past his knee, her eyes closed in concentration the whole time. Finally, she sat back and dropped her hands as she let the glow dissipate once again.

"There's a lot of damage to ligaments and nerves, and loss of muscle mass where they've atrophied from lack of use, but I think I can help. But I'd recommend that we wait until I've had a chance to rest. That's assuming you want me to try," she said.

"You've actually repaired that type of damage before? It's beyond anything the best clinics can manage," Dr. Littleton said softly.

"I've never attempted something like this," Kasie said. "But I can sense where the damage is, and a sort of - oh, how can I say it - a willingness for the cells to respond, I guess? I'm pretty sure I won't make things any worse, at least."

"I would be in your debt, if you can do anything to help."

"Well, then, I think we'll see what Kasie can do for you tomorrow," Mrs. Kilkarni said as the door opened to admit a dark-haired girl Alice took to be a year or two younger than herself. "And here's Sarah. Thank you for coming. Sarah Thompson, this is Dr. Littleton and his daughter, Alice. They've come to us under dramatic circumstances, and I expect they're rather tired. Alice especially, since she's just been healed. That's a side-effect of Kasie's treatments, but all in all, not a bad trade-off. Would you show them to rooms on the second floor of the student wing for the night, please?"

Alice suddenly realized that she was exhausted. A bed sounded perfect, so she got up and followed Sarah and her father from the room. She found she wasn't up to responding very well to Sarah's half-hearted attempts at conversation, so the other girl gave up and lead them to their destination silently. She showed them adjoining rooms, each with a private bathroom, said good night, and left. After giving her father a quick hug, Alice let herself into one of the rooms. She barely had the strength of will to strip off her bloody and ragged dress and make a quick job of washing the worst of the grime off with a wash cloth before slipping into the bed. She was asleep within minutes.

CHAPTER EIGHTEEN
Livin' for the Weekend

Alice woke the next morning to the sound of a light but insistent knocking at her door. It took her a few moments to remember where she was, and to wonder who knew where to find her.

"Who is it?" she called.

"Sarah," came the reply. "I've got some things here for you. And Mrs. Kilkarni asked me to give you a tour, if you're feeling up to it."

Alice got out of bed and cautiously opened the door, keeping it between herself and her guide. "Uhm, I don't think I'm really dressed for the tour. In fact, my dress is pretty much trashed."

Sarah smiled and held up a huge shopping bag. "That's where I come in. Mrs. Kilkarni had Coach Lane take me into town to pick up some essentials this morning. I think I've got most of the sizes right, or pretty close. Plus, that gave you a chance to sleep in, it being Saturday and all."

Alice accepted the bag and glanced inside. There were several complete changes of clothes, as well as toiletries, a hair brush, and a plain but functional pair of sneakers. "Oh, this looks great. Thank you, Sarah. Why don't you come back in about half an hour? I'll grab a quick shower and be ready to go. Uh, what time is it, anyway?"

"A little after ten. Your dad's already up. Coach Lane's been giving him his own tour."

"Okay, well, thanks again. See you soon." Alice closed the door, realizing as she did so that she was beyond hungry. She hurriedly cleaned up and got dressed. Everything fit well enough. Another knock sounded just as she was starting to brush out her hair.

"Come on in, Sarah, I'm just about ready."

Sarah stuck her head in, then walked over and sat on the edge of the bed when she saw Alice would be a couple more minutes. "You look great. Any idea where you'd like to start?"

"The cafeteria sounds good, if I can get something to eat. I'm starving," Alice replied.

"Oh, well the cafeteria's closed until lunch, and that's a couple of hours away. There's always the student kitchen, though."

"You have a kitchen just for students?"

"Well, this is a boarding school, and a pretty unusual one at that. I guess Mrs. Kilkarni thought our extracurricular activities might involve keeping unusual hours. So we have facilities to take care of things like eating whenever the mood strikes. It's actually pretty cool."

"Well, that's lucky for me. I could definitely do with a sandwich or something." Alice gave her hair one more swipe with the brush, set it down, and turned to the other girl. "Oh, I just realized something. That was your brother at the construction site last night, wasn't it?"

"Scott was at a construction site? What was he doing there?"

"Uh, flying around, making an awful racket, and probably saving my life, in no particular order."

"Really? I haven't seen him yet this morning, so he hasn't had a chance to fill me in. So I guess that's your job, now."

"Okay, I guess. But first, can I ask you something?" Alice and Sarah left her room and Alice allowed the other girl to select their

208

direction. "I've only been here about twelve hours and I've already met two kids with powers, which is two more than I'd ever met previously. How many students here are-"

"Special?" Sarah supplied. "Just about all of them."

"Wow. That's amazing. How many students go here?"

"Just thirteen."

"Thirteen. Still, that's a lot considering I was convinced I was a lone freak of nature on Monday. What's your power?"

Sarah stared down at the floor as she continued to lead Alice down the corridor, but said nothing.

"I'm sorry, is it considered impolite to ask? I don't know what the rules are here," Alice apologized.

"No, it's all right," Sarah hastened to reassure her. "It's just that, well, I guess you'd say I'm the part that makes the 'just about' necessary."

"So you don't have any powers?"

"No. But Scott and I are orphans. Our parents died less than a year ago, so I'm allowed to be here so we can stay close."

"Oh, I see," Alice said. Casting about for something to use to change the subject, she noted a flash of color as Sarah flipped her long dark hair to the side and combed through it with her fingers distractedly. "Oh, hey, neat butterfly!"

Sarah smiled and moved so that Alice could clearly see the tattoo on the back of her left shoulder. "Thanks. I begged my Mom to let me get it for weeks before she finally gave in. It was a reward for good grades, you know? Julio does some great designs, and he says he's going to open a parlor someday. Maybe I'll get one from him."

"Julio? Is he another student?" Alice asked.

"Yeah. You'll meet him soon enough. He seems, I don't know, a little sullen, or angry maybe. A lot of the other kids don't like him, but I get the feeling there's something there that they're missing."

"You like him?"

"Naw, not that way. He's not really my type. I'm an active girl; I need someone who can keep up with me. Of course, he can run like anything, but aside from that he doesn't seem the sporting type. Well, here's the kitchen."

The kitchen area was well stocked, though mostly with staples that would keep a long time in case the students didn't feel like flexing their culinary muscles. But there was milk, and a variety of cereals, which Alice decided was good enough for now. As she helped herself and settled into a seat at the small table, she filled Sarah in on the events from last night.

"Those two guys sound really creepy," Sarah said when she was done. "I've never heard of them before. Still, it could have been worse. Oglethorpe could have found you."

"He did. We were running when these two guys showed up."

"No kidding? Wow, that's some pretty serious bad luck. Still, you made it here safe, so all's well that ends well, right?"

"Yeah, I guess so," Alice said.

"Well, if you're done, why don't we finish looking around?"

Scott sat by himself at a table in the cafeteria. Due to his punishment for stowing away in the truck last night, he had spent the morning in his room. While he was grounded, he could only come out to go to class, eat meals, and report to LaRonda's lab for his duties there.

His isolation now was not a part of his punishment. Most of the students were off enjoying a day in town, and couldn't be bothered to come back for something as trivial as lunch. Aside from some teachers and staff, the only other student in sight was Min Ki. He was leafing through a graphic novel as he ate his lunch.

Scott was halfway through his meal when Sarah and Alice entered. He waved at them, and they came over after making their selections.

"Hey, Alice. I'm glad to see you're feeling better," he said as the girls sat down across from him.

"All thanks to you, and Kasie, of course," Alice replied. "I never got a chance to thank you for driving those guys off. It was very brave of you to jump into the fight like that."

Scott shrugged. "I can't say I really thought about it. When that generator was heading at you, I just reacted. I'm just glad I was able to come up with something that worked in the end."

"Me, too. What was that, anyway? Those guys seemed pretty well protected."

"I call that one my sonic stunner. You may have noticed I generate sounds and vibrations. Anyway, when I saw that my regular attack wasn't cutting through their defenses, I switched over to the stunner. It works on a different frequency, and the black guy's defenses couldn't cope as well."

"So you didn't kill him?" Sarah sounded relieved.

"Naw, but I'll bet he had one hell of a migraine when he woke up," Scott said. "I can't believe Coach Lane grounded me for saving his ass, though."

"It does seem unfair, but you really weren't supposed to be there," his sister replied. "Even knowing how things turned out, Alice's story scared me. Those guys were major league. You do know you got lucky, right?"

"Yeah, and the coach already read me the riot act. But I didn't know they were planning anything dangerous. I was just curious about what they were up to."

"Ms. Teresi's battle suit might have given you a clue," Alice said.

"I just chalked it up to her status as the resident mad scientist, though in her case it just means she's really angry all the time."

"Does she really run around in an Iron Man suit?" Sarah asked.

"Yeah. Last night was our third trip out where I saw it, but I haven't gone snooping in her lab too much. I wonder where she hides it when she's not using it?" Scott said thoughtfully.

"Hey, new blood! What's your name?" Min Ki said as he walked up to the table.

Sarah gestured at the newcomer as she looked at Alice. "Alice, meet Min Ki, one of the members of the combat team," she said.

"I thought Coach Lane was against putting students in danger," Alice said. "At least, he was pretty angry at Scott last night."

"You got into a fight? With powers? Radical! Tell me about it," Min Ki said, looking at Scott with a mixture of envy and respect.

Ignoring Min Ki, Scott responded to Alice. "He was upset because it was an uncontrolled situation. Team Red only spars under closely supervised conditions."

"What would you know about it?" Min Ki demanded. "Besides, we've all only been here about a week. Just you wait, I'll bet we'll really be cutting loose pretty soon, especially if I have anything to say about it."

"Why would you have anything to say about it? I'm just asking," Alice said as Min Ki visibly bristled at the question. "I don't know how anything works here."

"Team Red has their leadership match Monday," Scott explained. "Min Ki probably figures he'll win it. If enthusiasm counts for anything, he probably will."

"I see. Good luck, then," Alice told Min Ki.

"Thanks. So, are you going to be going here, too? What's your power?" he asked.

"I don't know if I'm staying or not, yet. My Dad and I had a run in with a guy named Oglethorpe, and we've been running ever since."

"You've seen Oglethorpe? Man, that's one bad dude. A few of us encountered him before we got here. I guess you could say we're hiding out from him."

"Really? Do you know anything about his friends? How many other supers does he work with?"

"From all I've ever heard, he works alone," Min Ki answered. "Not that I'd call that solid intel, if you know what I mean. He's got some way of finding people like us, so he could be fronting a huge organization. But in the field, he's never needed backup. The dude's unstoppable."

Just then, Dr. Littleton entered the cafeteria and walked up to the table. Alice noted he was still using his cane.

"Alice, Mrs. Kilkarni has asked to talk to us in her office. Are you just about done with your lunch?"

"Sure, Dad." Alice got up from the table.

"Hey, Coach Lane and Ms. Teresi just found you last night, right?" Sarah asked. Alice nodded. "So where was Oglethorpe? You didn't mention him when you told me what happened."

Alice looked down, and Scott thought she looked ashamed. "He's gone. I- I killed him."

Dr. Littleton put his arm protectively around his daughter as they left the cafeteria, leaving the others staring after them wordlessly. Only after they were out of site did Scott, Sarah, and Min Ki exchange glances. Then Min Ki gave voice to the thought ringing through all of their heads.

"No friggin' way!"

CHAPTER NINETEEN
A Fresh Start

Alice's father had obviously been given a more extensive tour of the school than the one Sarah had given her; he needed no one to guide him to Mrs. Kilkarni's office. It was on the second floor of the administrative building, which sat next to the lot where staff and visitors parked their cars. He knocked on the door, and immediately received a "Come in" in response.

The interior of the office was large and tastefully furnished. Maroon carpeting contrasted with the dark wood of the desk across the room. Two visitor chairs stood before the desk. To the left, bookcases lined the wall. A portrait of a man in his thirties, dressed in clothes long out of fashion, hung in a place of honor above a fireplace on the opposite side of the room, with a small light dedicated to its illumination mounted just above the frame. Two deeply upholstered chairs and a love seat were arranged before it, offering a more relaxed option for conversation than the utilitarian furniture.

Mrs. Kilkarni sat in profile, working at a computer on an extension to the desk. As the Littletons entered, she quickly suspended her work and rose to greet them. "Dr. Littleton, welcome. It's especially good to see you looking so recovered, Alice. How did you like the things Sarah picked out for you?" The Littletons sat in the chairs by the desk as she gestured towards them.

"Everything is fine. Sarah did a good job. Thanks for enlisting her to help me, Mrs. Kilkarni. I'd probably still be hiding under the covers, otherwise."

"Excellent. Well, I think we have a lot to discuss this afternoon, don't you? Where shall we start?"

"How about my class schedule?" Alice suggested. "I missed most of last week, but since I've been in classes for over a month and you've just started, I think I'll be able to get up to speed with the other students pretty quickly."

Her father looked at her in surprise. "Alice, Mrs. Kilkarni hasn't even offered you a spot here yet. Not to mention that we haven't even discussed cost, or what it would mean for us if you were to leave home to attend private school. Why are you so certain you're going to stay?"

"It's the Wonderland Effect again, don't you see?"

"The Wonderland Effect? I'm afraid you've lost me," Mrs. Kilkarni said.

"I'm drawn to the unusual, or it's drawn to me, maybe?" Alice explained. "Either way you look at it, it's no coincidence that I've wound up here within days of confirming that other paranormals exist. I'm meant to be here, probably to do something. So of course I'm staying."

Mrs. Kilkarni nodded thoughtfully. "Well, I guess it's a matter of perspective. I'd agree that you're not here by chance, since I've had people looking for you for over a week now. As for the rest-"

"No, you don't understand Mrs. Kilkarni. The Wonderland Effect brought me here at this specific time for a reason. I've got to be here."

"Alice, that's just not rational," Dr. Littleton said. "You've got some amazing abilities, but you're talking about probability manipulation on a macro scale."

"Perhaps not," Mrs. Kilkarni said thoughtfully. "A seemingly isolated event can start a chain of causation that stretches far beyond the area where it occurred. The trick would be in predicting how those effects would play out in relation to other random events. Perhaps some precognitive component? But whether the Wonderland Effect is real or not, or if some task lies before her, Alice is correct about one thing. My purpose here is to get her as a student for Prometheus Academy. Fortunately for me, she is inclined to accept. So that just leaves you, Dr. Littleton. What can I do to convince you?"

He looked at his daughter. "You really want to be here?"

"I need to be here."

He sighed. "Well, then I guess we're down to cost."

Elaine smiled. "We can work on that. I think it's obvious that this school was not made to generate money. Burning through as much money as possible isn't on the table either, but several students are here on what amounts to a scholarship. We can negotiate final terms later, but I'm certain we can come to an arrangement you won't regret too much."

"All right, but I have one stipulation of my own. I want to spend a little time here seeing the school in operation before I give final approval. If I'm satisfied with what I see after a week, I'll strike a deal with you on tuition. Until then, Alice is here on a probationary basis."

"That seems fair," Elaine said. "In that case, let's see what we can do about that schedule."

"Actually, I have a condition, too," Alice interrupted.

"Oh? I thought you had already settled on staying," Mrs. Kilkarni said.

"A request, then. Just a little something to make my time here more fun, and you might not even have to follow through on it."

♠ ♣ ♥ ♦

By dinnertime, Kasie and Regis had wandered back from yet another excursion into town, and Dr. Littleton no longer needed his cane. News had also spread among the students that someone new had joined their ranks. Consequently, Alice found herself the center of attention in the cafeteria.

"I am confused. Your power iz to grow und shrink?" Esme asked.

"That's not all!" Tweedledee said as he suddenly appeared nearby. "She's got lots of friends."

"Important friends," Tweedledum agreed. "In low places."

"Hmmm. Interesting," one of the Juliannas mused, poking at Tweedledum experimentally. "He feels real."

"And you're rude," Tweedledum accused. "I am real."

"Contrariwise, if he was a waxwork, you'd have to pay to see him. So cough up!" Tweedledee demanded.

"That's enough, boys," Alice scolded. "But basically, they're right. I have a lot of friends from the Wonderland stories, plus a couple of odd wrinkles on some of the episodes."

Autumn held out her cell phone to take a picture of the Tweedles. Esme noticed and elbowed Andrew in the ribs. "Camera," she whispered urgently.

Andrew sighed. "I got it; would you relax?" He looked to Alice. "So which team will you be joining?"

"Well, not Team Yellow, that's for sure," Levi sneered. "Ain't nothing elemental about a bunch of refugees from some fairy tale."

"Elementals?" Alice asked.

"Fire, water, and weather," Sarah explained from where she sat next to Alice. She indicated Levi, Autumn and Kip in turn as she spoke.

"Oh, well, I guess you're right. It doesn't sound like a very good match," Alice conceded. "What are the other teams?"

Scott, sitting across the table from Alice, gave Min Ki a friendly slap on the back. "Well, you could always join this guy on Team Red. You did pretty well during the fight last night."

"No, thanks. Combat's definitely not me," Alice replied. "But who else is on his team?" She glanced around at the rest of the kids clustered around.

"Constance here, for one," Kip said. "And Julio over there," he indicated a sullen youth sitting as far away from everyone else as possible.

"Oh, that's the artist you were telling me about, right Sarah?"

"Oh, don't waste your time worrying about him," Regis advised her. "He's obviously doesn't want to be here, and he lashes out at everyone."

"He's not that bad," Min Ki said.

"That's right," Constance added. "He does seem angry, but he really was sorry about those drawings."

Regis smiled condescendingly at them. "Well, it's nice of you to stick up for your teammate, but we all know what he's like. Alice, maybe you could join us. It's probably too late to try for the leadership position, but I think you'd fit in quite well on Team Blue."

"What's your focus?"

"Profiling. We had to predict how the city council is going to vote on an issue related to the school next week."

"Sounds a little, uhm, advanced for high school," Alice hazarded. "Oh, what's he doing here?" She quickly dismissed the Tweedles, banking on the crowd clustered around the table to mask their sudden disappearance.

Everyone looked around to where Alice was looking. A policeman had entered the cafeteria and walked over to the staff table.

"Uh oh, looks like they want you after all, Levi," Julianna whispered.

The policeman showed Mrs. Kilkarni something, and they both looked over at the group of students. She got up and came over with the officer, but they walked right past Levi with no more notice than was required to avoid bumping into him.

"Sarah, this is Officer Carpenter. He needs to talk to you."

"Officer, what's this about?" Scott asked. "I'm an emancipated minor, and Sarah is my sister. I'm responsible for her. Is she in trouble?"

"Possibly. Can you explain this, Sarah?" The policeman showed her a picture.

"Hey, get a load of this," Kip said. "Sarah's been running around town nekkid!" he leered. "But you've blacked out all the best parts, man."

Scott loomed over Kip and shoved him hard in the shoulder. "Get lost, this doesn't concern you," he said evenly. Kip glared at Scott and clenched his fists as a sudden draft of air caused his hair to stir uneasily. Mrs. Kilkarni cleared her throat loudly, and Kip glanced at her, then down at the floor. The tension in the air eased slightly, and Kip brushed past Scott, shoving him with his shoulder as he and Levi exited.

Alice looked at the picture. It showed a young girl with dark hair from behind in a nighttime street scene. As Kip had said, she appeared to be naked, but it had been carefully edited. "I can see why you'd think it's Sarah, officer, but you're wrong," she said.

"It's nice that you're trying to help your friend, young lady, but that is clearly her," Officer Carpenter replied. "We can't condone this type of behavior, so she's going to have to come to the station with me. You can come too, son," he told Scott.

"It can't be Sarah, sir. Look at her left shoulder."

220

Officer Carpenter looked at the photo with a puzzled frown. "I don't see anything special," he said.

"Exactly," Alice replied. "But Sarah has a butterfly tattoo on her shoulder. If your picture was of her, it would show up clearly."

"What? Let me see."

Sarah was still wearing the same top she had on when she gave Alice the tour earlier, and she quickly pulled her hair to the side so the mark was visible. The policeman looked back and forth between the girl and the photo. "Damn if your friend isn't right. How long have you had that tattoo? It's not a temporary transfer?"

"No sir. I've had it a year and a half, sir."

He sighed and shook his head. "Well, it seems I owe you an apology. I hope there are no hard feelings."

Scott reached across and shook his hand. "Not at all, Officer. If I didn't know better I'd have thought it was her myself. And thank you, Alice. You've saved us a lot of trouble."

"Yes. You might want to consider a career in law enforcement," Officer Carpenter suggested. "I bet you'd make detective."

"Uh, I'll think about it. Thanks."

The policeman nodded and turned toward the exit. Mrs. Kilkarni took his elbow and walked beside him. "Let me show you out. Under the circumstances, I hope you'll understand if I confess that I'm happy we weren't able to help you." Their conversation faded to inaudibility as they moved away.

The other students started to drift away, now that the excitement was over. Scott sat back down across from Sarah and Alice and breathed a sigh of relief. "Well that could have been a lot worse," he said.

Sarah looked down at her tray, shaking with reaction. "Yes, it could have," she said, so softly that only the two of them could hear her, "Because I think that was me in the picture."

CHAPTER TWENTY

Assessment

"Okay," Scott said as he, Alice and Sarah huddled in Sarah's room a few minutes later, "explain how you wound up running around town with no clothes, or even your tattoo."

"I can't explain all of it," his sister said softly, staring at the blanket in front of her as she sat hunched on her bed and clutched a pillow to her chest. "I've just been having really vivid dreams this last week, you know? I thought that's all they were, but the scene in that photo was too familiar for it to be a coincidence." She finally looked up at Scott, meeting his gaze. "I'm getting my powers, aren't I?"

Scott nodded somberly. "Looks like. The question is why they're putting you in such an embarrassing situation. And how."

Alice stood uneasily by the door. She hadn't really wanted to join the Thompsons for this discussion. There were no real precedents, but emerging powers seemed like a family matter. But Sarah had been insistent. Alice's eye for detail had deflected official attention for the moment and Sarah's cafeteria confession had brought Alice into the loop, willing or no. So here she was.

"What do you remember about the dreams?" she asked Sarah.

"I was searching for something. Or maybe someone? It was very important to find whatever it was soon. I think it has to do with Team Blue's assignment, but that's just a gut feeling, nothing I can explain, you know? Beyond that, it's just random street scenes at night."

"That sounds like a dream all right," Scott allowed. "Could you have been sleepwalking?"

"It's five miles into town from here! And I don't sleep in the nude. Even assuming I would strip in my sleep and go run a marathon, I would have been seen a lot more frequently than it seems I have been."

"That wouldn't explain the disappearing tattoo, either," Alice added.

"And I'm not sweaty or dirty when I get up in the morning. If I'd gone running that far without shoes, my feet should have been filthy, at least."

"Okay, that all makes sense," Scott allowed. "So if you're not sleepwalking, what is happening?"

His question was met with silence, as the three of them exchanged puzzled glances.

"So what do we do now?" Sarah asked.

Alice suddenly grinned as the answer came to her. "You get a roommate."

♠　♣　♥　♦

Alice's plan was actually pretty simple. They would set up a watch through the night to see if they could determine when and how Sarah's budding powers worked. Alice volunteered herself as Sarah's roommate because she could set one of her companions to stand watch and still get some sleep herself.

The dorm rooms were built to standard double occupancy designs, although with so few students everyone had opted for the more spacious solo living option. It only took an hour or so for the three of them to rearrange Sarah's room and bring in a bed from next door. Alice learned that Scott packed a lot of muscle power in his lanky frame. She figured he probably matched the capabilities of an Olympic weight-lifter without having to carry the same amount of mass. Given his age, he probably hadn't quite reached his full potential, either.

When the work of moving in was done, they just sat around in the girls' room, talking about little of consequence. No one seemed able to concentrate on maintaining the conversation as they all kept drifting back to the puzzle of Sarah's nighttime excursions. Finally, Scott rose and moved toward the door. "My room is right at the top of the stairs," he told Alice. "Come and get me if you need anything tonight. I'll try to stay awake for a while and watch out the window for anything unusual."

The girls went to bed shortly afterward, with a red rook standing sentinel at the foot of Alice's bed. However, when Alice awoke, it was to sunlight streaming through the curtains, and the five foot tall chess piece had not moved.

She crossed the room and shook Sarah awake. "Sarah, it's me, Alice. Did you have any unusual dreams last night?"

Sarah blinked up at the ceiling, considering the question. "No," she answered finally. "I don't remember anything about last night's dreams."

"Don't worry about it. Learning to take conscious control of your powers can take some time. At least, that's how it was with me."

"Really? What did you have trouble with?" Sarah asked.

"Well, my friends still pop in sometimes when I haven't called for them, but I guess that's to be expected. But I also tended to shrink things all the time. I remember once Dad was complaining to Mom that the newspapers were using microprint. The next day, I went to get his paper for him, and by the time I got it to the breakfast table he could have hidden it behind a piece of toast, fully open."

Sarah laughed. "I guess he wasn't so critical of the newspapers after that."

Alice smiled. "Well, anyway, don't fret. You'll get the hang of it soon enough. In the meantime, let's go get some breakfast."

♠   ♣   ♥   ♦

By Monday morning, Sarah still hadn't experienced another lucid dream. It was Alice's first day of classes at Prometheus Academy, but she felt she wasn't getting the full experience. Everyone seemed distracted as noon, the time for the Team Red leadership match, approached. All the students and half the teachers seemed to have bets on the outcome, and instructors weren't inclined to put forth much effort for students with minds firmly focused on the coming spectacle.

At 11:45 the bell rang, and everyone rushed out to the quad between the administrative, residential and classroom buildings. The gymnasium, which also housed the cafeteria, formed a third side of the open area. Opposite stood only a high hedge with a narrow, though obviously intentional, opening framed by a brickwork arch. The crowd was moving towards the opening.

"Alice, wait!"

Alice looked around and quickly found Sarah and Scott hurrying towards her. As they caught up, she fell into step with them. Soon, they stepped through the archway and Alice could see they were on a broad lawn on which an arena of sorts had been constructed. The perimeter was composed of concrete traffic barriers laid out in a circle fifty yards across. Within the ring were a number of obstacles, mostly free-standing walls twelve feet high by six wide, but there was also a mud pit in the center, covering a circle 20 yards across. Halfway between the mud pit and the concrete barriers, three pits five yards wide were spaced evenly around the arena.

The three combatants were already in the ring, standing on pedestals that left them a few inches above the surface of the mud, just a few feet in from the pit's outer edge. Each wore a harness with some sort of electronic assembly positioned in the center of their chest. Min Ki fidgeted, clearly anxious to get started. Julio stood with arms crossed, staring at a point between his teammates. Constance held her hands in front of her belly, fingers lightly touching but palms apart, with her eyes closed. Alice watched her for a minute or two while the last stragglers found positions in back of the barriers from which to watch the match. The girl was a statue. Most people would have swayed slightly as their center of balance shifted from moment to moment.

"Who do you like for leader?" Sarah asked, rubbing her hands together to keep them warm.

"I don't know any of them very well. Min Ki seems eager for the position, though," Alice answered.

"You have a flair for understatement," Scott said. He had his hands tucked inside the pockets of his jacket. "Most folk are betting he'll take the match out of sheer determination, but I'm not so sure. I'm not sure he can stay focused enough."

"So who do you like?" Sarah asked.

Before he could answer, Coach Lane appeared on another pedestal, slightly higher than the others, in the exact center of the ring. He carried a bull horn, and immediately put it to use addressing the crowd.

"All right, pipe down. We all know why we're here and what's on the line, so I'm just going to cover the rules before we get started. Each contestant is wearing a sensor that will register a hit on their body. Each hit will light up an LED on the display. Three hits will eliminate a combatant from the competition. Last one standing wins. Each participant is allowed to bring in any equipment that they wish, so long as they can actually carry it with them. Any questions?"

He scanned the students arranged around him. No one seemed to want to discuss terms, so he switched the microphone on again. "All right then. The combat will commence as soon as I leave this podium. Ready...set...fight!" Coach Lane vanished and Alice quickly noted his new position behind one of the barriers.

Taking the time to track Coach Lane almost prevented Alice from noting the opening salvo in the leadership match. As soon as the central pedestal was empty, Julio had rushed off his own, heading directly at Min Ki. He moved so swiftly, Alice was never sure where they came from, but he was suddenly holding two odd, silvery metal clubs.

Min Ki summoned his translucent armor as Julio left his pedestal. To Alice, it seemed it would only serve to protect him from a devastating blow, since the boy remained unarmed. But somehow, as they came together, it was Julio who went flying backward to splash in the mud, with his first LED lit.

Constance had not been idle as the boys went after each other. Her first move had been an incredible crouch and leap that propelled her higher than a tall man to somersault and land on dry ground twenty feet behind her initial position. As she landed, she reached into her tunic to retrieve a shuriken, which she immediately launched at Min Ki. The missile struck him squarely below one upraised arm and detonated. The force of the blast activated the first LED on his harness and toppled him sideways and into the mud puddle.

The students watching the match cheered as all three combatants assessed the threats facing them and made their decisions. Julio moved swiftly out of the mud onto dry ground and began running through the field of obstacles, using them for cover as he built up speed.

Constance decided to press her advantage against Min Ki. Several running steps brought her to the edge of the mud pit, where she jumped, landed in the center of the pedestal she had started out on, and then leapt forward again. The second jump propelled her across the entire width of the pit, poised to deliver a kick to her opponent, who was just getting his feet back under him.

Min Ki was not to be taken by surprise twice in succession, however. The legs of his armor extended instantaneously to twice their normal length, propelling him up and forward on a higher trajectory than Constance. The martial artist was unable to correct course in mid leap, and so was helpless to counter as Min Ki's left gauntlet shot out on the end of the extendable armor arm and grabbed her by her tunic just behind her neck as he passed her. Constance was yanked backward, and up and over Min Ki as he swept his arm around. A moment after he landed, he brought her down in a spread-eagled belly flop into the mud that made everyone present wince in sympathy.

"Ow, that must have hurt. Do you think she'll be able to continue?" Sarah yelled at Alice over the cheers of the crowd.

"I don't know. Kasie is standing by in case anyone needs to be healed, but that might disqualify the person needing the healing. Do you know how they're ruling on that, Scott?" Alice looked to her other side and was surprised to discover Scott was not there.

Before she could look around to see where he had gone, the question was answered for her as the sound of his powers activating rose over the sounds of the crowd. Scott lifted into the air, leaving a torn-up patch of soil in the lawn where he had been standing. Alice saw that he had removed his jacket, revealing a harness like the students in the arena wore. At once he flew out over the arena.

The combatants had taken notice, of course. Min Ki appeared to be shouting something at Scott, but no one could hear it over the buzz saw sound of Scott's flight power. Scott pointed at Min Ki, resulting in a small crater blasted into the ground when the boy dodged instinctively.

Min Ki quickly regrouped and held up a clenched fist toward Scott. Alice thought the armored lad was just venting his frustration at being unable to retaliate against the flyer, but quickly learned how wrong she was. One moment the fist of the psychic armor encased its

229

owner's physical hand, the next it was smashing into Scott's midriff at the end of the extended arm of the armor.

Oh, Alice thought, *now I know how he came out on top in his in exchange with Julio. He hit him with a short jab before the speedster could get in range for his attack.*

The force of the blow drove Scott backwards in the air, and he dropped several feet before catching himself with his flight power. He flew back towards the center of the arena quickly, lining up for a run on Constance, who had regained her feet and wiped enough mud away to see and function again.

Just before he reached the edge of the mud pit, Constance launched another shuriken at him. At the same time Julio, moving at the pace of a Nascar racer, cut through the mud field on a course that curved away from the flyer. This had the effect of throwing up a spray of mud that caught Scott in the face and upper chest. Scott wavered in his flight, and as the mud fell away, the audience could see the second LED on his chest light up. His erratic flight had saved him from the throwing star, however; it had flashed by harmlessly.

Or so Alice thought. A moment later, the projectile curved impossibly in its flight and came at Scott again, this time from the rear. He was unaware of the danger, and so had no time to react. The weapon struck him between his shoulder blades as Scott's eyes opened wide in surprise. The final LED on his harness lit up, and relative silence descended as his flight power cut out and he fell into the mud near the central pedestal.

"Scott!" Sarah yelled. She started to try to climb over the barrier to get to her brother, but before she could get a leg over, Coach Lane was there, restraining her.

"Relax, Sarah, this was all a part of the test. Mrs. Kilkarni wanted to see how they would react to a surprise on the battlefield," the instructor explained. "Scott's fine."

"But that was a shuriken. He could be bleeding out right now."

"Constance only took practice stars into the arena. They're rubber. He may be bruised, but that's all."

Sarah looked far from convinced, but stopped struggling. Coach Lane gave her a reassuring pat on the back and said, "Don't worry. The biggest problem you'll have is easing Scott's bruised ego. They took him out pretty quickly." Then he blinked back to his former position across the arena.

Alice returned her attention to the arena. Min Ki had learned from Julio's speed-assisted mud attack against Scott. He launched himself with his armor's legs once more, landing in the dry outer ring and quickly put one of the walls to his back. Constance likewise abandoned the central region and disappeared behind a free-standing wall on the opposite side of the arena. Julio continued his rapid circuit, zipping around obstacles with ease.

They've each got one strike against them, Alice thought. *It's still anyone's match.*

A moment later, Julio zipped behind the wall Min Ki was using for shelter, to the accompaniment of the sound of shattering wood. Julio was out past the wall again before the second LED on Min Ki's harness even had a chance to register the blow and blink on. The armored fighter looked back at the hole the speedster's silvery club had left in the wall and swore.

"Stand and fight, you coward!" he yelled.

"Says the guy in full armor," Julio taunted back. "What's the matter, not flexible enough to deal with reality? One more pass and I've got you beat."

"We'll see about that," Min Ki said. His armor's right arm extended as he whipped it around. As it intersected a pole ten feet away

231

from him, the arm bent and the section beyond continued to extend and sweep around until it grabbed the edge of another wall segment. It all happened in a second, and Julio found himself running into a psychic trip line as he approached to finish his opponent off. He went flying, tumbling as he lost his footing. He finally skidded to the edge of one of the pits and hung briefly on the edge before toppling in.

"Yeah! Hole in one!" Min Ki trumpeted. "Now who's finishing who off?"

"That would be me, taking you out," Constance called as she vaulted to the top of a wall segment nearby, touching down with only the lightest of taps before continuing her trajectory towards Min Ki.

"You wish," Min Ki laughed. Even as his right arm retracted, his left lashed out at Constance. But this time, he wasn't going for a simple punch. Amazingly, his armor's arm seemed to take on a life of its own, quickly wrapping itself around the martial artist several times, pinning her arms to her side and halting her progress simultaneously. For a moment, she hung in his grip ten feet in front of him before he swung her around and smashed her against the same wall Julio had smashed through earlier, just hard enough to activate the second LED on her harness. He brought his right fist up in line with her harness. "Nothing personal, you know. But say good night, Constance."

"Uh, uh, Min Ki. You haven't read her a bedtime story yet," Julio called. He had struggled to pull himself up to the edge of the pit with his arms hooked over the edge. As Min Ki turned to see what was happening, Julio threw a rock he had picked up from the bottom of the hole, putting so much effort into it that he lost his grip and fell back in. His aim was good, however, and the improvised projectile hit Min Ki's hip. His armor deflected it of course, but the damage was done and the final LED glowed to life.

Min Ki's disappointment was obvious, but his good humor at finally getting to take part in a powered scrimmage didn't desert him entirely. He cried out in mock agony as he collapsed and allowed his armor to dissipate, freeing Constance. "Curse you, hero. I'll be back, and my revenge will be terrible to behold!" He then fell still, simulating unconsciousness so his teammates could decide the match.

Constance walked up to the pit and looked down at Julio, who had managed to get back to the lip. She offered him a hand, which he took after a moment of uncertainty. She hauled him up to stand beside her with comparatively little effort, and he realized her dedicated training had given her more strength than he would have credited her with.

"Thanks for the save," she said.

"Uh, you're welcome," Julio said, trying to ease his hand from her grip.

"Not so fast, Mr. Blur." Before he could process that, Constance hooked a foot behind his leg and took him down, landing an open-handed blow with the heel of her hand on his harness's sensor pack just as he hit the ground. His final LED sprang to life.

"This match is concluded. Constance Crutchfield is the winner of Team Red's leadership challenge," Coach Lane announced over the bull horn.

With the match completed, Scott and Min Ki started climbing to their feet, but Constance remained crouched over Julio. Alice was just beginning to wonder what was up when Team Red's new leader suddenly bent forward and kissed the speedster soundly on the lips.

The kiss lasted a few seconds before the wolf whistles and cat calls started up, seeming to break Constance out of whatever trance she had fallen into. She looked around at everyone, and then down at Julio as her cheeks flushed a deep scarlet. The next moment she sprang up and dashed for the hedge leading back to the school buildings, choosing to execute another of her incredible jumps to clear the concrete barriers at the edge of the arena and one more to go over the hedge rather than take the time to locate the opening.

"Well," Sarah said as the winner disappeared from sight, "it will be interesting to see where that leads. It's bound to be someplace interesting."

Alice could only nod in agreement as she and Sarah reached up to help Scott as he climbed out of the arena.

CHAPTER TWENTY-ONE
Invitations

"Okay, pass me the toffee chips," Alice said, indicating the open bag sitting past Sarah on the counter.

Sarah relayed the candy to her, then went back to lining the cookie sheets with parchment paper. "This was a great idea. I haven't made cookies in ages. Not since..." She broke off as her throat closed up on her.

"Sarah?"

The dark-haired girl shook her head, then gave Alice a weak smile. "It's okay. I just realized the last time I actually made cookies was with Mom. We were getting ready for a school bake sale, and I was complaining that I wanted to be out with my friends. Pretty selfish, huh?"

"Pretty typical, more like. Did you get along with her?"

"Yeah, I mean, we had all the typical fights about appropriate clothes and stuff, but generally things were great. All this," she gestured at the half-made snacks in front of them, "just made me realize I've been avoiding some of our favorite activities."

"Sounds like it's time to reclaim territory, then. Actually, I'm a little jealous," Alice said as she finished mixing the dough and started spooning balls of it onto one of the prepared pans.

"Jealous? of what? My parents are dead."

"But you have good memories of them. Dad and I are tight, but I could never seem to please Mom. She finally went off and started a new family. Sometimes it seems like all my memories of her are of fights and her disapproval of me, and especially my powers. I can't help feeling like I should have been, well, different. Then maybe she would have stayed."

"I'm sorry. But maybe-"

"No, I'm sorry. I didn't mean to be such a wet blanket. We're supposed to be having fun here." Alice popped the first sheet into the oven and set the timer, then began loading the next. "Keep those cookie sheets coming. As soon as the smell of these little goodies starts spreading, we're going to be swamped with kids looking for a fix."

The two girls worked companionably for the next several minutes. True to Alice's prediction, Levi and Kip wandered into the student kitchen about the time the second tray was coming out of the oven.

"What are you making in here?" Kip asked. "It smells great."

"Alice is showing me her favorite cookie recipe," Sarah explained.

"Yep, Coffee Toffee Pecan Chip, my own invention," Alice said. "We've made plenty, so help yourselves."

Both boys did, and the room was soon filled with the sounds of appreciative groans of delight.

"Man, those are kickin' cookies," Levi said. "Better than my Ma's chocolate chip, and I never thought I'd say that about anything."

"You said it," Kip agreed. "I think I've got a new favorite."

Levi had taken two more cookies, but stopped and stared at Alice instead of immediately eating them, as Kip was doing with his share. After several uncomfortable seconds of this, Alice couldn't take it anymore.

"Can I help you with something, Levi?"

He blinked, seeming to only then become aware that he had been looking at her so intensely. "Sorry," he mumbled, "It's just that you don't add up."

"Excuse me? How's that?" Alice asked.

Levi had been looking down at one of the cookie sheets, but now he looked Alice in the eye, and his shoulders went back in challenge. "There's a rumor going 'round that you did for Oglethorpe, or at least that you claimed it. Is that really true?"

Alice blushed, but met his gaze squarely. "You make it sound like something to be proud of. Taking a life isn't something I ever thought I'd do, but he threatened me and my father. I'd really rather not talk about it, but, yeah, he's gone."

"How?" Levi pressed. "That dude came for me when I ascended, and he was freakin' unstoppable."

Ascended? Alice thought, though out loud she restricted herself to observing, "And yet here you are."

"Coach Lane showed up and teleported me out of there. Otherwise, I'd be dead, or where ever Oglethorpe wanted me to be. There's no way I could have taken him. So when some slip of a girl armed with nothing but some story book creatures claims to have taken him out, I'm skeptical. It doesn't add up."

"Why would I lie?" Alice asked.

"Maybe you're trying to impress us," Kip suggested.

"I didn't play that game back home, and I'm sure not looking to start now," Alice declared. "The only reason I mentioned it at all is that he seemed to have threatened at least half the people here directly, and I thought they should know. Believe me or don't; I really don't care."

"Well, I guess we'll see," Levi said. He grabbed a couple more cookies then nudged Kip with his shoulder. "Come on, we got better things to be doing anyway."

Kip looked at the girls, shrugged, and grabbed three more cookies before following his friend back the way they'd come.

Once they were out of earshot, Alice turned to Sarah. "Can I ask you something?"

"Sure."

"The night Officer Carpenter showed up with the photo, someone said the police must have decided they wanted Levi. Why would anyone suggest that?"

"Oh, Levi went into a burning house to try to rescue some trapped kids. Mrs. Kilkarni's first assignment for the elementals was to find ways to use their powers to aid the community without revealing what they can do. But the smoke got to be too much and they almost didn't make it out."

"So why were the police involved?"

"They thought it was suspicious that Levi showed up when he did, which kind of makes sense," Sarah explained. "They thought he might have set the fire so he could play hero. I guess some people do that. But they couldn't find any traces of an accelerant used to start the fire, so they're leaning towards labeling it an accident and letting it go. I'm sure it will all blow over before long."

"I see. Well, here come our next customers," Alice said as she spied Esme and Julianna approaching. "I hope they're a little more restrained than the boys, or we'll have to make another batch."

An hour later, most of the students were hanging out around the kitchen. Alice and Sarah had finished baking and washed the dishes, and people were chatting in small groups. The only kids Alice hadn't seen yet were Scott, Julio, and Constance. Constance hadn't been seen since the conclusion of the mock combat, and several students were holding some sort of grudge against Julio. And of course, Scott was still grounded.

Or was he? Alice had no sooner thought of him before she spotted his close-cropped red hair passing through the door. Before she could collect her thoughts, he was in front of her.

"Hey, Mrs. Kilkarni sent me to find you. She'd like to see you in her office, ASAP."

"Oh, uh, thanks. So they've got you running messages as part of your punishment now?" Alice asked.

"Nah, I was just the handy gopher that crossed her path first. I can see why, looks like everyone's here."

"Scott, catch!" Sarah called, and lobbed a baggie at her brother. He caught it easily, then held it up to look at the contents.

"Cookies?"

"Yeah, they're Alice's recipe and they're awesome. I was going to bring them by your room in a bit, but it looks like you saved me the trouble."

"They let me out of my box for pulling my surprise during the team challenge," Scott explained. "Come on, Alice, you shouldn't keep Mrs. Kilkarni waiting."

Alice nodded and got to her feet, feeling a bit of trepidation. The school administrator had promised she would let Alice know as soon as she made a decision about her special request, and now that the time had apparently come, Alice simultaneously dreaded the answer and

239

couldn't wait to hear it. She quickly walked out of the room with Scott at her side.

After a couple of minutes lost in her own thoughts, she noticed that Scott was behaving strangely. He kept looking at her, but tried to do it so that it wasn't obvious. he cleared his throat a couple of times, and she thought he was about to say something, but he never did.

Finally, she said, "I've been to her office before; you don't really need to play tour guide if you've got somewhere else you'd rather be."

"What? Uh, no, no place else at all. Actually, I was wondering..."

"Wondering what?"

Scott took a deep breath and said "How would you like to come flying with me Saturday morning? The sunrise is beautiful from 10,000 feet."

Alice stopped short. "Flying?"

"Yeah. Don't worry, I'm pretty strong and I can carry you, no problem. You'd be perfectly safe. You just need to dress warm."

Safe? Of course I'd be safe. Oh, he doesn't know though, does he? Alice smiled in spite of herself. "I, uh, I think that sounds great."

"Cool. Meet me on the first floor about 6:30. You're going to love it."

"I can't wait."

"Great. Well, uh, I guess I'll see you later then. I hope Mrs. Kilkarni has good news for you."

They parted ways, and Alice now found her thoughts drifting in two separate directions. Both were marked with anticipation and anxiety, but the flavors of each were quite different.

Soon enough, she reached the door to the office and knocked. Hearing a muffled but indecipherable response, she opened the door and entered.

Elaine was sitting before the fireplace tonight with a leather-bound book resting in her lap. Dr. Littleton was already in the room as well, sitting across from her in the other upholstered chair. Elaine indicated the love seat that remained and said, "Come in, Dear. We need to have a talk."

Alice felt her stomach drop. That wasn't a promising beginning, but she crossed to the indicated piece of furniture and sat in the middle, facing the adults.

"Now then, how are you feeling about Prometheus Academy after your first day?" Mrs. Kilkarni asked.

"Well, mostly it was just like a regular high school, except for the leadership match, of course. That was pretty intense."

"It was certainly that," her father agreed. "And that is the source of our concern. You've asked Mrs. Kilkarni to allow Miranda to come here as well. How do you think she'll feel attending a school where abilities like that are frequently on display? After all, it's not as if she has abilities of her own. Don't you think she'll feel like a fish out of water?"

"Please consider your response carefully, Alice. You may think you're offering your friend a chance at the adventure of a lifetime, but have you really thought about what life will be like for her here?" Mrs. Kilkarni asked. "I wouldn't want you to look back on this moment later and see it as just a selfish desire to keep a comforting influence in your life, despite any possible negative consequences for her."

Alice took a moment to collect her thoughts. *Am I being selfish? Miranda would love this place, wouldn't she? Or am I just projecting my feelings onto her?*

Finally, she looked up at Mrs. Kilkarni and her father. "In the end, I think it has to be Miranda's decision. And her parents, of course. But I think the important thing is that she is a good fit for your stated purpose in creating this school. You want to show the world that the empowered can coexist with normal people, right?"

"Ultimately, that is one of our aims," Elaine allowed.

"Then you should start looking for good, non-powered, candidates to bring into the school. You already have one precedent in Sarah Thompson." *Technically not true anymore, but you don't know that.* "Miranda is a good choice for the next regular student."

"And why is that?" Mrs. Kilkarni asked.

"Because she has a proven track record for keeping secrets. She's known as much as I do about my abilities ever since they first appeared, and she's never told a soul, not even her parents."

"Who may be a security risk themselves. We can't invite Miranda without informing her parents about what's really going on here," the principal said, tapping her fingers on her book. "Is there a reason you didn't entrust them with your secret as well?"

"Yes, but it wasn't that we were afraid that they'd tell anyone. We were more afraid that they wouldn't let Miranda see me anymore. And that wasn't based on anything more than a child's sense of how overprotective parents can be."

"And now?"

"I would still trust them to keep a secret. Miranda is who she is because of their influence, after all. As for the rest, I just don't know. We'll have to let them see behind the curtain and hope for the best," Alice concluded.

Elaine stared into the fire for a full minute, her fingers keeping up a steady rhythm on the book's cover. Finally, she nodded. "Your father's assessment of the Sullivans matches your own, and I think

242

you're right about the need for a human normal contingent for the student body. So I will take a risk. This Saturday, Coach Lane will transport you and your father home, where you can pack what you need for your time with us. While you're there, you can also approach your friend's family and extend an invitation for Miranda to join us."

CHAPTER TWENTY-TWO
Behind Closed Doors

After the humiliating ending to the Team Red leadership match, Constance had retreated to her room. She did not venture out again the rest of the day. No doubt there would be repercussions from ditching her afternoon classes, but that was the least of her worries. She had assumed the mantle of leadership, then immediately rendered it impossible for her to be in that role, at least for Julio. How could she have let her control slip so badly?

She spent the rest of the day meditating, systematically dealing with her embarrassment, doubts, and fears so she could get a good night's rest. When morning arrived, she felt ready to face her peers again, more than halfway convinced she could salvage the situation and re-establish a good working relationship with her teammates.

That sense of optimism vanished as soon as she walked into home room and was greeted with clapping and wolf whistles from Levi and Kip. As she blushed bright red, she surveyed the rest of the room's occupants.

Prometheus Academy had two home room groups. The upper classmen group consisted of the sixteen-year-olds and Scott Thompson, who was seventeen. Everyone else was in Constance's home room, where everyone was fourteen or fifteen. Aside from the two doing their best to send her running to her room in tears, the younger group included Andrew, Esme, Autumn, Min Ki and Sarah. Andrew was giving her a silly grin, but somehow he managed to keep it from looking like he was mocking her. Min Ki placed a fist to his palm and gave her a half-bow from where he was seated, looking calm and respectful. The girls were all looking at Kip and Levi with varying degrees of disgust on their faces.

Okay, that's two jerks and five supporters. Or, at least, kids that don't seem to care enough to give me a hard time. I can work with that. Constance straightened her shoulders and walked to her seat to the right of Min Ki's with her head high. Julio might be harder to deal with, but facing him would be easier after this relative victory.

♠   ♣   ♥   ♦

The key, Constance thought as she entered the cafeteria, is to make the first move. If I quickly establish a professional tone with him, maybe I can keep Julio from treating me like an overly emotional schoolgirl - even if that's more accurate than I want to admit.

Fortunately, she had not had a class with Julio this morning. That would change after lunch. Elaine had strong opinions about making sure all students worked together, so students of all ages frequently took classes together. Scanning the room, she quickly located her teammate just stepping out of line with his tray and walking towards the nearest empty table. Ignoring the wonderful smells for the moment, despite the fact that she had not eaten anything since yesterday morning, she headed straight for him.

She sat down across the table from him, and gave him a friendly smile, but not too friendly. "We've got a team meeting in the gym with Coach Lane this evening," she said, trying for a business-like, efficient tone of voice. "I just want to be sure you'll be able to make it on time. He says we've got a lot of ground to cover."

Julio grinned back at her. "Fortunately, covering ground is my specialty. I'll be there."

Constance nodded. "Good. By the way, I wanted to apologize."

"What for?"

"The, you know, the kiss. I was just so excited to have won the match. I, well, I hope you didn't get the wrong idea. It was just the thrill of winning, so don't think you've got to make it out to be anything more complicated. I shouldn't have done it, and I hope there are no hard feelings, you know?"

Julio just looked at her, long enough to make her nervous. *He's not buying it. Damn it, this is all going to blow up in my face. He's thinking I'm so hot for him I'd do anything for him, and...*

"No problem," Julio said finally. "I got it. Thrill of victory. Don't worry, we're good."

Constance sighed in relief. "Great. Thanks for understanding. Oh, good use of the tonfas during the match, by the way. What were those made of?"

"Aluminum. I rush ordered a set online after your demonstration. It's easier punching something with them when I run by than my hands. But you'll have to show me how to make best use of them. I still can't do all that grip changing stuff like you."

"Sure, no problem. We can start working on that tonight. Well, I'm starving, so I'm gonna go grab some chow. See you later."

Constance hurried away, relieved that the conversation had gone so well. Her relationship with Julio was firmly back on platonic ground. *So why does the smell of this food suddenly make me feel like puking?*

♠ ♣ ♥ ♦

Julio watched Constance leave, and mulled over their conversation. *She can say what she wants, but that kiss had nothing to do with winning a competition. I'm sure of that.*

Unfortunately, he wasn't sure about much else where his team leader was concerned. Julio had always been one to appreciate female company, but Constance hadn't even been on his radar until the end of the match. Now he was stuck trying to separate what the kiss had sparked from his real feelings about her. He knew he respected her; he didn't think her win was a fluke. Beyond that, his thoughts became a muddled, tension-inducing mess that made him feel like he was back in the mud in the arena, fighting for traction.

Well, if she wants to back off for a while, I guess that's fine with me. But I'm not promising to leave things there indefinitely.

♠   ♣   ♥   ♦

It was Tuesday evening. Kasie stood outside the Boulder City town hall and checked her phone's recorder app. It was working perfectly, and the phone's battery had a full charge. She was ready to preserve every statement and counterpoint in tonight's debate over the tax incentives for the school. All she had to do now was get in the room.

She glanced around, trying to see if any of Team Green's other members were around, but they were not evident. She wasn't really surprised. Esme's gift for languages was impressive, and no doubt useful, but she wasn't going to talk her way into the meeting. And Julianna's duplicates were even less likely to be overlooked during the proceedings. It looked like she had a clear field.

Kasie wandered around to the east side of the building, doing her best to remain inconspicuous. To aid in that effort, she had left most of her jewelry back at the school this evening. In truth, she felt practically naked without them, but the powers she drew from most of the stones would not aid her tonight. She retained only the pins for her piercings, since they were safely out of sight beneath her shirt.

After making sure no one was within her field of vision, she stepped into a recessed doorway for a side exit that was seldom used, switched on the recorder, and drew on the power of her jet stone.

Swiftly, her body lost all color and detail as she morphed into a two-dimensional shadow against the wall, barely visible against the stones in the gloom of the evening. She passed between the door and its frame easily. Having gained access to the interior, she made her way to the meeting room without further delay, gliding along the floor with no one around to notice the oddly mobile silhouette with no source. She slid beneath the door.

The conference room was laid out for public hearings, with a large area for citizens to sit and listen, or come forward to present their opinions. Beyond a wooden barricade sat the table, where the council members were already gathered. The entranceway was too far from the table for the politicians to have noticed a shadow on the ground, but it was also too great a distance for Kasie to make a good recording of the proceedings. She slipped closer, moving across the floor beneath the chairs, just in case anyone glanced in her direction.

Once she got to the wooden barrier, she let go of her phone, which immediately reverted to its normal dimensions and composition. Her shadow form could not manipulate its controls, which was why she had turned the recorder on before entering the building. Now, all she had to do was wait for the meeting to conclude, retrieve the phone, and exit as she had come. Fortunately, her shadow form was comfortable. The cramped space beneath the chairs was quite spacious by her current standards.

CHAPTER TWENTY-THREE
Taking Flight

Following her interview with Mrs. Kilkarni, Alice was fit to bust with excitement. She was going to see Miranda again! And maybe bring her back to the school!

She was aching to tell her friend all about Prometheus Academy, but she was under a strict signal blackout order. No one knew exactly what the organization behind Oglethorpe was capable of, so no one associated with the school was supposed to use any sort of electronic messaging to communicate with those who weren't in on the secret. She wasn't even responding to Miranda's increasingly frantic pleas to let her know she was all right. It was hard, but the secret that was Prometheus Academy was not hers to endanger, and she knew she would never forgive herself if she lead the enemy here. She would just have to wait until she could see Miranda in person.

The rest of the week passed slowly, and Alice focused on her school work to distract herself from her worries about what Miranda was going through. She also had the anticipation of her flying date with Scott to occupy quiet moments. She discovered, quite to her surprise, that she was interested in Sarah's brother. Maybe that had something to do with his actions back in the construction yard, but Alice thought that she probably would have liked him regardless. He was athletic, handsome, and had an easygoing, optimistic outlook on life that made him fun to be around.

The rook still kept vigil in the girls' room each night, but so far there hadn't been any indication that Sarah had taken another excursion, and she reported that she had not experienced the lucidness in her dreams that she associated with her power's activation. Alice suspected her own intrusion into the other girl's life, along with Sarah's awareness of being watched throughout the night, had placed a temporary damper on her emerging abilities. Until the new arrangement became routine, Sarah was likely to remain in her bed.

When Alice's alarm went off Saturday morning before dawn, she took a moment to savor the thrill that this long-awaited day was finally here. It promised so much potential, she could scarcely contain herself. She hopped out of bed, heading toward the bathroom, when Sarah's sleepy voice stopped her.

"What's up? Did I do something?"

"No, I'm just getting an early start," Alice said. "Scott's taking me flying, remember?"

"Oh, okay," she said sleepily. "Hardly seems worth it, just to be carried like a special delivery package. It would be different if I could fly under my own power. But have fun." Sarah burrowed back under the covers as Alice continued to the bathroom and took a quick shower. Then she quickly dressed in several layers of warm clothes, purchased just the day before, and let herself out.

Scott was waiting for her when she got to the first floor. "Hi, you look great. You ready for this?" he greeted her.

"You bet. Did I dress warmly enough?"

Well, it's pretty cold up there. We'll probably both be ready for some hot chocolate when we get back, but trust me, it will be worth a little discomfort," Scott said. "Speaking of which, you'll need these."

He gave her a pair of earplugs. Alice had seen cops on TV shows wearing similar stuff while practicing on indoor shooting ranges. "Are these really necessary?"

"Yeah. My power isn't exactly designed with stealth in mind. Without these, your hearing will be impaired for the rest of the day. Prolonged exposure can probably lead to permanent damage."

Alice grimaced. "Okay, I'll put them in just before we take off, then. Don't you get a pair?"

Scott shook his head. "Nah, it's one way my body's adapted to my power set. My hearing can't be overloaded, so I don't need them."

"Handy," Alice observed. "Well, where do we start?"

"Out back, on my launching pad," Scott answered, starting to lead the way. Alice followed.

"You have a launching pad?"

"You'll see," he replied.

As soon as they stepped out the door into the pre-dawn air, Alice was grateful for every stitch of her clothing. The temperature was just above freezing, and a stiff breeze did its best to snatch away what warmth her body was producing. The sky was still covered with stars, though a rosy glow was beginning to displace the blackness to the east. Scott walked to the back corner of the quad where a square cement slab, about a foot and a half on a side, was set into the grass.

"I don't really need it to take off," he explained as he took a stance in the middle of the surface. "But without it, I'd tear up a significant section of the lawn. I really don't want to get Adrian upset."

"Adrian?"

"The groundskeeper and handy man. He's a nice guy, and there's no reason to make extra work for him. You ready?"

Alice nodded, inserted her ear plugs, and then stepped close to Scott. He scooped her up, supporting her under her knees and across her back as she put an arm around his neck. He smiled at her, looked up into the sky, and launched.

Launch is the perfect word for it, Alice thought as the ground dropped away. Scott's flight relied on raw power to overcome gravity, and she felt several times heavier than normal as they accelerated. Somehow, she had expected a more graceful and gentle translation. *Not that this isn't exciting and fun, just different from what I expected.*

After a few seconds, Alice found she had to close her eyes, which were beginning to tear up from the force of the wind their passage was kicking up. She didn't want Scott to think she was scared, though, so she kept a smile on her face as the acceleration continued, because the roar of his power rendered speech all but impossible.

Finally, after what seemed like minutes, they reached what Scott apparently considered cruising altitude and Alice felt the force lessen. She opened her eyes and looked around in wonder.

Of course, her gliding power meant that she wasn't completely new to the sensation of hanging unsuspended in the air, but this was very different. For one thing, she had never achieved this much altitude, and at a guess, she had never flown as fast before, either. So she didn't have to force the sense of wonder onto her face as she took in the view.

The pre-dawn glow in the east had intensified greatly in the time she had kept her eyes closed, no doubt in part to their higher position. But the sun still had not crested the horizon. There was sufficient light to make out some details, however. Boulder City spread out just to the west, still illuminated by streetlights. Few vehicles could be seen moving along its streets at this time of day. North and east, the surface of Lake Mead was a vast, black flatness in the gloom, contrasting with the lighter shades of the desert floor elsewhere.

Just before the edge of the sun became visible, Scott banked and turned Alice to face the mountains to the west, hovering in place. Sunlight streamed past them, and moments later, the sun was high enough to illuminate the peaks of the hills. They acquired a golden glow, and then light poured down the slopes as Sol rose higher over the horizon. Alice laughed in delight, her discomfort with the temperature completely forgotten.

A moment later, Scott turned the to the north and east, and they moved out over the surface of the lake, watching the world come awake far below them. Soon, they could see light reflecting off the surface, as the formerly flat expanse was revealed to consist of peaks, valleys, and whitecaps kicked up by the steady wind.

Alice tapped Scott in the center of his chest to get his attention. When he looked at her, she leaned forward and kissed him. She felt his muscles tense in surprise at first, but as the kiss continued, he relaxed and returned it enthusiastically. When they finally ended it, Alice smiled warmly at him, stroked his cheek with one hand, and then rolled out of his grasp and plummeted toward the lake.

She had caught him by surprise with that move, and he continued on his course for several seconds before he was able to react. Even then, his speed was such that he had to turn in a fairly wide arc to sweep around and reorient on her falling form. Alice applied her gliding power subtly to slow her descent in order to maintain some altitude; she figured Scott was too panicked at the moment to notice. She fell with her arms tucked to her side, head slightly downward, enjoying the sensation of the near free fall.

Then, as Scott swooped down to intercept, she suddenly flared out, turning her plummet into a shallow horizontal glide that cut above his path. She laughed as he flashed by, then directed her glide back toward the lake shore. She expected Scott would come around again to match her in a moment.

He did, but when she looked toward him with a look of pure joy, she was startled to see Scott looking back with his face contorted in rage. He glared at her for a moment, then suddenly accelerated away, back toward the school.

255

Alice watched him go in shock. *Looks like this date is over. What gives?* She had anticipated a little grumpiness after her prank, but it served him right for just assuming she was entirely dependent on him for her safety today. But she had counted on his better nature to help him appreciate her surprise pretty quickly. She was completely unprepared for this level of overreaction.

Unable to match Scott's speed, Alice continued to glide toward the shore. She doubted she had the altitude to make it all the way back to the school. so she was in for a bit of hike after she landed. She would have lots of time to think about how things had gone wrong between her and Scott.

She was still several hundred feet up as she reached land, and was considering landing quickly just in case there were any early morning nature lovers out and about when movement against the ground below caught her eye. She pulled up short, trying to convince herself that her eyes were playing tricks, but really, what was the point? Wasn't this exactly what Sarah had asked for less than an hour ago?

The figure couldn't possibly be anyone else. All dark hair and flesh tones, Sarah had chosen an extremely inconvenient time to reconnect with her powers. *Flight is an unexpected wrinkle*, Alice thought as she removed her earplugs, *but it could explain how she had made it into town and back without attracting more attention or getting dirty feet.* But now that she had ventured out during daylight hours, she might soon attract quite a bit of attention, especially considering the sound of her laughter and whoops of delight.

Alice shook her head and altered course to intercept. Fortunately, Sarah wasn't moving much faster than Alice's top speed, but she was moving erratically, lost in the sheer joy of the experience, and that made predicting her future position difficult. This early in the day, Alice's chances of finding an updraft were effectively nil, so she was only going to get one chance to catch her friend.

256

"Sarah, come this way! It's me, Alice!" she called as she closed in. If Sarah was still asleep, she might not hear her, or heed her if she did, but Alice felt she had to try. Fifty yards out, she despaired of catching Sarah as her course veered away from her. But then, just as quickly, Sarah changed direction again. Alice yelled "Gotcha!" as her hand came down on Sarah's calf before she could slip by.

To her astonishment, her hand passed right through the other girl's leg. She was so surprised, she dropped several feet before she re-established control of her gliding power. However, the contact had been enough to get Sarah's attention, and she turned around and came back to hover before Alice.

"Alice?" She glanced around quickly. "This isn't a dream, is it?"

Alice shook her head. "No. Aren't you cold?"

"No, why would I be?" Sarah asked. Then, after glancing down at herself she let out a dismayed squeak and tried to cover herself with her arms. "Oh, I see what you mean. But I feel fine. Why is that?"

"I have an idea," Alice said. "Try to take my hand."

She reached out and allowed Sarah to grasp her hand, but received another surprise when she felt Sarah's hand grasp hers as solidly as ever.

"Okay, so what does this prove?" Sarah asked.

"That your powers are weirder than I thought," Alice responded. "A moment ago my hand passed right through your leg. I wonder..." Without warning, Alice suddenly swept her free hand in an arc in front of her, and was rewarded by the sight of her hand passing through Sarah's form without resistance.

"Oh!" Sarah exclaimed. "That was...odd."

"I'm sorry, did that hurt?"

"No, I was just, uh, aware of it. I can't really put the sensation into words."

"Uh huh," Alice muttered, filing that bit of information away. "Let's land. I want to try something."

Sarah readily agreed and the two girls were soon on the ground. Alice started searching through a number of small items in a belt pouch she wore strapped to her waist.

"Can we make this quick? I don't want anyone to see me like this," Sarah said, looking around anxiously.

"Of course, That's part of what I'm hoping to fix right now. After all, it's a long way back to the school from here." Alice pulled out a small package, about the size of a small matchbox. "This should do it."

"What's that?"

"A plastic rain poncho," Alice replied.

"But it's so tiny," Sarah said, looking at it dubiously. "Was it made for a Barbie doll?"

Alice smiled. "Nope, it's just shrunk. Watch." She pulled a candy from a pocket and ate it, concentrating on the packet in her hand. It quickly grew to the size of a stack of index cards. Alice opened the package and removed the poncho, shaking it out.

"You were able to grab my hand. See if you can take this from me."

Sarah quickly grabbed the garment and clutched it to her front, looking relieved. "Cool, I did it," she said. "Now I'll just slip it on..."

But before she could match actions to words, Sarah disappeared. The poncho, however, remained where it was hanging in midair. Then it ballooned out from its flattened shape, as it had been when she was holding it against herself, until it appeared to be draped over an invisible person.

"Curiouser and curiouser," Alice muttered. "What just happened, Sarah? I can't see you."

"Uh, I'm not sure," Sarah replied. "I can still see you and everything, but I feel weird. It's like my body just became really flexible." The material of the poncho rippled wildly. "Huh, let me try something."

The poncho suddenly twisted , bunching up into a line like it was a washcloth someone was wringing out.

"Sarah?" Alice exclaimed. "Are you all right?"

"Yeah, I'm fine," she replied. The poncho went back to looking like it was draped over an invisible person. "Does any of this make sense to you? I haven't got a clue how I'm doing any of this."

"Maybe," Alice said, pulling out her cell. "What's Scott's number?"

Sarah gave her the number, then the poncho swiveled around. "Where is he, anyway? Weren't you guys supposed to be-"

"I'll explain later," Alice interrupted, working on her phone's keypad. "I need him to check on something for me." She finished her text message, then put her phone away. "Well, it's a long walk back from here, so we'd better get started. I've got to be ready to go home later this morning."

Alice started walking towards a road they could follow back towards town. The poncho drifted along beside her. She wasn't sure what to call Sarah's current mode of movement; even though the garment bobbed as if she was walking, the poncho stayed well above the ground. "Can you still fly?" she asked.

The poncho rose into the air and performed a loop-de-loop before settling back beside her. "Yep." After that, the poncho just drifted forward instead of bobbing along as before.

Alice's phone rang, and she retrieved it from her pocket. "Hello, Scott?'

"Alice, what's up? I checked on Sarah like your text said, but I can't wake her up. Do I need to call 911?"

"No, it's okay. She's with me."

"What? I'm looking right at her!"

"I'll explain when I get back to the school. Come and get me if you want the details quicker, because I've got a long walk ahead of me. Or send Coach Lane or someone if you're still angry. I'm sorry about my little stunt, by the way."

"Uh, we'll talk about that later. Right now I'm worried about my sister. See you soon."

Alice hung up and looked over at the poncho. "Well, I think I know how your power works, Sarah."

"Really? So what am I doing?"

"It's actually pretty simple. You're a ghost."

CHAPTER TWENTY-FOUR
Reconnecting

"Sarah is having out-of-body experiences, or projecting her astral body, depending on what label you want to put on it," Alice said. She, Scott and Sarah were back in the girls' room. Scott had flown out to collect Alice and his sister, and they had all made it back here without being spotted. There had been some initial confusion about how to get Sarah back into her body, but after sending Scott out of the room for a minute, she and Alice eventually figured out that she could "put down" the poncho to revert to her visible, insubstantial body, and then "pick up" her physical body to reintegrate.

"But why am I always naked? I'd never choose to do that!"

Alice shrugged. "Maybe because your astral form is your essence? You don't even take your tattoo along in that form, so it makes sense clothes would be left behind. Maybe with training you'll be able to mentally add clothing or something deliberately. It's worth a try, anyway."

Scott sat brooding in a desk chair, chin on one hand. "But you said Sarah was able to take your hand, even though she was like a hologram the rest of the time. And how was she able to grab the poncho at first?"

"There's definitely a few differences between Sarah's power and what most of the literature recounts about astral projection."

"There's literature on this?" Scott asked.

"Sure," Alice replied. "There are lots of people who have reported spontaneous out-of-body experiences. A few even claim to be able to induce them at will. I read a lot of metaphysical stuff after my powers developed, looking for some answers about how they worked. Nothing really seemed to fit, but I kind of know what the standard scenario would be like, if there is such a thing."

"So how are my powers different?" Sarah asked.

"Well, right off the bat, we can see you. For most people, they'd just be an invisible observer wherever they went in that state. They also aren't able to interact physically with anything. A lot of the people who write about this think they're actually just using some sort of remote perception, and not leaving their bodies at all. In your case, I'd say it's pretty definite that you are leaving your body."

"Yeah, lucky me," Sarah said. "So what happened with the poncho?"

Alice started playing absently with a lock of her hair as she considered the question. "I think you adopted it as a temporary body," she finally offered.

"What?" Scott and Sarah said in unison.

"Think about what we know," Alice said. "Or maybe start with what we don't know. Out-of-body experiences are one line of proof some people offer to argue that there is some part of us that survives death. So if this spiritual essence is the part of us that's really, uh, us, how does it make a body work? Scientists have worked out electric signals and hormones and stuff that regulate the body, but on some level, doesn't there have to be a sort of telekinesis, or something, that allows that spiritual consciousness to move the body?"

"I -, I can almost follow that," Scott said, a puzzled look on his face. "I'm not sure I'd agree with it, but I can follow it."

"Good. So what I'm thinking is that Sarah retains that telekinetic ability when she leaves her body. If she concentrates, she can use it to pick up objects with her astral body, but if she concentrates too closely, she actually merges with it."

"Do you really think that's how my power works?" Sarah asked.

"I don't know," Alice replied. "It's one way of understanding what you do, but it's not my power. If you have a better framework for relating to it, I'd say go with it. But I think the 'how' of it isn't as important for now as the 'what', you know?"

Sarah nodded thoughtfully. "So what's next?"

"That's easy. I'm going home."

♠   ♣   ♥   ♦

"Hi, Mrs. Sullivan. Is Miranda home?" Alice tried hard to keep her tone light as she greeted her best friend's mom, all too conscious of the tricky discussion she might soon be having with her – if Miranda decided she wanted to transfer.

"Alice, this is a pleasant surprise. Miranda said you and your father were out of town."

"Yeah, we just got back."

Mrs. Sullivan gave Alice a brief hug and then stepped back, holding her by the shoulders as she looked into her eyes. "Is everything all right, dear? Miranda hasn't said anything, but I can tell she's been worried this past week or so. I assume there was some sort of family emergency to draw you and your father out of town in the middle of school terms."

"Yeah, it's been a busy time, for sure. I'm transferring to a new school," Alice said.

263

"Oh, now I understand. Miranda must be devastated that you won't be around anymore. But why wouldn't she say anything about it?"

"Well, actually, she doesn't know that part yet. I'll explain it all later, but I mostly came to let her know. She can fill you in on the details later."

"I see," Mrs. Sullivan responded. "Well, she's in her room; you know the way." She gave Alice another hug. "We'll miss you. I almost feel like I'm losing a daughter."

Alice returned the hug, then followed the familiar hall to Miranda's room. The door was closed, so she knocked.

"Yes?" Miranda called from the other side.

"I've returned from beyond time and space to bring you momentous news," Alice said in a comically deep voice.

Alice scarcely finished before a screech of excitement assaulted her ears and the door was snatched open. Then she was smothered by her friend's enthusiastic greeting. "You're here! Oh, thank goodness. I was so worried! Why didn't you call me?"

This statement seemed to trigger a memory, because the next moment Miranda released her and stepped back, a look of consternation on her face. "You didn't call me! Don't you know I've been worried sick? Where have you been? What's been happening?"

Alice crooked her head back towards the front of the house, where Miranda's parents were watching a movie and said "I'm sorry. I wanted to call, but we need to have this conversation face to face. In private."

Miranda glanced in the direction Alice had indicated and nodded her head, drawing Alice into her room and closing the door. However, she still looked sulky as she sat on the edge of her bed and looked at her. "This had better be good."

"I don't know if you'll think it's good, but it's definitely interesting. But before I tell you anything, you've got to let me know. Have you seen anyone following you or anything?"

"No, but thanks to you I've been setting new records in paranoid behavior ever since..." Miranda stopped, hand to mouth as she remembered. "Oh, listen to me. I'm a terrible friend. Here I am grumping at you, and you've been through so much. Is Ches really gone?"

Alice nodded somberly. "Yeah, the card soldiers, too. I am sorry I haven't been responding to your texts and all, but I've got a secret that's not mine to risk. I can tell you about it, but only like this. We were afraid my communications with you might be intercepted, otherwise."

"Okay, so dish! What's been going on? Start with what happened between you and that fake FBI agent, and don't you dare leave anything out!"

Alice spent the next forty-five minutes doing just that, with frequent interruptions from her friend to clarify points or detour into speculations about what Oglethorpe or the two supers who had taken Alice and her father to the junk yard were really after. Finally, Alice got to the point of mentioning her plans to transfer to Prometheus Academy.

"Wait! You're actually transferring to this boarding school for new mutants?"

"Hey!"

"Sorry," Miranda said, struggling not to look too upset. "It's just, well, I can't believe you're leaving. I'll miss you."

"You didn't let me get to that part. You don't have to. I talked Mrs. Kilkarni into offering you an admission. If you want it."

"What? You want me to come to... How is that supposed to work? I don't have any powers!"

"That's okay," Alice explained. "Part of the mission statement for the school is to show that normal folks and the empowered can coexist peacefully. The fact that you don't have powers is actually your 'in'. That, and the fact that you already know that the empowered exist."

"Oh, so now I'm your token norm?"

Alice opened her mouth to reply, but then realized she had no idea how to respond. Until Miranda laughed at her, that is.

"Oh, the look on your face! That'll teach you to let me worry for no good reason!"

Alice did her best to look stern and condescending, but it was difficult with the smile struggling to break out across her features. "Off with her head. That will put this peasant in her place." Then she couldn't hold it in any longer, and she laughed along with her. Then the moment passed and Miranda grew thoughtful.

"Do you really think it's a good idea for me to be there, though? I mean, how would I stack up against a bunch of supers? Do they bench press cars and stuff like that?"

"I haven't seen anyone do anything like that, though I'll admit they have some pretty awesome abilities. But they're not all physical or overbearing like that, anyway. Julianna just splits off duplicates of herself, and none of them have any other powers, so she's pretty normal when you get right down to it. And Esme is a linguistic type; she doesn't have anything really amazing going for her either. So you wouldn't stick out too much. Plus, hopefully, we'll get more non-powered students in the future."

"Well..."

"Oh, come on! You can't tell me you don't want to be there."

"I do. I'm just wondering how to convince Mom and Dad to go along with this," Miranda said.

266

"We're going to have to let them in on my secret, obviously. And Dad will come over to talk to them when we're ready; that should help."

"Yeah, I guess."

Alice pulled out her phone to call her father. "Then are you ready to shake up your parents world?" Miranda nodded, and Alice dialed.

♠   ♣   ♥   ♦

Several hours later, Alice found herself in her bedroom, finishing up her packing. She hummed to herself as she worked, happy to know that Miranda was doing the same thing, getting ready for Coach Lane to transport them both back to Prometheus Academy.

Convincing Miranda's parents to approve of the transfer had been a two-step process. First, they had needed to convince them that super powers were real. This had actually been the easy part. Alice's father showing up without his cane had laid the groundwork; something unusual had clearly happened to him. A quick demonstration of Alice's abilities had overcome their inclination to disbelieve the explanation, though it had taken a while for the implications of this revelation to sink in.

Once the initial goal was accomplished, they had faced the even greater hurdle of convincing Miranda's parents to allow their daughter to attend a school for empowered students. Mrs. Kilkarni had gone so far as to offer Miranda a full scholarship as a reward for her demonstrated discretion in regards to Alice's abilities, and due to her status as one of very few non-powered students aware of the school's secrets. Even so, it wasn't until Dr. Littleton pointed out that, once news of the empowered broke, whenever that might happen, anyone with experience with and connections to the empowered community would be in high demand with both corporate and government agencies to act as liaisons that the Sullivans decided that the opportunity was too good to pass up.

While Alice and Dr. Littleton were busy with the Sullivans, Houston had been scouting their neighborhood for any signs that their house was being watched. Alice had no idea how he set about performing this task, but as the leader of Mrs. Kilkarni's field team, she figured he knew what he was doing. So once Miranda's transfer had been agreed upon, she accepted his assurance that it was safe for her and her father to return home without question.

Alice closed her final suitcase, then took a quick sip from a glass of water close at hand to shrink it to a fraction of its former size. The reduced weight might not make much difference to Coach Lane when it came time to teleport everything back to Prometheus Academy, but it would certainly make things easier on her as she carried her baggage to the living room. Aside from clothes and other essentials, she was bringing some of her favorite books and a few knick knacks to make her side of the dorm room feel more like home, including Barello, her stuffed monkey.

She took one last look around the room, idly wondering how long it would be before she saw it again. Brushing those thoughts aside, she stacked her three shrunken suitcases on a hand cart, strapped them down, and wheeled them out of the room and down the hall to the living room. Her father sat there, watching news on the television, while Houston paced up and down near the windows, one hand on the grip of his Bowie knife.

"I'm ready," Alice announced. "As soon as Miranda gets here, we can be on our way."

Her father looked at her with a melancholy smile and sighed. "I knew this day would come, I just didn't expect it to be so soon. Even when you started college, I was half hoping you'd stick around and attend here."

Alice crossed to him and hugged him as he rose from his chair. "I'll miss you, Daddy. But don't worry, I'll call you every day. Well, every week, at least."

Suddenly, a frantic knocking sounded from the front door. Houston pulled aside the edge of a curtain to look out and see who was there.

"That can't be Miranda, surely," Alice said.

"It isn't," Houston replied as the knocking came again. "It's a woman, but I don't recognize her."

Alice took a peek and gasped in surprise. "Mom?" She quickly crossed to the door and threw it open. Meredith entered immediately. She was clearly agitated; her eyes were wide, her hair disheveled and her clothes were wrinkled. It was such a stark difference to her usual, carefully maintained image that Alice and her father were both troubled, expecting news of some disaster.

Her father recovered first. "Meredith, what's wrong?"

Her mother focused on him, pushing past Alice without a word or a glance. "Arthur, you've got to help me. I don't know what to do. Please, help me!"

"Of course I will, but you've got to tell me what's wrong. What do you need?"

"I don't know how to handle her, Arthur! You've got to help! Samantha's gone wild and I don't know what to do!"

CHAPTER TWENTY-FIVE

Surprises and Complications

Arthur guided Meredith to a chair and gently eased her into it, staring intently into her eyes the whole time. "Dear," he said, unconsciously slipping back into former manners of address, "I can see something unusual has happened. It has something to do with Samantha? Let's calm down a bit and you can tell me all about it. Take a deep breath and hold it...that's it. Now release it slowly...good. Once more...and release. All right, now tell me what's happened."

"It's Samantha, She's done something to Alan. I know it."

"Samantha's done something to her father? Okay, you're going to have to start at the beginning so I can understand. When did this happen?" Dr. Littleton asked.

"Sometime this morning. I was out picking up a few groceries. When I got home, Alan was on the floor. I tried to rouse him, but all he did was groan a little. I couldn't get him to focus on me at all."

Houston stepped up beside Dr. Littleton and put one hand on his shoulder. "This looks like a family matter. I'm going to call the school and let them know we may be returning late. I'll be just outside if you need me."

Arthur nodded, and as Houston stepped out the front door and pulled his phone from his pocket, he returned his attention to his ex-wife. "Did you call 911?"

Meredith frowned, her gaze on the front door. "Who is that man?"

"Alice's new teacher," Arthur summarized. "Now, did you call 911?"

"Of course. The EMTs rushed Alan to the hospital, and they've run a bunch of tests. There's no sign of a stroke, nothing unusual in the blood work...they don't know what's wrong with him. All he does is groan and stare off into space."

Alice glanced out the window, uncertain what to do. Meredith's car was in the driveway, and she thought she could make out a figure in the back. "Is Samantha in the car?" she asked.

"Yes," her mother replied. "She's almost as unresponsive as Alan. Her eyes followed what me and the EMTs were doing, and she follows directions. She just won't talk. It's almost like she's having a really bad sulk about something."

"It sounds more like whatever happened to Alan traumatized her as well," Arthur suggested.

"Maybe, but there's something... She looked so smug whenever she looked at Alan. I know it sounds crazy, but I can't shake the feeling that she's responsible."

"Meredith, that's nonsense, and you know it."

Meredith looked pointedly at Alice. "Is it?" She turned to look her ex in the eye. "Can you, of all people, really tell me that's impossible?"

Alice swallowed. She could almost feel the waves of anger and hatred emanating from her mother. Things had gotten a little better between them in the years since the divorce, but suddenly it was like the disastrous birthday party had happened just yesterday, and she had a strong urge to put some space between them. "I'm just going to go check on Sam," she said, and hurried outside before anyone could object.

Coach Lane had wandered over in front of the closed garage door. He spoke into his phone softly, his deep bass rumble unintelligible from this distance. Alice walked in the opposite direction, to where her mother's car sat at the entrance to the long driveway, barely far enough in to be clear of the street.

Looking through the side windows, she could see her half-sister in the far side back seat. It was obvious, even at this distance, that something was wrong. A normal child would have been impatiently clambering around the inside of the car, probably wrenching the steering wheel about and leaning on the horn. But Sam just sat there, arms limp at her sides, staring vacantly at the driver's seat in front of her. The straps on her child seat hadn't even been buckled.

Alice opened the near-side door and climbed into the seat next to Sam. The younger girl did not respond, and Alice felt her fear swell on Sam's behalf. "Sam," she said softly, barely more than a whisper, "it's me, Alice. Can you look at your big sister, please?"

Sam's head turned toward her obediently. Alice thought she might have seen the barest trace of a smile pass across the little girl's lips. That was somewhat encouraging, given what their mother had said about Dr. Casey's condition, but it was such a faint response compared to the gleeful squeals and hugs their meetings usually produced that it just made Alice's heart break all the more. Her sister was in there somewhere, probably hurting. She had to find a way to break through to her.

Alice took one of Sam's hands in her own. It felt as warm and alive as ever, if she discounted the limpness. She reached across and brushed Sam's hair back from her face so she could see her eyes clearly. *They're definitely focused on me*, Alice assured herself. *But there's no sense of recognition or emotion. No sense of her.*

"Hey, Runt, I hear you've had a rough morning. I'm worried about you. Can you talk to me? Please?"

Sam's eyes suddenly changed. The eyelids closed slightly, as the disinterested gaze suddenly became focused and intent. Alice felt a momentary thrill of hope, but before she could vocalize any further encouragement, Sam's eyes blinked.

♠ ♣ ♥ ♦

Alice looked around. It took her only a moment to identify Samantha's bedroom, and at first she thought her sister had teleported her here. But after a moment, she realized that this new space might look like the bedroom she had visited in the past, but it was actually quite different.

First, there was the bed. Samantha's parents had splurged on a mini loft bed with an enclosure of printed cloth stretched on thin flexible rods around the mattress to make it a castle play area as well as a simple sleeping area. But as Alice focused on it, the cloth walls seemed to recede even as they gained substance. In a moment, she was looking at a distant castle with pennants fluttering in a breeze. The slide that descended from the bed had transformed into a fine, broad roadway. And yet, somehow, the entire edifice remained within Samantha's room. Feeling more than a bit nauseous, Alice looked away and the room resumed its usual appearance. Though now that she thought on it, the room looked bigger, cleaner, and more sparkly than she remembered it.

"Hey, Big Sister," Samantha said from just behind her. Alice spun around to find her half-sister looking more animated and alert than she had been in the car, though still less bouncy and carefree than usual. "You're just in time."

"Just in time for what?" Alice asked.

"The tea party, of course, silly. We always have a tea party. But it's better in here, don't you think?"

Alice gasped as a table and chairs suddenly appeared in the middle of the room, which fluidly expanded to make room for everything. The chairs were white with carved and painted flowers and pink accents, and all but two were occupied by Samantha's favorite toys and dolls. They had all grown to about two feet high, but still sat immobile, like the stuffed dollies, bears and bunnies they were. A tablecloth of some sheer yellow fabric covered the tabletop and draped off the edges at the corners. The table was covered with fine porcelain place settings, a fancy tea urn and accessories, and plates of delicious looking cupcakes and cookies. Alice could smell the frosting and the tea steeping in the urn from where she stood.

"Uh, yes, it does look...impressive," Alice ventured. "What do you mean by 'in here', exactly?"

Sam gave the question a bit of serious thought before answering. "I think I'm using my 'magination," she said. "But it's a lot better now."

Alice walked to one of the empty chairs and sat down because she felt she needed to get off her feet before she fell over. *If everything here is a product of Samantha's imagination, then she's probably using some sort of telepathy to share a mental...playroom?...with me. We're probably still in the car. I hope so, anyway.*

Sam skipped over and climbed in the chair next to her, then picked up her cup and held it out to Alice. "Tea, please!"

Alice shrugged mentally and reached for the teapot. *Well, I wanted to talk to her, and we are communicating. Maybe if I play along I'll be able to find out what's happened.*

As she filled Samantha's cup and added cream and three lumps of sugar, Alice glanced at the girl sitting next to her and tried to make her tone casual as she asked, "How long has your imagination been this good?"

"About a week," Samantha said, but her smile vanished. She helped herself to a fancy frosted cookie, refusing to look at Alice.

"Did something happen then?"

275

"You haven't offered Mr. Jumpy any tea yet," Samantha said shortly as she indicated the bunny on Alice's other side.

Okay, she's definitely touchy about something. Alice decided to play along and turned to the stuffed toy. "Would you care for some tea, Mr. Ju--?" Alice stopped as her gaze settled on a figure seated behind the party guests. The corner was unusually gloomy, given the brightness in the rest of the room, but she now saw that the figure sitting in the chair facing the wall was not another stuffed animal, as she had originally thought. It was...

"Dr. Casey?" Alice called softly.

She started to get up, but Samantha grabbed her wrist. "No!" she shouted. "You can't talk to him!"

"Why not, Samantha? What's going on here?"

"Daddy was bad, so he has to sit in the corner," Samantha explained.

Alice felt chilled. "You've trapped your daddy here?"

"No," Samantha pouted. "Why would I want to do that? That," she indicated the form in the corner, "is just his dollie."

"Oh, I see," Alice said, relieved. *It's just another bit of her imagination after all.* "Can I please take a look at it? I promise I won't touch it."

"Well...okay."

Alice got up and moved closer to the figure. For a doll, it sure looked life-like. Skin and hair appeared natural, and the clothes were certainly in the style that Dr. Casey favored. Still, she had just seen a cloth castle transform itself into a seemingly real fortress, so this was nothing to be too surprised about.

But as she crouched beside it, the figure suddenly turned and looked at her. "Alice, fancy meeting you here," Dr. Casey said, a vacuous smile on his face.

She reared back, startled, then moved back towards the man in the chair. "Dr. Casey? Are you...all right?"

He nodded. "Why wouldn't I be?"

"Samantha said you had been bad and had to sit in the corner. What is that all about?"

Dr. Casey laughed shrilly. "I'm sure I don't know. I'm just sitting here thinking about how to advise one of my masters candidates. David is facing quite a dilemma..."

Alice tuned out his explanation. *If this is just a bit of Sam's imagination, wouldn't it make up an excuse a six-year-old would use? She wouldn't know anything about how her father works with students at the university.*

"Dr. Casey, could you help me with something?" she interrupted.

"Well of course. What's on your mind?"

"Uh, I've got this project for school. We have to describe the common uses for several plants, and I'm stuck on one of them. There's something that's made from the willow tree isn't there? Something about the bark?"

"Yes, that's right. Extract from the bark from the white willow contains salicin. The human body processes it into salicylic acid, which is basically a natural form of aspirin. The aspirin you buy in the stores today is a slightly different compund..."

Alice stood up and returned to the table quickly, noticing as she did so that she was shivering. *There's no way a six-year-old*

277

produced that piece of classroom lecture. So what does that imply for me?

"Sam, you lied to me just now, didn't you?"

Samantha looked up from her earnest conversation with a stuffed bear across the table from her - a bear that did not move or speak, Alice noted. "I didn't!" she said.

Alice got down on Samantha's level to try to keep from intimidating her. "It's all right, Sam. I'm not mad. But I really need to know what's going on, okay?" She indicated the figure of Dr. Casey, which had gone back to staring absently into the corner. I just had a talk with your dollie, and he told me things I don't think you know. "

Samantha just shrugged. "Of course. Daddy knows lots of stuff I don't know, so his dollie does, too. That's what dollies are for."

"I don't understand." Alice looked back at the figure. "So you're saying that really isn't your daddy?"

"Of course not."

"But it's something like your daddy? Something that knows what he knows?"

Samantha clapped her hands. "Yes. Now you've got it. It's a dollie."

Alice thought for a moment, then asked, "Did you make the dollie?"

"Yes."

"Why?"

Samantha fidgeted. "Well, I like it here. I don't have to clean my room. This one cleans itself. I don't have to do any chores or...other stuff. But it gets lonely."

"So the dollie keeps you from being lonely?"

"Sort of. A dollie's not as good as having someone here, like you. But Daddy's dollie is better than Mr. Jumpy."

"Because he moves and talks?"

"Yes."

When I leave, will she have a dollie of me? Alice wondered. She couldn't quite bring herself to ask Samantha, though.

"Sam, do you know something has happened to your daddy?"

Samantha immediately looked away and began playing with the sugar cubes in the bowl. Alice gently reached over and took both of the little girl's hands in her own, turning her so they faced each other. "Sam, look at me," she coaxed. "I'm not angry, but I need to know what happened. Did you do something to your daddy?"

Samantha raised her head slightly, but still refused to look directly at Alice. "He asked me to," she said defensively.

"He asked you to do something? What?"

"He asked me to make him feel good."

Alice felt her fingers tighten reflexively. *Oh, no. Dr. Casey wouldn't...*

"Only I didn't like doing what he wanted me to do. So I just did it."

Alice blinked, and forced herself to relax slightly. "I don't understand, Sam. You didn't like what he wanted you to do, but you did it anyway?"

"No, I just made him feel good so I wouldn't have to do it."

Alice pushed her emotions into a mental box and sat on it. Later, she would have the screaming fit she wanted to have, but right now, she needed to be strong for her sister. And possibly for Dr. Casey.

When she felt she had enough control to speak quietly, she asked, "How did you make him feel good, then?"

"Like this."

Normal perception was suddenly washed away in a kaleidoscope of memories that were not only auditory and visual, but which engaged all the senses. There were recent memories, like the electric thrill of victory after defeating Raptor to rescue Billy, and the taste and sensation of Scott's lips during their airborne kiss. But more distant memories were there as well - the first seconds after getting the joke that lead to a five-minute belly laugh when she was ten, her first taste of coconut cream pie fresh from the refrigerator, the discovery of each new power she had ever developed. All of these and scores of additional memories burst fully on her consciousness at once, each as vibrant as the moment in which they first occurred. All were pleasurable, though they varied in intensity, and her mind flitted from one to another, the relative highs and lows creating a symphony of pleasure from which she was unable to detach herself.Every nerve ending throughout her whole body overloaded, sending wave after never-ending wave of pulsed energy directly to the pleasure center of her brain, and her sense of self almost melted under the onslaught.

It was her memories of Samantha that saved her. Her consciousness wavered, focusing on individual sense memories for microseconds. But every time she encountered a memory of Samantha, she clung to it briefly before being swept away again by the psychic current. Each time, she managed to hang on just a bit longer, until finally, she had enough time to assemble a coherent thought, a purpose. *I'm no good to Samantha like this. I've got to make this stop.*

And just like that, it did stop. Alice's eyes focused, and she discovered she was sprawled on the floor beneath the tea table. Her limbs still felt watery and ached with the echoes of her greatest joys, so she just lay there and breathed deeply for several minutes. Then she slowly pulled herself up onto the chair she had chosen when she first sat

280

down at the table. She looked over at Samantha, who simply stared back solemnly.

"Wow. Don't ever do that to me again, kiddo. Promise me."

"You didn't like it?"

"I liked it too much."

"That's silly. If you liked it--"

"Never do that to me again. It's important. Promise," Alice ordered.

"Okay, I promise."

Alice heaved a sigh of relief, flavored with just a bit of regret. "Good."

♠   ♣   ♥   ♦

A few minutes later, Alice came to herself in the back seat of the car after asking Samantha to allow her to leave the tea party. She could still feel the tingles from the ecstatic overload. She decided to leave Sam in the car for now, until she had a chance to talk to her father. Coach Lane looked at her oddly as she made her way back up the drive, but did not say anything, so she let herself back in the house without speaking to him.

Her father was alone in the living room, apparently lost in thought. However, he revived as she entered the room. "How's Sam?" he asked.

"Not good. We need to talk. Where's Mom?"

"She went to the kitchen to get something to drink."

Alice considered, then said, "Can we talk in your office, then? I don't want Mom in on this until we figure out how to explain it to her."

He looked troubled, but nodded and quickly got to his feet and lead the way to study. Alice closed the door behind them, and after a slight hesitation, locked it.

"Okay," she said quietly, "Samantha's got powers, and she is responsible for Dr. Casey's condition, which isn't nearly as serious as it would be if I had anything to say about it."

Dr. Littleton raised an eyebrow. "That's quite a bit of information and feeling for such a brief statement. I hardly know which question to ask first. Why don't you start by describing her abilities?"

"She's a telepath. She's got a mental playhouse she just sucked me into when I tried to talk to her. We're talking total virtual reality, Dad, completely under her control."

"I see. And how does that relate to Dr. Casey's condition?"

"He's traumatized her. She's retreated into her mental fortress because nothing bad can happen to her there. But before she did, she gave her father what he wanted in spades. I think Dr. Casey's been molesting her."

Her father raised a fist, touching one knuckle to his lips as he closed his eyes and absorbed the statement. "That's a serious charge, Alice. What did Sam tell you, exactly?"

"Just that he asked her to make him feel good, but she didn't like what he wanted her to do to make that happen. So instead, she just hit him with an endless, full intensity replay of every positive moment he's ever experienced, in simulcast. The creep's probably never been happier."

"I see...You seem to be speaking from experience," he prompted.

"Yeah, she hit me with the mojo, too. It's powerful. And it only stopped when I gathered enough force of will to *want* it to stop."

"Hrmph, talk about poetic justice," Dr. Littleton observed. "I doubt her father has the strength of will to ever want it to stop. If there's not some sort of time limit on this thing, I doubt he's going to recover."

And how do I feel about that? Alice wondered. *Well, at least he can't hurt anyone else, now.*

"That still leaves us with a huge mess," she observed aloud. "Someone's got to coax Sam out of her shell, and that's not going to be easy."

"You're right. It's a job for professional counselors," Dr. Littleton said as he crossed to the door and unlocked it. However, he paused before opening it. "Don't worry; I'll talk with your mother and make sure she makes the proper arrangements. And just so we're clear, there's no reason to mention our suspicions about Alan to her unless he recovers. I want her focused as much as possible on making sure Samantha gets the care she needs. Right now, Meredith only has a vague suspicion about her, and that will allow us to insist that she treat Sam as the trauma victim she really is."

With one last look at his daughter to make sure they were on the same page, Dr. Littleton opened the door and made his way back to the living room. Alice followed, and they found Meredith pacing before the window. With assurances that they would look in on Alan soon, Dr. Littleton hustled his ex-wife out the door. "We'll need to get Samantha to a counselor, of course. She's the only one who saw what happened to Alan, and getting her to talk about it may give us our best chance at helping him. I know just the--"

A sudden blast of electricity split the air above the driveway, slamming into Houston and driving him back into the garage door. Alice blinked as the electricity faded, fighting to clear the spots from her vision so she could make out what was happening. When she finally could see, she had to bite back a scream.

Oglethorpe stood at the end of the driveway beside her mom's car. The rear door was open, and the villain already held Samantha in the crook of one arm as he leered at Alice across the top of the vehicle.

"Alice, there you are! You know, I came here looking for you. Imagine my delight at making the acquaintance of this young lady. She seems much more malleable than you, so I think I'll let you wait for another day. But never fear, we will meet again."

"No!" Alice screamed. "Leave Samantha alone!" She started forward, knowing even as she took her first step she was too far away to reach them in time. The only one who would have stood a chance of reacting swiftly enough was--

A bestial snarl sounded from the road, and Oglethorpe glanced over his shoulder. "What? How many times do I have to kill you?"

Alice, halted and stared, confused and hopeful. *It couldn't be him, could it?*

Oglethorpe teleported away from whatever lay out of Alice's sight on the far side of the car, reappearing much closer to the house in order to put something between himself and...

"Ches!" Alice cried as the feline bounded to the top of the car, tail lashing and with a predator's gaze locked upon his foe.

Before Alice could force herself into motion again, her mother pushed past her, charging at Oglethorpe. "Give me my daughter!" she yelled as she closed the distance between them.

Oglethorpe ignored her, reserving his attention for the cat. "Sorry, can't play today, Kitty. Go roll on a bag of catnip!"

Ches leaped at the pudgy man facing him with such apparent disdain, just as Meredith reached him and grabbed for Sam. But Ches merely passed through empty space where a knot of people had stood a moment before. Oglethorpe, Meredith, and Samantha had vanished.

CHAPTER TWENTY-SIX
Back to School

Alice screamed. In the space of less than a minute, she had experienced three momentous revelations, and she couldn't process it all. Two horrible facts and one wonderful one all clamored for her undivided attention, so she couldn't focus adequately on any of them.

Oglethorpe is alive!

He's got Sam and Mom!

Ches is alive!

Surprisingly, the scream helped. Ches winced and ducked his head at the shrill sound, and the familiar mannerism broke the gridlock. Alice became fully conscious of how huge a hole had been torn in her life back in that clearing, and now the missing piece was back. Oglethorpe and her family were critically important, of course, but in this instant, there was nothing she could do to locate him and rescue them. But she could deal with Ches.

"Ches, you're back!" she yelled as she threw herself on the cat, hugging him around the neck as if she'd never let go. "You're really here! How is it possible? Never mind, I don't care, you're here!"

"Well, of course I'm here," Ches said, seemingly perplexed by all the attention. "Why are you carrying on like this?"

"Because you were dead," she said.

"Dead? Don't be ridiculous. Honestly, you take one little trip to London to visit the queen and people react like you never intended to come back."

"But--" Alice began, then stopped herself. Discussions with Ches could be circular or twisted; they were seldom to the point. If he wanted to avoid the topic of his apparent death, she wasn't going to get him to talk about it. Nor did she really care. His simple presence was enough, at least for now. "Oh, never mind. I'm just glad you're home."

A groan from the direction of the garage shifted Alice's attention, and she and her father hurried over to Houston, who was attempting to sit up.

"No. lie back down," Arthur ordered him. "I'll call an ambulance. You need medical attention."

Houston waved him off as he sat up. "I'm fine. I'm tougher than I look. I was stunned, but other than that I've just got a couple of burns Kasie can fix when we get back."

He turned his attention to Alice. "Well, I guess your Boojum didn't quite do for Oglethorpe after all."

Alice shrugged. "I can't explain it. I saw him disappear. It did something to him."

Houston grunted. "Ain't nothing ever certain where that one is concerned. Don't worry about it. I'm just sorry I let him get the drop on me."

"What do we do now?" Alice asked.

"Pick up your friend and get back to school, STAT. Ain't nothing else to do."

"But we've got to find Mom and Samantha," Alice protested.

Houston sighed and draped his arms over his knees as he sat staring at the ground between his feet for a moment, then looked back to

288

her. "Look, we'll do what we can to try to help, but this isn't our first run-in with Oglethorpe. We've been dancing with him for years. Sometimes we get to the kids first, and sometimes he does. If he recruits some of them like you're saying he tried to do with you, we don't have a clue where he takes them. We're lucky he doesn't know where we are."

Houston got to his feet. "We need to get you to safety. That's our first order of business. If we can locate Oglethorpe's facilities, we may be able to do something, but don't hold your breath. You may just have to get used to the idea that you might not see your mother and half-sister again."

"And if I can't do that?"

"Could be a long, frustrating life."

Alice was on pins and needles the entire time they were at Miranda's house. She feared that Houston would tell her friend's parents that a dangerous paranormal had resurfaced and might target the school they were sending their only child to, but apparently he did not believe that this was important information. If the Sullivans picked up on Alice's mood, they probably put it down to excitement over her move to her new school. But most of their attention was focused on Ches, whom they were meeting for the first time because Alice wasn't about to let him out of her sight anytime soon.

Miranda knew Alice's moods better, plus Alice had told her Ches was dead. She knew something was up, but eight years of friendship had given the girls a catalog of nonverbal cues to work with, and Alice was able to signal her friend that she would explain later.

"Last item before we take off is your PA communicator," Houston said, handing each of Miranda's parents a device that looked like a cell phone. "These are on our own proprietary system, optimized for voice and video communication. You won't be able to load apps on these or anything like that, but you can talk to Miranda any time she isn't actually in class as long as she has her unit with her, and there's never any charge to you."

Alice noticed that Coach Lane didn't mention the school's concerns over the possibility of regular electronic communications being traced, and wondered about the implications of that while Houston explained how to use the devices to Mr. and Mrs. Sullivan. *Could Mrs. Kilkarni really want Miranda there that badly, that she'd avoid telling parents about possible dangers? Or is she trying to keep me happy? Or is Coach Lane editing the information he gives out on his own initiative? I could believe that he's pragmatic enough to convince himself that Miranda has the right to choose her own path and act to prevent complications for her. It's irresponsible, but I can't say I'm sorry about it, whatever the explanation.*

Soon enough the explanation was done, Miranda and her parents had said their good-byes, and it was time to go. Alice and Miranda both had their things packed in several suitcases that were piled in the middle of the living room floor. Houston motioned the girls and Ches to take up position near the luggage. His power did not require touch, and he could teleport multiple targets at once. A moment later, they were in Miranda's new room, near Alice and Sarah's.

"OK, both of you report to Mrs. Kilkarni's office. I'll move Alice's luggage to her room and you can unpack when you get back," Coach Lane instructed.

The girls nodded and headed out. Ches kept pace at Alice's side, and she constantly reached out to stroke his head, neck or shoulder as they made their way to the office. The cat got stares from everyone they passed, but staff and students were all used to the unusual here. The looks were curious, not afraid.

When they arrived at Mrs. Kilkarni's office, Alice knocked, and the group entered the office after receiving a muffled acknowledgement from inside. It was late afternoon, and Elaine was relaxing by the fireplace with a red, leather bound book open on her lap. She closed the book and set it aside as she rose to greet her visitors.

"Welcome back, Alice. I see everything went well, since I'm assuming this is Miranda Sullivan, whom I've heard so much about." She turned her attention to Miranda. "I'm glad you decided to join us, dear," she said.

"Uh, thank you, ma'am," Miranda responded. "It was generous of you to invite me."

Elaine smiled. "Well, I won't pretend I don't have my own reasons for bringing you here. We are trying to foster good relations between everyone, after all. I actually think I'm lucky that you're here. You have a good character, and sometimes it seems like that's almost as rare as powers these days."

"Well, you may not feel lucky for long," Alice said. "Oglethorpe is back, or didn't Coach Lane tell you?"

"He did mention it in passing the last time he called. Somewhere in the middle of a long string of expletives. I take it the encounter didn't go well for him."

"You could say that. Oglethorpe hit him with a lightning bolt from hiding, so Coach Lane missed the whole thing. I'm sorry."

Elaine looked puzzled. "Why should you feel sorry?"

"I was the one who told you all that Oglethorpe was gone – deader than dead. If I hadn't said that, he would have been more alert."

Mrs. Kilkarni shook her head. "Vigilance is all well and good, but Houston knows better than most how hard it is to guard against a teleporter. He's used that fact to his own advantage often enough. What happened wasn't your fault, or his. It's just how things work."

291

She knelt down in front of Ches, stoking him behind one ear. "And this must be the Cheshire Cat. I've been looking forward to meeting you."

"Of course you have," he replied.

It was Alice's turn to look puzzled. "You don't sound surprised to be seeing him."

"That's because I'm not. I figured he'd be back."

"Why? I told you... what happened. Why would you think he'd return when I didn't?"

Elaine continued to pet Ches as she answered. "Because I had a theory about your companions, as you call them. Tell me, in all your time in Wonderland, did you ever see more cats like Ches, here?"

"Uhm, no, now that you mention it."

"Or any humans other than those who had a part in Carroll's stories?"

"No. In fact, a cardinal once told me he'd never seen people before I got there."

"Exactly," Mrs. Kilkarni said, as if the conclusion was obvious. It wasn't to Alice.

"So what does that prove?"

"Come now, Alice, use a bit of that logic Charles Dodgson loved so much. If there was no pride of Cheshires to produce this magnificent specimen," Ches purred loudly at the compliment, "or people to produce Hatter or the Carpenter, where do they come from?"

Alice shook her head. "I guess I never really thought about it. When they started appearing, I was so young, and as I grew older they were such a constant part of my life I never really questioned it. They were just there." She nibbled at a fingernail as she considered Elaine's

292

question. "But I see what you mean. They can't exist in a vacuum, can they?"

"Not if they're natural creatures in their own right."

"So what are they?"

Elaine considered Alice carefully, as if judging the impact her next statement might have on her. Finally, she shrugged. "I'd say they're you. Psychic manifestations of your subconscious mind, to be precise. Which means, if they take enough damage, they might be disrupted for a time, but you'll probably be able to call on them again within a few days."

Miranda snorted. Then she giggled. Alice looked at her in confusion, and that broke her self-control, and she laughed out loud.

"What's so funny?" Alice asked in an irritated tone.

"Oh, I'm sorry," she replied, sobering up at once. "After everything that's just happened, I shouldn't be laughing at you now, but I just can't believe this is really a revelation to you after all this time."

Elaine rose and gave Alice a comforting hug. "Ah, yes, your mother and sister, right? Houston filled me in on the kidnapping. It's a terrible tragedy, but we'll try to put it right."

"How?" Alice whispered, not trusting her voice not to crack if she tried to talk any louder.

"I'm not sure. We've been looking for his base for a long time now, but maybe you'll help us find it. Maybe that's why your Wonderland Effect brought you here, since you seem so confident your arrival is no accident. Goodness knows we could use a break like that."

"But how is that supposed to happen? It's not like I can control it."

"Then trust it. It's brought you this far. Perhaps it will reunite you with your family when the time is right."

293

Alice closed her eyes and drew in a deep breath. *Trust it. I can do that.*

"Oh!" Alice said, as something suddenly occurred to her and she straightened up, pulling away from Elaine's embrace.

"What is it, dear?" Mrs. Kilkarni asked.

"I was just thinking how easy it is to talk to you. It's kind of like talking to Ches when I'm worried about something. And then I remembered what you said about him. If he's really a part of my subconscious, that means I've been talking to myself for eight years and didn't even know it! I'm certifiable! Mental! Bonkers!"

"Nonsense. Self-talk is a well-documented method of working through problems. Everyone does it."

"Really?"

"Really," Elaine said. "I'll show you the journal articles if you're interested."

"That's all right," Alice said, kneeling by Ches and giving him a hug around his neck. "Talking things out with this guy is such a habit, I don't know how I'd give it up. It's just nice to know self-talk is normal."

"Of course it is," Ches purred. "And we do it better than anyone."

♠ ♣ ♥ ♦

After a bit more chat, including an informal school orientation for Miranda, the girls returned to their rooms to unpack. Alice set to the task with gusto, happy to finally be able to personalize her half of the room. Sarah was nowhere in evidence, so she worked contentedly on her own.

Alice was adding clothes to the bottom drawer of her dresser as Ches lounged at the foot of her bed and she heard, but was not conscious of, the sound of a zipper being slowly manipulated. As she closed the drawer, she heard a loud, plastic CLICK from across the room and felt something small forcefully make contact with her bottom. She spun around, scanning the room as she rubbed at her buttock, but she and Ches were alone in the room.

"Who did that?"she asked Ches.

"Did what?"

Alice glanced at the floor and stooped to pick up a foam dart with a blunt plastic tip. "Who shot me with this dart?" she clarified.

"I didn't see anyone," Ches replied disinterestedly. "Are you sure some*one* did it?"

Alice frowned. The stress Ches had placed on the syllable was significant; she was sure of that. She was also sure that was as much information as he intended to convey. The rest was up to her. She scanned the room again.

The sound had come from the vicinity of Sarah's desk, but there was no dart gun in sight. In fact, the desk was suspiciously clean, now that she thought about it. The area was pristine save for a backpack in the shape of a teddy bear hooked over the back of the chair. Alice's eyes narrowed. The zipper on the backpack was halfway open, leaving an opening from the bear's neck to the middle of his belly.

"Sarah, that's not funny," she said, though secretly a bit amused. "Don't forget, you'll have to sleep in your own bed sooner or later. If you don't want to wake up with a permanent marker mustache, give it up right now."

The bear's head rose to look directly at her. "Spoilsport. I was betting I'd get at least three shots off before you figured it out." The bear reached inside its body and pulled out a multi-shot toy gun, seemingly oblivious to the fact that it had no opposable thumb, or any fingers whatsoever. It pointed the gun at Ches. "It was you, wasn't it? You tipped her off."

The dart gun fired, but Ches simply vanished and reappeared on Miranda's bed as the missile harmlessly impacted on the wall behind his vacated position. The bear looked around, saw him, and tossed the gun carelessly over one shoulder so it landed on the empty desk. "Cool trick," Sarah said.

"Well, look who's mastered her powers," Alice said, settling onto her own bed. "You've got a pretty good trick of your own going there."

"Thanks," Sarah replied. The straps on the backpack unhooked themselves from the back of the chair and the teddy bear dropped to the floor. Then it walked toward Alice's bed on its two rear legs, dragging the straps behind it. "I was going to use this as my Halloween costume, but then I had a better idea. But I didn't want to let this one go to waste."

Alice grinned in spite of herself as the teddy bear reached the bed and held up its arms to be picked up. She bent down and easily lifted it to the bed beside her. Then she frowned. "Hey, why can't you just fly up here, like you did with the poncho?"

"I could, but it doesn't fit the dignity of my current body," Sarah said as the bear gave her a bow worthy of a courtier. "Besides, I just wanted to see if you'd pick me up."

Alice stuck her tongue out at the bear. "You're going to look so cute with that mustache. I may even add a goatee."

Sarah laughed as the bear held up its paws in surrender. "Okay, I promise I'll be good. Mercy, please."

"All right, I'll forgive you, just this once."

"Good. Now, let's talk about important issues. Like, what are you wearing to the Halloween party?"

Alice slumped back against the headboard and sighed. "Sarah, I've had a really bad day. I don't think I'll be in much of a mood for a party."

"It's still four days away! What could possibly have happened to put you in a funk for that long?"

"Oglethorpe is back, and he kidnapped my Mom and my six-year-old half-sister."

There was a long pause, then Sarah said "That would do it. Oh, Alice, I'm so sorry. Give me just a minute." The bear collapsed on the bed as Sarah's astral form appeared, then zipped through the ceiling.

A minute later Sarah rushed in wearing her physical body and immediately engulfed Alice in a hug. "I'm so sorry. You've just had a terrible tragedy and here I am pranking you. I'm horrible."

Alice returned the embrace. "No you're not. You couldn't have known. I don't mean to be a wet blanket, either. You'll have a better time at the party without me. I'm just not going to be much in the mood for having fun."

"All the more reason you need to be there. Come on, at least pop in for a few minutes. Trust me, you'll want to see the other kids' reactions to my costume."

Alice was intrigued despite her current worries. "What is it?" she asked.

"You'll just have to come and be surprised like everyone else," Sarah said.

CHAPTER TWENTY-SEVEN

Halloween

"Come on, you've got to go. You don't have to dance or anything, but you've got to at least show up," Scott said.

"Why?" Alice asked.

"Because if you wallow in misplaced guilt and worry, you'll not only fail to come up with a good plan for rescuing your sister, but you'll probably overlook any opportunities that present themselves. You need to get on with life, at least in little ways, to keep yourself functional," Scott responded.

It was lunch time on Tuesday, the day before Halloween. Alice sighed. She had insisted since the weekend that she wasn't in the mood for a party, but Scott, Sarah, and Miranda had made it their mission to drag her into the midst of student activities in spite of herself. "Fine, we'll go. But you're responsible for costumes. I'm not in the mood to think about it."

"Great," Sarah said, "I can't wait to see the expression on your face when you see my costume."

"Yeah, about that," Scott replied, "why all the secrecy? Just tell us what it is."

"Ask around, big brother. Is anyone telling what they're doing? No, they're not. Half the fun of the night is surprising people with your big entrance. And mine's gonna blow your mind."

Alice turned her attention to her lunch. *Say whatever you want about Prometheus Academy, no one can say we don't eat well. At this rate, I'm going to gain ten pounds by the end of term.*

Scott got up from the table. "I'm going to go grab a dessert. Anyone want anything?"

"You haven't even touched your lunch yet," Sarah protested.

"If I wait, all the chocolate cupcakes will be gone," Scott explained. Then he hurried across the room to the cart parked outside the swinging doors leading to the kitchen.

Sarah shrugged and started eating her own lunch. "How are you two getting along, now?" she asked Alice.

She sighed and considered how best to answer as she finished a mouthful of her own meal. She swallowed and said, "Well enough, I guess. He apologized for overreacting to my little stunt during our first date. He said it really had nothing to do with me and it just reminded him of something he didn't want to talk about. So I apologized for diving out of his arms, and we just dropped it." She took a sip from her milk carton, then continued. "I'd say we're still feeling a bit awkward around each other, but I hope the feeling will pass. I do like him."

Sarah grinned. "Good. I think you're good for him. He seems more...animated since you showed up." She looked past Alice as something else attracted her attention. "Oh, now that just pisses me off!"

Alice looked where Sarah was, and felt her own face flush with angry heat. Miranda had entered the cafeteria, followed at a distance by Kip and Levi. As Alice watched, Kip gestured, and a sudden, unnatural gust of wind blew the back of Miranda's skirt up. Alice could tell this wasn't the first time he had done it; Miranda already looked to be on the verge of tears. Several of the teachers had also noticed what was happening and Mr. Honeycutt was already starting to get up from the staff table to deal with the situation.

300

Before he could move away from the table, Marchie suddenly appeared between the boys and Miranda. "Teatime for two troublemakers! Lump it and lose it!" he cried, and threw a sugar cube at Kip, striking him in the chest.

Immediately, a whirlwind formed, engulfing the two miscreants and lifting them from the floor. They tumbled about in the air helplessly as the miniature twister lurched drunkenly about, upsetting more than one table as the diners scrambled out of the way. After several seconds of mayhem, punctuated by the boys' cries of consternation, the twister suddenly dispersed and they were thrown clear.

Right into the dessert cart.

Following the crash, all was silent in the cafeteria for a score of heartbeats. Then, the clapping started. At first, it was just Julianna, but soon other girls joined in, and then the boys. Even a couple of the teachers joined in. Alice blushed at the applause, punctuated by cries of "You show 'em!" and "That's the way to give them their just desserts!" from a couple of her more enthusiastic admirers.

She rushed over to Marchie and took the sugar bowl away from him gently and set it down on the edge of a nearby table. She took one paw in her hands and stroked it, saying softly, "It's all right, Marchie, calm down. They won't do it again."

Mr. Honeycutt arrived and surveyed the damage as Kip and Levi got unsteadily to their feet. "Well, I trust you have both learned a valuable lesson. But just to drive it home, you're both on clean-up duty. I expect this dining area to be spic and span before dinnertime. Mrs. Fields will show you where to get the cleaning supplies. Are we clear?"

"What about her?" Levi said, pointing to Alice.

"She's welcome to stay and watch if she wants," Mr. Honeycutt said, "though why she'd want to look at your ugly mugs any more than necessary is beyond me."

This was met with laughter and catcalls by the assembled students, and Levi looked down at the mess around his feet, his fists clenched in anger.

Scott stepped up beside Alice and Miranda, who was looking at her friend with wide-eyed amazement. "Would you ladies care for some refreshment?" he asked, proffering two chocolate frosted cupcakes - the only items to have survived the cart's destruction.

Alice looked at him with a raised eyebrow and Scott shrugged. "Well, I told you they'd be gone if I didn't hurry."

♠ ♣ ♥ ♦

The theme for the Halloween party was "Come as you aren't – or as you'd like to be!". Alice thought it showed a lack of commitment on the part of the planners; anything could fit into that definition. But then again, maybe that was the point.

Alice and Scott were late because Alice balked at Scott's choice for their costumes. "You've got to be kidding me."

"You said you didn't want to think about it, and I didn't have much time to plan," Scott replied. "These costumes are simple and didn't take too long to throw together."

"But we need at least two more people," Alice dodged.

Scott shrugged. "We waited too long. Everyone was already a member of another group or had their individual costumes all set to go. If anyone asks, we'll just say we're from early in the movie."

"All right. Did you at least get me a basket?"

Alice kicked him out of her room, changed into the costume, and added one additional accessory. Then she joined Scott and they headed for the gymnasium.

"Where's Sarah?" Scott asked as they crossed the quad from the dorms.

"Beats me. She disappeared on me a couple of hours ago. I assume she's getting her costume assembled."

"Well, she's always loved Halloween. But she's really excited this year. I can't wait to see what she's come up with."

As they reached their destination, Scott opened the door and the music, which had been muted up until that point, blasted out, mixed with excited chatter and laughter. Apparently, the students were having a good time. However, the lighting inside was sufficiently dim that it took Alice a few seconds after entering before her sight had adjusted to allow for a visual confirmation of that fact.

The bleachers, capable of seating hundreds of people when extended, were recessed against the walls to give as much area over to the party as possible. Tables were set up at one end of the floor. Each was draped with a tablecloth and had some sort of spooky decoration serving as a centerpiece. The one closest to them had an animated head within a crystal ball that dispensed portents of doom whenever someone wandered too close. Not surprisingly, no one was seated at that table; it would have been virtually impossible to have a conversation around the thing. A huge buffet table, holding far too much food for the number of people attending the party, sat against the far wall, with a bubbling cauldron of punch on an elevated platform in its center. Thick mist poured down from the bowl, half-hiding the food nearest to it. The far end of the room was the dance floor, currently occupied by about half of the students, which meant it was virtually empty.

Alice felt a momentary pang of loneliness at the sight. *There's so many more of us than I suspected just a few weeks ago, but it doesn't take much to emphasize how few of us there really are.* She shook her head to get rid of the unpleasant feeling and focused her attention on the costumes.

Miranda, ever the social butterfly, was dancing with Min Ki. Her winning personality and apparent comfort around her fellow students had made her so popular that Team Red had invited her to round out their group while Alice was still resisting her friends' urgings to come to the party at all. With a dark dress and wig, she made a stunning Wednesday Adams to complement Min Ki's Pugsley. Julio and Constance, as Gomez and Morticia, laid down moves the tango-loving duo would never have contemplated. Nearby, Esme and Andrew provided counterpoint to the goth-fest the others were putting on, though they hadn't bothered to coordinate their costumes. Esme was a ravishing Cleopatra, while Alice thought the boy's outfit was supposed to evoke David Copperfield, or some other famous stage magician.

Julianna was just inside the door in a business suit with a skirt, wearing a wig. It took Alice a moment to make the connection. "Barbara Walters?" she guessed.

"Yeah," Julianna replied, obviously pleased. Then pointed to her dupes scattered throughout the gym. "And Katie Couric, Deborah Norville, Ashleigh Banfield, and Jane Pauly."

Scott looked a little dazed. "Wow, way to take a theme and run with it, Julianna."

Alice nudged him and gave him a reproving look. Switching back to Julianna, she asked, "So are you going to be a journalism major?"

She nodded. "That's the plan. I hope my power will let me cover several different arenas simultaneously. You know - politics, business, and entertainment."

Alice considered this. "Your power works that way? How far can your dupes get from you? Is there a time limit? What happens if you get assigned to a story in LA and your dupe needs to go to Iraq or something?"

Julianna bit the tip of her thumb thoughtfully. "I haven't noticed any limitations yet, but you make a good point. I think I'll have to do some tests. Maybe I'll bring it up with Mrs. Kilkarni. Well, don't let me keep you. Autumn headed for the rest room a few minutes ago, but she was sitting at that table if you want to wait for her." Julianna indicated one of the tables as far from the dance floor as possible.

"Thanks," Alice said doubtfully. "Not that I don't like Autumn, but why would you think we were looking for her?

Julianna looked pointedly at Alice's costume. "Well, let's see. Blue and white gingham dress, red shoes, and a picnic basket. The only thing missing is a little dog."

The picnic basket shifted in Alice's grip and yipped. Julianna raised one eyebrow at her. Alice grinned and lifted one side of the cover to reveal a small terrier.

"You got a dog just for your costume? How? When?" Scott asked.

"Once Alice finally made it into the garden from the hall of doors, she met a puppy. Most people forget because they've only seen the movies and never read the book," Alice explained.

"Anyway, I rest my case. If you're not Dorothy Gale, this is the worst costume I've ever seen," Julianna concluded. "And you are obviously the scarecrow," she said to Scott."

"Yeah. So?"

"So you didn't coordinate with Autumn?" Julianna laughed. "Oh, this is too good. Come on, you've got to see her."

She grabbed Alice's hand and pulled her toward the table she had indicated, but continued past it. As they reached a door leading from the gym toward the girl's locker room, it opened and Autumn stepped through. She was dressed all in black, wore a pointed hat, and had green makeup covering every inch of exposed skin.

"Oh," Alice said, immediately getting it and playing along. "Scarecrow, what are we going to do? The Wicked Witch of the West has found us!"

"Aye, me pretty. And now I'll be having those ruby slippers," Autumn said in a fake-scary voice.

Scott laughed. "Are you a wicked witch or a pirate?"

Autumn wrinkled up her nose at him. "Augh, you're right, that does sound more like a pirate, doesn't it? I'm not too good at improv, I guess."

"It was fine," Alice said. "Don't pay any attention to the critic behind the curtain." She held the picnic basket in front of Scott's face as a stand-in for the drapery.

Scott gently pushed the basket down, drawing another irritated yip from its occupant, who was peeking out from under the cover. "Easy, Toto, I don't think she means us any harm."

"So, Autumn, how did you decide on the wicked witch?" Alice asked.

"Elphaba, if you please," Autumn replied. "I love the musical, and I thought it fit the 'come as you aren't' part of the theme. I practically live in water, and Elphaba can't even touch it, you know?"

"Ooo, nicely done," Alice said, dropping a curtsey to the other girl. "Scott and I were just heading for the buffet. Care to come?"

"Sure, why not?" Autumn replied. Julianna begged off, saying she had to check on Mr. Frankel, the economics teacher, who was manning the DJ booth for the evening.

Alice scanned the room as they crossed to the table. Regis Adair, dressed in white lab coat, steampunk goggles, and huge rubber gloves was Dr. Horrible, which would make Kasie, sans gems tonight and in very plain garb, Penny. Kip, the beefiest of the students, had been recruited to play the doctor's nemesis, Captain Hammer. A tall, dark figure, easily seven feet tall, dominated the space in front of the food table. It was dressed in a flowing dark robe and hood, with a black, spiked crown on its brow.

"And who do we have here?" Alice asked as she approached. "Sarah, is that you?"

"Sarah?" an irritated, thin, but masculine voice issued from the impressive figure. It turned, revealing Levi ensconced inside a huge paper-maché construct that sat on his shoulders. The figure's upper arms were molded vertically against the chest, and Levi's arms emerged to form the forearms. His face was peeking out of the torso, just below its sternum, although it looked like a flap of fabric could hide him when he wasn't eating. His face was at a higher level than normal as well; Alice assumed he was wearing painter's lifts, adding about a foot to his height.

"Sorry, Levi," Alice apologized, tapping her head. "It's just that Sarah's been keeping her costume a secret, and I had just about everyone else accounted for."

Scott gave the other boy a thumbs up. "You really went all out. Who are you?"

Levi took the praise as his due, holding up one hand to show off a huge, thick, and definitely fake gold ring on one finger. "Sauron, scourge of Middle-Earth and forger of the one ring. Bow before me, mortals, and I may let you live."

Autumn, fell to her knees, holding her hands up in mock terror. "You had me at Sauron," she said. "Please don't hurt me."

Alice was about to compliment Levi on his work, when the current song ended and a momentary lull in the noise levels was suddenly filled with a shouted, "Where is my head?"

Everyone looked around for the source of the voice, but the acoustics made pinpointing the speaker's location next to impossible.

Suddenly, an eerie green light shone from the girders high above the gymnasium floor. Alice saw the light was from a jack o' lantern, held aloft in a heavily gloved hand. The rest of the figure was dressed in clothes that looked like they came from the Revolutionary War, including a heavy cloak and breeches stuffed into high leather riding boots. But the figure had no head, just a ragged stump of a neck and a wash of blood down the front of its shirt.

"Speak, fools, before I slay you all in my wrath! Where is my head? I will have it!"

There was a gasp of surprise from many of the spectators, because the mouth of the jack o' lantern moved in perfect synchronization with this speech.

"Is that Sarah?" Alice asked Scott.

"Yeah, that's her," he confirmed. "I'd recognize that fake-deep voice anywhere. But this is way better than anything she's ever put together before."

Before anyone could react, the figure leapt down from the girder, plunging over thirty feet to land in a crouch in the middle of the dance floor with one hand flat on the wood surface and the other still holding the gourd head aloft. Slowly, it rose to its feet and turned, surveying the entire room. "Well, where is it? Or shall I take yours to replace my own?" it said, stabbing a finger at Min Ki menacingly.

Suddenly, Alice felt her basket lurch and Toto was running across the floor at the figure, barking angrily. Before she could take more than a step or two to follow it, the dog had latched onto one boot just above the ankle and started worrying at it, trying to haul it away.

The Jack o' lantern's carved grimace suddenly transformed into a happy smile. "Oh, how cute." Sarah's voice rang out in its normal tones. "Hey, little fella, it's okay. I'm not really mean. Who do you belong to, huh?"

Toto was having none of it, however, and nipped at the gloved hand as Sarah bent down and tried to pet him. Then he jumped back and started racing around her feet, barking furiously.

"All right, pup, that's quite enough," Alice said as she got close. "Back to the story book with you, since you can't behave." The dog vanished in an instant.

"Let's hear it for Sarah Thompson, folks," Alice encouraged the crowd, "a.k.a the Headless Horseman." A round of polite, but reasonably enthusiastic clapping ensued.

Before it died away, Mrs. Kilkarni was there, surveying Sarah's costume at close range. She gave particular attention to the jack o' lantern, with its animated expressions. "Well done, Miss Thompson," she said finally. "Am I to understand you have had a break though?"

"Um, yes, maam. I--"

Elaine smiled. "No need to go into details tonight, child. It's nothing that can't wait until after breakfast. Shall we say in my office, 8:30?"

"Um, yes?" Sarah hazarded.

"Good. Well, then, on with the party," Mrs. Kilkarni said as she turned back to the staff table.

Cell phone cameras had been snapping pictures of Sarah's costume from several angles. A sudden commotion at the edge of the dance floor drew everyone's attention as Andrew suddenly slammed a drink cup on the top of a table he and Esme had been sharing and shouted at her. "For crying out loud, Esme, I don't care about the freaking cameras anymore. Get the stupid thing removed, already; I'm tired of covering for you. I thought having you as a girlfriend was fantastic, but you're driving me crazy. Just go away!"

He stalked off, leaving Esme staring after him with wide eyes. He did not look back as he slammed through the main door, apparently heading back to the dorms. Esme looked around at the people around her, several with half-raised cells forgotten in their hands. Then she bolted for a different exit, sobbing. In a moment she had vanished into the night.

"Well, I guess it isn't a party without a little drama, eh?" Kip observed to no one in particular. He got no response, but people started drifting back to their own concerns as the music started back up. Alice grabbed Sarah by a forearm and pulled her toward a table. "Well, this is impressive," she said, having to look up to see even the neckline of the figure before her.

"Yeah, there's only one drawback," Sarah sighed, half turning toward the buffet. "My body is across campus, and that food looks great!"

CHAPTER TWENTY-EIGHT
New Assignments

"Before our meeting gets underway, let's welcome our newest member, Alice Littleton. Welcome to Team Green, Alice." Kasie lead a round of polite applause from Esme and Julianna, who had elected to attend without her dupes. It was early evening and they were using one of the classrooms that contained a large table for use during group projects.

Alice accepted the recognition with a certain degree of trepidation. Mrs. Kilkarni had assigned her to the group, so she was to be faced with the same challenges as the other girls. However, based on what she had heard about the contest to claim the leadership position, she wasn't sure she wanted any part of it. Eavesdropping on closed-door sessions of local government struck her as a morally gray area, even if no attempt had been made to profit on the information gleaned.

Kasie had been appointed as the team leader, but she had been shocked to learn that Esme had also successfully completed the task and produced a transcript of the meeting.

"I didn't see anyone else in the room except the town council members," Kasie said. "How did you manage it? Did you hide a recorder in the ceiling?"

Esme gave her a lazy grin. "Zat vould be telling," she said. "I only did it to show how rezourceful I can be. Don't vorry, your position is secure."

That's hardly the point," Kasie returned. "As team leader, I should have a clear idea what my people are capable of."

"I'll tell you vat, you ask me ven you need to know if I can do zomething, and I'll let you know."

Kasie seemed inclined to argue the point further, but Mrs. Kilkarni spoke up from her position at the head of the table. "Enough posturing, girls. Kasie, a good leader knows how to instill trust in the members of her team. If Esme doesn't feel comfortable bringing you and the others into her confidence, perhaps you should take it as a challenge to your ingenuity rather than your pride."

Kasie hesitated, but finally nodded. Elaine stood up, drawing every eye to her. "Now, it is time to give you your next team challenge. This will be different from your last assignment, in that this time I expect you to work together to achieve your goal. Any of you can suggest a strategy to employ, but it will be up to Kasie to select the plan she thinks has the best chance of success and coordinate its execution."

The girls all nodded their understanding, and Elaine continued. "This task will challenge your ability to think creatively and work subtly. Your task is to bring me the mayor's cell phone and then return it to him without him becoming aware that it has ever left his possession."

Alice's trepidation turned to outright panic. "I can't do that! I won't do that."

Elaine regarded her calmly. "And why is that, dear?"

Alice found herself struggling to put the obvious into words. "Because it's wrong, of course. It's a violation of his privacy, and theft, besides."

"Tell me, Alice, are you familiar with the American plains Indians' concept of counting coup?" Mrs. Kilkarni asked.

"No, I'm not."

"A warrior for the tribe was given a stick. Not a spear, not a club, but a light-weight stick. He would approach his enemy openly, and attempt to touch him with the stick. That's all. Not hurt his enemy, but merely to demonstrate his skill by touching him. But the enemy had no idea of the warrior's true intentions, and so would react as if the warrior had lethal intent."

"Okay..." Alice said, having no idea where the administrator was going with this detour.

"I want you to think of this exercise as our equivalent of counting coup," Elaine explained. "Our target will have no idea our intentions are merely to test our own skill, so if you get caught, the consequences could be severe. Not as severe as an apparent open attack against a foe on his guard, but enough that you have a real incentive to avoid being detected. And the phone will be returned to him immediately. So there will be no harm of any sort."

Alice wanted to object. The exercise went against everything she stood for, everything she had been taught growing up. But a small voice in the back of her mind whispered *How else is she going to train students with your kinds of abilities?*

She looked at the other members of her team. Kasie seemed deep in thought, already working out a strategy to pull this off. Esme toyed with a lock of her hair, seemingly unconcerned with the moral aspects of this challenge. Only Julianna was looking at her intently, as if waiting to see which side she would come down on.

Oh, well. In for a penny and all that. It's not like I have to follow through if I don't like what we come up with. Aloud, she said, "All right, I'll go along, at least until we decide how we want to do this. But I'm not promising I'll participate unless I'm satisfied with the final plan."

"Excellent. Now if you'll excuse me, I need to go and give Team Blue their next assignment." Without another word, Mrs. Kilkarni walked out the door, leaving Team Green to organize their thoughts.

A half an hour of discussion failed to produce anything workable, and they decided they needed more information. After Kassie gave each team member a research assignment, the meeting broke up.

"Alice, may I speak vit you in private? It vill only take a moment," Esme asked as they were all gathering their things.

"Uh, sure, I guess," Alice replied. Esme remained sitting as the rest of the team gathered their things to leave, so Alice stayed with her. She noted that Kasie gave the duo still at the table a disapproving half-sneer before she tossed her hair back over her shoulder and departed. Julianna didn't even spare them a glance. "What's up?" she asked once they were alone.

Esme did not answer immediately. Instead, she toyed with a lock of her hair and stared at the table in front of her. Alice was amazed, and a bit troubled. In the time since Alice had joined the school, Esme's behavior had been consistent. Esme was bold, always going straight for whatever she wanted at any given moment. This hesitant, quiet version was a little unnerving.

"I need some advice, and I'm not sure who to turn to," Emse finally said. "You remember what happened on Halloween? At the dance?"

"You mean your break-up with Andrew?"

Esme nodded.

Alice closed her eyes and blew out a breath, then looked at the other girl closely. "Are you sure you want to talk to me about this? You wouldn't be more confortable with Kasie or Julianna?"

Esme snorted. "You know vat they call Team Green? The other students?"

"Sure. Ever since the leadership was determined, you've - well, I guess now it's 'we've' - been Kassie and the Hardliners."

"Correct. Zey tink ve are all alike. All vit heads filled with nothing but fashions and make-up. Zat ve are all about being popular."

"If that's what they think about me, they're going to be so disappointed," Alice said. "I've pretty much been the opposite of popular, in fact."

"You are right. You don't fit in here. Zat's ze point."

Alice shook her head. "I don't follow."

"Ven Andrew broke up vit me, Kasie told me it vas about time. She had been planning to tell *me* to dump *him*. She said it vouldn't do for someone like him to be seen around her so much."

"Sadly, I have no problem believing that of Kasie," Alice replied. "Okay, so why me?"

"I heard you helped Sarah vit her powers."

"Well, sort of, I guess. Well, if I'm going to help, I need to know what's up. What was your fight about, anyway?"

"I needed Andrew's help vit something. I'll admit, at first, I only came on to him to get vat I vanted."

"What did he help you with?"

"He...he helped me keep a secret."

"Oh, and now you're afraid he'll tell it to everyone?"

Esme shook her head. "No, he doesn't know it. I tricked him into helping. But I don't think he vould tell even if he did."

"If he didn't know your secret, how did he help? Did he provide a cover story?"

"Uhm, sort of."

315

"Oh, I see. Esme, are you a lesbian? Because it won't make any difference to anyone worth worrying about."

"No," Esme replied hurriedly. "Zat vasn't the type of cover he vas providing for me."

Alice assessed Esme's reaction and decided she was probably telling the truth. "All right, so Andrew was being hoodwinked into keeping your secret, but now he's out of the picture. And you want me to help you figure out how to patch things up with him so you can keep your secret longer?"

"No! Zat's not important. I vould tell him vat it is, and how he has been helping me, but..."

"Go on," Alice encouraged her.

"I am afraid. Afraid ze secret itself vould drive him away from me."

"It's that bad?"

"Not in itself. But he vould think I vas only telling him now to get him to keep it hidden."

"So if you're not worried about protecting your secret... Oh, I see. You started out trying to use him, but now you've started to develop a crush on him, right?"

Esme nodded. "And I can't just apologize, because then it will seem like I'm just trying to play him again."

"So tell me about him. What got through to you?"

"Vell, he makes me feel important to him. He interrupts whatever he's doing to talk to me or handle something for me. I know he cares." Esme stifled a sob. "Cared."

After a moment, she regained control and continued. "But I tink vat really got to me are his illusions."

Alice nodded. "Right, he's a light manipulator. He must have a real artistic streak if his illusions made that much of an impression."

Esme gave a small, hiccupping laugh. "Not those illusions. He practices stage magic. You know, sleight of hand. He could do so much more if he just used his light manipulation abilities, but he's a purist. At first, I thought he was being silly, but he really does treat it like an art, you know? In the end, his tricks have to be something he could pass along to anyone else."

Esme stared at her fingers, apparently trying to contort them into some difficult configuration before she gave up and gathered them into a loose fist. "I've watched him practice, and he makes some of those moves look so easy, so natural. Then I try them and I'd swear I'm about to break my hand. And he does it all just because it fascinates him, and occasionally lets him pull some little trick in public."

Alice searched the other girl's face. *How sincere is she? I won't help her take advantage of Andrew again.* It was the falling shoulders and downcast eyes that finally helped her decide.

"Esme, if you want my advice, here it is. You need to decide what's really important to you. If it's Andrew, then find a way to apologize to him that proves you mean it. Then be sure to treat him right."

Esme looked up at her, tears glistening in her eyes. "I tink I can do that."

♠ ♣ ♥ ♦

"I received a very interesting call from the mayor yesterday," Mrs. Kilkarni said. Team Blue, their ranks bolstered with the addition of Miranda, sat in another classroom around a similar table to the one Team Green was currently using.

"Interesting in what way, Mrs. Kilkarni?" Regis asked. As the newly appointed leader of Team Blue, he took it upon himself to move the conversation along.

"Apparently, something has been drawing a significant amount of energy from the local power grid lately."

"And he asked for your help?" Miranda asked. "Why would he do that? As far as he knows, this is just a small private school, right?"

"It was less a request for help, more a demand for answers," Elaine explained. "He said the timing of the power draining events coincides with our opening, so he wanted to know just what we're up to out here."

"Is there any chance he's right?" Andrew asked. "We do have some features you won't find in a normal school, after all. Ms. Teresi's lab, for one. We don't really know what she's up to down there, but there are all sorts of rumors. Could she be behind it all?"

"Her lab is not connected to the local power grid at all," Mrs. Kilkarni replied. "But that was a very good observation, Andrew. But I am confident that we are not behind these events. Since the mayor sees things differently, I think it would be a good idea for us to figure out what really is going on."

"So you want us to track down whatever facility is causing the power drains? How are we supposed to do that?" Sarah spoke up. "Doesn't the power company have some sort of detectors that can tell them where the energy's going?"

"Not in this case apparently," Elaine replied. "That's one of the reasons the mayor is so concerned."

"I still don't see how we're going to track them down, then," Sarah persisted.

"I'm not leaving you without resources. I have managed to procure times for the power drain events, as well as a general sense of how much power was drained each time. In addition, I can tell you that all indications are that the source of the events is fairly close. Almost definitely on our side of town."

"But--," Sarah began.

"No problem, Mrs. K," Regis interrupted. "We'll get right on this."

Elaine smiled. "I knew I could count on you, Regis. I'll leave this with you and your team. Report directly to me when you've made a discovery." Then she rose and walked out of the room without more than a benevolent smile for her students.

"Are you crazy?" Sarah turned on Regis as soon as they were alone. "We don't know the first thing about power grids or anything like that. How are we supposed to figure this out when the power company is stumped?"

"We'll use our own special talents," Regis replied. "It shouldn't be difficult. Just bring that city map up to the rec room, and we should have an answer within a few minutes. Let's do this, people."

CHAPTER TWENTY-NINE
Dinner Conversation

The Prometheus Academy Round Table Dinner was a tradition less than a month old. Alice had missed the inaugural event, since she and her father had been on the run from Oglethorpe that Wednesday night. She had made it to the school for the next session of dinner and powers-centric discussion, but she had largely just sat and listened. Last week's dinner had been pre-empted by the Halloween party. So tonight was only her second time attending, and Miranda was a complete newbie.

Unlike other nights of the week where the students and staff ate together in the cafeteria, the Round Table was hosted in a formal dining room. The actual piece of furniture was a fat oval, and the food was served in courses by staff from the cafeteria in order to limit distractions that might otherwise result from having to pass dishes up and down the length of the table. Attendance was limited to students, Mrs. Kilkarni, and the two empowered members of the faculty. LaRonda slouched in her chair with her cheek resting on one hand, predictably grumpy about the imposed time away from her lab.

Once everyone had received their choice of soup or salad, Elaine signaled for attention by tapping her wine glass lightly with a knife from her place setting. Idle conversation died quickly as students turned their attention to the principal. "Good evening, students," she said.

The students responded as they had been trained, repeating "Good evening, Mrs. Kilkarni," more or less in unison.

"Does anyone have anything they would like to discuss this evening?" she invited.

"I do. I would like to clear up a misconception," Esme responded, drawing intense scrutiny from several attendees who picked up on the sudden absence of her characteristic accent.

Elaine gave Esme an assessing look. "Are you sure you want to do this? Once you do, there's no going back."

"I'm sure," Esme replied. After receiving a nod from Elaine, she continued. "You all have the wrong idea about my power. It does not make me omnilingual."

"That can't be right," Levi exclaimed. "I've heard you speak a bunch of languages. More than I can name, for sure."

Esme rolled her eyes. "Americans," she said deprecatingly. "You're so monolingual as a rule you'd be willing to believe anyone fluent in even three languages must have some sort of paranormal edge. I do speak many languages, because growing up my family travelled all over Europe. I learned early on I had a natural gift for languages, and took advantage of every opportunity I had to learn more. But it took work. My paranormal abilities lie in an entirely different area."

"Why did you keep it a secret? And why tell us now?" Scott asked.

Esme hesitated, then said, "The stress of keeping my secret has damaged relationships - one in particular - that I value more than the pretense I've been trying to keep up. Coming clean now may be too little, too late, but I won't risk repeating the same mistakes."

"And that has something to do with why you've been driving me crazy for three weeks?" Andrew challenged her.

"Yes," Esme answered. "You see, when I was offered the chance to come here, I was determined to make a fresh start on my own terms. I wanted to be exotic and popular. So I adopted that silly accent, and made sure you all saw me as just what I wanted to be."

"That doesn't sound so terrible," Sarah said. "You're beating yourself up over giving yourself a makeover?"

"It went a little deeper than that," Esme said as her form blurred before their eyes. In a moment, she went from a slim, athletic young girl with thick wavy hair and a flawless complexion to a plumper, rather plain-looking girl with straight, light brown hair and freckles. It took Alice a bit of effort to discern traces of the student she had thought she knew in the person sitting across the table.

"You're a shape shifter?" Andrew exclaimed.

"No, my body never changes. I modify how you percieve me. I could walk out of this room right now and come back in as you've known me up 'til now, as any one of you, or President Obama. I could even prevent you from taking notice of me at all."

"Oooh, now I get it," Kasie said. "The night of the city council meeting--"

"I was the first to arrive, and I was sitting in the middle of the public area, tape recorder in hand," Emse confirmed.

"So what was the deal with the cameras?" Andrew asked.

"A camera doesn't have a mind to cloud," Esme explained. "It just records what's actually there. At first, I thought I just needed you to replace me with an illusion for the school picture. Then I realized I'd show up in any picture anyone took of me, and I freaked out a little. For what it's worth, I'm glad I stayed around you long enough to really get to know you, and I'm sorry for nagging you about the cameras so much."

Andrew just frowned and shook his head. He sat back in his chair, arms crossed, and looked anywhere but at his former girlfriend. Esme let out a resigned breath and started picking at her food, though with little apparent interest in actually eating any of it.

323

"All right, I think that's enough on that topic," Mrs. Kilkarni cut in. "If no one else has anything...?" No one motioned otherwise, so she continued. "Tonight is something of an anniversary, for an event that I think it worth our time to consider. There are obvious parallels to our potential situation. Has anyone here heard of *Kristallnacht*?"

The children exchanged glances around the table. Finally, Kasie said, "No, but it sounds pretty. Does it have something to do with gemstones?"

Esme snorted in disgust, earning her an angry look from her team leader, but she stared back boldly. "It wasn't pretty. In fact, it was a brutal offensive by one of the worst dictators in history."

"Softly, dear," Elaine said. "It was 74 years ago, so I think Kasie can be forgiven for not making the correct association right off the bat. Since you seem to know about it, why not fill in your classmates?"

Esme grimaced, but nodded her acceptance. "*Kristallnacht* is German for 'night of crystal" but history more correctly remembers it as the "Night of Broken Glass". Hitler and his ministers staged what a simple-minded six-year-old might have accepted as a spontaneous uprising against Jews living within the Third Reich, supposedly in retaliation for the killing of a government official. With the full blessing of the government, the rioters trashed Jewish homes, businesses and synagogues, leaving broken glass in the streets. Authorities only acted to prevent fires from spreading to non-Jewish structures."

Alice, who was not a particularly good history student, was shocked. "Okay, I get that Hitler was bad, and a major nut job to boot, but why would he do that?"

"That is a question historians have discussed at length," Elaine supplied. "His cover story, such as it is, is that he believed in a conspiracy among Jews all over the world. I think it's a bit simpler than that. Hitler was a thug, and his ideology demanded an enemy to suppress. The Jews were a convenient collective scapegoat."

"Why the Jews in particular?" Amber asked.

"For starters, they had a strong sense of community and fellowship among themselves, but lived in communities scattered all over the world," Elaine said. "That worked to Hitler's advantage. It made it easier to sell some people on the idea that these people with no homeland of their own, but still with a strong nationalistic sense of purpose and destiny, were up to something that ultimately served only their own ends. But there were other factors.

"As a people, the Jews had a strong work ethic, and many were doctors, lawyers, and other professionals, or successful business owners. The influence they had within society made those who bought into the propaganda uneasy."

"So Hitler stirred up people against the Jews because he needed someone to bully in the name of national protection?" Min Ki asked.

"Some would say that lacks a certain nuanced understanding of the situation," Elaine allowed, "but basically that's how I see it."

"So how did that lead to all the broken glass?" Levi asked.

"Hitler had decided to expel all the Jews from the Reich," Mrs. Kilkarni explained. "But he couldn't do it all at once. So he rounded up as many as he could and told them to get out. In many cases, the countries where they had been born could not or would not accept so many refugees at once, so the Jews wound up in concentration camps. The son of one of the couples in a camp near Poland, Herschel Grynszpan, shot the German official in the Paris embassy assigned to help him, one Ernst vom Rath, exactly 74 years ago tonight. Vom Rath died two days later, and the Reich seized on the excuse for the supposedly spontaneous riots of *Kristallnacht*."

"So Hitler did all that just to punish the Jews for what one man did?" Julio asked.

325

"It was probably more to see how well his propaganda against the Jews was working with the average man on the street," Elaine explained. "The lack of outraged response to the Jews' plight from the masses was good news as far as he was concerned. It meant he had succeeded in planting his seeds of distrust. The Reich issued a decree that the Jews had brought this misfortune on themselves through their collective actions, fined them heavily, and seized the insurance payments that would have gone to the home and business owners to pay for damages in order to satisfy that debt. It was the opening salvo in his real agenda against the Jews."

Silence descended on the dining room as the students considered this depraved chain of reasoning and action.

"So, does anyone see any lessons in this for us today?" Elaine finally asked.

The students exchanged nervous glances. No one really wanted to take up this mental exercise, but finally Sarah raised her hand. "You're saying governments could view empowered like Hitler did the Jews. Even if we don't self-identify most strongly with other empowered first, and with our nations second, some politicians might accuse of that anyway."

Elaine nodded. "Of course, we can hope that our leaders have learned the lessons history teaches, and have the wisdom not to go down that road. But even here, ambitious men might try such a gambit as a means of attaining power, casting themselves in the role of humanity's defenders. They wouldn't even need to believe in the threat, necessarily. They might just use it to create a groundswell of support that they hope will carry them into a position of power."

"If so," Alice thought aloud, "our own strengths would be turned against us, just as the Jews' positions of influence were against them. If people are taught to mistrust us, our abilities would just make us seem even more of a threat to normal people."

Min Ki shook his head. "Man, that would suck. There's no way to win in that situation. If you try to act harmless and innocent, like most of the Jews, you wind up in a concentration camp somewhere looking at the gas chamber. Try to fight back, and you give your enemy an excuse to come down on all your people hard."

Elaine nodded. "Of course, some might say the Jews would have done better banding together to resist the Reich's actions against them. Given the Holocaust and its aftermath, one could argue they couldn't have done much worse than what they actually experienced in the end."

Miranda shook her head, venturing into the conversation for the first time. "I don't buy that. That just would have proven every lie that Hitler and his friends had been telling about them all along, at least in the minds of the masses. Look, I'm here with all of you, and I'm not afraid, because I know you. That's the key. You've got to educate people and make them understand and believe that there's no hidden agenda, and you just want to live like everyone else. Right?"

Elaine rewarded Miranda with a light round of applause. "Very well said, Miranda. And that is exactly one of our purposes here at Prometheus."

Julianna looked thoughtful. "But how do you do that? Educate the people when you're so outnumbered and lots of them have reasons, valid or not, to mistrust you?"

Elaine smiled grimly. "That, as they say, is left as an exercise for the student."

CHAPTER THIRTY
Plots and Preparations

"Want to catch a movie Saturday? *Skyfall* is opening this weekend," Scott suggested. He and Miranda were lounging on a couch in the rec room. Alice was lying on the carpeted floor in front of them with her head on Ches' side. Her unfocused eyes stared towards the ceiling and her teeth worried at her lower lip.

Scott glanced at the other girl, who simply shrugged when she failed to respond. Alice had been withdrawn all day after Elaine's history lesson the previous evening. So Scott raised his voice slightly and said, "Or I could get Ms. Teresi to hook up a big vat of sulfuric acid to the sprinkler system and we could run through the spray until we're nothing but skeletons. Sound like fun, Alice?"

"Sure, let's do that," she responded.

Scott shook his head in exasperation. He pointed his finger at her and let loose with a very low-powered burst of energy. "Wrong answer," he chided.

"Hey, what's the deal?" Alice exclaimed, shocked out of her reverie by the vibratory poke.

Did you hear my last suggestion at all?" Scott asked.

Alice thought for a moment. "Something about the sky falling?"

"Ah, then he's settled on *Chicken Little* for his English book report," Ches said. "May I be the first to congratulate you on reaching for new literary horizons."

Scott grinned in spite of himself, but tried to look severe as he shifted his attention to the cat. "Laugh it up, fuzzball. But I'll have you know there are depths there that few have understood. Anyway, you're just sore that I wouldn't read *Mrs. Frisby and the Rats of NIHM* to you."

"Couldn't, you mean. All that stumbling over the words that had more than two syllables--"

"Enough!" Alice cut in. "I get it, I'm a terrible person for tuning out. I'll try to be good."

"Good," said Miranda. "So how about catching *Skyfall* this weekend?"

"I don't know. I wouldn't be very good company. I keep on obsessing on the fact that Oglethorpe's out there somewhere. I've got to do something, but I'm not sure what."

"I don't know what you can do," Scott replied. "He's out there somewhere, but even if we knew where, he's probably beyond our reach. It's not like we've got a jet in the basement waiting to whisk us off at a moment's notice. And we sure don't want to bring him here."

"No, of course not..." Alice's reply drifted off into silence as she appeared to consider the idea. Her eyes suddenly locked on Julio, sitting in a corner of the room with his sketch book, with Constance and Min Ki talking quietly nearby. She got up and walked over to the table. Scott and Miranda followed after her.

"Hi, Julio. How are you doing?"

Julio glanced up suspiciously from where he had been working on yet another page in his samples book. The theme for this one appeared to be clocks and other timepieces. "Fine. What do you want?"

"I need the help of an artist. Could you make me a sketch of Oglethorpe?"

Julio returned his attention to his sketch book. "Sorry, I've never seen the guy."

"But I have. I could describe him to you. Please, it's very important," Alice pleaded.

"I don't work that way. It's not easy to get someone to describe something in enough detail to make an accurate drawing. It would just be a waste of our time."

"I'll pay you," Alice offered. "If it doesn't come out in the end, it's my fault, and it was my time to waste."

Constance reached over and put one hand lightly on Julio's arm when he hunched his shoulders and appeared ready to protest again. "Come on, Julio, it's obviously really important to her. Besides, you could use the practice. What are you going to do when a customer walks into your shop and wants a custom job?"

Julio looked up at her, and seeing nothing more than an encouraging smile, he allowed some of the tension to ease out of his frame. "Fine," he said, flipping to a blank page towards the back of his pad. He pushed out a chair on his other side and jerked his head towards it. "Have a seat, *chica*, and let's see what we can do."

Alice sat down and looked at the vast expanse of blank page and realized Julio had a point. This wasn't going to be as easy as she had hoped. "Where should I start?" She asked.

"Start with the basics," Julio replied. "How tall is he? Describe his general body shape and clothes he tends to wear. We'll try to get more specific as we go."

"Okay. Well. he's short and kind of pudgy, probably in his mid-forties. He wears a rumpled black suit that looks too big for him, with a white shirt and thin black tie."

331

"What's his hair like?"

"Dark, and cut short. Not quite a buzz cut, but short enough it would be hard to ever call it messy. It looked to me like he was going for low-maintenance over attractiveness."

They worked for about half an hour as the image slowly took shape before them. Autumn Glassford drifted over towards the end of the session to see what they were doing. "His neck should be thicker, and darken the eyebrows a bit," she offered.

"Oh, good catch," Alice said. "I knew there was something off, but I couldn't put my finger on it. When did you run into him?"

"About three months ago, down near the docks in a south Florida port. He tried to snatch me off the street. Houston showed up just in time and took me back to my parents' ship. He made his sales pitch to us, and before I knew it I was here at the school. They were still finishing up final details in the construction."

"How's this?" Julio asked.

"It looks good. I think it's about as accurate as we're going to be able to manage," Alice said after giving it a critical review.

"Yeah, I think so too," Autumn seconded.

"Okay," Julio said. "Give me a couple of minutes and I'll make you a clean copy without all the eraser marks."

"So what are you going to do with it?" Scott asked as Alice reached into her belt pouch for her wallet.

"We're going to set up an early warning system," Alice replied.

♠   ♣   ♥   ♦

"The idea is pretty simple," Alice said.

"It always is with you," Scott replied.

Alice gave him a playful punch in the arm. "Hmm. As I was saying, I'm going to put out the word among the local bird population that I need to know if this man appears in this area," Alice explained. She and her friends had relocated to the student kitchen area. "If one of them spots him, it will come and find me so we'll know to be on guard."

"Let me see if I've got this straight," Scott said. "You're going to walk around town and show this picture to birds, and ask them to come find you if they see Oglethorpe around?"

"Not exactly. That would take too long. The last time I tried this, I had one bird spread the word to have a bunch of birds meet at a prearranged location and spoke to all of them at once. It just took some bird seed to make sure they attended. I figure it will work as well this time. We can use the area where Team Red had their leadership match."

"Why birds in particular?" he asked.

"They cover a lot of ground when they're looking for food and stuff, and they see a lot. They're just our best bet of turning something up in time to be useful."

"But how long do you think a bird can stay focused on a task like this?" Miranda asked.

"Good point," Alice responded. "Last time I got results within a couple of hours, but that was a case of searching for something that I knew was almost certainly out there in my search zone. In this case, it could be weeks or longer before Oglethorpe appears in the area, if he ever does. I'll probably need to reinforce the instructions weekly to make sure our network stays on the job. And I'll also have to start spending as much time outdoors as possible so I can receive any reports coming in."

"But does this even have a chance of working?" Miranda asked. "You told me Oglethorpe is a teleporter. Wouldn't he just suddenly show up here?"

"I don't think so," Alice said thoughtfully. "However he gets his information, it probably doesn't come to him complete right at first. He probably has to scout an area to zero in on his target. I'm going to assume that's the case, anyway, because otherwise we've already lost."

"Okay, so if this works, we get a warning that Oglethorpe is in the area," Scott said. "What do we do when the warning comes? From everything we've heard, he's almost unstoppable."

"Tell Mrs. Kilkarni, I guess. Maybe she has an evacuation plan."

"Then shouldn't she know what we're doing?" Miranda asked.

"Yeah, you're right. Scott, would you go into town and buy a 50-lb. bag of birdseed? I'll go talk to Mrs. Kilkarni and then find a bird or two to spread the news. We'll set up the network Saturday morning at dawn."

♠ ♣ ♥ ♦

Early Sunday morning, Sarah tumbled along the ground, apparently drifting with the wind. Actually, what an observer would have seen was nothing more than an empty plastic shopping bag that she had adopted as a temporary body. In point of fact, although her starting position had been carefully chosen to make her approach plausible, her path was anything but random. She had a specific objective in mind.

When Team Blue adjourned to the rec room with a map of the area over a week ago, Sarah hadn't had a clue what Regis was planning. She and the others had simply followed his directions when he told them to tack the map up on the wall. They had no sooner finished when Regis plucked a dart from a board hanging on the wall, said, "I wonder where the power drains originate from?", and tossed the dart over his shoulder. The missile missed Andrew's head by a fraction of an inch and thudded into the map.

"Hey, watch it," Andrew exclaimed. "At least give a guy a chance to get clear before you do something like that!"

"Relax, you were never in any danger," Regis said, totally unconcerned about the glare he received from the other boy. "Let's see what we have, shall we?"

Regis stepped up next to Andrew, followed a moment later by Miranda, who at least had the decency to give Andrew a sympathetic shrug before turning her attention to the map. Andrew gave a frustrated snort and snatched the dart from the wall so he could look at the spot more closely. Sarah hung back.

"Well, there's definitely some sort of structure there," Regis observed. "It's even further east of town than we are, which is saying something. Well, let's see what we can find out."

Regis moved to one of several computers in the room and started up Google Earth. In less than a minute, he was studying the area in question.

"According to the tag someone's dropped on the site, it a manufacturing plant and warehouse owned by Solomon's, Inc. Let's see what's known about them." He switched to a browser, typed in a search term, and quickly opened several relevant results in separate tabs.

Sarah moved closer and read over his shoulder as he started perusing the results.

"Hmm. this doesn't make much sense," Regis said. "Solomon's appears to be a company that manufactures components for washing machines and other household appliances. Why would they suddenly start using more power than normal? And drawing it in a way that's not traceable?"

"Are you even sure this is where the drain is coming from?" Andrew challenged. "I mean, all you did was toss a dart at a map. You're staking a lot on--"

"This is the place," Regis said, taking his eyes off the screen to look directly at Andrew. His tone left no room for doubt or debate.

"Maybe not," Sarah said as the next screen flashed up. "According to this, Solomon's went bankrupt over a year ago. There shouldn't be any manufacturing going on there at all."

"Maybe, maybe not," Regis hedged. "Somebody's obviously taken over the property. The question is who, and did they do so legitimately?"

"So that's it, right?" Miranda said. "Mrs. Kilkarni said to find out where the power drains were coming from. So we just point her to this warehouse and get our next assignment?"

Regis shook his head. "The next assignment will be to find out what's going on there, so we might as well get started on that without having to be told. Sarah, why don't you chase down the Solomon angle? Find out if the warehouse was sold to anyone, and what happened to their other assets."

"What about the rest of us?" Andrew asked.

"Stand down for now, or you can help Sarah with her inquiries. I'm going to see if I can trace any activity at the site over the past several months. We'll meet again in a week to compare notes."

When they met again, they had much to discuss.

"The Solomon case is still tied up in the courts," Sarah said as the meeting started. "I found out by asking a paralegal at a law firm in town for help with a case study for a school project. She said that this sometimes happens, though she was kind of surprised it happened with the Solomon case. On the surface, there's nothing there to suggest that the whole thing couldn't be over and done with by now, but for some reason it's never been settled."

"So there's no way anything should be going on out there," Andrew mussed. "I wonder how long the new operators have been in residence?"

"About eight months," Regis said matter of factly.

"How could you possibly know that?" Miranda asked.

"I paid for access to satellite imagery for the greater Boulder City area for the past year," Regis explained. "And it's been a very interesting picture I've put together from those shots."

He flipped around his laptop to show others the screen, which displayed a zoomed-in view of the manufacturing plant from space. It was a nighttime shot, though, and it was difficult to make out much detail.

"This is one example of activity at the site that doesn't match up with any normal patterns for the business which used to run it. It's one of the easier ones to make sense of, though, because there was a full moon this particular evening," Regis said, then pointed to a rectangular object on the road. "I'll draw your attention to this truck."

"Why?" Andrew asked. "So someone made a delivery or something. We already knew something was going on out there, assuming your dart pointed us in the right direction."

"This isn't a delivery. What's interesting about it is what it's carrying away from the site," Regis said.

"Okay, I'll bite. What is it hauling?" Sarah asked.

"Dirt."

"Dirt? And you find that interesting?" Andrew asked.

"Yes, I find it very interesting. This truck is far from the first to be carrying soil from this facility. We're looking at a picture taken about six months ago, so we're talking about two months worth of this activity, all carried out in the middle of the night, by the way. The same

337

is true of deliveries made during this timeframe. All activity around the area happens at night, at least until recently."

"I still don't get it," Sarah said.

"Perhaps this shot will help," Regis replied smugly. "It was taken at noon, so it's easier to see what's there. Or, rather, what isn't there."

The rest of the team looked at the next picture for over a minute before Miranda's eyes opened wide. "Oh, I get it. There's no holes anywhere on the property. So where did all the dirt come from?"

Regis gave her a genuine smile and pointed at her. "Good! Miranda gets the gold star. That's it exactly."

"So you think they've been expanding the plant underground?" Sarah asked.

"It's the only conclusion that makes sense. In addition, someone's erected a privacy fence with barbed wire strung around the top around the whole place. Why? The area out there is desolate. The road doesn't even go anywhere; it just turns into a dirt track out beyond the warehouse and finally disappears into the desert. There's no reason for anyone to be out there, unless they're going here." Regis indicated the complex they had been investigating.

"So is anyone going there?" Miranda asked. "You just said the pattern changed recently?"

Regis nodded. "Right. For a little over a month now, cars have been arriving at the facility, and later departing, on a regular schedule. In short, people are working there. And we need to find out who they are and what they're doing."

"How are we supposed to do that?" Andrew asked.

"If my understanding of how she pulled off her impressive Halloween costume is correct, I think this is a job for Sarah," Regis replied as he sat back in his chair contentedly.

♠　♣　♥　♦

And that was why Sarah was currently approaching the facility disguised as a bit of litter. As she approached the fence, she flew up into the air, twisting as if caught in a minor dust devil. She then drifted down into the parking lot and scooted under a car near the entrance. Then she waited.

She had timed her arrival well. Within a few minutes, a vehicle passed through the security gate into the lot and parked. As a uniformed figure emerged and headed toward the entrance, Sarah slid along the asphalt and then tumbled in a breeze that wasn't quite blowing in the right direction to account for her path. She allowed herself to get hung up on a bush for just a moment, in order to time her approach to the door correctly. As the worker swiped his badge at the door and pushed it open, she broke loose from the vegetation and fluttered across the intervening space, following the man into the interior.

CHAPTER THIRTY-ONE
Sarah and the Secret Base

The area just inside the door was a small security zone barely large enough to hold five or six people standing in an uncomfortably tight cluster. There were no chairs; apparently no one was expected to need to wait here very long. The only features were a trash can with a hinged door in its cover, an inner door with another badge reader beside it, and a window looking into a room with a desk, screens showing views of the parking lot and some interior hallways, and a guard in another uniform.

"Good morning, Master Sergeant Taylor," the guard said, standing and saluting as Sarah scooted into a corner below the window. The guard had "U.S. Air Force" stitched on his uniform shirt above the breast pocket. She assumed the master sergeant's uniform matched, although his coat prevented her from verifying this fact.

The master sergeant Sarah had followed in returned the salute in a perfunctory manner. "Airman," he acknowledged, then jerked a thumb towards the floor. "I'm late for the morning briefing. Take care of that trash."

"Yes, sergeant," the other responded. The master sergeant scanned his badge and disappeared through the door. The guard emerged before it had fully closed, grabbed the bag Sarah was inhabiting, and shoved it in the trash can. Sarah heard him key the door again to return to his desk as she took stock of her new situation.

Enough light leaked in around the openings in the lid for her to make out that her bag rested on top of a sizeable collection of half-empty paper coffee cups and bags from various fast food franchises and donut shops. Apparently, she had come as far as possible with her current cover. She released her hold on the bag and reappeared in her natural astral form, making sure to remain within the confines of the container. This meant her body was occupying much of the same space as the trash, but as she was insubstantial this didn't particularly bother her or disturb the can's contents. The smell was another matter altogether, and gave her an incentive to choose a course of action quickly.

Regis had briefed her on several possible scenarios before she left on her scouting trip, and the likelihood that her litter disguise would not get her very far into the facility had been high on the list. It would have been nice to see more of the rooms and passages near the entrance, but the real area of interest lay below her, where the new construction had been carried out. She sank through the bottom of the container and the floor, reoriented herself so her head faced downwards and began slowly inching downwards through the foundation and ground, angling slightly towards the center of the structure. Her astral form required no air to breathe, but she was in complete darkness. She strained to pick up on any sounds, as this seemed like her best chance to receive a warning when she was about to return to open space.

The staccato tap of footsteps reached her just before her face emerged into a corridor with rough, unfinished walls like a swimmer breaching the surface of a still lake. The hallway was illuminated by bare bulbs in fixtures mounted directly to the ceiling, with exposed cable runs strung between them and fastened every few feet with simple metal strips screwed into place like enormous staples. Master Sergeant Taylor was walking away from her and approaching the door to a conference room. She could see several people seated around a table inside the room through a window to the right of the door. She also noticed a security camera mounted high on one wall, but it was pointed downwards to focus on anyone walking along the hallway. Her position at the ceiling was out of its line of sight.

Sarah pulled her head back up into the ceiling and glided forward until she was above the conference room. This space, at least, had been finished to a greater degree, including the installation of a drop-down ceiling composed of acoustical tiles. Thus, Sarah found herself in a crawlspace looking at the back sides of lighting fixtures and data cable runs. She settled in for a good eavesdropping session as she heard the door open below.

"Good morning, Master Sergeant. Glad you could join us," a gruff voice said.

"Sorry, sir. I had a bit of car trouble this morning. It took a few minutes to arrange for a jump start." Sarah heard the sound of a chair being pulled away from the table and then scooting back into position.

"Hrmph. Well, I guess these things happen. Let's get down to business, then." There was a sound of shuffling papers before the voice continued. "Lieutenant, what's the status of our target?"

A woman's voice responded. "Activity at the school remains normal. As far as we can tell, the staff and students remain unaware that they are under observation."

"And the status of the threat assessment report?"

"Nearly complete, sir. We've catalogued a wide variety of abilities including flight, various forms of energy projection, and force constructs, all of which could have devastating effects in real world encounters. There's at least one speedster in the group, capable of attaining speeds in excess of 200 miles per hour, and one adult capable of at least short range teleportation. And that doesn't even cover all of the students present on the campus."

"Do we know anything about the remaining students?"

343

"No, sir. Our remote observation capabilities only allow us to account for phenomena with fairly obvious effects on the environment. If there are telepaths or others with similarly subtle capabilities present, we might not learn about it until those powers are used against us."

I'm learning so much, thought Sarah. *Like, now I know an astral body can't get chills. If I was hearing this in my physical body, I'd be covered in goose bumps.*

The first voice continued. "And how likely is it that these capabilities will be employed against us?"

The woman's voice replied without hesitation. "At this point, I rate the threat level as low. The gathering of these widely disparate individuals into a group is noteworthy, but there is no indication that they have an agenda against any outside person or group."

"How can you say that after the--" Sarah heard more papers rustling about, "Drafton boy's activities?" a new voice interjected.

"With all due respect, Major, Levi remains an unclassified risk. He may be a fire projector or manipulator, but since we have no witnesses to describe how the house fire began, we can only speculate," the lieutenant replied.

"A house goes up in flames just as a boy from this school for mutant misfits passes by and you're having trouble classifying him?"

"Yes," the lieutenant rejoined, calmly but firmly. "There are at least two possibilities, which speak to two entirely different motivations. He could be, as you suggest, a fire manipulator who knowingly set fire to a house with young children inside. In this case, we would be dealing with a monstrous pyromaniac, and he would pose a clear and present danger."

"And the other possibility?' the gruff voice prompted.

"A precognitive who went to the scene of an imminent house fire intent on saving lives," the woman concluded. "As for the school as

344

a whole, however, neither possibility necessarily affects my overall threat level assessment, since there is no indication that this incident was sanctioned by Mrs. Kilkarni, or anyone else in a position of authority there."

"So your conclusion is that Drafton is best dealt with on an individual basis, should that become necessary?"

"Yes, sir."

"Very well, let's move on to our next item then. Master Sergeant, bring us up to speed on countermeasures."

Countermesures? That sounds ominous.

"Yes, sir," Taylor said. "Well, as I've mentioned before, these new delivery systems are a pain to work with. They're so advanced my crew and I have virtually no useful experience to draw on when it comes time to fix something that's screwed up. The targeting circuitry seems to work just fine, though it's hard to be sure since we don't want to test them while they're still sitting in the launch bay."

"Bottom line, how many units can you give me if we have to launch today?"

Today? That's just hypothetical, right?

"Best guess? forty-eight to fifty-three."

"So about half the fleet?"

"Yes, sir."

"Well, given the experimental nature of the systems, that's not too bad. Hopefully it will never come to deployment..."

Whew! Hypothetical after all.

"Before our timetable calls for it," the voice concluded.

What? He couldn't be saying what I think he just said, Sarah thought, trying desperately to come up with some other way to interpret that statement. *But there isn't any other conclusion that fits. He just said that they're going to attack our school, just as soon as they're ready or feel justified. I've got to get a look at these weapons!*

Leaving the conference behind, Sarah glided forward in the crawlspace. *They couldn't have excavated too big an area,* she reasoned. *Whatever they've got stashed here must be close by.* Within a few yards, she came to a concrete wall that cut off the space she was in from whatever lay beyond. Pausing to take a mental breath she didn't currently need, she eased through the barrier.

Her face emerged into a hangar, or at least that was her first impression. There were work areas marked out in painted lines on a vast expanse of concrete flooring, with work bays and tool chests. The ceiling wasn't as high as she expected for a typical hanger.

But then again, this one is anything but 'typical', isn't it?

On the far side of the hanger, the weapons systems stood in neat rows.

Robots. Why did it have to be robots?

The robots were almost stick figures rendered in metal. They consisted of bare, nine-foot frames designed to provide mobility and mounting points for weapons, plus what looked like jet-powered wing assemblies attached to the spine of the skeletal forms. About half sported what appeared to be conventional guns chain-fed from drums mounted below the shoulder joints. The remainder were outfitted differently, but Sarah couldn't make out details from her current position. She needed to get closer.

She quickly scanned the area, noting several cameras scanning the huge room. Again, they were all focused slightly downwards, leaving the ceiling unguarded. But several people were working on robots away from the main group standing in readiness. *Those they're working on would be the half the fleet that's still not ready for deployment. But the people are the real problem. If any of them look up while I'm trying to cross the room, they'll be sure to see me. Well, if I can't go over or through, I'll just have to go under. There's one of the units with the weird weapon mount close to the side wall. If I time it right, I can come up next to it and get a good look while the camera is on the far end of its scan. Then it's time to clear out of here!*

Suiting actions to thoughts, she withdrew back into the wall and dropped down - right into an open room! Fortunately, this area was just a storage room lined with metal shelving units, and currently unoccupied. For a bonus, the room's contents apparently weren't considered worthy of a dedicated security camera, so she hadn't given herself away by her mistake. Resolving to learn from the near disaster, she reoriented herself head downward and lowered herself through the floor. After traveling for several feet, she concluded that the base had only a single subterranean level and she was below the level of the hangar floor. So she turned herself horizontally and moved to where she thought the robot she wanted to examine was parked and slowly raised her head above the surface.

She had carefully noted the position of the camera that scanned this section of floor from her previous position high on the wall, and sought it out immediately. She was horrified to see it pointing straight at her, and braced for the intruder alert that would bring armed men and women running, but it didn't sound. As the camera rotated away, common sense accounted for the lack of reaction.

Only the top of my head was visible, and unless someone happened to be looking directly at the monitor that camera connects to just as I popped up, chances are they'd overlook me on a casual scan. There's a lot of clutter on the ground here. Still, best to finish what I'm here for and stop tempting fate.

347

She turned her attention to the robot, which was held in a semi-reclined position on some sort of rack, as she moved toward it. Sarah was still intersecting the floor and ground beneath it from the bottom of her rib cage down, presenting as low a profile as she could while still being in a position to see everything of interest.

The first thing she noted up close was that the robot's hands were not designed for manipulation; there were no thumbs at all, and the fingers were nothing more or less than supports for three long, sharp blades, like a mad mechanic's idea of talons. The ten-inch spike projecting from the front of each foot made her doubt the units were programmed for soccer, either. This model featured a futuristic-looking probe sticking out from the chest area on some sort of swivel mount to allow it to orient semi-independently of how the robot faced. Sarah guessed the cables that ran to the rear of the device from some sort of box mounted where a human's intestines would be provided power, which would make the device in the chest some sort of energy projector.

Sarah had allowed herself to become too engrossed in her examination of the automaton. As she concluded her assessment of the thing's likely capabilities, she became aware of footsteps behind her just as someone came around a cabinet, placing her directly in his line of sight.

"What the--," he exclaimed, followed by the sound of something solid dragging across cloth and a *click-clack* Sarah was depressingly sure she knew from a short lifetime of television shows and action movies. "Halt," came the command from behind her. "Hands where I can see them, and turn around slowly."

She glanced over her shoulder as she raised her hands about head high, fingers splayed to show she wasn't holding anything. She found she was looking at a young man of about twenty years who held a pistol leveled at her and looked utterly astounded by the sight of a naked girl half sunk in a concrete slab. "You know, a gentleman would offer a girl a coat to preserve her modesty," she suggested. *Did I really just say that?* she thought in amazement. *I wouldn't have thought I'd be so glib facing someone with a gun pointed at me, but maybe it's because I know it really can't hurt me.*

The young man hesitated only a second before electing to punt this problem to his superiors. Keeping the pistol pointed at Sarah with one hand, he said "Don't move," before removing a radio from his belt and thumbing the switch. "Central, this is Airman Miller. I have a paranormal intrusion in work bay Alpha Charlie Seven. Repeat, paranormal intrusion in Alpha Charlie Seven."

Two seconds later, the alarm Sarah had dreaded earlier sounded in earnest. Shortly after that, a calm female voice cut in, muting the alarm slightly. "Paranormal intrusion detected. Repeat, paranormal intrusion detected. Begin preparations to activate Response Sequence Vulture. Repeat, activate Response Sequence Vulture."

Damn, what do I do now? Sarah thought. *I guess I can let them take me prisoner. It's not like they could do anything to me in my current form, and maybe I can defuse this situation if I can talk to the commander and make him understand we're not a threat.*

So she just stood there as men and women ran to various predetermined points in the hangar, though no one made an immediate effort to reinforce Airman Miller, which struck her as odd. What could be more important than securing the prisoner?

"Uh, any chance of getting that coat?" she finally tossed back over her shoulder, just before the robots standing in formation suddenly shifted into a more upright stance, like soldiers coming to attention, as their eyes lit up. As the front rank took an initial step forward in perfect unison, a series of small explosions sounded from the roof at the end of the hangar the mechanized walkers faced. Supports gave way and the ceiling came crashing down onto the floor, followed by massive amounts of sand and even some desert bushes.

At first, Sarah had the wild thought that her friends had somehow learned of her discovery and were coming to rescue her. *But that's silly. Only Team Blue knows I'm here, and I don't really need saving, anyway.* But as the torrent of dirt and vegetation slowed to a trickle, revealing a perfectly rectangular opening to the sky, the real purpose of the collapse became clear. The front rank of robots' jet packs came to sudden, roaring life and lifted them through the opening, followed a handful of seconds later by the next rank, which had been following in their wake with mechanically perfect timing and precision.

Great galloping goose eggs! she thought in dismay. *They're launching their attack on the school and no one knows it's coming! This is all my fault!*

CHAPTER THIRTY-TWO
The Attack

"So this is your master defensive plan?" Miranda asked disbelievingly. "You're going to take long walks around the campus?" The girls were walking near the hedge that lead to the arena where Team Red had fought.

"Don't forget the pep rallies for the birds," Ches chided. "That's a key element, you know. They totally set this apart from a pathetic and doomed attempt at establishing a healthier lifestyle."

Alice felt her cheeks coloring at her friends' ribbing. "All right, I know it's not much, but I've got to do something! Mrs. Kilkarni said to trust that my powers would bring me and my family back together when the time was right. Well, how can they if I don't give them room to operate?"

Miranda placed a hand on her shoulder and gave her a brief squeeze of support. "Sorry. I'd probably be a basket case if it was my mom that had gone missing. If this helps you deal, I'm all for it. I don't even mind the long boring walks that much."

At that moment, they all heard an exuberant "Yahoooo!" from overhead as Min Ki came bounding over the top of the hedge, the legs of his armor that had propelled his leap already retracting as he reached the apex of his flight. It was only then that everyone realized he was on a collision course with Miranda. Alice was certain he had too much speed and momentum to recover, but at the last possible moment an arm projected into the ground in front of her friend, giving the boy an abrupt upward boost. He cleared Miranda by inches and hit the ground in an awkward sprawl, then tumbled a good fifteen yards further before coming to rest on his back. The armor winked out of existence.

"Still bored?" Ches inquired, but Miranda and Alice were already running towards Min Ki to check his condition. Ches sighed as he followed slowly. "Why do I bother?"

Min Ki raised his head slightly as they approached. "Everyone all right?" he asked.

"Yeah," Miranda said. "How are you?"

Min Ki frowned. "I must have hit my head on something. I could have sworn there were only two of you a second ago. But now I'm seeing Sarah, and she's naked. That can't be right."

The others all looked behind them, where Min Ki was focused, and discovered that Sarah was indeed there, just as Min Ki had described. She literally flew at them, her feet a good foot off the ground.

"Hey guys, guess what? I can teleport this way! I was thinking, 'I really need to be back at the school', and here I am. Good thing too!"

"Why's that?" Alice asked blankly.

"We're about to be attacked by giant robots!" Sarah said, pointing to the East. "Come on, we've got to warn the others and find some cover!"

Min Ki's face lit up like a toddler's at Christmas and he scrambled to his feet. "A robot attack? Seriously? Cool! How soon?"

The entire group was moving swiftly towards the quad now, and Sarah pointed to a rank of flying silver forms that swept up into the air as they topped a rise in the desert floor about a quarter mile out from the school grounds. They quickly reoriented and started a controlled, yet swift descent obviously intended to leave them on their feet at the edge of the lawn. "About thirty seconds. Damn, they're quick. We haven't managed to warn anyone else yet, and we're stuck in the open!"

Tweedledum and Tweedledee suddenly appeared next to a heavy wooden picnic table set by the side of the path. They quickly started tipping it onto its side, presenting the top to the robots' landing area.

"Never fear, fair maidens, we shall defend thee!" Tweedledum shouted happily.

"Certes! Take refuge in our impenetrable fortress while we teach yon fools a lesson!" Tweedledee cried.

"It's better than nothing!" Alice said, and hastily scrambled behind the makeshift shield with Miranda and Sarah. Min Ki simply armored up again and stepped out in front of the table as the first contingent of robots came crashing to the ground, balanced perfectly in a crouch on two feet and the back of one hand. As they straightened up, explosive bolts released the wing assemblies, which dropped to the ground. The robots stepped forward, oriented on Min Ki and the Tweedles, and bullets started stitching out a trace on the ground that raced at the three targets.

Min Ki ran forward, heedless of the bullets. His confidence proved well founded, as the projectiles glanced harmlessly off his psychic protection. He got within range of the enemy just as the second wave of robots landed. As his armor's arm extended a full twenty yards in less than a heartbeat, his fist connected solidly with one of the lead construct's head. He knocked it off its shoulders in a shower of sparks, and it fell forward, deprived of its control functions.

Meanwhile, the Tweedles were targeted by several of the other mechanical forms. Alice screamed as she saw their bodies shake in response to the first impacts. They might actually be nothing more than psychic projections, but she still considered them as something closer to pesky, mischievous little brothers. But her scream cut off as she realized they appeared unhurt. Then she heard the sound of bullets striking metal. She risked a quick look over the top of the table and saw the sparks caused by projectiles striking the bodies of the robots firing on the boys. She ducked back down as several shots impacted in the wood of the tabletop.

Miranda looked at Alice in astonishment. "Why didn't you tell me they were bulletproof?"

"You think I tested them to find out? They're actually reflecting the bullets back at their opponents!" Switching her attention to the Tweedles, she waved them forward. "What are you waiting for? Go have fun!"

The Tweedles needed no further urging. They drew their wooden swords and charged ahead. The swords were shot to kindling before they had gone a dozen paces, but neither seemed to care, or even notice. And the reflected bullets were having a cumulative effect on several of their foes, damaging joints and wiping out sensor arrays in the heads.

Ches was getting in on the action, too. He teleported onto the shoulder of one of the blaster-equipped units and swiped his tail across its eye sensors. The robot turned to the side suddenly to assess this new threat in its environment, but the suddenness of the move brought the blaster to bear on its neighbor, and it fired before its systems could compensate for the change in facing. The blast twisted the arm of the robot it hit, immobilizing it. Ches teleported away to another robot's back just as a robot in the rank behind opened fire on his former position; bullets shredded the first robot's head, putting it out of commission.

Sarah suddenly shook her head as if waking from a bad dream. "What am I doing? We've got to warn the others! I'll try the PA system in the office!" A second later she had vanished.

By now, several ranks of robots had landed, and Min Ki was in danger of getting swarmed by their numbers. He was effectively in hand-to-hand combat now, and unable to carefully aim his powered punches. Where he made contact, he left dents and broken components, and even managed to drive individual robots back a step or two. But for every one he damaged, another stepped up to take its place. What was worse, the robots armed with the blasters were powerful enough to punch through his defenses, and even the blades on the ends of the fingers had enough force behind them to leave shallow cuts on his arms and chest. Alice thought the attacks were doing relatively little damage, but how long could Min Ki withstand a constant barrage? He was being driven back, and other robots were about to encircle him.

"Hatter!" she called. "Give Min Ki a dose of hyper time."

Hatter popped in beside her, standing fully erect and oblivious to the chaos all about. He focused on the armored lad for a second, fiddling with his watch. Just as Min Ki started moving quicker in relation to the robots, one of the units locked on to Hatter and hit him with a blaster bolt in the center of his chest. He wound up splayed on his back several feet away.

"Hatter," Alice called, "are you okay?"

He groaned in reply. "All things considered, I'd prefer to be in the Queen's croquet grounds."

Sarah reappeared beside Alice and Miranda. "We should have help soon. I sure surprised Ms. Wisson, though. Stay here; it looks like Min Ki could use some help."

Sarah ran through the table, right through the midst of the battle, and stopped by the side of one of the robots that had lost its head. Alice risked another look and saw her reach out and touch the metal frame, only to disappear a moment later. Then the robot got up and started attacking its fellows, striking with its talons and kicking with the foot spikes. She was forced to return to cover before she could assess the effectiveness of Sarah's attacks.

Light, sound and movement from the direction of the school buildings drew Alice's attention. The cavalry was coming, and not a moment too soon, as the last of the robots landed and dropped their wing assemblies. Julio was leading the charge, running faster than Alice had ever seen him run before. His arms pumped in time with his rhythm, the metal tonfas flashing as they caught the sunlight. He targeted the units in the rear, striking out at knee joints as he sped by. Wherever he struck, joints jammed or shattered altogether. Several robots attempted to orient on him to fire with blasters or bullets, but he outpaced their targeting systems easily.

The buzz of Scott's flight power heralded his arrival, and he began targeting heads and the blaster assemblies, which seemed particularly vulnerable to his attacks. He managed to stay ahead of the invaders for several seconds, dodging about and suddenly hovering to launch targeted attacks. He put three robots down with head shots and had ruined the blasters on four more before his luck ran out. As he lined up another shot, a blaster from another robot caught him in the side. The roar of his flight power cut out instantly, but he didn't drop. The force of the blast sent him arcing through the air to crash into the upper portion of the nearby hedge wall. The force of the impact produced a hole that failed to punch completely through the hedge, leaving Scott supported in a hollow twelve feet off the ground. Only his legs remained visible, twitching feebly.

Kasie arrived shortly after Scott, and Alice stared at her in amazement. She was like a kid's cartoon come to life. She was surrounded by a yellow aura as she flew effortlessly through the air, and her left side was protected by a translucent green shield that seemed to emanate from the emerald on her bracelet. It shrugged off blasters and bullets alike as she approached the scene of battle.

Kasie held up her right arm before her, elbow bent with her hand flat and parallel to the ground. As Alice watched, light forms rose from the star sapphires in the ring she wore. As they grew to the size of dinner plates, Alice recognized them as six-armed stars from the gemstones, floating free and bright enough to pick out easily. Kasie swiftly straightened her arm, and the stars flew like Constance's shuriken. Alice gasped as they struck three different targets. The spikes on the stars looked insubstantial, but their effect belied the appearance, as one jammed the ammunition feed on a robot with standard guns, another rendered a blaster assembly inert, and the last punctured a head and dropped a robot to the ground.

Whoever said diamonds are a girl's best friend never saw Kasie in action, Alice thought. *Though come to think of it, I don't know what she can do with those, do I?*

By now, almost half of the invading machines were down for the count, and several of the remaining ones showed significant damage. Enough targets were actively engaging the robots that none seemed inclined to target Alice anymore, so she was able to observe things more openly, though she remained behind the table. The arrival of Scott and Kasie had allowed Min Ki to retreat sufficiently to keep from being surrounded and completely overwhelmed, but he continued to fight. As Alice watched, he looped one arm several times around a robot's leg and pulled, upsetting its balance and bringing it down, at least temporarily.

One of the Tweedles took a hit from a blaster, and while it shredded clothing, it did not seem to cause him much discomfort. Alice did notice that it did not reflect back on the source, however.

Autumn came running from up to the scene. Alice was surprised that she had responded to the call. Sure, as a swimmer she was very fit; she noted that other girl didn't seem particularly winded, which would definitely not have been the case if Alice had had to cover that distance quickly. But what did she plan to do against robots?

357

The answer came quickly, as Autumn raised her hands and sent a jet of water several inches across and backed by incredible force at a group of robots still trying to target students with ranged attacks. Most were victims of Julio's strafing runs, and therefore had severely limited mobility, so guns and blasters were about all they could bring to bear unless someone ventured too close. The high pressure water attack was devastating. The sheer force was enough to knock most of them over, hampered as they were. But the water also forced itself into electrical systems, shorting out the robots within moments.

Ches popped up next to Miranda and Alice, thoroughly soaked and looking indignant. "She could have warned us," he said snippily.

Alice gave him a sympathetic pat on the head, but the battle was winding down and she had more urgent concerns. As the others mopped up the remaining automatons, Alice popped a bit of candy in her mouth and ran to the hedge even as her form grew to fifteen feet. She reached Scott and peered anxiously into the hole in the vegetation. "Are you all right?" she asked.

Scott groaned. "I think that blast fractured a few ribs," he gasped. "Getting down from here is not going to be fun."

"Be still; I'll get you some help," Alice replied. She looked back over her shoulder and waved for attention. "Kasie, Scott could use some healing over here."

She drifted over, still sporting her cheery yellow glow, and took in the scene. "How bad is he?"

"Several broken ribs, at least," Alice replied.

"Okay, we're going to have to be careful, then. Step back."

Alice moved away from the hedge as Kasie raised her left hand, which bore her amethyst ring. A purple beam shot out of the gemstone and encircled Scott, lifting him gently from the hedge so that

Kasie could lower him to the ground. She landed next to him, and soon the white glow Alice had come to associate with Kasie's healing power played over Scott's side.

Once she was done with Scott, Kasie turned her attention to Min Ki, who bore several bruises and shallow lacerations from his scuffle with the robots. As he waited for her to finish, he looked at the sole invader remaining upright. "So how long are you going to animate that thing?" he asked.

"Until I can drop it in private," Sarah replied, her voice coming from the space where the robot's head once sat. "The emergency is over, so I'd just as soon not flash anyone else, thank you very much."

"Damn," Min Ki said regretfully, though his grin and a wink conveyed more good-natured teasing than anything else.

"Hey, I thought you were with me," Miranda objected. "Remember Halloween?"

"Forget it," Autumn advised. "He's a teenage boy."

"Oh, no," Miranda countered. "Give him that much slack now and by twenty he'll be a lost cause. I'm drawing the line in the sand, right here, right now. Understood?" She glared at her boyfriend, who nodded nervously.

"Well, good luck with that," Alice said. "I think you're overlooking the bigger problem, though."

Miranda looked confused. "What's that?"

"You don't find it the tiniest bit disturbing that, confronted with a naked girl and the prospect of fighting robots, he was more excited about the robots?"

"I'm standing right here, you know," Min Ki interjected.

"Don't be silly, Alice. When is he going to get another shot at robots? A girl, on the other hand..." Miranda's voice trailed off as a thoughtful frown replaced the airy, unconcerned expression on her face. "Hmm, you know, you may have something there."

"Hey!"

"Face it, girl, you've fallen for a budding workaholic," Alice said.

"Well excuse me for saving your lives," Min Ki said, taking Miranda by the arm and leading her away. "Come on, Miranda; just ignore Ms. Bad Influence."

Miranda giggled in spite of herself, glancing over her shoulder at Alice as she let herself be lead away. "He's got you there," she said cheerfully.

"So what do we do now?" Autumn asked, watching the couple make their way toward the school.

"Head back inside and regroup," Sarah said. "I've got some things to tell you all, and you're not going to like them."

CHAPTER THIRTY-THREE
A Bug's Tale

"I say we go knock some heads together," Kip exclaimed angrily.

"Seriously? That's your answer?" Miranda scoffed. "You're attacked once and you're ready to go all Brotherhood of Evil Mutants on their butts?"

"Why not?" Levi shot back. "It sounds like they've already decided how they feel about us. That's 'us' as in 'everyone sitting around this table except you', by the way. What makes you think you even get a vote on this?"

"She gets to express her opinion because I say so," Alice replied. "She's my best friend, and what affects me affects her."

"Besides," Sarah cut in, "you missed the point where the officer in charge of the threat assessment argued against classifying us as a risk. Not everyone over there is convinced we're the enemy."

"Sounds like it's a minority opinion, though," said Regis. "She didn't manage to prevent the attack."

"It's still an opening," Autumn argued. "I'm not ready to declare war on the government until there's no other option. Besides, we don't know how high this operation goes. I can't believe they're really authorized to attack civilians like this."

"If they're really part of a rogue op, all the more reason to go and show them how big a mistake they've made," Kip said. "If Sarah's report is accurate, they've thrown everything they had ready at us; let's not give them a chance to fix the rest."

Alice found her attention drifting from the debate that had been dragging on for almost half an hour now. It wasn't that she didn't find the topic compelling, but there was something about the attack that bothered her, apart from the fact that it had occurred at all. She picked up her phone from the tabletop in front of her and flipped through the photos she had taken of the robots, looking for something to scratch the mental itch that wasn't letting her concentrate. She settled on one she had snapped of the headless robot Sarah had animated, staring at the claws and the blaster assembly in its chest. *What am I not seeing here?* she thought.

She suddenly became aware that the room had grown very quiet. She glanced up from the phone, looking to her right, then left, to discover everyone at the table was staring at her.   "What?"   she asked.

"Are you in, or out?" Levi asked.

"In or out of what?"

"Girl, where have you been?" Levi slumped back in his chair in exasperation. "I can't work with her."

Alice looked to Scott, still puzzled, and now with spots of color rising on her face. "Sorry, I must have zoned out for a minute."

"Try fifteen," Scott said. "We decided to send a delegation to the secret base to see if we can bring this misunderstanding to a peaceful conclusion. The question is, do you want to come?"

"Isn't that, you know, dangerous? Just dropping in unannounced on a bunch of nervous military types with lots of guns at their disposal?"

362

"That's what I said," Miranda mumbled, but loud enough for everyone present to hear. She had physically withdrawn from the table; her chair was pushed back and her arms were crossed over her chest.

Scott shrugged. "Most of us who want to go think we have abilities that will keep us from getting hurt."

Alice looked at him in shock. "Us? You're going on this stupid... What makes you think you won't get hurt? You're not bulletproof."

"I can help if things get dicey, and I trust my teammates to keep me safe. Or patch me up, at least."

Alice shook her head. "I wish you'd reconsider." Addressing Levi, she said, "I'm out."

Levi smirked at Kip. "Told you Miss Fairy Tales would chicken out."

Alice scowled. "Let me guess, our diplomatic experts," she gestured at Kip and Levi, "came up with this idea and sold the rest of you on this madness? It'll be a blood bath."

"Not everyone," Autumn said. "Most of us don't like the idea. Only a few are going."

"Who?" Alice asked. Min Ki, Constance, and Kasie raised their hands in addition to the three who had already expressed their intentions. *Constance might have a chance at talking to whoever's in charge over there without it ending in violence. But only if Kip and Levi aren't there to provoke the other side.* Aloud, she asked, "Has anyone asked Mrs. Kilkarni about this? It's her school, after all."

"She's not here," Julianna reminded her. "She went to check out a lead on another potential student."

"Enough talk," Kip stated. "The longer we wait, the more they're going to dig in. Let's go."

363

The half dozen who committed to the trip got up from the table, along with several others. Alice got up as well, intent on trying a last minute plea to keep Scott from going. As she and Scott turned from the table, a cockroach scurried across the floor towards them, then suddenly stopped as their movement registered. Scott raised a foot to crush it, but Alice suddenly stumbled into him, shifting his balance and ruining his aim. The cockroach scurried under a heavy bookcase before anyone else could react.

"What was that for?" Scott asked.

"Sorry, my leg was numb after sitting there for so long. I lost my balance," Alice explained. Switching the topic of conversation, she said "Please, Scott, don't go over there. They're scared; there's no way they're going to be reasonable."

"All the more reason for me to be there to support the others," Scott replied. "We've got to make the effort; otherwise things are just going to spiral out of control. Better to at least try to calm the waters before someone really gets hurt."

Alice snorted in frustration, then wrapped her arms around Scott and gave him a deep kiss. "You're an idiot," she said when they finally surfaced. "Try to at least be a careful one. I won't forgive you if you don't come back."

"You worry too much," Scott said. He gave her another quick kiss, then broke away from her and left with the other members of the away team.

Most of the other students were drifting away as well, Julianna grabbed Julio gently by the shoulder before he could leave. "Are you sure you don't want to go with the rest of Team Red?" she asked.

"I never wanted to come to this school in the first place," Julio said. "There's no way in hell I'm fighting for it. If they attack again,

I'll already be packed up. I'll be over the horizon before the first shot is fired." He quickly passed through the doorway and out of sight.

Miranda stepped up beside Alice. "You want to go drown our sorrows in mint chocolate chip ice cream until the men folk get back?"

Alice winced inwardly. Miranda was trying to play it lightheartedly, but years of friendship told her that she was actually as scared for Min Ki as she was for Scott. But she couldn't afford to lose focus right now. So she turned her attention to her phone again, pulling up the picture of the robot once more. "Maybe I'll join you in a bit. Something's not right here, and I think I've almost coaxed it to the surface. I just want to be alone for now, okay?"

Miranda was obviously disappointed, but accepted her explanation with as much grace as she could. She and Sarah left together, probably heading for the student kitchen on their way to one of their rooms. When they left, Alice found herself alone in the room.

She forced herself to study her phone for a full minute after they left, before suddenly crossing to the doorway. She quickly checked that no one was in sight in either direction before she pulled her head back in and closed the door. Then she sat down on the floor in front of the bookcase.

"It's okay, you can come out now. Everyone else is gone," she said.

The cockroach appeared below the bottom shelf, cautiously sensing the room before finally scurrying across the floor and coming to rest in front of Alice.

"Now then," she said, "what's this news about Oglethorpe?"

♠ ♣ ♥ ♦

Twenty minutes later, Alice was approaching the top landing on the staircase in the administrative building. The area wasn't exactly off limits to students, in the sense that they had not been told 'don't go there', but it was definitely off the beaten track. Alice had had no more inclination to go there than the cafeteria's receiving dock. If anyone had asked, she would have assumed it served some boring, mundane function for the school, though in truth she had never given it any thought whatsoever. Not until Rizzo the cockroach reported that Oglethorpe had been there.

It seemed unbelievable that Oglethorpe had found the school at all. Yet Rizzo had been quite confident in his report. He had observed the sketch on the table from his vantage point in a high cupboard in the student kitchen while Alice had explained her plan to Miranda and Scott. *And isn't it just a little freaky that my ability affected him with no conscious intent on my part?* Alice thought. *It must be getting more powerful, or maybe bugs are just easier to influence. Either way, it turned him into an Oglethorpe-seeking drone, scouring all of the buildings in the school until he found him.*

Alice glanced up above the door to the main area. A security camera stared back at her. That, at least, seemed to suggest there might be something beyond the door worth protecting, and therefore something that might attract Oglethorpe's attention. But what would draw his attention away from the smorgasbord of powers on display elsewhere in the school? Alice grabbed the doorknob to find out.

Only to discover the door was locked. Fortunately, the door was not flush with the floor; a gap at the bottom let light leak through from the area beyond. Alice thought the gap was wide enough to be useful.

She took a sip of water from the bottle she had brought with her, and shrank to her smallest size. She laid down and eased under the door, then fought to force her way through a tight carpet weave on the other side, but eventually she stood up on the far side of the barrier.

As she ate a bit of candy to return to her normal size, she tried the door again. It opened easily from this side. She secured a bit of duct tape from a roll from her fanny pack over the latch to keep it from locking again, in case she had to come back. Then she examined her new surroundings.

At first, nothing looked interesting enough to attract Oglethorpe's attention. In fact, the only feature was an elevator to her left at the end of a short corridor, with the opening from another hallway leading straight ahead for someone exiting the lift. Alice walked to the corner and looked down the passage.

Now this is more like it, she thought. The new hallway ended in a security door with a control panel on the wall to the right. It would require a code entered on a keypad to get through the door. As Alice approached, she noted that her previous trick wouldn't work this time. The door was not simply flush with the floor, it was actually set down into it. She decided that the door probably slid into one wall to allow passage to whatever lay beyond.

Okay, so the presence of something valuable enough to be worth stealing is confirmed. The only question is, did Oglethorpe get what he came for? If he needs to see the area he teleports to, this might keep him out. Of course, he could probably knock it down, but maybe he wants to keep his presence a secret.

After mulling the situation over for a bit, she admitted defeat. She couldn't get beyond this point, and there were too many unknowns for her to accurately guess whether her foe had achieved his objective. She would just have to inform Mrs. Kilkarni that there was a good chance they had been found, and let her determine the best course of action from here. She just hoped the administrator returned soon. Alice felt convinced that time was precious now.

As she headed back to the stairwell, Alice tried to come up with some way of effectively dealing with Oglethorpe if he decided to attack openly. Surely with all the abilities collected here, they could come up with something. They just needed to sit down together and compare notes. Constance had her awesome martial arts and exploding, guided shuriken, Kasie had her sapphire stars (plus whatever she could do with diamonds?), Scott had his sonic blasts. Even Ms. Teresi could help with her armor and...

Alice stopped cold on the landing beneath the security camera. She pulled out her phone, quickly located the picture of Sarah animating the robot, and stared at the weapon mounted in the mechanical chest.

I am so dense! I didn't see it because of the difference in sizes, but that blast projector is the same. I've seen that shape before. On the arm of LaRonda's armor!

CHAPTER THIRTY-FOUR
An Overdue Confrontation

Alice hurried to Scott's room and searched through his desk drawers until she found his key card for accessing Ms. Teresi's lab. She couldn't start throwing around accusations without some sort of proof. The first step would be to get a closer look at her armor and make sure that she was remembering the energy projector accurately. A part of her hoped she was wrong, and that she'd see differences in design once she had a chance to compare the assemblies. After all, she had been hurt, and her mind focused on other things, the night she actually saw her armor.

Even if they do look the same, that still might not mean anything. Maybe it's a case of form following function - the projectors might have to look the same in order to work. The real smoking gun would be to find emails or other communications between LaRonda and the Air Force or someone discussing the sale of the technology.

Alice slipped the card into her fanny pack and opened the door cautiously. No one was in sight, but she heard the sound of excited voices. She followed it to the Rec Room, where most of the other students had gathered. The away team had returned, and no one looked any the worse for having made the trip. Alice allowed herself to relax slightly once she confirmed that Scott and Min Ki, specifically, were still healthy and whole.

She quickly ran to Scott to give him a hug and a quick kiss. "You're back so soon! What happened?"

"Nothing," Scott replied. "The entire base was trashed and empty. They must have started in on some sort of bug out procedure as soon as they launched the attack. The other robots and all the electronics in the base were destroyed with some sort of controlled explosives, and it looks like any papers were shredded, then fed right into an incinerator. We couldn't find anything we could use to prove who had been there."

"So where does that leave us?" Alice asked.

"Flapping in the breeze, waiting for the next attack," Levi said. "There's no way to tell when or where it'll come from, but we're sure on someone's list."

"You said it," Kip affirmed.

"Well, maybe Mrs. Kilkarni will have some idea how to handle it once she learns about the attack," Sarah said. She was staying close to her brother and frequently reaching out to touch him, as if she needed assurance he was really there. Across the room, Alice noted Miranda was seeking similar reassurance from Min Ki.

There didn't seem to be much more to say about the problem for the moment. Alice considered talking to Scott privately to share her suspicions about LaRonda, but decided against it. He would still have to work with the teacher if she was innocent, and by proceeding alone, Alice would leave him able to claim ignorance about her plans. Besides, her abilities provided her with her own back up for dangerous situations.

Alice's emotional side urged her to head straight to the lab right now and find the armor. But her rational side argued that the search would yield more fruit with less risk if she went at night, when there was less chance of encountering Ms. Teresi. Besides, the realization that someone in the school might be working for Oglethorpe had frightened her, and she felt the need for friends around her. She couldn't seek their reassurance directly without letting them know about her plans for the evening, but she could take comfort in their presence and implied support. They all felt the weight of impending danger following the morning's assault.

"Come on," Kip said to Levi, heading for the door. "Let's put our heads together and come up with an appropriate greeting for our next batch of visitors,"

"Straight up," Levi said, joining his friend.

A few seconds after they left, Min Ki walked over with Miranda. "We shouldn't allow ourselves to be taken by surprise again," he said to Scott. "I think a watch is in order."

"What do you have in mind?" Scott replied.

"I'm going to go hang out on top of the Administration Building for a while. I'll scan the area regularly and try to give us warning if there's any sign of another attack starting. I can call the office so Ms. Wisson can use the PA again."

Scott nodded. "Okay, I'll come spell you in a couple of hours. I doubt they're ready for a follow up so soon, but better safe than sorry."

Miranda gave Alice a quick hug. "I'm going to go keep Min Ki company," she said.

"Don't distract him too much," Alice teased, but her voice was flat with worry.

Miranda stuck her tongue out at her. "Did you figure out what was bothering you earlier?"

"Yeah, I'll fill you in later, though. You holding up all right?"

"As well as can be expected, I guess." Miranda started to follow after Min Ki, but turned back long enough to say, "I guess maybe you were right about the Wonderland Effect, after all. I sure feel like I've been stuffed down a rabbit hole." With a playful wink, she was gone.

Alice and Scott sat down on a sofa, legs not touching, but holding hands. Sarah perched on a stool nearby. The TV was on, but the sound was turned way down, and no one was watching it. Alice glanced around the room at the other students and noted the same brooding expression on every face. Andrew sat in a chair by the window, absently flipping a coin back and forth across the backs of his fingers, and occasionally making it disappear altogether. Esme, stripped of her glamour, played listlessly at darts with Autumn. Both girls repeatedly tossed darts at the board and then retrieved them, mechanically going through the motions without seeming to care about anything as ephemeral as a score. Esme's attention frequently wandered to the coin dancing on Andrew's hand, however. Other students stared into space or flipped through books or magazines without any apparent interest.

"Kind of weird no one else noticed the attack, don't you think?" Scott asked after a couple of minutes.

"Not really," Sarah responded. "From launch to the end of the fight, the whole thing only took a few minutes. Plus, we're well outside the developed part of town, the better to play with powers without attracting attention, and the base is even further out. There's nothing between us and it but a couple more miles of empty desert. At most, someone in town might have heard something like distant jet engines."

"We should probably clean up the battle site in case someone does come by, though," Alice said.

This proved to be relatively easy. They enlisted Kasie's help. Alice used her powers to shrink the robots to a tenth of their initial size, then Kasie used her amethyst to pick up the pile of scrap metal and dump it in one of the pits in the combat arena. Then she scooped up enough sand to fill in all of the pits, so that the symmetry of the layout didn't point out where something of interest might lie.

After that, the afternoon passed in a dull haze composed of equal parts boredom and fear. When Scott went to relieve Min Ki, Alice had finally had enough and returned to her room with Sarah. But after a few minutes, Sarah got up and headed for the door.

"I can't just sit here. I've got to do something to work off some energy or I'll burst," she complained. "I'm going to go for a bike ride. Want to come?"

Alice declined; physical exertion had never been one of her favored coping mechanisms. So she spent the remainder of the day fruitlessly fretting over her plans for that night. She went to dinner when it was time, although she had no appetite and scarcely touched her food. In this, she was not alone. Soon afterward, she plead mental exhaustion and went to bed. Surprisingly, she actually did fall asleep.

♠　♣　♥　♦

The alarm on her phone, which Alice had tucked under her pillow to muffle the sound, woke her up at 11:45. She quickly silenced it and glanced over at Sarah's bed. She detected no movement, and decided that Sarah was either so deeply asleep she hadn't noticed the brief disturbance, or she was out and about somewhere. Either option suited her just fine.

Alice got out of bed and quickly dressed in the dark, then eased out of the room and shut the door softly behind her. Ches and Hatter appeared at her side as she headed for the lab.

"So, do you have an actual plan?" Ches asked.

"Maybe we'll find a signed confession sitting out on a work bench," Hatter suggested.

"Everybody's a critic," Alice complained. "Actually, I don't have a fully formed plan, but we've got to start somewhere. I'd like to get a look at her armor, of course. After that, we'll just have to see what we can find. Maybe there will be something suggestive we can challenge her with, assuming she actually is guilty. We won't know until we get there."

373

They made the rest of the journey in silence, and arrived at the lab door without incident. Alice swiped the badge over the reader by the door and cautiously pulled it open. The interior was dimly lit by a single fluorescent tube mounted above a work bench. Nothing moved in the relative gloom.

"Okay, looks like we're in luck," Alice whispered. "Ms. Teresi's not here, so spread out and -- YAAAHH!" She screamed as every light in the room came on simultaneously as she stepped over the threshold. She looked wildly around, expecting to see LaRonda leveling some sort of death ray at her, but there was no one else in the room.

Hatter sauntered towards a computer sitting on a desk across the room. "Motion sensor," he observed calmly. "Ms. Teresi doesn't care to waste effort on trivial things like flipping a light switch."

"Motion sensor; yeah, I knew that," Alice said, closing her eyes as she willed her heart to stop trying to escape from her chest. "Okay, anyone see the armor?"

"Negative," Ches said, "but this looks interesting. What do you suppose it does?" He was circling the three-foot sphere resting on its support platform in the middle of the room.

"Probably the force field generator Scott told me about when I first got to Prometheus," Alice answered. "Pretty cool, but not helpful, since none of the robots were equipped with anything like that. Keep looking."

Hatter straightened up from the computer. "Well, this difference engine is a bust. It wants a password, but I can't figure it out. I tried 'teatime', 'raspberry scones' and 'oolong', but it didn't like any of them."

"Check under the keyboard," Alice suggested as she looked beyond equipment racks into other parts of the lab. As near as she could figure, the lab was one large room divided unevenly into six or seven ad

374

hoc work areas by shelving units and random clutter that almost seemed to have sprung up naturally at a distance around each project, like weird tech fairy rings. There was no sign of the armor, however.

After a brief pause, Alice heard the click of the keyboard being used again, and Hatter grunted. "What the heck is a Heterodyne?"

"I haven't got a clue," Alice responded.

"Well, it got us in, anyway. What do you want to look for?" Hatter asked.

Alice hurried over to the computer and gently displaced Hatter so she could manipulate the mouse and keyboard. "Here, let me," she said. She opened the email program as well as a file browser and spent several minutes perusing their contents.

"Well, I don't know whether to be happy or sad. There's nothing here that--"

The sound of high-power circuitry coming on line interrupted her, just before she heard Ms. Teresi's voice behind her. "If you're looking for the answers to next Friday's quiz, I haven't written it yet," she said.

"Oh, there's the armor," Ches observed, looking in LaRonda's direction.

"Yay?" Alice offered as a sick sensation settled in her belly.

"Miss Littleton, would you care to explain yourself?"

Alice swiveled around in the office chair slowly to face the instructor, who stepped out of an elevator in the back wall; the door had opened silently behind Alice as she studied the computer screen. LaRonda was wearing everything except the helmet for her armor, so Alice could see the angry scowl focused on her. One of LaRonda's arms was extended so the blaster assembly on the arm pointed directly at the chair she occupied. *And it looks just like the ones on the robots,* Alice noted.

"Well, you see, I'm, uh, looking for... Ah, damn, you were right. I was looking for the test answers. I'm so embarrassed," she said, playing the busted teen miscreant for all she was worth. "Uhm, sorry?"

LaRonda just stared at her for several seconds before shaking her head. "No, that's not it. Who sent you?"

Alice looked at her blankly. "Uh, what?"

"Don't play innocent with me. Someone sent you here to steal my inventions, didn't they? Not that most of them could be reproduced by conventional manufacturing methods, but there's still companies out there that would love to reverse engineer my devices to better direct their research efforts. So which one got to you?"

Alice gulped. If LaRonda thought she was after her designs, she was treading on dangerous ground. Alice was certain that the mad scientist would fight to protect them with all the fervor of a wild animal protecting its young. She made a spur of the moment decision to come clean.

"None of them. After the robot attack today, I just thought maybe you had something to do with it. I was looking for evidence, but I can see that I was wrong now, and I'm really sorry."

Ms. Teresi scowled at her. "What nonsense are you spouting off? I'm warning you, girl, I'm about to lose my patience. Now who sent you?"

Alice was shocked. How could Ms. Teresi be unaware of the attack? No one in the dining room had talked about anything else that night. But as she thought back on dinner, she realized she didn't remember seeing the science teacher there. With Mrs. Kilkarni away, LaRonda must have taken advantage to spend more time in her lab and gotten distracted by her latest project.

376

"You've been in your lab all day, haven't you?" she asked.

"Yeah, so what of it?"

"Well, while you were working down here, the Air Force attacked the school with about fifty robots they were hiding in a secret base just east of here. Several of them were armed with blasters similar to the ones on your armor, so I came to check it out." LaRonda was looking even more angry, prompting Alice to hold up her hands in a calming gesture as she blurted, "Look, I have proof!"

"Proof?"

"Yes," Alice said as she pulled out her phone. "Look, I took pictures after the attack. See this one? It has a blaster mounted in its chest, see?" She held out her phone, displaying the picture of Sarah's robot.

LaRonda took the phone, her skepticism plain to see. But when she got a good look at the image, her expression changed to shock. She swiped at the screen, looking at the other pictures Alice had taken. As she viewed more pictures, her eyelids started twitching. She swiped back to the first image, and the whole right side of her face started trembling.

"Watch out, she's gonna blow!" Ches warned in an urgent undertone. Alice nodded, but didn't dare move; she didn't want to draw attention to herself.

The next moment, the phone fell from LaRonda's hand as she clutched at her head and shrieked in pain. The screen cracked as it hit the floor, then LaRonda's armored knee crushed it as she collapsed on top of it. She shrieked again, pulling at her dreadlocks as if she wanted to pull them out by their roots. Alice and her companions exchanged glances, uncertain what to do. Then, with a final cry of anguish, LaRonda fell forward, striking her head on the concrete floor, and then sprawled loose-limbed. As her cries ceased, the room became still enough for Alice to hear the faint hum from the lighting fixtures.

"The lady doesn't seem to care for robots," Hatter observed. "I wonder how she'd react to a dressmaker's dummy?"

Alice dove forward out of the chair and pulled on LaRonda's shoulder, but was unable to budge her due to the weight of the metal encasing her. "Help me!" she snapped at Hatter, who hastened to do her bidding. Even Ches helped once they had raised her up a bit, getting under her with his head, then shoulder. Finally, they succeeded in rolling the woman over onto her back. Alice checked her over as well as she could, then sat back with a sigh of relief.

"She's breathing easily, so that's something. She doesn't even seem to have hurt herself too bad with that last lunge at the floor."

"Perhaps," Ches observed, "but that's a long way from saying she's well. Something about those pictures set her off."

"Well, they're gone now, so I can't even look them over again to try to figure out what it was. Maybe we should--" Alice cut off as LaRonda twitched and mumbled something incomprehensible. "Maybe she'll come around soon," she said hopefully.

"Then maybe we shouldn't be here when she does," Ches suggested.

"No, I think it will be all right," Alice said. "I don't know what just happened, but I think Ms. Teresi is more victim than villain. We've got to try to revive her."

"Leave it to me," Hatter declared. He promptly sat down, legs crossed, and positioned LaRonda's arm in his lap. He removed a butter knife from one pocket, then removed his hat, revealing a butter dish perched on top of his head.

"You've got to be kidding me," Alice said, reaching across to stop Hatter as he prepared to smear a bit into the inside of the armor's elbow joint.

"Why not? It's the best but--" Hatter replied.

"No," Alice interrupted firmly.

"Oh, honestly! You just can't help some people," Hatter huffed as he tossed the dish over his shoulder. LaRonda's eyes drifted open as the dish shattered.

"Would you please just go away and let me die in peace?" she said.

"Ms. Teresi! What happened?" Alice bent over her in concern. "Can I get you anything? Some water?"

LaRonda nodded. "Some water would be nice. A shot of bourbon would be better. There's a bottle on the bookshelf to the right of the computer desk."

"Are you sure? You really don't look well."

"Good, 'cause I'd sure hate to look like a freaking debutant while I feel this bad. Get me the bourbon."

"All right, but just a bit." Alice motioned to Hatter, who retrieved the bottle. Together, they helped her sit up enough to take a big sip of the whiskey. LaRonda sighed and relaxed a bit as she reclined again afterward.

"Try a bit yourself, if you'd like," LaRonda invited.

"Uh, no thanks," Alice declined. "You know, a teacher really shouldn't be offering this stuff to a student."

"No problem, I'm not a teacher. Not anymore."

"Why not?"

LaRonda looked Alice directly in the eyes. "You were right. Those robots were my designs. I made every one of those things with these two hands." She held up her gauntleted fists. "The only thing is, until I saw those photos, I couldn't remember any of it. Can you believe it? The better part of eight months of my life was a complete blank, and I never even noticed."

"How is that possible?" Alice asked.

"I don't know. But I'll bet it has something to do with this place, and rather than stick around to figure it out, I'm thinking getting the hell out of Dodge is a better plan. If you're smart, you'll go, too."

"You want me to come with you?" Alice said, confused.

"Did I say that? Do I look like a social worker? Just grab your stuff and run while the gettin's good."

Alice shook her head. "No, I've got to know who's behind this, and what's really at stake. If you're smart, you'll help me."

"Girl, I can't even sit up right now. How much help do you expect me to be?"

Alice waved a hand dismissively. "You'll be on your feet again, soon enough. You're already sounding steadier. I think I know where I can get some answers. I just need you to go on as usual for a bit longer; just pretend your lost memories are still lost. You'll be safe enough."

LaRonda grimaced. "Maybe, but why should I stick around a moment longer than necessary? What's in it for me?"

"Two things. A chance to find out who blocked your memories, and what they really want."

"Not nearly enough."

Alice smiled. "You interrupted me. That's only the first part of what you stand to gain."

380

"So what else is there?"

"Friends and allies," Alice answered. "People who can watch out for you, and maybe remove that memory block if it ever gets slapped back in place."

There was a long pause. Finally, LaRonda sighed. "Fine, I'll think about it."

"Good. Now, while you're thinking about it, I need to borrow a couple of things."

♠ ♣ ♥ ♦

A short time later, Alice was back on the stairs in the administration building. I've got to find out what's behind that door. Something tells me if I do, I'll know what needs to happen.

Her tape was still in place on the door at the top of the stairs, and she let herself into the hall leading to the elevator bay. She walked to the cross corridor and peeked at the security door at its end. No one was in evidence, so she rounded the corner and stopped several paces from the door, contemplating her options. She was determined to get past the barrier, but if she had to break down the door, she might wind up giving Oglethorpe exactly what he wanted. She wanted to avoid a brute force approach, but unfortunately, that didn't seem possible.

Before she could act, however, the door slid open, and Elaine Kilkarni stepped through. She was reading from a clipboard she held in the crook of one arm, but stopped when she sensed a presence in front of her. The door slid shut just behind her as she looked up, adopting an expression of mild surprise. "Miss Littleton, what are you doing here? How did you get in?"

"Mrs. Kilkarni, thank goodness. I know this is going to sound, uh, pushy, but I need to see what's behind that door. Please let me in."

Elaine frowned. "I'm afraid that's impossible. What's on this floor is off limits to all students, even the resourceful ones. It is, quite simply, none of your business."

Alice shook her head. "You're wrong, Mrs. Kilkarni. I don't know exactly what's in there, but it's something Oglethorpe would find very interesting, am I right? So, I'm guessing you got back from your trip this evening and learned about the robots that attacked the school today. So you rushed up here to make sure that whatever is in there is still secure. Now you're heading off to bed, convinced that it's safe, and Oglethorpe still doesn't know where we are." Elaine's expression had shifted from annoyance to astonishment as Alice had proceeded. Now, Alice jerked her chin forward defiantly. "So tell me, how am I doing so far?"

Elaine didn't say a word, which Alice interpreted as a tacit acknowledgement of her points. So she continued to press her attack. "You're wrong, because I have eyewitness testimony that Oglethorpe has stood in this very room. He knows exactly where we are, and that brings up a lot of interesting questions, doesn't it?"

Elaine shook her head in denial. "No, it's not possible," she whispered, more to herself than to Alice.

"Don't you see? Whatever you're hiding in there is so important to Oglethorpe that he's ignoring a school full of powers, ripe for the taking, because he'd rather have it than us. But once he's got it, he won't be satisfied. That thing you're protecting is drawing him to us like a magnet, and he'll suck us up in his wake as soon as he's ready."

Elaine dropped the clipboard and covered her face with her hands, weeping quietly.

"Mrs. Kilkarni, please! You've got to trust us. Tell us what's really going on here, and let us help. Once the other students and I know what's at stake, we'll do everything we can to defy him, but we're probably going to have to do it somewhere else."

382

Elaine dropped her hands and looked at Alice, and shook her head as a bit of her self confidence returned. "I can't do that, dear. I'm sorry you don't like it, and I'll understand if you want to leave the school, but I won't let you in."

Alice sighed to herself. It looked like it would have to be brute force after all. She reached to the small of her back and withdrew one of the items she had borrowed from LaRonda, leveling it at Elaine. "I'm sorry, too, Mrs. Kilkarni, but that wasn't really a request. Open that door," she said as the handheld blaster powered up.

To Alice's surprise, Elaine did not show any sign of fear or shock. Her eyes merely narrowed to slits and her mouth became a straight, short slash in her stony countenance. "I will not be threatened in my own school, young lady. You are not getting past this point, no matter what you do. Now put that thing down and--"

Alice shifted her aim to the right and fired suddenly, discharging the weapon into the wooden frame beside the security door. She hoped the show of force and determination would make the administrator cave and open the door, but she misjudged the strength of the blast. The wood shattered, and splinters flew in all directions. One of them grazed Elaine, tearing a deep, jagged furrow in her cheek.

Alice gasped in horror. She hadn't really intended to hurt Elaine, and she found herself instantly rushing to apologize. "Elaine! Oh, no, what have I done? I'm so..." Her voice trailed to nothing as, impossibly, she saw the wound knitting itself back together almost instantly. But Elaine doesn't have any powers. The only person I've ever seen regenerate from a wound that quickly was...

Alice turned to run, But Elaine teleported in front of the elevator doors, blocking her access to both it and the stairs. Ches immediately crouched, preparing to spring at her, but Alice called out to him. "Ches, don't, she'll only kill you again. Or, is it he'll kill you again?"

Elaine laughed as her form shifted to Oglethorpe's familiar features, the voice shifting downward as well, In less than three seconds, Oglethorpe stood before her, though incongruously dressed in Elaine's business suit with the skirt. "Damn, I had you going for a while there, girlie. You have a really bad habit of forcing my hand, though, don't you?"

CHAPTER THIRTY-FIVE
That Ain't No Rabbit Hole

Alice's temper flared, momentarily overriding her concern for her own safety. "What have you done with Elaine?" she demanded. "And how did you get through the door?" Alice imagined Oglethorpe forcing Elaine to open the door, taking whatever was hidden beyond, and then exiting wearing her form. *Maybe it's her body he doesn't want me to see back there.*

Oglethorpe laughed as if he'd just heard the best joke ever, then wiggled uncomfortably. "Just a second, girlie." His form shifted again, and Elaine reappeared. She sighed in relief. "That's better. Oglethorpe is useful, but he doesn't fit my clothes well." She contemplated Alice thoughtfully with one finger resting on her chin. "I guess it's time to decide what to do with you, dear."

Alice backed up as she realized the truth. "It's been you all along, hasn't it? Oglethorpe is just an alter ego?"

"He's not a separate personality, if that's what you mean," Elaine explained. "He's just a role I sometimes find convenient, made possible by a shapeshifting power I picked up a while back."

"From someone you recruited to your shadow organization?"

Elaine made a dismissive gesture. "From someone who had to be retired. He lacked vision." She seemed amused.

"Retired? You mean murdered? Why would you do that? Why would you even create this school if all you're after is more power? It doesn't make any sense."

"You have no idea what I'm after!" Elaine retorted. "But I think it's time you learned. Otherwise, you won't be in a position to make an informed decision."

"If you're asking me to join you again, my answer hasn't changed," Alice said.

"I hope that I can change your mind, dear," Elaine said. "It would be a shame to lose a young woman with so much potential."

Alice shook her head in disbelief. "Really? You're threatening me now? Isn't there a saying about honey and vinegar that might apply here?"

"Quite right, my dear. Please understand that I do not want to hurt you. But I cannot allow anyone to disrupt the plans I have set in motion. Too much depends on them."

Right. Cue maniacal super-villain monologue, and that's my cue to exit, stage left. Alice summoned her looking-glass, prepared to leave Elaine cackling to herself, but before she could step through, Elaine teleported into the space the mirror occupied and grabbed Alice by the throat, pushing her back before she could break the plane of the glass. Alice felt her feet leave the floor and she was slammed back against the wall, struggling for a breath that would not come.

"Did you really think I hadn't anticipated that?" Elaine mocked her. "I will give you one last chance to hear me out, and I urge you to pay attention." She glanced behind her, to where Ches once again crouched, but dared not attack while Elaine had Alice in such a compromising position. It would take less than a second for her to break Alice's neck. "Now, get rid of the mirror and kitty so we can finish our talk in peace."

Alice complied. Immediately, Elaine released her and Alice dropped to the floor, gasping for air through her sore throat. Elaine waited a bit for her to regain her composure and the ability to breathe more quietly before she spoke again.

"Let me show you my true form," she said. Her body altered again, though the transformation was subtler this time. The lines on her face retreated and disappeared and her hair grew fuller and more lustrous, until she stood before Alice as a woman in her early twenties, yet still recognizable as Prometheus Academy's founder.

"Okay, you've made your point. You're an overachiever," Alice said. "You've reached the heights of villainy at such a young age. Color me impressed."

"Alice, this will go so much more smoothly if you would just tone down the sarcasm, difficult as that may be for a teenage girl. I'm trying to explain myself to you, and trust me, that in itself is a compliment." Alice rolled her eyes, but motioned for Elaine to continue. "Very good. Now, in point of fact, I am actually much older than I looked even a minute ago. I was born in 1832, you see.

"I won't bore you with too many details right now, but suffice it to say that, by the time of the Civil War, I was married to a businessman and living in New York City. Joseph had a gift for predicting the future performance of stocks and commodities, so we were very well off, though neither of us realized the nature of Joseph's ability until I happened to rest my hand on his shoulder while he was looking over the previous day's stock report in the paper one morning at breakfast. His was the first power I ever duplicated, you see."

"You expect me to believe powers have been around and undetected all that time?" Alice asked.

"As near as I can tell, that was about the time that paranormal abilities first appeared. But early abilities were usually limited and expressed themselves less spectacularly. Joseph's precognition was limited to the markets, for example. Otherwise, he would have anticipated the plots his supposed friends were laying against him. Two of the more common abilities were enhanced strength and healing. In any one individual, neither was too remarkable, but I duplicated those abilities from multiple individuals over time, and they reinforced each other exponentially. Now, I can out-lift all but the largest cranes and the regenerative effect even counteracts aging, so I'm effectively immortal."

"So you've got money, power, and all the time in the world to enjoy it. Sounds like you've got it made. Why all the deceptions and murderous rampages?"

"Compassion, and the desire to protect our kind," Elaine answered. "Don't you see? Relatively speaking, we're among the first individuals to express the characteristics of humanity's next evolutionary phase. But we are still rare in the population. If humanity becomes aware of us too soon, they will rise up against us and overcome us through sheer strength of numbers. Mankind's progress will be set back, maybe even be halted altogether, through envious short-sightedness. That cannot be permitted."

"Still not seeing the compassion, particularly since you just admitted to killing a shapeshifter, and tried to do the same to me the first time we met," Alice challenged.

"Survival of the species outweighs the survival of any one individual," Elaine said. "Besides, I wasn't trying to kill you in Wonderland. The Oglethorpe attack scenario has been effective in herding many young people to Prometheus' welcoming arms. I will admit that you surprised me, though. No one else has ever fended me off so well. Until you came up with the Boojum, I had planned to use you to motivate LaRonda to greater efforts. You were to be a poor innocent lamb lost to the wolves. As it turned out, you disrupted our timetable and LaRonda had to suit up several nights in a row, and young Mr. Thompson stowed away repeatedly, before Houston was able to locate you again."

"Yeah, that brings up a good point. How did you survive the Boojum?"

"I survived because you do not understand the Boojum's nature. It is not an embodiment of death, despite the portrayal of Mr. Carroll. But if I had not copied your looking glass previous to that encounter, then I most certainly would 'never be met with again', at least not in this world. You see, just as I can teleport myself, or turn that power outward to teleport someone else, you have the ability to travel to other worlds via your looking-glass, or send others there with the Boojum."

"Other worlds? You mean more than one?" Alice asked.

"Yes, it would seem there are an infinite number of worlds out there, just as the physicists have speculated. I can attest to that, since I visited several after our encounter in Wonderland before I finally made it home," Elaine confirmed.

Alice was stunned. *After finding Wonderland, I never even thought to try to reach another world.* "Are there people in those other worlds?"

"Wonderland is unique in lacking humanity, or at least it appears to be an aberration," Elaine answered. "But we've drifted off the point. I was explaining my purpose. Do you know what the greatest evil is in this world?"

"I can think of one, but I'm sure you're about to tell me something different," Alice replied.

"War," Elaine said, brushing past Alice's verbal barb without regard. "In my long life, I have borne many children, and without exception, they have been lost through the short-sightedness of men who ought to know better, who hurl countries into conflict for the sake of land, resources, or perceived slights to their pride. Well, enough is enough. I intend to put a stop to it."

389

"Let me guess," Alice theorized, "you'll take over and the world will become a utopia. It will never work, you know."

"No doubt there will be a cost, and it will take time," Elaine conceded. "But time is a luxury I can well afford, and I have advantages no other leader has ever enjoyed. In the end, I will succeed." Elaine spoke with the passion of a fanatic, and Alice realized it would be almost impossible to sway her from her course. She found that conclusion more than a little frightening.

"Just to be sure I understand you, let's recap," she suggested. "You intend to wage the biggest war anyone has ever seen in order to protect the empowered from persecution, even though that means lots of empowered will die in the fighting. But you think it's worth it because in the end, you'll rule forever and you think that somehow, that's going to cause everyone to make nice with each other. Stop me if this sounds crazy or anything."

"You're overlooking something," Elaine said. "The empowered are the greatest resource humanity has ever encountered. We can give humanity clean, renewable energy, fresh water for crops and drinking – the list goes on. With the empowered in charge, there won't be a need for war, because resources will no longer be scarce. *homo sapiens* will be freed to achieve their fullest potential before being replaced, quietly and peacefully, by the empowered, as our kind supplants them through natural selection."

"Even if I believed that, your plan would cause the deaths of millions before you could have a hope of gaining control. Even more would die trying to break free from your rule. It's not worth it."

"You can help me reduce the cost, Alice. Give me the Boojum," Elaine said.

The suddenness and absurdity of the request halted Alice's thoughts. When she could finally formulate a reply, she said, "You've got a hundred powers already, and that's going to solve your problems?"

"You exaggerate," Elaine replied. "In point of fact, I have copied less than a dozen distinct abilities, and I don't think I'll be copying many more. I sense I'm getting close to some sort of limit, and so now I only copy powers that offer unique opportunities. Your looking-glass was one, and the Boojum is another."

"Ah, I see," Alice said. "You can't have everything, so you created Prometheus Academy to collect kids with worthwhile powers so you could keep them close to you. But that still doesn't explain why you want the Boojum so badly."

"Exile has long been considered a humane alternative to execution," Elaine said.

"Humane! You want to tear your enemies away from everything they've known and worked for all their lives. Their friends and families would have no hope of ever seeing them again, and your victims would have to start over again in some random world with no resources or companions to turn to. And you call that humane? In some ways it's worse than an outright killing!"

"Perhaps," Elaine replied calmly. "But I would only need to use the power sparingly, against truly irritating leaders. The rabble would get the message that resistance is futile pretty quickly, and, lacking direction, would disperse back into the general population. Trust me, used properly, the Boojum can shorten the coming conflict substantially."

"Used as a weapon of terror, you mean," Alice said, backing away. Her hand moved to her fanny pack, but she made no move to try to open it. "Well, I swore never to summon it again, and nothing you've said is changing my mind. So forget it; you'll never get it from me."

Elaine sighed. "I was afraid you would be stubborn. Added to that, your new knowledge makes you dangerous, and your ability to shift between worlds makes it extremely difficult to try to contain you. So, regrettably, that leaves only one option."

She held up a hand with electricity arcing between her fingers. She flicked her wrist, and a bolt of lightning flashed towards Alice, only to spread out along the surface of an invisible hemisphere and ground out on the floor five feet from its target.

Elaine looked surprised. "What new trick is this?"

Alice unzipped her fanny pack and removed a metal sphere about four inches across. "I found this when I raided Ms. Teresi's lab using Scott's access card earlier tonight. Scott told me all about her force field, and it sounded like it might be useful, so I shrunk it and brought it along," she said smugly.

"Resourceful, as I noted before," Elaine said with a regretful smile. "We could have accomplished so much together. But since that is not to be, I'll send you on your way. Enjoy the sights on your last trip."

Elaine twirled her wrist, ending with two finger pointing straight up, and then everything surrounding Alice vanished.

♠   ♣   ♥   ♦

Alice felt herself falling in darkness, and immediately activated her gliding power to compensate. Her eyes quickly adjusted to her new surroundings, and she realized she could see stars, more stars than she had ever seen before. They were brilliant and somehow more accessible than she could ever recall, and they were all around her.

"Cool, from here it looks like a big ball of yarn," Ches said from behind her.

Alice turned around, a task made easy by her limited flight ability, to see the cat suspended in mid-air, batting his paws at something that wasn't there. Then she looked down.

"AAIIIIEEEEE!"

The Earth lay far, far below her feet. She was so high the curvature of the planet was obvious. In fact, it looked like video she had seen from the space shuttle. The sun was currently eclipsed by the planet, and the only details she could make out were the lights of major cities, where they weren't blocked by clouds. She screamed again and clutched at Ches as her mind tried to make sense of it all. To her surprise, Ches bared his fangs and snarled at her, causing her to recoil from him.

"Ches?"

"Have I got your attention?" he asked. "Good, now snap out of it. You haven't got much time." When Alice looked at him uncomprehendingly, Ches sighed. "Do you remember how long Scott said the force field would last?"

"Uhm, about five minutes, I think."

"Exactly. So you've got less than five minutes to get back down to the ground before this air bubble pops and you suffocate. Any ideas?"

"I can just let myself drop," Alice said, letting her gliding power lapse. She felt the effect in her stomach as she returned to freefall.

Ches rolled his eyes. "Do you happen to remember how long it took Felix Baumgartner to make his jump?"

Alice thought back to Miranda's recap before her adventure rescuing Billy. "About ten minutes, I think."

"You see the problem. We might even be higher up; it probably depends on what Elaine was capable of. What else have you got?"

"You, all of the characters from the Wonderland stories," Alice said, racking her brain for anything from the books that might help. *Hatter's time manipulation won't do; time would pass more quickly for both me and the force field, so it would still fail at the same place relative to the ground.*

"No good," Ches replied. "What else?"

"Uh, I could shrink myself to use less oxygen, but that won't make a difference when the field drops. Growing won't make me fall faster. Oh, this is hopeless!" Alice felt the panic rising again. She was going to die up here!

"Focus!" Ches snapped. "What do you have that can move you quickly across a distance?"

"The looking-glass moves me between worlds, but I'll still be--. Oh, the drift factor! But that's random; I can't control it!"

"You can't prevent it," Ches corrected her.

"But I might be able to direct it?"

"Have you got a better idea?"

"No."

"Then get going," Ches directed. "I'll see you on the ground."

Ches vanished, leaving Alice to face the void without distractions. She fought down her fear and concentrated on moving towards the ground as she summoned her mirror, which appeared several feet away between her and the Earth. She fell through it, noting that it was much larger than usual. It was big enough for the entire sphere of the force field to pass through. The planet below her was now completely dark, since Wonderland lacked any cities to brighten the night. She summoned the mirror again to return to Earth, and the lights reappeared.

But are they any closer? Alice couldn't tell, and started trying to find some way to measure her progress. After a couple more transitions, she noted that a star that had been just at the horizon was now eclipsed by the planet's atmosphere. She felt a small thrill of hope, which was dashed almost instantly as the star reappeared after the next passage. But it disappeared again the next trip through the mirror, and did not reappear through three more. *Okay, so it looks like the motion is somewhat random, but probably tends towards the direction I want to go,* Alice concluded. All that remained was to see if it would be enough.

After a couple more hops between realities, Alice thought to wonder if she might get to falling too fast and run into heating issues when she got to denser atmosphere. Reasoning that most of her progress would have to come from her use of the looking-glass anyway, she reactivated her gliding power to slow herself down.

She began to feel tired. She usually didn't feel any strain from her jumps, but she had never made so many of them in such a short period of time. She found herself drifting into a semi-hypnotic state as her weariness grew. She watched the progression of lighted world – mirror – dark world – mirror – lighted world over and over, sometimes losing precious seconds when she would forget to summon the looking-glass again for the next transition.

Sound shocked her back to her senses. Aside from her brief talk with Ches at the start, her fall toward Earth/Wonderland had been unnaturally quiet. But suddenly, there was a whisper of sound caused by air brushing past the surface of the force field. She had reached atmosphere! She refocused on the mass below her, confirming it was Earth by the lights. She was still very high, but her field of vision was noticeably less than it had been the last time she took conscious stock of the situation.

She took a moment to slow her descent further, then passed over to Wonderland again. The looking-glass was harder to summon this time, and as she completed the passage the bubble of her force field suddenly slowed, causing her to fall painfully onto its interior. *I must have made a sudden jump into denser air.* The thought made her welcome the pain. She was getting closer to breathable air.

Alice returned to the center of the area encapsulated by the force field, where the metal sphere hung, motionless relative to the boundary. She slipped it into her fanny pack and zipped it up. She reached for the strength to summon the looking-glass once more, barely managing to make it appear so she could return to Earth's environs. She felt a tug on the pouch at her waist as friction slowed her descent even more.

Just as she wondered if she could manage two more transitions in hopes of getting still lower, the force field collapsed with no warning. Instantly, she became chilled by the passage of icy air and she started tumbling uncontrollably. She gasped as the cold further muddled her thoughts, uncertain what to do. She struggled to keep her eyes open and use her gliding ability to orient herself, finally managing to cancel her unwanted rotation. The lights of a big city remained far below and off to one side, but her eyes refused to focus and her eyelids kept drooping, cutting off her vision.

A trickle of fear passed through her, but it was a distant thing. She was aware that she was still in danger, needing to fight the pull of gravity to come to a safe landing, but her reserves were depleted. She forced her eyes open, and tried to slow her descent, but couldn't tell if her efforts were having any effect. In spite of herself, her eyes closed once more. The sound of rushing wind was the last thing she was aware of before she lost consciousness.

CHAPTER THIRTY-SIX
Waking Up

"Alpha Wolf, I have the target in site and I am in position."
The disembodied voice had a mechanical edge to it, as if it was coming
from a cheap speaker. Alice twitched as she started to become aware of
the world around her again, but she kept her eyes closed. *If I'm lucky, I
can get back to sleep.*

"Roger that, Black-and-White. Keep your distance and
remain unseen until the rest of the team is in place. We will commence
the operation on my mark." The second voice spoke with a clipped
rhythm, and placed the accents on different syllables than Alice would
have expected. It made her think of Africa, or somewhere equally far
away. However, it was clear of mechanical distortion. Though she could
not associate a name or face with the voice, the speaker was obviously in
the room with Alice.

This realization caused a pang of regret. She was warm and
comfortable, and just wanted to rest, feeling the reassuring weight of the
blanket and pressure of the bed below her.

Blanket? Bed? Alice's eyes snapped open and she sat up
abruptly as she realized she had no idea where she was or how she had
come to be here. Her last memory was of falling; she could not reconcile
that predicament with waking up...at all, let alone wherever she was
now. The room she found herself in did nothing to help her orient
herself.

She was on a cot with a thin, dark wool blanket draped over her. A small pillow similar to ones flight attendants sometimes provided on long flights had supported her head. The rest of the room appeared to be the common area of a small apartment, judging by the counter and kitchenette at the far end of the room. The room did contain a number of things Alice would have expected to find in a living room. A television was mounted on the wall to her right, fro example, while to her left a love seat and a couple of upholstered chairs faced it from beneath a window. The rest of the room, however, looked like some sort of eclectic museum had moved in. Display cases held models of planes and military ships, or examples of native crafts like baskets and carved masks or animal figures. The walls were covered with pictures of dark-skinned people in tropical settings, often featuring beaches or the ocean, and black-and-white pictures of more ships and planes. Where the walls were not supporting the pictures, native spears, and banners for something called the Quartermaster Corps were prominently displayed.

Alice took in the sense of all of this in the space of a couple of seconds as she attempted to ground herself. Her attention quickly narrowed to the man sitting on a stool in front of a laptop perched on the counter between the main room and the food preparation area. Soldier Boy wore the same tan uniform she had seen him in at the construction site. As if the outfit wasn't enough of a giveaway, she could see a couple of the tattoos dotting his face from her position mostly behind him as he concentrated on the screen. Her gasp of surprise drew his attention, and he turned to flash her a smile with teeth that looked amazingly wide and white against the dark background of his skin.

"Igneous, I am passing command of this operation to you," he said. "Alpha Wolf, AFK."

"Roger that," a new voice responded. "This is Igneous. Team Retribution, commence attack in three..two...one...Go!"

Soldier Boy adjusted the volume, then turned completely away from the keyboard, giving Alice his full attention as he removed a headset with a microphone attachment. "Excellent, you're awake. Are you hungry?"

Alice ignored the question as she took a closer look at her surroundings. She didn't feel particularly threatened, despite her previous encounter with her host, but she was uncomfortable enough to want someone she could trust beside her. Ches and Hatter responded to her silent summons. Ches adopted a wary half crouch, facing the man from between him and Alice. Hatter, however, immediately became distracted by a mask in a case beside him, mimicking its teeth-baring grimace.

"Where am I, and how did I get here?" Alice asked. Her throat still felt raw and sore from Elaine's grasp.

"My name is Kirdja Putu," the man replied by way of introduction. "You are in my apartment above my store, South Seas Surplus, in San Diego. Hector and I found you last night, and brought you here to recover from your ordeal."

"Hector," Alice repeated thoughtfully. "Moves things without touching them, dresses like a lumberjack?"

Kirdja nodded as the sound of a heavy tread on metal stairs came from a door near Alice's end of the room. "That's probably him now. Don't be alarmed; he's likely to be emotional when he sees you're awake, but we mean you no harm."

Alice wanted to ask why a virtual stranger and former adversary would have any strong feelings about seeing her awake, but before she could pose the question, the door opened. Lumberjack – *Hector,* Alice corrected herself – stood in the entrance looking tired and dejected. As soon as he saw Alice, his expression became animated, and he rushed forward, arms open as if he intended to hug her. "You're awake! Thank God --"

He stopped, both physically and verbally, as Ches suddenly teleported before him, snarling and showing claws extended. Hector lowered his hands, but still kept them away from his body, as his gaze dropped to his feet. "Pardon me, *senorita*, I forget myself. It's just, I've waited so long to meet you, and I need your help so badly."

"Wow, that's a lot to absorb in one go," Alice responded. "Before we get too far along, can we clear the air a bit? The last time I ran into you two, you tried to kidnap me, so why should I want to help? Why should I trust you?"

Hector clenched his fists, but made no move toward her. "We were not trying to kidnap you. I told you at the construction site that we meant no harm. We were trying to prevent you from being swept up by another group that was searching for you. I guess we failed."

Alice thought back to their first meeting. "I couldn't understand you. At the time, I was operating at an accelerated time rate; it garbles sounds, especially speech." *And there was definitely someone hunting me with less than altruistic motives, so that checks. Houston and LaRonda scooped me right up, and took me directly to my worst enemy. I just didn't realize it at the time.*

Her eyes roamed the room and came to rest on the laptop. *Even so, that's not proof that these are good guys.* "But that doesn't explain why you were there in the first place. How many empowered teens have you two collected, and what do you do with them?"

Kirdja looked confused. "We do not collect teenagers, empowered or otherwise."

"Don't give me that," Alice snapped, pointing at the laptop. "I heard you. Just before I woke up I heard you talking to a team of your commandos, or whatever you call them. You were about to launch an attack on someone."

Kirdja's jaw dropped and he stared at her for the space of a half dozen heart beats. Then he started laughing. It was not the uncomfortable chuckle of someone caught in nefarious activity, but one of sheer delight that quickly grew to the gut-wrenching belly laugh of someone who has just heard the funniest joke of their life. Even Hector covered his mouth and tried to suppress a chuckle. Unsuccessfully.

"What's so funny?" Alice asked hotly.

"This master criminal will keep no secrets from you," he said, then gestured to the laptop. "Come, see the fruition of my plans."

Alice looked at Ches and Hatter. "Watch him," she said, indicating Hector, then approached the counter that supported the computer. Kirdja retreated to the kitchen in deference to her obvious skittishness. She knew she was probably being paranoid, but she had been quick to trust Elaine, and that had almost cost her everything. She would err on the side of caution until she believed she understood who her new associates were and what they really wanted with her.

The laptop's screen was at an oblique angle to the far end of the room, so she hadn't been able to see any details from the cot. Now the screen had blacked out due to lack of activity, but she could hear the chatter from the Kirdja's team, full of admonitions to "take the right flank" and "watch your six". She reached out and tapped the touchpad to reactivate the screen.

She had expected to see video footage from helmet-mounted cameras, or something similar. What actually appeared was so far removed from that, she had trouble processing it for a moment. "What is this?" she finally asked, feeling her cheeks heat up as the first stirrings of embarrassment swept through her.

"World of Warcraft," Kirdja answered. "The dwarf there is Igneous--"

Alice waved him to silence. "You've made your point," she acknowledged. As the tension that had been building up in her body released, she suddenly felt weak and grabbed the counter and stool for support.

"You're still tired," Kirdja observed. "Sit down. Drink this," he suggested, pouring a light yellow liquid from an urn into a mug and handing it to her.

Alice accepted it, enjoying the sensation of warmth against the palm of her hand. She took a cautious sip, then made a face at the slightly spicy, but mostly muddy, flavor. "What is this?"

"*Kava*," Kirdja replied. "It's good for you; it'll put hair on your chest!" And he laughed again. Alice smiled in spite of herself and took another sip from her cup. The word was unfamiliar to her, but she guessed it was some sort of medicinal plant from wherever it was Kirdja called home.

She also realized she was ravenous. "You said something about eating a few minutes ago?" she prompted. Kirdja nodded and started bustling around the kitchen, extracting meat and eggs from the refrigerator, spices from cabinets, and pans from cupboards. Soon, the smell of grilling steak and scrambled eggs was making Alice's mouth water.

Ches and Hatter had relaxed their guard when Alice appeared satisfied that the men were not an immediate threat. Now Hector walked over calmly and stopped a few steps away. "Have you filled her in, yet?" he asked Kirdja.

"No time; she just woke up," the other replied.

"Hey, that reminds me, how did I get here, and how long was I out?" Alice asked. "The last thing I remember I was falling, then I think I passed out. Personally, I wasn't about to place any bets on getting myself to the ground safely."

402

"You would have lost that bet if you had, *senorita*," Hector replied, entering the kitchen to pull out utensils and a napkin and set them in front of Alice. "We caught you and brought you here when we couldn't find any injuries, aside from those bruises on your neck. You've been asleep for a little more than ten hours."

"You caught me? Two guys I had run into before just happened to be in the right place to catch me as I fell out of the sky in the middle of the night? That sounds a little far-fetched."

"There was nothing 'just happened' about it. We were told where to go and when to be there," Hector replied as Kirdja set a plate with the steak and eggs in front of Alice, along with an assortment of condiments.

Alice was so hungry, she took the time to cut off a huge hunk of the steak and eat it before asking the obvious question. "Told by who?"

"My ancestors," Kirdja replied.

Alice was too busy attacking her food to reply verbally, but crooked an eyebrow at the two of them to prompt an explanation. Hector supplied it. "You remember the ghostly forms that protected Kirdja during the dust up at the construction site? Well, they offer advice as well, and they seem to have short-term precognition. When they think we need to be somewhere, they give us a heads up and we check it out."

"All right," Alice said, doing her best to hide her skepticism, "but why would they take an interest in me?"

"Because, in some way, you're crucial to helping me with a problem," Hector explained. "My sister and her family went missing several months ago. Kirdja has been using his special resources to help me find them. Twice, now, they have lead us to you."

"The ancestors have warned me of a brooding evil whose aura hides Hector's family from them. You are fated to face this evil.

You must defeat it, or it will grow to swallow us all. The ancestors brought us to you so that I might guide you, and that you might reunite Hector's family."

Alice set down her knife and fork as she suddenly discovered she wasn't hungry at all anymore. "Well, it looks like fate's already caught up with me. I've faced the evil you're talking about, and she's way out of my league. I haven't got anything that will touch her."

"The ancestors say you're wrong," Kirdja responded. "You've lost a skirmish, but you're alive. You will face this woman again, and you alone have the ability to end her threat once and for all."

"Well, your ancestors are full of it!" Alice shouted, suddenly furious at this scrawny, dotted man in his ridiculous uniform. "She heals from any injury almost instantaneously, is stronger than a locomotive, and that's just scratching the surface of her powers! I'll be doing good if I can just get my friends away from her."

"She sounds formidable," Hector allowed. "What plan is she hatching with all of her abilities?"

"She's running a boarding school in Nevada," Alice replied. "It's a place that takes the phrase 'empowered student body' to a whole new level."

She looked at Hector. "I'm guessing Julio Zarzosa is your nephew?" He nodded eagerly. "Well, you'll be glad to know he's in good health. I haven't met your sister or her husband; Julio says they abandoned him at the school because they couldn't cope with him anymore."

"That's ridiculous," Hector replied. "My sister has electrical powers of her own, so she knows what it's like to try to keep that sort of secret. His parents are proud of his abilities, as am I. They've never been a source of friction."

Alice's head slumped forward. She stared at the half-eaten plate of food without seeing it. She didn't want to be the one to tell Hector, but she couldn't see any way around it if she wanted to be able to look at herself in the mirror without seeing a coward. She decided to start with the easy point first.

"I just determined yesterday that Elaine – she's the big bad – has some sort of memory alteration power. I guess she used it on Julio to give him a reason to stay at the school. As long as his family didn't want him, he was as good off there as anywhere else until he graduated and could start his apprenticeship."

"Apprenticeship?" Hector asked, puzzled.

"All he talks about is becoming a tattoo artist and opening his own shop someday."

"He is a gifted artist, but I've never heard him express such plans before. Perhaps it is a side effect of whatever she's done to him. Do you think Elaine did something like that to my sister and brother-in-law's memories?"

Alice's eyes filled with sympathetic tears as she shook her head, and she could tell from his expression that Hector had more than half expected this response. "Her plan seems to be to try to catch the empowered when they're young enough to brainwash. She's been selling us a bill of goods to make us believe the government has decided to eliminate us, and it's been pretty convincing. But I got a peek behind the curtain last night. When I wouldn't agree to join up with her voluntarily, she teleported me into space."

She glanced down at her hands, which she had clenched together with fingers interlaced. "See, Elaine's ability is to copy powers from other paranormals. She copies the powers of anyone with an ability she deems sufficiently useful. If it comes from a kid, I guess she alters his memory to make him forget, then finds a way to get the kid enrolled at the school. But adults that threaten her plans are eliminated. I'm betting they get the same treatment I got; I mean, who thinks of teleporting someone into space on the spur of the moment? The victim would die of exposure to vacuum, and the body would either burn up on re-entry, or maybe just fall into the ocean. The chances that it would be recovered are probably pretty slim, and even if it was, who could connect it to her?"

"How did you survive?" Kirdja asked.

"I had borrowed a device from a friend that generates a force field. It only lasts a few minutes, but it was enough to let me reach atmosphere before its charge ran out."

Alice looked up to find Hector standing in a braced position, legs apart with his arms bowed to bring his clenched fists together in front of his sternum. He brought his gaze up to Alice and Kirdja. "We will go and save my nephew from this monster," he said evenly.

"As you say. We'll fly there tonight," Kirdja responded.

"You can fly?" Alice asked.

"I'll charter a plane," Kirdja replied.

"Of course," she said, embarrassed by her mistake. "I guess the people I've been hanging out with have warped my expectations."

CHAPTER THIRTY-SEVEN
Cargo Ritual

Alice returned to her interrupted meal, leaving Kirdja and Hector to make plans for their trip. She had no trouble admitting to herself that she was terrified of the thought of returning to Prometheus Academy. Elaine could get rid of her with a simple gesture, and most likely would as soon as she saw her in order to keep her from telling the rest of the students what was really going on at the school. Despite her fear, she knew she had to go back to warn her friends.

She tried to come up with a way to warn them remotely. She couldn't simply call or text Miranda, for example. Knowing what she did now, she could see the real purpose behind Elaine's restrictions on electronic communications. The proprietary cell phones given out to all students were no doubt controlled by Elaine. Alice suspected she could filter out any communications she wanted to block, so all she would accomplish by calling her father and having him relay a message to Miranda, for example, would be to let Elaine know she had survived. Elaine probably also monitored internet usage, so any message Alice might post anywhere Miranda would have a chance to see it would be as likely to come to Elaine's attention first. In the end, she decided that preserving the element of surprise was her best option. She would just have to get into the school undetected and deliver her news in person.

Once she had finished eating and found the bathroom, Alice spent some time wandering around the apartment, looking at all of the items on display. A lot of the pictures and models dated to WWII, with an emphasis on the conflict in the Pacific. However, aside from place names and terse descriptions of the planes and ships, she was not able to assemble much of a picture of how everything fit together. After about half an hour of this, she found she was getting tired again and returned to the cot. Ches came and lay down on the floor beside her, and she stoked his fur as she drifted off to sleep once more.

She woke to find Hector standing over her, shaking her shoulder gently. Ches and Hatter had departed while she was sleeping. Judging by the sunlight filtering into the room, several hours had passed and it was nearly sunset. "It's almost time to go," he said. "But I thought you ought to see what Kirdja's up to before we leave."

Alice sat up and ran her fingers through her hair to get the worst of the knots out of it. "Why, what's he doing?"

"Nothing to be alarmed about," Hector assured her. "He's conducting the evening ritual for his people. Whatever happens when we get to the school, it's probably going to get pretty intense. We're going to need to trust each other, so I thought it would be good for you to understand Kirdja's belief system. It's a little unorthodox, to say the least."

"I've seen folks using some pretty weird powers for the last few weeks. I don't think there's much that can surprise me," Alice said.

"I don't doubt that," Hector said. "But Kirdja, while he accepts that the empowered – that is, people whose genetics allow them to express unexplainable abilities – exist, he doesn't see himself as one of them."

"I've seen him throw a spear made of light. In fact, I took a pretty nasty wound from it. If he's not empowered, what is he?"

Hector made a see-saw gesture with his hand parallel to the floor. "It's not so much what he is, as how he sees himself. Have you ever heard of cargo cults?"

"Nope."

"Okay, let's see, where to start then?" Hector took a moment to organize his thoughts. "I had to research all of this after I met him. Kirdja and his people come from an island in the South Pacific, and as I understand it, many people in that part of the world tend to engage in ancestor worship, or at least they used to. The basic idea is that when someone dies, their spirit moves on into the realm populated by gods. So in a sense, the departed becomes like a minor god himself, able to influence the physical world in ways the living can't. So the living seek to leverage the departed spirit's sense of a familial bond to act on their behalf, usually by performing rituals to honor the ancestor. The ritual can be simple or complex, depending on the circumstances. Generally, simple rituals suffice to request a small personal favor, while the complex ones seek blessings for an entire community of people."

"Sounds kind of odd."

"It's not unique to the South Pacific. Chinese folk religion taught people to honor their ancestors for similar reasons. Now, way back when the cultures of the islands came into contact with Westerners, mostly European explorers, they were thrown for a loop. The explorers did things that the islanders couldn't comprehend, and had access to things the islanders couldn't make for themselves."

"I don't understand what you mean," Alice confessed. "How would that cause a problem?"

"Well, it happened lots of different ways, but since Kirdja focuses on the WWII era, let's use an example from that period. During the campaign, Kirdja's people saw a group of men, U.S. soldiers, come ashore on their island from big metal ships. These men cleared long strips of land of all vegetation and smoothed it out, set up a little hut with this stick-like projection attached to the roof, and a man inside the hut sat down and started talking to a box sitting on a table. What do you suppose happened next?"

Alice thought through the scene Hector had just painted with his words. "I guess the strips of land were for airplanes?"

"Got it in one. And once the planes landed, the people on the planes gave the men who had cleared the land all sorts of wonderful things. Prepackaged food, metal tools, weapons, blankets...the list goes on."

"Well, of course. That was why they cleared the landing strips in the first place, because they needed to be resupplied," Alice observed.

"Except that where you and I see a necessary relationship between those two events, the natives saw it as cause and effect. To them, it seemed like they had just witnessed the magic ritual to end all magic rituals, and it had succeeded beyond anything the natives could have imagined before."

"Wait, you mean they thought the soldiers had used magic to summon supplies when they built landing strips?" Alice asked in astonishment.

"Yes, that's exactly what I mean. So the natives tried to recreate the ritual for themselves. They cleared strips of land, built their own hut with sticks up top, and set a man with coconut shells over his ears to talking to a box inside. And then they waited."

"Waited for what?"

"For the planes that would bring them all the same wonderful things the soldiers received, of course."

"But that's crazy. They didn't have people on another island or on the mainland to send stuff to them," Alice protested.

"But they didn't think those things came from other people. They thought they were gifts from the gods, and the people in the planes were the soldier's ancestors, responding to the ritual their descendants had just performed."

Alice hid her face in her hands, trying to wrap her mind around this misconception. It had a certain Carroll-ish logic to it. She could almost see the Hatter and Marchie deciding to give it a try the next time they ran out of fresh scones at the tea party. "So what did they do when it became obvious no planes were coming?"

"They tried to fix the ritual, of course. They had other men march around in formation with sticks in place of rifles, built warehouses to receive the cargo they expected, and even built replicas of the airplanes out of the local vegetation and set them by the sides of their runways. They generally did everything they could to mimic what the visitors were doing to such great effect."

"So when Kirdja's powers manifested..."

"He thought he had finally stumbled onto the right ritual," Hector confirmed.

"But he's so young! He certainly wasn't there during the war!" Alice thought of Elaine's claim, then had to add "Was he?"

"No, certainly not," Hector replied. "Don't get the idea that the islanders have focused on this exclusively all this time. Most learned better over time - learned about manufacturing processes and everything that has to take place before those planes can land. But in the backwaters, there were still outbreaks of these cargo cults from time to time. Over time it got mixed in with Christianity and all sorts of things."

"Christianity?"

"All good gifts come from our heavenly Father," Hector quoted.

"Oh, right," Alice said. "So when Kirdja conducts his ritual, what happens?"

"Typically, the ancestors give him something small, but very valuable, to share with his people," Hector replied.

411

"Like what?" Alice asked.

"A few weeks ago, it was a bar of gold an inch thick, about the size of an index card."

"Wow, that must have been...handy," Alice allowed.

"Yep, they were able to convert it to pretty big pile of cash once they melted it down. The bar had a symbol molded into it I had never seen before, kind of a stylized octopus or something. Anyway, why don't we go see what the ancestors are bringing tonight?" Hector swept an arm towards the door in invitation, and Alice got up and preceded him down the stairs. Halfway down, they made a U-turn, then exited through a swinging door at the bottom of the stairs into a store. As Kirdja had indicated, it was stocked with all manner of military surplus items, including uniforms, camping gear, and MREs. Hector swept past Alice and took the lead, guiding her through display cases and bins to the rear door.

They exited the store into a large open area enclosed by a high cinder block wall. About twenty people of varying ages were gathered along the rear wall of the store. Alice estimated there were three or four families, plus a few individuals. The youngest was a boy of about two, while the oldest person was a woman who was probably in her late 60s. Some stood about talking in small groups, but everyone was paying at least partial attention to the far side of the enclosure.

"Is that - or should I say was that - a Lockheed C-60A cargo plane?" Alice asked.

"Yes," Hector said, his surprise at her ability to identify the craft evident in his voice.

Alice shrugged. "There was a model of one upstairs," she explained. "It was in much better condition."

"I don't doubt it," Hector said.

The plane was shoved into the back corner of the enclosure with its tail close up against the side wall. The side door and much of the cowling around the engines were missing, and even in the fading light, Alice could tell that there were several birds' nests in places that clearly indicated the engines hadn't functioned in quite a while. The fuselage was badly weathered as well, to the point where bare, rusty metal showed through the paint and primer in several places.

On the opposite side of the yard, a man sat before an antique shortwave radio set that looked like it had about as much chance of working as the plane. The stool and table were out in the open and situated much closer to the store than the derelict aircraft. This was apparently to make room for an altar set in front of a three-pronged prop assembly approximately ten feet high that was mounted on the wall opposite the plane. It apparently came from another C-60A, and it was obviously intended as a stand-in for a crucifix, despite the absence of a figure stretched across the blades.

Kirdja stood behind the altar holding a clipboard. Bowls of burning incense sat on either side of the altar, and an antique wind-up phonograph sat in the center. About halfway between the front of the altar and the nose of the plane, four wooden crates had been arranged to form a rectangular platform and draped with parachute silk, which rippled in a steady breeze. Several items were set out on top of the makeshift covering; canned food and fresh vegetables, bottles of wine and soda, and a carved native mask were just a few of the items Alice could make out.

Kirdja tapped a wooden pencil against the side of his clipboard. The crowd immediately fell silent. He turned to the man at the radio. "Let the ancestors know we are ready to begin," he commanded. The man faced the radio and began flipping switches and turning dials at random, all the while keeping up a steady stream of vocalizations in a language Alice could neither understand nor identify.

413

A few moments after the radioman began, Kirdja switched on the phonograph and set the needle on a record already in position on the turntable. The sound of a big band filled the courtyard, and then the Andrews Sisters launched into their jazzy rendition of "Don't Sit Under the Apple Tree with Anyone Else But Me". Alice was just starting to enjoy the number when Kirdja began leading the rest of the group in the yard in a chant in that unknown language that somehow created a harmonizing counterpoint to the big band recording.

As the music continued, Kirdja walked around to the front of the altar in measured paces and approached the platform, which Alice suddenly realized held offerings for the ancestors. He set the clipboard in an open space on the platform. Then, while the spectators continued the chant he had begun, Kirdja switched to a monotone, droning string of verbalizations, arms stretched wide above his head, which was turned to the heavens.

Alice didn't see how it started, but fire suddenly blossomed in the center of the silk-shrouded platform and spread to encompass it all, at which point Kirdja fell silent. Her attention was so captivated by the fire that she wasn't sure afterward when the next phase of the ceremony began.

It was motion that drew her gaze to the derelict plane. The craft was outlined in a faint green-white glow, and the propellers were spinning, gaining speed as she watched. Soon, they were stirring up a strong wind in the enclosure, although Alice did not think the props were spinning fast enough to actually move the plane. Since both front tires were flat, she figured it was a moot point.

Alice began to wonder if she needed to reassess that conclusion when the tail of the plane lifted off the ground and the plane assumed the position of an aircraft in flight. However, it remained immobile, though she could now see two ghostly figures seated in the cockpit, apparently guiding the craft in its non-flight.

414

After about a minute of this, the Andrews Sisters ended their song, the onlookers ceased their chant, and the tail settled gently back to the ground. The semi-transparent pilots appeared in the doorway, climbed out, and approached the burning offerings. They reached into the flames, obviously untroubled by them, and lifted each votive item. Alice watched closely as one of the pilots took the carved mask. A glowing representation of the mask appeared within the insubstantial hands moving it, but the physical mask remained in place for a moment. Then, as if some essential quality had been removed, it collapsed into a pile of ash. The pilot appeared to pass the glowing mask to an invisible bystander, and it vanished as he relinquished his hold. As Alice watched, this sequence played out again for every item on the platform.

The final object lifted from the platform was the clipboard. The pilot examined the glowing essence as the original disappeared into dust, then said something to the other apparition. Kirdja smiled in the throes of religious rapture as the first ancestor approached him and they began to converse. The other returned to the doorway of the plane and reached inside, removing a wooden container about the size of a large shoe box. He approached the others and handed the box to Kirdja. As soon as he grasped the box, it lost the other-worldly glow and became substantial. As the exchange took place, the first ghost gestured toward Alice; Kirdja glanced her way and nodded.

"What do you suppose that was about?" she asked Hector quietly.

"I'm sure we'll find out soon," he replied. "The ritual is almost complete."

Sure enough, Kirdja's ancestors finished talking with him and returned to the plane. As they disappeared through the doorway, the plane lost its faint glow. At the same time, some subtle shift occurred in the light coming from the fire. Alice could not say what had changed to save her life, but some quality had changed, and it was suddenly just the remains of a backyard bonfire. Kirdja closed his eyes and took in a deep breath, then released it. His face wore an expression of contentedness as he approached Alice and Hector. He set the box down in front of her.

"A gift for you," he said.

"What is it?" Alice asked warily.

"Open it and see."

Shrugging, Alice bent down and released the latches holding the box closed. She lifted the lid carefully and peered inside. There was nothing there but a thick black electrical cable. She looked up at Kirdja. "Uhm, how thoughtful?"

"The immediate future is difficult to see; much depends on seemingly trivial choices you and others will soon be called upon to make. If you follow one particular path, this may be what you need for the coming confrontation," he explained. "If you take a different path, you may still succeed, in which case you will find this useful later on."

Alice reached in to lift it out, then grunted in surprise at its weight. It wasn't that it was a strain to lift it, but it required more effort than she had anticipated. The reason became apparent as it came free of the box and she got a look at the plug. It was shaped like a plug for a standard electrical outlet, but it was huge. In fact, it was larger than a plug for a washer or dryer. She checked the other end of the cable, but it was only somewhat larger than a standard female end for a computer or stereo.

"Odd," Hector said. "You'll never find a receptacle big enough to plug that into."

Just like that, Alice finally made the connection, and reached for the metal ball resting in her fanny pack. "Oh, I bet I will," she said. "Anyone got a bottle of water?"

CHAPTER THIRTY-EIGHT

Clearing the Air

Once Alice got back inside the apartment and shrank the cable, she was able to confirm that the ends were a perfect match for a standard electrical outlet and the power receptacle on the force field generator. "My compliments to your ancestors, Kirdja. It couldn't have been easy to produce this."

"That's nothing," Hector said. "Minor gods are nothing if not versatile." Kirdja just smiled and sipped his *kava*.

"What's that supposed to mean?" Alice asked.

"Just what I said," he responded. "Despite what you've seen, I think you still see Kirdja as one of the empowered whose abilities just happen to be dressed up with tribal-themed special effects."

Alice looked at Kirdja to see how he was taking this. Hector's comments seemed rude, almost as if he was ignoring his friend's presence and sensibilities. However, Kirdja did not react at all; he simply watched the two of them and took another sip from his mug. She shrugged. "Well, what if I do? My own abilities entail a fair amount of window dressing, so I understand how that might work."

"Fair enough. But there's a considerable amount of evidence that his abilities, amazing as they appear, are even more profound."

"I don't see where you're going with this," Alice confessed.

"One of the biggest questions mankind faces is whether some part of us survives bodily death. I think Kirdja's interactions with his ancestors gives us the answer. I've been watching them for several months now, and the more I do, the more certain I am that they are just what they appear to be."

Alice thought about Sarah. "It's not that I don't believe in something after this life. I have a friend with different abilities that could be seen as evidence of that. The problem is, no matter how reproducible the effects his ancestors create are, the abilities of other empowered mean that they aren't definitive proof. People can always interpret events however they like."

Hector shrugged. "I'm just saying you should be open to the possibility that Kirdja's power really is the ability to contact his dead."

"And that for him, material goods really are gifts direct from God? Seems to me evidence of the afterlife would be more, uhm, universal, you know?"

"I cannot speak for your ancestors, or Hector's," Kirdja interjected, "but mine are distinct individuals. I know them as much by their personalities as by their faces. And the ways they choose to help are often new and unexpected."

Alice was inclined to discount personalities as proof that Kirdja's ancestors were actual spirits of the departed based on her own experience with her Wonderland companions. However, not wanting to be overly argumentative, she kept that point to herself. Instead, she responded to the last part of his statement. "Such as?"

"They helped us catch you out there in the desert," Kirdja offered.

"Yeah, you said they told you where to go and when you needed to be there."

"They were a little more helpful than that," Hector said. "Think about it. We were out there in the middle of the night. It was pitch black. The moon is just past new now and had set early in the evening; we got there much closer to midnight. We weren't sure what we were supposed to do. It should have been impossible for us to notice you even a few hundred feet above the ground, assuming we had been inclined to look up in the first place. And if we did spot you, and caught you with my telekinesis at that point, the sudden stop would have killed you just as surely as if you'd hit the ground."

Alice realized she hadn't considered this. She had just accepted Hector's earlier statement at face value. "So what happened? How did you save me?"

"When we got out there, I prayed to my ancestors to light our way so that we could fulfill their purpose for us."

"I guess they took him literally, because suddenly there was a full moon hanging in the sky," Hector added. " I looked up at it in surprise, just in time to see you. The moon framed you perfectly as you fell past, and I took to the air immediately. You were still pretty high up then, and I was able to get you in range of my power in time to slow your fall gradually before bringing you back to the ground next to the car. But it was a near thing."

Alice considered this carefully before asking, "How could they suddenly give you a full moon? They didn't just shift its position in orbit. Surely someone would have noticed."

"Agreed. I shudder to think of the damage that would cause; the sudden shift in tides would probably wipe out most coastal settlements," Kirdja said.

"And the effect does not appear to have been widespread. There were no news reports about an unexpected full moon last night, for example. Believe me, I checked," Hector added.

"So what happened?"

Kirdja shrugged. "The ancestors work in mysterious ways. They allowed us to see what was necessary."

"Maybe the rest was just our minds' attempt to interpret the effect in a way that makes sense based on past experiences," Hector added. "The point I'm trying to make is that they often respond to requests for aid in unexpected ways, just as you'd expect from actual people."

"But enough about that. We need to make plans to confront this woman, Elaine, you told us about," Kirdja said. "I will make the arrangements for our travel, but I need to know where we are going, exactly. Where can we find her?"

"And Julio," Hector added.

Alice looked from Kirdja, with his calm face marked by the pattern of dots, to Hector, his expression pleading for resolution more eloquently than any words could, and made a decision. Her looking-glass appeared beside her, and Ches crouched between her and Hector, his low growl a testimony to his readiness to cause mayhem at a moment's notice.

"Uhm, is something bothering you?" Hector asked in surprise, eyes on the huge feline. Alice could see the wariness in his eyes and imagined he was preparing to catch Ches with his telekinesis if it became necessary. That was fine with her; Ches was intended to act as a distraction.

"Very perceptive of you to pick up on that," she answered wryly. "Yes, there are a couple of things we need to discuss, and I'll warn you now that if I don't like your answers, I'm out of here." She gestured to the looking-glass.

Hector looked panicked, and opened his mouth to object, but Kirdja simply leaned forward and held up a cautionary hand to him as he looked at Alice calmly. "Of course. You have been through much in the last day or so. Please, share your concerns."

"Okay. Look, it's not that I'm not grateful for the assist last night. That and the power cable for the force field generator buys a lot of goodwill." Alice hesitated, looking at her feet as she ordered her thoughts. Then she looked up at Kirdja's eyes. "But I've got a lot of friends in danger right now because we trusted someone too easily. Heck, I put one of them in the middle of all this because I was too selfish to let her stay where she was safe. I've got to be certain that if I tell you where they are, I'm bringing them help, and not someone else who'll try to exploit them a different way."

Alice pointed at Kirdja. "Most importantly, I can't forget that the first time we met, you stuck me with a spear. Yet you claim you were trying to save me. So how did something like that happen?"

Kirdja fidgeted uncomfortably in his chair. "You were charging at me, a giantess wielding a wheelbarrow. It was very intimidating. I was getting ready to throw my spear at the noisy, flying boy, but switched to you, as the more immediate threat. I only intended to hit your leg to hobble you until we could get you away, but I rushed it." He shrugged. "It may sound weak, but I can't do better than the truth."

"Besides, it wouldn't really have helped us if you had come with us then," Hector said thoughtfully.

"Uh, once more with clarity?" Alice requested.

"Kirdja's ancestors told him you would be key in bringing me and my nephew back together," Hector explained. "But you hadn't met him then, and never would have if you hadn't gone with the others who showed up. Maybe that was what the ancestors intended all along."

Alice pursed her lips. "Could they really know enough to set up something like that?"

"Limited precognition," Hector reminded her.

Kirdja nodded. "They might not have understood how it would all play out, but they might have sensed it was important to be there to lose one battle in order to win the war."

Alice considered the answer. *It's not really all that different from my own belief that the Wonderland Effect tends to manipulate events to put me where I need to be. For that matter, there's nothing to say that both conjectures aren't right.*

She turned her attention to Hector. "So this all really hinges on whether or not your story is true. Can you prove you're Julio's uncle?" Hector nodded eagerly and scrambled for something in his back pocket. "Slowly!" Alice warned him.

Hector halted, then slowly resumed extracting his wallet from his pocket. "I have pictures of me and his family together. It's not really proof, *senorita*, but it's the best I can do for now."

The Duchess' frog footman appeared beside Hector and extended one hand. "Let him bring it to me," Alice instructed, and Hector readily gave the wallet to the amphibian. The footman flipped it open, confirming that it contained nothing more menacing than debit cards and identification as he conveyed it to Alice.

She accepted it and quickly scanned the photos in their plastic sleeves. Julio was not in all of them, and several of the ones he did appear in did not show Hector. But three did show them together, along with a couple that could only be Hector's sister and her husband. One showed the group at an amusement park, another at a picnic.

The last one showed Julio, his parents, and Hector posing around a painting of a young man walking away from the viewer in a street scene. Behind him, store fronts were dirty and showed weathered signs and a couple of boarded up windows. But in front of the young man the shops looked prosperous and well-kept. Even the man himself seemed caught in the middle of a transformation; the old, ratty sneaker on his back foot was replaced with a shiny black dress shoe on the forward one, and a crisply pressed pair of slacks was replacing the worn jeans from there to just above the knee. The picture filled Alice with a sense of optimism. Beside the canvas, Julio held up a blue ribbon triumphantly.

Alice folded the wallet and handed it back to the footman to return it to Hector as her looking glass blinked out of existence. "All right, I guess I'm convinced. Heaven knows I'm going to need help, and it isn't likely to come from anywhere else."

She pulled the force field generator from her fanny pack and attached the power cord. "Elaine's last name is Kilkarni. She runs Prometheus Academy, located just outside Boulder City," she told her new allies.

"Excellent. I have a friend who runs a charter plane service. I'll give him a call and we'll be ready to leave in about an hour," Kirdja said.

"That's not going to be enough time to get me much of a charge on this thing," Alice said, plugging the force field's cord into an outlet. The lights immediately dimmed, and Alice looked around in surprise. "Wow, it really sucks it in, doesn't it?" She turned her attention to the controls and used her fingernails to spin a tiny knob to the left. As she did, the lights slowly brightened, returning to their full radiance when the dial was set to about a third of its maximum setting.

Hector gave the unobtrusive device a calculating look. "I hate to think how fast the dials on the electric meter are spinning right now," he said.

Kirdja chuckled as he rose to go pick up the phone. "It's in a good cause. Once I've booked our flight, we'll have a bite to eat and discuss just what we'll do once we arrive."

CHAPTER THIRTY-NINE

"The First Casualty of Battle..."

Alice glided through the cool night air above Prometheus Academy. She had managed to convince Kirdja and Hector that stealth was their best option to get things moving their way at the school, and her current size of just three inches offered their best chance to communicate with the students and remain undetected. The only drawback was that she had to leave the force field generator behind, along with the other contents of her belt pouch. Once she shrank an object, she could not shrink it further. Consequently, the generator was now taller than her and heavier than her diminished strength could lift.

She tried not to let the loss of the protection bother her. It wasn't easy given her memories of Elaine's lightning bolts and fire balls, but she kept reminding herself that the protection only lasted a short time, and she was far more likely to be returned to space to suffocate in any event.

So let's REALLY focus on not letting Elaine see us.

It had been easy to set up her initial approach to the school. Once the plane was within sight of Boulder City Municipal Airport, which lay to the southwest of the town, Alice had summoned her looking glass to bail out to the corresponding skies above Wonderland. A second transition placed her close enough to the school to reach the dormitory before her glide path intersected the ground. She still had nothing like pin-point control over her spatial displacement when she passed through the mirror, but the more she attempted to control the direction and magnitude, the better she was getting at it.

Alice had come to realize she could sense...something. The best label she could come up with was waves, though she had no idea what they were composed of. The sense was subtle; she had never noticed it before, when she was trying to anchor herself in one spot during her transitions. Furthermore, the waves came at irregular intervals, from all directions, like water surging about in a lagoon during an earthquake. But she was often able to anticipate a wave going in the direction she wanted, and time her transition to ride it to a greater or lesser degree.

As she drifted down to the windowsill of the room she shared with Sarah, Alice did her best to mimic the flight pattern of a sparrow. The rooftops of Prometheus Academy sported any number of odd metal projections. If any of them were sensors to track objects in the air above the school, there had to be loopholes in their programming to keep whoever monitored them from being driven crazy by false alarms. Alice's size alone would probably allow her to slip through the hypothesized sensor net safely, since it would likely be prioritized to scan for flying people or vehicles, but she thought she might still be mistaken for a remote controlled drone. To play it safe, she tried not to present a series of movements that would look too odd compared to a small bird's flight.

As soon as she landed, Alice rested the tip of the nail she carried on the sill and leaned the head against the window pane. A shrunken plastic shopping bag hung on her left arm, holding half of a normal-sized peanut. She extracted it, holding it like an oversized sandwich, and took a bite to trigger her growth. When she had doubled her height, she stopped and picked up the nail.

Sarah was sitting at her desk, listlessly moving the mouse about as she stared at her computer screen. Alice was relieved; getting in would have been much more difficult if Sarah had been asleep, or worse still, out on an astral excursion. Alice tapped sharply on the windowpane with the nail to get her roommate's attention.

Sarah glanced curiously about until she zeroed in on the source of the sound, then scrambled excitedly to the window when she caught sight of Alice on the ledge. She quickly unlocked the window and heaved it up to let Alice in.

"Where have you been? You were gone when I got up this morning. At first, I just figured you needed to get an early start on something, but when you didn't turn up and no one had seen you by lunchtime, I started to get worried."

"It's been an interesting time, and not in a good way," Alice replied as she stepped off the window sill and glided gently to the floor. "But I don't have a lot of time to repeat myself. I need you to go and get Miranda and your brother and bring them back here. Tell Miranda to invite Min Ki. Don't let anyone else know about this, or tell anyone else you've seen me, and I mean anyone. Can you do that for me?"

"Uh, sure, but... No, nevermind, you'll explain when we get back." Sarah ran to the door.

"Don't run. You can't afford to draw attention to yourself," Alice called softly, yet urgently, to her.

Sarah took a moment to compose herself and offer Alice an acknowledging thumbs up before she opened the door just wide enough to slip through before it closed.

Alice ate the rest of her peanut to regain her usual size, then sat on her bed to wait. She wanted to get the word out to the rest of the students as quickly as possible, but gathering all of them together at once would be too likely to draw attention from the staff. She was going to have to trust her friends to spread the information to the others. She had another matter that required her attention as well, and she was anxious to attend to it. She believed she had a pretty good idea what was hidden behind the security door.

427

Within a few minutes, the door opened and Scott entered. He closed the door behind him as Alice rose from the bed. They came together with a hug and a quick kiss in the center of the room.

"Where have you been, and what happened to your neck?" Scott asked as he caught sight of the bruises on her throat.

Alice shook her head and embraced Scott again, her ear pressed to his chest so she could hear the reassuring rhythm of his heart. "Wait. We'll get through this quicker if I only have to explain it once. Just hold me for a minute, please?"

She could sense his impatience for answers in the tension in his body, but after a moment she felt him relax slightly. She closed her eyes and gave herself up to drinking in every sensation she could – the warmth radiating from him, his scent, accented by spices from his favorite body wash, and the sensation of his breath whispering through the hair on top of her head. They stayed there until the door opened again, and she reluctantly released him.

"I'd say 'get a room', but it looks like you already did," Min Ki said with a grin as he lead the others through the door. "Ow," he added as Miranda smacked him in the shoulder with the back of one hand as she swept past him to catch Alice in a hug of her own.

"Sorry my boyfriend has no manners. I'm working on it."

"Never mind," Alice said, "we've got more important things to worry about." As she let go of her friend, she gestured to her bed and the desk chairs. "Have a seat, everyone. I've got news, and most of it's terrible."

Alice remained standing as the others found places to get comfortable. "Okay, so yesterday I noticed something about the robots that attacked the school. I didn't say anything initially because I didn't want to raise potentially false accusations against Ms. Teresi until I had a chance to check things out."

From there, she filled her friends in on the series of discoveries and events her investigation had lead her through, enduring frequent interruptions for questions. It amazed her to think all of it had unfolded in less than twenty-four hours; it felt like a week.

There was a long silence when she finished as the others digested her news. Finally, Min Ki looked up at Alice and asked, "So how do we beat Elaine?"

"We don't. To use LaRonda's expression, we're getting the hell out of Dodge. I need you all to spread the word to the other students. We all need to be out of here before dawn."

"But I thought Kirdja's ghost pals said you can beat her," Min Ki objected.

"If you believe them, and that's a pretty big 'if'. They said I'm capable of it, but I have no idea what I could do to her," Alice corrected. "Maybe I'll figure it out somewhere down the line, but for now there's no percentage in a fight when flight is so much easier and effective. Besides, even if I do beat her, there's no telling what the cost will be."

"Where are we going to go?" Scott asked. "If we go to anyone's home, Elaine will find us pretty quickly. Not to mention we don't have much money."

"Kirdja and Hector hadn't been able to find Elaine and this place until they managed to meet me. Hopefully, Elaine will have just as much trouble finding Kirdja's place. We'll go there to start. And that brings us to you," she said, facing Min Ki.

"Huh? What do you mean?"

"I didn't invite you here just because you're dating my best friend," Alice explained. "You're also Julio's best friend, and reuniting him with his uncle is what brought Kirdja into this whole business in the first place. I've hardly had any interaction with Julio, so I don't know if he'd listen to me. So I'd like you to ask Julio to do you a favor."

429

"Like what?"

"Ask him to run into town and pick up a package. Tell him, oh, a friend of the family offered to stop off in town on their way to Las Vegas or something. Tell him they just called from the parking lot at the Coffee Cup, and he needs to get there quick."

"The Coffee Cup isn't open this late," Min Ki objected.

"I know that, but hopefully Julio doesn't. If he does, tell him your friends agreed to wait there for half an hour before they give up and leave. The important thing is to get him to go. Tell him anything necessary to make that happen."

"Is it really that important?" Min Ki asked.

"Look, as near as I can figure from what happened with LaRonda, being confronted with something directly related to suppressed memories tends to break the mental block," Alice explained. "The problem is that it's debilitating. I guess it takes time for the mind to reintegrate the old memories and identify the fake ones as garbage. If Julio has a hard time with it, I want him away from here when it happens. If he winds up comatose for a few hours or something, it had better not be when we need to move him. Besides, it's not fair to him to put him through that in front of everyone else."

"Well, since you put it that way, okay."

"Thank you. Trust me, you're doing your friend a big favor," Alice said. As Min Ki let himself out, she turned to her best friend. "Miranda, I need you to start quietly spreading the word among the other students. Min Ki can help you once he sends Julio on his way. Make sure everyone's ready to leave no later than 3:30. There will be a small charter bus waiting beyond the rear school gate past the loading dock to take us all away before any of the staff are awake."

"Aren't you going to be telling anyone else your story? I mean, you are the witness, after all," Miranda said as she paused, one hand on the doorknob.

"I'll meet up with you all before we leave and try to deal with any skepticism anyone feels about what I've discovered. But right now I need to stay out of sight, plus I need Scott and Sarah to help me with a rescue mission. Elaine kidnapped my mom and sister, disguised as Oglethorpe, and I'm pretty sure I know where they are. We're not leaving them behind. Plus, if Elaine didn't kill Julio's parents, they might be there, too." Miranda nodded her acceptance and left.

"Why would she kill Julio's parents?" Sarah asked.

"My guess? They told her they wouldn't be sending Julio here and she wouldn't accept 'No' as an answer," Alice replied.

Sarah looked at Scott with sudden, fervent intensity. "I'll bet that's what happened to Mom and Dad," she said.

Scott rubbed his forearm, his eyebrows drawn together. "What do you mean? It was just a car crash."

"Maybe not. Dad was always a careful driver. It wasn't like him to run a red light like that. You were there. Do you remember anything unusual?"

"What? No, it wasn't--"

"Think!" Sarah said, pacing excitedly. "It might have been something really subtle. I bet there's a dozen ways Elaine could have caused the crash!"

"She didn't!" Scott objected.

"You can't be sure of that," Sarah countered. "I'm going to make her pay for ripping our family apart like this, just you wait and see!"

Scott halted Sarah by stepping in front of her and grabbing her shoulders. "Listen to me. You go up against Elaine and you're going to die. For nothing! I won't let you do that."

"You don't know everything she's done. It would fit in with everything we've learned about her."

"It would, but you've got to believe me, she didn't do this."

"How do you know?" Sarah challenged, her voice raised in frustration.

"Because it was me!" Scott shouted back.

Sarah stopped struggling to get loose from Scott's grip, staring into his face in horror. Then she wrenched herself free, taking a step back. Scott's arms remained stretched out toward her for a moment before dropping listlessly to his side. Sarah licked her lips and shook her head, her eyes filling with tears. "No, you wouldn't do something like that. You couldn't!"

Scott stood with head bowed, eyes closed and fists clenched uselessly. When he spoke again, his voice was low and threatened to break repeatedly. "I wouldn't," he agreed, "not on purpose. It was a stupid accident. But that doesn't change the fact that it was my fault."

Sarah stared at her brother, her breath coming in short, rapid bursts. "Tell me," she demanded.

"We were on our way to pick you up from tennis practice so we could all go to dinner," Scott said as tears started sliding down his own cheeks. "I was in the back seat, playing around with my vibration jet power. I was keeping the force way down and modulating the frequency. I could kind of sense that I was closing in on a tone that would do something unusual. Mom told me to knock it off because the sound was annoying. I...I should have listened to her."

"So what happened?" Alice prompted when he fell silent.

432

"You remember the last attack I used on Kirdja at the construction site? That's when I discovered it. I accidentally let the beam intersect Dad's head just as I locked in on the frequency, and he just collapsed. That's why he ran the light, and the semi smashed into the car. I'm so sor--"

Sarah slapped him across his face, cutting off his apology. "You idiot! Why didn't you tell me this before now? I have a right to know why!"

"I know. I know. I just couldn't. I... didn't want you to hate me." Scott finally looked up at his sister, long enough to look into her eyes and say, "But I'd rather have you alive and hating me than let you try to take on Elaine."

Sarah spun away from him and smashed a fist into the wall. It left a smear of blood behind, layered over a slight indentation in the surface. Scott reached out for her shoulder, but she shrugged him off. "Leave me alone," she growled. "I can't deal with you right now."

Scott stepped back, head drooping in defeat. Alice stepped up beside him and rested one hand on his shoulder. She leaned in, giving him a quick kiss on his cheek, and tasted the saltiness of his tears on her lips as she whispered in his ear. "She'll come around; it's just a lot to take in at once. But I need her right now if we're going to rescue anyone. The room next door is empty. Wait there and I'll join you in a few minutes." Scott nodded mutely and left.

Alice guided Sarah into a chair and gently took her by the forearm to look at her hand. She snatched a couple of tissues from a box on the desk and started blotting at it so she could assess the damage. "How does your hand feel? It doesn't look like anything's broken, aside from the skin across a couple of knuckles."

Sarah sniffed and looked at the scraped up skin dismissively. "I'll be fine. I've had worse out on the BMX track." She took a deep

433

breath and let it out in a rush. "Okay, you've got some plan in mind. Fill me in."

"You sure? You just got blindsided with a major emotional bomb."

"That's why I need to do something to take my mind off it," Sarah replied.

"That's what I wanted to hear," Alice said, grasping Sarah's shoulder encouragingly. "I need you to act as a scout for us. If Elaine does have prisoners on the top level of the administration building, we need to know how many and how to get them out. Take a look behind the door and see if it's easier to open from the inside. If it isn't, we're going to have to take the noisy approach, and that means we'll have less time to get clear once we start."

"Gotcha. Give me a minute to birthday suit up."

A minute later, Sarah leaned out the wall of her room and examined the open area between the dorms and the administrative building. It was almost 11:00, so she was not surprised to note that no one was loitering about. She flew across to the top floor opposite and eased her astral body through, prepared to pull back immediately if she encountered Elaine or any of the staff. However, she made it through the stairwell, hugging the ceiling to avoid the security camera Alice had warned her of, and the hallway leading to the security door without seeing any sign that the area was occupied.

She approached this door cautiously. Whatever secrets Elaine harbored lay just beyond this doorway, and Sarah was certain that she had employed every safeguard she could come up with to keep them safe. What if she had some sort of super science device that could disrupt an astral form? But her fear proved unfounded and she passed through with no trouble. It was only once she was on the other side that it occurred to her that she could have gone through the walls and avoided the portal altogether in light of her concern. She resolved to do better in the future.

She looked around quickly. What light was available came from doorways further along the hall and was barely enough to allow her to make out details around her. She was at the end of a corridor with institutional linoleum tiles making up the floor. The walls were some pale color and bare of any decorations. The most prominent feature was a keypad similar to the one she had seen outside. Exiting would be no easier than gaining entry in the first place. Sarah supposed that made sense if this area served as a prison.

She floated down the hallway, glancing through open doorways as she went. There was an office and what looked like a chemical lab, followed by a medical examination room. The hallway ended in a heavy door in the left-hand wall secured with a magnetic lock and another, smaller, keypad. This door had a narrow, vertical window set into it towards the unhinged side. The area beyond was in darkness. Sarah passed through quickly, conscious of the passage of time.

As she had expected, the next area contained six detention cells. She could barely make out the steel gates in the light from the window in the door; the darkness in the cells themselves was impenetrable.

"Mrs. Casey, are you here?" she called. At first there was no response, but when she called again she heard a grunt, as if someone had been startled into wakefulness. A moment later lights came on as she heard movement in the first cell to her right. Looking in, Sarah could see two cots, a toilet, and a sink. A middle-aged woman was sitting up on one of the cots, and a smaller figure stirred feebly under a blanket on the other, apparently a child who was still asleep.

"Who are you, and why aren't you wearing any clothes?" the woman asked as Sarah approached the door of the cell. Then she gasped

435

in shock as Sarah entered the enclosure, passing through the bars effortlessly. "Oh, no, not another one. Go away, I'm not cooperating."

"Mrs. Casey? You've got it wrong. I'm not with Elaine, or Oglethorpe. My name is Sarah; I'm a friend of your daughter."

"You know Alice?" The woman sounded hopeful now. "How on earth did you find us? I don't even have any idea where we are."

"You're at Prometheus Academy. Alice and I attend school here with a bunch of other empowered students, but we just discovered Elaine's secret. We're leaving, but don't worry, we intend to take you with us."

"Thank heavens! Do you really think you can get us out?"

"Leave it to us. We're having to make things up as we go, but Alice has been searching for you and Samantha for weeks. She's not about to abandon you now that we've found you."

Mrs. Casey nodded. "So what happens now?"

"I'm going to go tell Alice I've found you. We'll make a plan and be back to get you out in a couple hours. We don't want to tip our hand before our ride gets here, okay?"

Mrs. Casey looked worried. "That will seem like ages, but I guess it makes sense." She paused, then said, "Tell Alice I'm sorry."

"Sorry for what?"

"She'll know. Just tell her for me."

"All right. I'd better go. Don't worry, we'll all be out of here before you know it."

Sarah clasped the prisoner's shoulder reassuringly, eliciting a look of surprise from Mrs. Casey, who hadn't expected this type of interaction from an insubstantial girl. Then she floated back through the bars and checked the remaining cells, which were all empty. Then she floated back through the door at the entry to the cell block and into the corridor leading to the security door with the keypad.

Sarah knew she could just fly out the side of the building and return to Alice with her news, but she wanted one last look at the door by the elevator. Now that it was certain they'd need to come through it, she wanted to see if she could find any way of opening it quietly.

However, she wasn't very far along the corridor at all when she heard a faint chime and the door began to slide open. To her surprise Miranda was standing there, looking scared and unhappy. She heard a boy's voice, and darted aside into the medical examination room before she could see who it was with Miranda and be seen in turn. But she listened intently.

"--can't leave her out there spreading Elaine's secret through the whole school now, can we?" the voice, which Miranda suddenly realized belonged to Regis, was saying. "We'll have to keep her here until Elaine can come decide what to do with her."

"I get that," Levi replied. "But why did you send Kip off before we brought her here?"

"He has to locate Min Ki before he lets the cat out of the bag. Once he's attended to, we can drop in and visit Alice. I'll bet her boyfriend and his bratty sister will be with her, so we'll want to play it cool, like we're coming to her for confirmation of what we've heard. Then the three of us will overpower them and bring them here too."

"That's a lot of students to go missing in a school this small," Levi observed.

"No problem. Elaine will just wipe the memories for most of them, and we can come up with some explanation for whoever is left. Miranda here probably just got homesick; couldn't cope with being a norm among the empowered, right?"

The group was moving down the corridor as they talked, and Sarah realized they couldn't help but see her when they passed the open door, but she didn't want to leave Miranda until she knew what they intended to do with her. Glancing around quickly, her gaze settled on a syringe lying on the counter. Quickly, she reached out to touch it, then vanished as her astral body bonded with the object.

She was just in time. To her surprise, Regis forced Miranda into the examination room, then shut the door once he and Levi were also inside.

"Sit down and keep quiet," he told Miranda, gesturing to the exam table. At first, she looked like she intended to resist, but Levi held up a hand, suddenly covered in flames. Miranda took the hint and perched on the end of the table.

Dropping the flames and his hand, Levi turned his attention to Regis and said, "So you were the first person she told about all this?"

Regis smiled, shrugging in false modesty. "What can I say? I'm just lucky, I guess."

438

CHAPTER FORTY
Collision Courses

Hector put the bus in neutral, switched off the engine, and let it coast down a slight incline toward the delivery entrance to the academy grounds. When the forward momentum had fully played out, he put it in park and set the brake. "Well, here we are," he said. He turned in the seat to face the front seat across the aisle. "How are you feeling?"

Julio looked at his uncle, a grim smile on his features. "A little wobbly, but I'll be fine before long. Then I'll be ready to take this place apart, along with anyone who tries to get in my way."

Kirdja rested a hand on the boy's shoulder. "Patience. If all goes well, we'll be leaving quietly. We don't need to fight to win."

"Tell that to my mom and dad," Julio said heatedly. "I can't believe that bitch killed them and had me believing they abandoned me. That's not something I can let go unanswered."

Hector clenched his hands in frustration, staring at them as he recalled Julio's report once the youth had regained his memories. He told them Elaine had lured the Zarzosas to the school for a tour with the promise of a full scholarship. After the tour was done, though, Julio's parents decided that the school wasn't a good fit for their son, and declined Elaine's offer.

At that point, Elaine dropped her pretense of powerlessness, locked the door to her office remotely with a button hidden beneath her desk, and informed Julio's parents that he would be attending the school

439

regardless of their wishes. When Mr. Zarzosa remained defiant, Elaine teleported him away.

Serena, Julio's mom, responded in force, striking Elaine with a lightning bolt. Elaine collapsed, and Serena quickly went to check on her, probably hoping to learn what had happened to her husband. But as she crouched next to her, Elaine reached out, grabbed her by one forearm, and squeezed. Julio heard the bones in her arm snap over Serena's cry of pain. Serena gave her opponent another jolt, but Elaine seemed to absorb it with even less effect then the first time, and then her own fingers crackled with an electrical charge. But rather than use it on Serena, she simply pushed her away, gestured again, and Serena disappeared.

The entire attack had taken less than a minute. Julio was so shocked, he hadn't even tried to run before Elaine teleported behind him, grasped his head between both hands, and dropped him into a trance to begin the process of editing his memories. In addition to blocking his access to the events that had just transpired, she had modified several incidents relating to his parents' reactions to his abilities, and then magnified their importance in his mind so they negatively colored Julio's recollections of what had been a healthy and happy home life.

"We will settle accounts," Hector told his nephew, "but after we get the others to safety. Undoing all of her work here is just the start."

Julio looked his uncle in the eye, assessing his words. Finally he said, "All right, I'm going to hold you to that."

♠ ♣ ♥ ♦

Kip found Min Ki as he reached the landing to the second floor of the dorms. "Hey," he greeted the other boy casually. "I just saw Miranda. She was knocking on Kasie's door and looked pretty freaked out. She told me to find you. What's going on?"

"Man, Alice just got back, and she dropped a huge bombshell. Elaine's been lying to us! She's got a bunch of powers, including shape-shifting. She's actually Oglethorpe, or I guess I should say Oglethorpe is one of her disguises."

"No way! And you actually believe her?"

"Well, yeah," Min Ki replied, though he seemed uncertain for a moment. He shook his head and looked back up at Kip. "Even if you don't believe Alice, you can't deny something weird is going on here. Alice thinks we should all get out of here, and if there's even a chance that she's right, I agree. We can sort out the rest later. Right now we've got to warn the others."

The two boys had been walking along a hall and had reached a doorway leading to a series of dorm rooms. Kip gestured for Min Ki to lead the way. As he stepped through the doorway, a strong gust of wind slammed into him from the side and Min Ki's head smashed solidly into the door frame. Kip caught him as he slumped, unconscious, and heaved him up over his shoulder.

"Sorry, dude, we have other plans," Kip said as he carried his classmate away.

♠ ♣ ♥ ♦

Sarah was frustrated. Miranda needed her help, and Alice and Scott needed to know that there were students actively working with Elaine. But she could not leave without first reassuming her astral form, and that would alert Regis and Levi that their duplicity was known. There was no telling what they might then do to Miranda before she could get back with help. So she just sat there as a syringe on the counter, waiting for an opportunity and trying to learn as much as possible about Elaine's plans by observing and listening to her minions.

Regis disconnected from the call on his cell phone and grinned at Miranda. "Good news," he taunted. "You get to live. Elaine's going to edit your memories. You'll recall coming here and watching Alice's powers go to her head. You'll go home convinced she turned on you, belittling you for being a powerless inferior, so you probably won't even care when you hear about her death. So everyone wins. Except Alice, of course."

Miranda's face paled. "I don't want to remember my friend that way, and I'm certainly not going to stand by and do nothing while you try to kill her."

"Not my problem, and not your choice," Regis responded.

"So where is Elaine, anyway?" Levi asked.

"Rousting LaRonda and Houston out of bed to help with containment. We've got the job of picking up Alice, Scott, and Sarah."

"Three against two," Levi observed. "Not the best odds. Scott's vibration blasts could make it a tough fight."

"You worry too much," Regis sneered. "With my luck, we'll mop them up--"

He was interrupted by the sound of the chime on the security door. Regis crossed to the exam room door and opened it to look down the hall. A moment later he backed up and opened the door wide to allow Kip to stagger in with Min Ki draped over his shoulder. Miranda quickly vacated the exam table, and Kip dropped his burden on it.

"Whew. That little runt gets heavy after a while," Kip said, stretching to ease the muscles in his back and arms.

"What did you do to him?" Miranda asked hotly, doing her best to look Min Ki over for signs of trauma she could treat.

"Relax, sweet cakes, he'll be fine. I just introduced his head to a door frame."

"Knew you couldn't take him in a fair fight, so you had to hit him from behind?" Miranda mocked. "Yeah, that sounds about your speed."

"What, that little wimp? I'd mop the floor with him any day of the week."

"Can it, you two," Regis snapped. "Levi and I have a job to do, so you," he indicated Kip, "get to babysit our guests here."

Sarah mentally tensed for action. The syringe she was animating was full of some clear liquid. She had no idea what it was, but if she and the prisoners were left alone with Kip, she would fly the needle into him and see what effect the contents had on him. Then she could revert to her astral form and deal with whatever happened. In a fair fight, she might not have much of a chance against Kip, but in this circumstance she could hit him while he couldn't land a punch on her in retaliation. Add her martial arts classes from the Y into the mix, and she felt pretty confident that she could put him down for the count if it proved necessary.

She eased the plastic sheath off the collar that held it in place over the syringe's needle as Regis and Levi moved toward the door, but it opened before they got there to permit a much younger version of Elaine than Sarah was used to seeing to enter the room.

Alice paced nervously in the room she shared with Sarah. The other girl's body lay on her bed while her astral form was off getting the lay of the land on the top floor of the administration building. Alice put it down to her current mood that she looked more like a coma patient than someone merely asleep. After ten minutes with no sign of Sarah's return, Alice couldn't stay there any longer. She slipped out of the room and went next door to see how Scott was doing.

The answer, as it turned out, was 'not well'. He sat on the one piece of furniture that Alice had not moved next door when she and Sarah had decided to share a room, because there was already a window seat there. He was slumped forward, his head resting in his hands, almost at the level of his knees. Alice quietly crossed the room and sat beside him, resting her hands on his back and one leg.

"She's never going to forgive me," he said. "Not that she should."

"Hush," Alice murmured. "I'll admit you haven't done yourself any favors by hiding it from her for so long, but she'll come around eventually. You're family. You need to stick together."

"You really think so?" Scott asked, finally looking up at her.

"Yeah, I really do," Alice answered. She took the hand nearest hers and gave it a reassuring squeeze as she made small circles on his back with her other. "Just give her time, let her work through it, and most of all, let her be angry."

Scott didn't answer, so they just sat there for a minute, sharing the silence. Alice marveled at how quickly the wheel had turned. *Just half an hour ago it was him comforting me. I guess love really does make us stronger.*

Finally, she gave him a firm pat on the back and stood up. "Come on," she said. "Sarah will be back from scouting Elaine's secret lair by now. Let's see what we're up against."

♠   ♣   ♥   ♦

Regis tapped lightly on the door to Alice's room, then opened it when there was no response. A quick scan as he and Levi entered revealed only Sarah, asleep on her bed.

Or was she asleep? It was certainly late enough that most students should be sleeping, but Sarah was fully dressed and lying on top of her covers. Regis approached her, noting that she was breathing

444

normally. But she remained totally unresponsive when he lifted a hand, prodded her shoulder, and finally, slapped her lightly across her cheeks.

"She's out there somewhere, probably getting ready to cause us problems," he told Levi. He pulled out his cell phone, quickly redialed the last number from the phone's memory, and waited for Elaine to pick up.

"Hello? Alice and Scott aren't here, and Sarah's apparently out flashing people somewhere, which can't be good for us. What do you want me to do?"

Elaine suddenly appeared next to Regis, looked at Sarah's body on the bed, and gave a sigh. "Honestly, I really have to do everything myself." She picked up Sarah, snapped, "Find Alice and Scott, immediately," and vanished.

♠ ♣ ♥ ♦

Min Ki groaned and opened his eyes. He was lying on an exam table, and Miranda was standing by his side, holding one of his hands. He put his free hand up to his face, cautiously exploring the extent of the damage his skull was already informing him of in great detail. "What happened?" he asked.

Miranda hooked a thumb at Kip, who Min Ki now noticed leaning against the counter at the other end of the room. "Captain Cowardice cold cocked you. He's working for Elaine, along with Regis and Levi."

"Don't get any bright ideas about suiting up, either," Kip said. "Your armor might protect you, but your girlfriend here could easily get damaged in a scuffle. No one wants that."

"More to the point," Miranda said, casting a dark look Kip's way, "Elaine is here. She just popped out, but she could be back any second. You're in no shape to take her on, even if you did squash this annoying ant."

Kip scowled, but before he could come up with a rejoinder, Elaine appeared holding Sarah. Seeing Min Ki was awake, she ordered, "Get up. If you can't stand, you can use the chair in the corner."

Though he was actually beginning to feel much better, Min Ki made a show of relying on Miranda's assistance as he got up and made his way to the chair. Elaine laid Sarah's body on the exam table, looking at it thoughtfully.

"What?" Kip asked after a minute of this silent contemplation.

"Hmm? Oh, I was just wondering. Sarah's ability is truly amazing. What do you think? If the body dies, would she hang around as a perpetual ghost, or simply blink out like a light?"

♠　♣　♥　♦

Alice stepped back into her room with Scott just behind her, then pulled up short in surprise at seeing Regis and Levi there. Casting a glance at the empty bed, she asked, "Where is Sarah?"

"We didn't--" Levi began.

"We don't know," Regis cut in smoothly. "We just came in a moment ago looking for you. Min Ki gave us some wild story about you returning, claiming that Elaine is Oglethorpe. We figured he was smoking something, but we came to find out what's really up. Nothing, I assume."

"You assume wrong," Scott informed him.

"No kidding? That's a pretty outrageous claim. How sure of this are you?"

"Elaine's been hiding her powers from us all, including her native ability to duplicate others'. I personally saw her shape shift into Oglethorpe, then she tried to kill me."

"O-kay," Regis said. "That's pretty conclusive. So what do we do about it?"

"Sarah was scouting Elaine's secret lair on the top floor of the administration building. There's a keypad on a security door I couldn't get through, so she was going in astrally. Her body was here when I left. You say it wasn't when you got here?"

"No," said Levi.

"She must have found something really urgent, couldn't find us, and went to try to deal with it on her own. We've got to get over there and help," Alice said.

"Let's go," Regis said.

"But we still can't get through the door," Scott said.

"Leave that to me," Regis replied.

♠ ♣ ♥ ♦

"Well, there it is," Alice said, indicating the door and the keypad. "So what's the plan for getting us in?"

Regis removed a small plastic box from his pocket and shook it suggestively, producing a rattling sound. "I'm feeling lucky. I think this will do the trick."

"What's that?" Scott asked, looking over Regis' shoulder as he flipped open the case.

"Gamer's dice," Regis answered. "With my power, I find them useful for finding the best option among a number of choices in a wide variety of situations. This one is a ten-sided die. Now watch me work."

Regis turned to the keypad and rolled the die in the lid of the carrying case. He punched a 7 into the keypad and rolled the die again.

Scott and Alice exchanged doubtful glances. "It can't really be that easy, can it?" Alice whispered.

"I guess we'll see," Scott replied.

During their exchange, Regis had added a 2 and a 6 on the keypad. He rolled the die again, pressed the 4, and then the Enter key. The door slid open with a soft chime. He gestured grandly for Alice and Scott to precede him, then flipped the case closed to return it to his pocket. The others stepped cautiously through the doorway, moving towards the far end of the brightly lit hall as silently as possible. Regis fell in at the rear of the procession and the door slid closed.

Alice peeked through the open doorways into an office and a lab, then moved on when they proved to be empty. The two remaining doors in the hallway were both closed, though one had a vertical slit of a window, through which light streamed to illuminate a bare strip of paint on the opposite wall. Even though this one was further away from her, Alice decided to investigate it first, since she wouldn't have to open it to get a sense of what lay beyond.

Peering through the narrow viewport, she whispered excitedly, "It's a cell block, but I can't see past the side walls to see who's in there. Regis, can you use your dice to get through this door, too?" Then, in her mind's eye, Alice saw Regis once again enter the 4 on the first door's keypad and then move decisively to the Enter key. "Uh, Regis, how did you know how many digits were in the code for the security door?"

She turned to see him standing beside the other door, one hand already on the knob. "Nice catch, Alice, but a little too late, I'm afraid." With no further hesitation, he pushed open the door to the examination room. "We're all here now, Elaine. What do you want to do with everyone?"

Elaine appeared in the doorway, a seemingly genuine smile on her lips. "Alice, there you are, and none the worse for wear, apparently. You simply must tell me how you survived."

Alice just glared at her silently, her mind scrambling desperately for some means of dealing with the threat before her, and coming up blank. *Damn Kirdja's ancestors. Why couldn't they have just told me what I need to do?*

Elaine tilted her head to one side, unconcerned with Alice's obvious hatred of her. "Well, perhaps a bit later, then. Don't just stand around like a bump on a log, come in." When neither Scott nor Alice moved to obey, Elaine dropped her smile and snapped impatiently, "Oh, just admit you're beaten and get in here. I have several of your friends here who won't enjoy a chance to see the stars as much as you did, so there's no point in delaying the inevitable."

Alice glanced at Scott, then dropped her gaze to the floor and shuffled forward.

CHAPTER FORTY-ONE
Prometheus Aflame

Even though the exam room was larger than normal for this type of facility, it was beginning to get a little crowded, with one mad overlord, a comatose body, four prisoners, and three henchmen all competing for space.

Not to mention a useless witness in a syringe. Sarah thought. *I've got to do something, but what?*

Elaine apparently agreed with Sarah's assessment, because she clapped her hands for everyone's attention, not that she didn't already have it. "All right, this just won't do. I need space to work. Regis, you and the boys take these three," she indicated Scott, Miranda, and Min Ki, "to the cells. Alice and I have some things to discuss."

Elaine turned to the students being herded out the door. "And lest any of you think about making trouble, don't forget I've still got Sarah's body here. I don't have to tell anyone what happens if there are problems? Good. Now move along. Memory alterations take time, but we'll have you back in classes with nothing more than the recollection of a bout with the flu to trouble your thoughts."

When the others had left, Elaine leaned against the door with one shoulder. "Now let's see, where to start?"

"How about with why you're walking around openly looking young and trampy?" Alice suggested.

"Hmm, I see recent experiences have done nothing to teach you any manners," Elaine said. "But if you must know, it will help when

I start altering your friends' memories. A few unbelievable elements added to the real memories will help the mind classify them as dreams, making it easier for the false memories to supplant them. Plus, I just prefer looking this way when there's no compelling reason to play a different role. But you're trying to divert me. You know perfectly well what we need to discuss."

"You mean your demand that I give you the Boojum? My answer hasn't changed."

"But circumstances have. You have chosen to make my secrets public, and that's very dangerous information to have. If you don't want your friends to pay the price for your snooping, you'll do as I say."

"You wouldn't! They're too valuable to you as pawns on your chessboard."

"You've seen how easily my memory alterations can be circumvented. Truthfully, the trick is only useful to gain a little more utility from an asset. That's why I use it sparingly. If a subject recovers memories at the wrong time, tremendous harm can be done before I can rectify the situation. Now give me the Boojum."

"That's not happening," Alice replied.

"My patience is wearing thin." Elaine turned and held out one hand toward Sarah's body on the table. "You know, I was just thinking earlier that Sarah might well be able to survive as a ghost if her body were to die. Shall we put the theory to the test?"

"Wait!" Alice shouted. When Elaine simply looked at her, she slumped in defeat. "All right, I'll do it. But I'll need something to send the Boojum after."

"Excellent. I'm so glad you've decided to start being reasonable," Elaine purred. "And a victim for your predator shouldn't be a prob--"

452

Elaine cut off as the building shook, badly enough that both she and Alice had to take a step to keep from being thrown to the floor as they heard cries of shock and concern from the others in the hallway.

"What is the meaning of this?" Elaine spat, but they were staggered by another quake, and cracks appeared in the ceiling, accompanied by the sounds of breaking brickwork and sparking electrical connections, before Alice could even consider a reply. As the lights flickered, Alice staggered over to the exam table and started trying to move Sarah's body. Before she had managed to do any more than pull it into a sitting position, there was a final jolt and the ceiling disintegrated as the lights finally went out for good.

Alice screamed and tried to shelter Sarah's body with her own, a task made all but impossible due to the fact that Sarah was sitting higher and hunched into a forward-leaning, boneless sprawl. Light returned, almost as bright as before, but whiter; it seemed to come from floodlights mounted on the roof of the other campus buildings and reflected off scattered clouds that had moved in over the school. Sarah, from her viewpoint in the syringe, saw Alice look up in amazement as the entire south-eastern corner of the building's roof peeled up and flew away, though not far judging by the sound of falling material striking the ground outside.

Sarah looked up to the suddenly open sky and saw two men who could only be Hector and Kirdja hovering in the air. Hector looked tired, as if he had just moved a mountain, which Sarah figured wasn't too far from the truth.

Elaine was furious, but rather than waste words, her hands glowed as she prepared to hurl fire and lightning at the interlopers. Sarah decided she wasn't going to get a better opening, so she quickly hurled the cap over her syringe's needle away and zipped the hypodermic across the room and into Elaine's side, pumping its entire contents into Elaine's system at once.

♠ ♣ ♥ ♦

Alice felt a muted sense of relief upon seeing Hector and Kirdja coming to her rescue. But Elaine remained a force to be reckoned with, and Alice interposed her own body between that of Elaine and Sarah in hopes of preventing her foe from carrying out her threat. This proved needless, as she saw Elaine stagger and clutch at a wall for support, though Alice could not determine what had happened to inconvenience the older woman. She had no doubt Elaine would recover in a few seconds, though.

She barely had a chance to register that Elaine's ability to act was impaired before Sarah blinked into existence at the older woman's side. "This won't last," Sarah said, "so make the most of the opportunity. I'm going to rally the troops."

A line of fire arced up into the air, directed at Hector, from the other side of the wall that separated the room Alice was in from the corridor, though without the roof Alice wasn't sure the terms applied. The flames splashed harmlessly off Hector's force field far enough from his body that he probably only felt uncomfortably warm. But almost instantly, the flames tracked to the left, away from both flying figures, and Alice heard Regis yell, "No, I think they're here to help!"

That statement made no sense, but Alice couldn't afford the time to think about it. She quickly summoned not only her card soldiers, but also most of the chess pieces. "Fan out and break anything that looks even remotely fragile, but don't attack any people." she directed them.

As they started to go forth in search of things to hit, Alice snagged a red bishop and hauled him next to Elaine. "I've got a special job for you. Her you can hit as hard and often as possible." If it had been anyone else, Alice would have felt guilty for giving such an order, but in this case, she knew she was only buying herself precious seconds. At least, that's what she told the accusing voice in her head to make it shut up as the bishop set to work with his mace.

♠ ♣ ♥ ♦

Hector was surprised to discover that he was reveling in taking action. Julio had made a quick turn at scouting the grounds shortly after they had parked the bus, and had seen Kip carrying Min Ki across the quad into the administration building. Hector's nephew had shown good judgment; he had remained in hiding until he saw Regis and Levi lead Alice and Scott into the same building, then returned to the bus to report on recent developments.

A hasty discussion had followed, during which they decided that it was likely that the rescuers had not only lost the element of surprise, but were being deceived or picked off by Elaine's forces. They decided the situation called for decisive measures, and subtlety was discarded in favor of shock and awe tactics.

Now, Hector ignored the blast of fire that momentarily licked at his defenses, before the boy who directed it at him was more or less tackled by another standing in the remains of the hallway he had revealed when he peeled a huge section of the roof off the building. It had been tricky, making sure he wasn't losing his psychic grip on any piece big enough to hurt someone if it happened to fall on their head, but he had managed to keep control.

An area to his right was a cell block; he had managed to uncover three cells with his initial effort, one of which was occupied. It wasn't his sister and brother-in-law, as he had hoped, but the sight of the prisoners gave him a surge of hope.

He gently scooped up the woman and little girl in his power and raised them up to join him and Kirdja. As they came close, he called, "Are there any other prisoners in the cells?"

"The woman shook her head and said, "No, it's just the two of us." She gestured between herself and the girl.

455

Hector tried not to let his disappointment show. He had known the odds were slim going in, and there were more than enough people here in need of help to make the effort worthwhile. He scooped up all the remaining children, leaving only Elaine and Alice's minions, many of them disappearing into sections of the building still covered by the intact portions of the roof.

As he moved the entire airborne group away from the damaged building, flames started leaping up from the wall of the exposed hallway, where the fire projector's power had set it alight when his friend pushed his arm to the side. A moment later, a muffled explosion sounded from deeper within the building, and thick gray smoke started pouring from the edge of the hole.

"Sounds like some of the card soldiers had a little too much fun in the chemistry lab," Alice called.

Hector started moving himself and his charges towards the rear entrance to the school and the waiting bus, though it occurred to him that driving out might not be an option any longer, now that Elaine was alerted to their presence. Even so, it would be easier to load the kids in the bus and then fly it out than to maintain a telekinetic grip on over a dozen individuals. However, he had not gone far before the school's PA system came to life with an electronic thump and a squeal of feedback.

"Good morning, Prometheus! This is Sarah Thompson, with breaking news. Elaine is Oglethorpe, and has been trying to brainwash us all against the government. Guess she wants a super-powered army. In other news, classes have been canceled. Meet in the quad for departure on a permanent field trip. We may have to fight our way out of here, because Regis, Levi and Kip are on Elaine's side. This is not a joke! Move it, people! Oh, and don't trust any teachers or staff."

Hector decided to land everyone in the quad to wait for the other students. It seemed like a good idea to keep folks together, rather

456

than leave one group unprotected by the bus while coming back for the others.

♠   ♣   ♥   ♦

Julio and Constance were in his room when Sarah's announcement came over the PA. He had slipped back into the school shortly after Kirdja and Hector had started their assault. Hector had originally wanted to keep Julio with them, but the speedster argued that his abilities were useless while he was suspended in empty air. Kirdja agreed with him, so Hector reluctantly allowed Julio to take on the task of rousing the students who were still asleep.

"Damn, I should have thought of the PA system," Julio said. "But at least everyone should be awake now."

"You still would have needed to come back for those," Constance said, indicating the aluminum tonfas he had just pulled from their cloth storage bag. She carried her own wooden pair tucked through the cloth belt at her waist, along with a pouch of throwing stars and the staff she held in one hand. "Still, it wouldn't hurt to reinforce Sarah's message, in case anyone thinks this really is a prank."

"Right. I'm faster, so I'll take the upper floor. You check the rooms on this floor, and we'll meet at the stairs."

Without waiting for confirmation, Julio dashed off, running as fast as he dared in the enclosed space of the hallways. It was far from his top speed, but he dashed up one side of the hall and then down the other, shouting, "You heard the lady, everybody out!" and using his tonfa to splinter door frames as he rushed past. He figured the sound of cracking wood served to underscore the urgency of his call, and he certainly didn't care about the damage at this point. It would have been more efficient to just visit the rooms that a student actually lived in, but Julio wasn't close enough to most of them to know for sure which rooms they had selected.

He arrived back at the top of the staircase leading to the ground floor. Constance was already there, with Julianna and Autumn by her side. Esme hurried down the hallway to join them, and a moment later Andrew clambered down the stairs Julio had just descended.

"Is this everyone?" Julio asked in surprise. "You'd think there would be more people asleep this time of night."

The sound of more falling rubble came from the quad. "That sounded like a building collapsed," Esme gasped.

"I'll check it out," Julio called, already halfway down the stairs. "Come on, we'd better get out in case the dorms are next."

♠　♣　♥　♦

As soon as Hector set everyone down, Regis grabbed Kip and Levi by the wrists. "Okay, before the telekinetic can figure out we're the ones working with Elaine, we've got to get to work. We've got to make sure no one leaves. Get over to the rear gate and disable that bus, then herd anyone who tries to head in that direction back here, got it?"

"Yeah," Levi replied. "but what are you gonna do?"

"What I do best," Regis replied. "Now go."

♠　♣　♥　♦

Scott ran to Alice as soon as he was in control of his movements again. "Are you all right? What did she do to you?"

"I'm fine," she replied. "Elaine threatened me, and Sarah. I was on the verge of giving her the Boojum when Hector ripped the roof off. Come on, let's see what we can do to neutralize Regis and the others working with Elaine."

She had taken only a step, however, when a loud crack echoed across the quad from the direction of the administration building. Alice looked and saw the bishop's head sailing up into the air, and then down to bounce along the ground. "Uh oh, looks like Elaine's recovered. Keep an eye out for trouble."

The words were no sooner out of her mouth than a mechanical arm suddenly smashed outward through the exterior brickwork in the middle of what Alice had always taken to be a poorly executed attempt at a decorative frill on the back of the administration building. Four-foot wide ridges of brickwork stuck out from the back of the building at each end, with two additional ridges spaced evenly between. Each ran from the ground all the way to the roof, with only a slight curvature at the top to relieve the severity of the lines they cut. But now they were revealed as camouflage as robots smashed their way out into the chill night air. One robot broke its way out at the level of each story in each section. The robots on the second and third stories jumped to the ground, one to either side, as the one at ground level simply stepped forward. Two more emerged from each cavity, for a total of thirty-six of the nine-foot tall mechanoids.

"Uh, I spy, with my little eye, trouble with a capital T," Scott said. "These look tougher than the first batch, too."

Alice could see he was right. The first batch of robots, from the *faux* Air Force base, had been light weight and relatively flimsy, because they had needed to fly with the help of the jet packs. It occurred to her that they had probably also been intended to instill the students with a false sense of superiority when they went down relatively easily.

By contrast, the units facing them now were heavily armored, and the arm and leg pieces were thicker. Even the joints were protected by plates as much as possible without sacrificing too much in the way of mobility. All of these units seemed to have come equipped with arm-mounted blasters rather than conventional guns, as well.

Alice turned to Miranda. "This might be a good time for you to try to get to the bus."

"What about you? You're not exactly bullet-proof either."

459

"I'll be useful, indirectly. Don't worry, though. I'm not about to try to take on one of those things by myself."

"Okay, but you'd better make it to the bus before we leave, or I'm going to give you a scolding like you've never had before," Miranda said, trying to keep her tone light. Then she dashed off towards the corner of the gymnasium where the cafeteria complex and the loading dock were located.

♠　♣　♥　♦

Kip and Levi landed next to the bus as the miniature tornado Kip had conjured to carry them in its eye dispersed. "Okay, it's all yours, dude," Kip said.

Levi pushed open the door, which had not been locked, and climbed a couple of the steps so he could see the length of the bus. Then he sent a wave of flames washing down the length of the vehicle from his hands and quickly exited the way he had come. The entire passenger compartment was ablaze in moments, including the drivers seat and controls.

"Ain't no one driving away in that tonight," Levi said with satisfaction. "Let's go play sheepdog." He stepped in front of Kip again, and the whirlwind formed once more to carry them off to their next encounter.

♠　♣　♥　♦

Elaine appeared in front of her mechanical goliaths. Coach Lane appeared by her side a moment later, and LaRonda stomped around the corner of the admin building just after that, wearing her full battle gear, including the helmet. "Playtime's over, kids. Tell your new pals to stand down before I have to do something we'll all regret," Elaine ordered.

Min Ki suited up, an eager light in his eyes. "We can do this, guys. Who's with me?"

"Easy, bud, we agree with you, but we can't go off half-cocked," Scott replied. "We've got to have a plan."

A blur of motion and rush of wind interrupted Scott. By the time he turned to follow Julio's progress, the speedster had already attacked several of the robots, striking at knees and wrists as opportunity presented itself. However, the results for his efforts were lackluster, as the reinforced joints took the blows with little more than small dents in the armor plates.

"Or we could just go for it," Alice observed as the first blaster bolts traced Julio's path.

♠ ♣ ♥ ♦

Constance and the group exiting the dorms had an excellent vantage from which to see Julio's attack. "Anyone who considers themselves noncombatants, make for the loading dock and get to the bus," she said. "The rest of you, let's go."

She dashed ahead, heedless of who chose to follow her.

♠ ♣ ♥ ♦

Miranda pulled up sharply at the corner of the cafeteria. She could hear something approaching along the other side of the building, so she crouched down behind a picnic table. Suddenly, a glow and the crackle of flames was added to the sound of fast-moving air, and the source of it all rounded the corner. Kip and Levi once again stood in the eye of a miniature tornado, easily twenty feet off the ground. Levi's left hand was held out low to one side, pumping a never ending stream of fire into the twister, forming a truncated cone of heat and light that ended a foot above the ground.

The boys and their creation swept on past her position before they could spot her. She watched them move toward her friends, thinking furiously. There had to be something she could do. Her gaze

461

turned to the lunchroom and inspiration struck. Miranda scrambled to her feet and ran for the door.

♠ ♣ ♥ ♦

Hatter appeared at Alice's side in response to her silent summons. She had already recalled the chess pieces and cards from the administration building, which was already showing open flames from several locations in any case, and deployed those that remained between her friends and Elaine's robots. About a third of the chess pieces failed to reappear, meaning they had been killed out by the results of whatever mayhem they had caused earlier. Only three of the card soldiers remained, though Alice supposed that was to be expected, since they were highly flammable.

"This is shaping up to be downright unpleasant," Hatter observed as the robots began to advance.

"You took the words right out of my mouth," Alice replied.

Hatter patted the pockets of his coat, searching. "Did I? I wonder what I did with them."

"Focus, Hatter, I need your help. Coach Lane is trying to teleport into position to hit Julio, and he's going to get the timing right pretty soon. I need you to slow him down. Then start working on the robots. If they're being controlled remotely, maybe we can use the time differential to disrupt communications."

"Egads, that's brilliant," Hatter replied. "Leave it to me."

Meanwhile, Scott had taken to the air, and was directing blast after blast of vibratory energy at the robots. He had learned his lesson from the first encounter, though, and eschewed hovering for continuous swoops and climbs, with frequent changes of direction. This made his own discharges miss the mark with some frequency, but those that did land disrupted the delicate electronic circuits of his foes. The robots thus affected frequently stopped moving for fifteen or twenty seconds before lurching back into motion. Twice, he was able to follow up shots that temporarily stalled robots with head shots that put them down permanently.

Min Ki was also active, though he was having a hard time of it. His punches, powered by the sudden stretching of his psychic armor, were powerful, but not very effective. The robots' armor was designed specifically to deflect blunt force attacks, so he was reduced to following Scott's lead and trying to strike at heads. Even then, it took him several blows to sufficiently batter a robot into an immobile metal sculpture, and in the meantime he took several direct blaster hits, though his armor seemed to protect him from most of the force of each attack.

"Ches, you're up!" Alice yelled.

"You bellowed?" Ches said calmly from behind her.

Alice didn't even spare him a glance as she surveyed the battlefield. "I think you're the natural choice to play a little cat-and-mouse with Coach Lane. Take him down, but don't kill him if you can help it." The Tweedles appeared as Alice gave Ches his orders. She simply gestured towards the wonders of battle spread before them and they dashed off to have fun.

LaRonda was next to Elaine, using the blasters on her armored forearms to take pot shots at targets of opportunity. Several chess pieces had already met their ends from her withering fire, and Alice feared she would need to keep her promise to free her from Elaine's control once more.

To Alice's right, Kirdja was hurling his light spears at anything that came within range, and an occasional shade blinked into existence to take the brunt of an attack directed against him. It was hard to tell what Hector was up to in all the confusion, but Alice thought he was probably using his telekinesis to pummel robots with pure psychic force. All in all, the battle was not going too badly.

Then Scott dodged to his left, right into the path of a spear Kirdja had just released. It took him high on the right shoulder, and he tumbled from the sky. The relative silence as his flight power cut out was filled by Alice's scream of anguish. *Of all the bad luck...*

Alice halted in her rush towards Scott's position. He was moving, so her immediate fears were relieved, but that last thought had alerted her to a danger she had lost track of in the chaos.

"Where's Regis?" she yelled, her eyes searching the quad frantically.

♠ ♣ ♥ ♦

Julio cheered silently within his head as he finally managed to batter through the defensive plates and break the knee joint of one of the robotic attackers. It had taken far more passes than he had anticipated, but at least he finally had confirmation that he could be effective against the behemoths. He changed course to orient on his next target.

Then a blazing blue star whipped past him. The missile curved in flight, finding the gap between the joint covering and the elbow on another robot's arm. The next second, the covering was blown off by a muted explosion.

"Take it out, Julio!" Constance yelled from behind him, even as several more blue streaks struck successive targets in a line.

Julio flashed Team Red's leader a grin as he flashed past the robot with the exposed elbow joint and smashed the joint into immobility with a single blow.

♠ ♣ ♥ ♦

Hatter finally managed to maneuver himself close enough to where Houston appeared after one of his teleports to slow the passage of time for him as he tried to strike at Julio.

464

Having achieved his first objective, Hatter moved on, dodging through the chaos to approach a cluster of the robots. He succeeded in altering their time rates as well. However, after observing them for several seconds, he determined that they were not being controlled remotely, because they continued to show as much purpose in their movements as previously.

Unfortunately for him, Hatter had failed to keep adequate track of the other robots, and he was caught flat-footed by a shot from another unit as he turned to find more subjects for his time manipulation. The shot caught him dead center in his chest, driving him back several feet to topple backwards onto the ground. Smoke wisps drifted from the wound for a moment, then Hatter disappeared.

♠ ♣ ♥ ♦

Houston cursed to himself as he did his best to fend off the thrice cursed Cheshire Cat. Everything was moving much faster than it should, and he realized Alice had turned Hatter's time manipulation power against him. As a result, his biggest advantage, of being able to appear next to targets unexpectedly for a quick attack before blinking away, was severely compromised. It became a struggle to think far enough ahead to anticipate where his targets would appear with sufficient accuracy, and even when he did appear close enough to attack, his victims were often able to dodge the blow.

As he teleported to the edge of the quad near the hedge to regroup, he found himself under attack by the cat. Fortunately for him, the feline was keeping his claws retracted, restricting himself to blunt force attacks with his heavy paws, but even that hurt. His attempts to teleport away were matched blink for blink by his adversary, who moved quickly enough to smack him again before he could move himself to yet another location.

He was on the verge of teleporting away from the battle entirely when time lurched back into normality. *Right,* he thought, *now*

465

we'll see who has a better grasp on teleportation tactics. Here, kitty, kitty...

♠ ♣ ♥ ♦

Julianna, Esme, and Andrew attempted to make their way across the quad to the loading dock. They were far enough away from the robots that they did not draw much fire, but they still had to be cautious, because the mechanoids' fire was unnervingly accurate. Fortunately, the robots' movements included a tell of sorts, a sudden shuddering halt in the tracking of the arm relative to its target, just before each shot was fired, so as long as they remained alert they had a second to dodge if they thought they were in the sights. Even so, there had been a couple of very close calls when a shot from a source one of them had not noticed missed only due to random body movements.

Suddenly, their progress was blocked by Kip and Levi riding a flaming whirlwind. Julianna tried to dodge around them in one direction, and the twister moved to head her off. Esme headed the other way, and Levi took advantage of a momentary drop in the wind velocity to launch a fireball to drive her back. "Yippie-ti-yi-yay, losers. Just to let you know, your bus is toast, so why don't you just sit down and wait for Elaine to finish with the others. Trust me, you'll be better off working with her."

Esme shook her head stubbornly and made another attempt to dodge around. Levi responded with a fiery whip, lashing her across her leg. She collapsed, crying out in pain and beating out the embers left on the edges of the rip that had appeared in her jeans. Julianna hurried to help, as Andrew's face contorted in anger.

"Leave her alone!" he shouted. Andrew was suddenly at the center of a hemisphere of quasi-darkness, where the light from the roof-mounted lamps and the fire from the twister were much less effective. The next second, a laser beam shot out from his fingertips, striking Levi in his side. He responded with his own howl of pain, and the fire faltered and went out.

Levi was not out, however. Though obviously hurt, he turned his attention from examining the damage where his right hand clutched his side to the light manipulator. "Congratulations, you just won a trip to a barbecue, and you're the main course," he snarled.

♠ ♣ ♥ ♦

Kirdja reached Scott's side and knelt to check his injury. As the boy started to try to rise, Kirdja grasped him by his uninjured shoulder and gently restrained him. "I'm sorry for your injury, son. Please give me a moment to treat it."

"But the robots, and Elaine, they'll attack us if we stay here."

"Trust me, we'll be safe for a moment," Kirdja replied, and began chanting in a rhythmic language Scott did not understand. Ghostly tribesmen fended off attacks around them as Kirdja continued his invocation, and Scott's pain lessened.

♠ ♣ ♥ ♦

Houston had his bowie knife in his hand. Before Hatter slowed him down, he had restricted himself to using it against Alice's summonings. Elaine still considered the students valuable resources, and he had no intention of stirring her anger against him by killing off her charges.

The cat was another matter entirely, and now he was ready to draw him in and finish their little dance. He blinked away after taking another hit from one forepaw, then immediately spun about and thrust with his blade.

He had timed his attack well, though his aim was a bit off. Ches appeared next to him reared up on his rear legs, the better to batter him once again, and the blade slid easily between his ribs, sinking in to the hilt. But it missed his heart.

467

Ches brought his rear paws up, claws extended, and raked them down Houston's front. Cloth and flesh alike parted, leaving deep gouges in Houston's side and upper legs.

Houston cursed again, but retained enough concentration to port to the side and strike again. This time, he landed a lethal blow, and Ches fell heavily to the ground. Houston fell on top of him as his legs refused to support him any longer, then found himself directly on the ground as the feline disappeared.

♠ ♣ ♥ ♦

Miranda ran up beside Andrew, more than a bit out of breath. She pulled on his arm as Levi prepared to hurl a massive fire ball. "Come on, don't just stand there, we've got to move."

Andrew allowed himself to be lead, narrowly avoiding the worst of the heat as the fire ball impacted the ground where he had been standing. As he followed Miranda, he heard Levi urging Kip to give chase, and a voice calling "Where's Regis?", but he was unable to determine its source. Instead, he focused on the girl before him, who held something small and cylindrical in her hand. "Where did you come from?" he asked as they darted across the open ground.

Miranda ignored him, looking for something or someone in the midst of all the activity. Andrew decided she must have spotted it, because she suddenly took a straight path towards the dorms.

"Can you do something to slow them down for just a second?" she asked.

"Sure, just a sec," he replied.

"No, not yet! Wait until I tell you."

"All right," Andrew said, puzzled by her request, but willing to help her since she seemed to have a plan.

A few more running steps brought them within a lesser lit area in the lea of the dorms, and Andrew spied Regis crouched by the base of the wall. He stood as the duo arrived, totally unconcerned by their presence.

"What do you think you're--" he began, but Miranda gave him no chance to finish.

"Now, Andrew!" she yelled, simultaneously jerking the hand holding the cylinder towards Regis. Without waiting to see what she was trying to accomplish, Andrew turned back to Kip and Levi's fiery tornado, which was rapidly closing the distance.

Andrew raised his hands, and a bright flash of light burst into the faces of the approaching villains. Andrew's power prevented him from being blinded, but they had no such protection, and the tornado hesitated for just a second as Kip struggled to clear his vision.

A wracking cough and strangled cry brought Andrew's attention back to Regis, who seemed to be in the middle of some sort of fit or asthma attack. Miranda spun back in the other direction and hurled the entire cylinder at the tornado, which was once again moving forward.

At first, it seemed to have no effect, and Levi cracked his fire whip menacingly above their heads. "No place to run, now, losers! It's frying time!" He coughed once as a bit of smoke wafted into the twister's central area, then the whip flickered and faltered as both he and Kip were engulfed in thicker tendrils and began coughing. Soon tears were streaming down both of their faces, and a moment later the tornado and fire both lapsed completely and the boys crashed to the ground, where they continued experiencing great difficulty with the simple act of breathing.

Andrew looked at Miranda in confusion. "What was that?" he asked.

"Ground cayenne pepper from the kitchen," Miranda replied. "The effects won't last long, so I think we ought to make sure they're down for the count before they can recover." Then she kicked Regis in the head, apparently with a great deal of force and satisfaction, leaving him spread-eagled and unmoving.

"And that's what you get for not taking me seriously," she spat.

♠   ♣   ♥   ♦

Elaine stood back from the battle, assessing everything that unfolded. She occasionally struck a Wonderland creature that strayed too near with a lightning bolt, disrupting the conjuration. Alice was filling the area with as many of her companions as she could, though they did little save to distract her robots from attacking higher profile targets that actually posed a threat to them.

Still, Elaine was confident enough of the eventual outcome to devote most of her time to watching the students and noting how well or poorly they made use of their abilities. This was, after all, one of the primary reasons she had created the school in the first place. Once she had altered their memories, they would have no recollection of the night's events, but she would have a far better grasp of their capabilities.

So far, Julio, Constance, and Min Ki had managed to render eight of the new robots inoperable. But Elaine knew that Constance carried only twelve of her throwing stars, which she was charging and using to open vulnerabilities in the robots' defenses for Julio to exploit. Min Ki, after a poor showing initially, had come up with a more effective strategy. He would extend one arm of his armor and wrap it around the legs of an advancing robot, tripping it. Then, as it attempted to rise from the ground, he took advantage of the opportunity to aim a blow with his other fist into the relatively immobile head, smashing it into the ground. The pace at which he was taking his mechanical opponents out had increased significantly.

Even so, she expected he would go down before all of her robots were taken out of commission. The blaster bolts that hit him did have some effect, even through his protective shell, and the consequences of the accumulated damage were unavoidable.

Elaine became aware of an odd booming sound just before the rear doors of the administration building, the top floor of which was now fully ablaze, burst off their hinges. At first, she couldn't tell what the thing coming through the doorway was, but as it straightened she recognized the statue of Prometheus that had graced a pedestal beside the decorative archway over the school's main driveway until this evening. The bronze figure had been equipped with a gas flame that burned in a thick metal plate held aloft in its right hand. Disconnected from its fuel source, the flame had gone out, but this did not keep it from being effective. As Elaine watched, the statue, almost as tall as the robots themselves, stepped up to the nearest one and slashed at its head with the edge of the plate. Even Elaine's eyebrows raised as sparks flew, along with the top of the robot's head.

I haven't given Sarah enough credit, she thought. *She's just coming into her abilities, and she's already as effective as any student here.*

A window on the top floor of the dorms shattered into pieces, frame and all, and fell to the ground. Immediately afterward, Kasie flew through the opening, engulfed in the yellow aura of her flight power. Her emerald shield glowed at her left wrist, and she paused to scan the battlefield.

"Yeah, reinforcements!" Miranda said as she and Andrew moved back toward Julianna and Esme, who were attempting to meet them halfway.

Andrew looked worried. "Uh, not to be a wet blanket, but didn't we just knock out her boyfriend, who was working against us?"

Miranda slowed in her forward progress as she considered this fact. "Oh, damn."

Kasie finished her review of the scene and immediately took action. She extended her right hand, aiming the ring with star sapphires surrounding a diamond, and a beam of white light shot out, striking Min Ki between the shoulder blades. Min Ki was driven forward as if he had been hit by a delivery van. He bounced off the leg of a robot nearby, winding up flat on his back. His armor vanished, and he did not attempt to get back up.

"Min Ki," Miranda cried, and dashed towards the prone figure.

♠   ♣   ♥   ♦

Julio paused as he saw his teammate struck down by Kasie's attack. "Watch out," he called to Constance. "We've got to be careful until we can find a way to counter her."

"I can take her if you can make me an opening," Constance replied confidently.

"If you say so. Be ready," Julio replied and took off at top speed.

He dodged another white beam from Kasie as he closed the distance, then started running in a tight circle below the flyer's position. Kasie ignored him for a moment, electing to launch a trio of sapphire stars at Constance, after catching the other girl's blazing throwing star on her shield. That moment of inattention proved her undoing.

Julio stirred up his own twister with his tight circuit, flashing by the same point dozens of times per second. The force stretched upward, catching Kasie in its rotation. She spun in place, fighting to regain control. But in the few seconds it took her to regain her orientation and rise above the worst of the whirlwind's effect, Constance acted.

Constance had avoided Kasie's attack, using her staff to vault out of the path of the light-based missiles. As soon Kasie started suffering the effects of the twister, Constance took two running steps and leaped. Planting one foot on the shoulder of a robot in her path, she leaped again, changing her trajectory to intersect with Kasie as the other girl rose higher.

She struck Kasie in the back, driving the breath from the flyer's lungs. Her momentum carried them beyond the area where Julio's twister was even now dissipating as he ceased running. Before Kasie could recover, Constance locked her staff under her opponent's chin and pulled it tight, cutting off her air.

"I'd really recommend landing before you pass out," Constance suggested, whispering in Kasie's ear. "I can leap away, but you'd probably break a leg from this height, at the very least."

♠ ♣ ♥ ♦

Elaine decided that matters had progressed as far as she was willing to permit. Her resources, though vast, were not unlimited, and more than half of her robots were damaged. The students she counted among her allies were neutralized, and she considered the likelihood of seeing anything new and interesting from the other students still on their feet vanishingly small; it certainly wasn't worth the cost of allowing the conflict to continue.

Still, she needed leverage to convince the others of the futility of further resistance. Accordingly, she teleported behind Alice, grabbed her roughly by the shoulder, and blinked back to her previous position with her.

"Enough," she shouted, her voice filling the courtyard easily and drawing everyone's attention to her as the robots ceased their barrage of blaster fire. She shoved Alice to her knees, grabbed her by her ponytail, and pulled her head back, easily holding her immobile with her augmented strength. Her other hand crackled with energy, less than a foot from Alice's ear. "You've all performed better than I would have expected for children with as little experience as you've obtained, but unless you want to see your friend here die, you'll surrender now."

Scott pushed Kirdja away, though his shoulder still appeared to pain him slightly as he rose to his feet. "Alice said you've already tried to kill her at least once. Why should we think you won't do it anyway?"

"For one thing, she still has something I want. Besides, you're all more useful to me alive than dead, her included. Now that everything is out in the open, we can move ahead as a team once she gives it to me."

"I won't give you the Boojum," Alice replied. "And I won't support whatever mad schemes you're plotting. Do what you want; I'm done with you."

"Me too," Scott added. Across the courtyard, the statue of Prometheus nodded its head in agreement.

Elaine felt her irritation with these ungrateful whelps spike. She was prepared to offer them the world, and all they did was whine and dig in their heels. *Very well, I can wait a few years for a generation of empowered with more vision.*

She twisted Alice's head, forcing her to look at her. "I urge you to reconsider, dear. I don't doubt that you're willing to die rather than give me what I want. But are you ready to watch him die, instead?"

Lightning blasted across the open space, striking Scott in the chest. He collapsed to his hands and knees, then drew one arm in across his front, gasping in pain.

"The next shock will be sufficient to kill, Alice. So choose. Will you give me the Boojum, or would you rather watch him die?"

♠　♣　♥　♦

Alice stared in dismay at Scott, and knew she was caught. She could not allow him to die for her defiance, even knowing that Elaine might well kill them all once she had the Boojum anyway. At least if she did, Alice wouldn't be at fault for what happened to them.

Besides, what did it really matter in the end? Elaine had amply demonstrated that she could counter anything Alice or the others could bring to bear against her.

She was preparing to open her mouth to give in to Elaine's command when Marchie suddenly appeared beside Kirdja. Startled, she looked at him. Why was he there? She hadn't summoned him. What would be the point? He was the most timid of all her companions, and easily confused besides. He was the last of her allies she would think to bring into a fight.

Then, in a sudden, glorious flash of insight, she knew what she had to do. She had to give Elaine what she wanted in order to be free of her.

♠   ♣   ♥   ♦

Scott struggled to focus through the pain of the electrical burns across his chest. *Don't do it. Don't give in, no matter the cost.*

But to his dismay, he heard Alice reply, "No, don't do it. I'll...I'll give you the Boojum."

Scott looked up from the ground in disbelief, his heart heavy as he saw Elaine grasp Alice by her left arm and twist it behind her back painfully. "Excellent," she gloated. "I just need a good grip to duplicate the ability once you summon the Boojum - and to make sure you don't try anything."

Alice grimaced, trying to shift her position to ease the pressure Elaine exerted on her arm. "I won't. Look, here it is."

Scott saw the Boojum manifest a few feet in front of Alice, looking just as she had described it. It was a vague outline of some sort

475

of large bird, defined only by the distortion around the edges. It darted forward and lunged at Coach Lane, who lay hunched in a ball on the ground, huddled over his injuries. He cried out, then faded away in a matter of seconds.

"Yes! The Boojum is mine!" Elaine cried happily. But then she looked down at Alice in anger. "But you've cost me my best lieutenant. You'll have to pay for that." With a sudden, seeming careless twist, Elaine brought Alice's arm higher behind her back, and Scott heard the sound of the bone snapping as Alice screamed in pain.

"Now, I think I'll take this beastie for a little test drive," Elaine said. The almost invisible form of the Boojum appeared again, somehow sleeker and more menacing. It oriented on Scott, who looked to Alice. If he was about to be swept away to another reality, he wanted to take the memory of one last vision of her with him.

To his surprise, he saw that Alice was holding a garish, multicolored ceramic bowl full of sugar cubes in her right hand. Before he could properly take stock of that, Alice got her left foot under her, spun around, and smashed the entire bowl into Elaine's hip. "Time to take your lumps, you slithey bitch," she yelled.

Instantly, the Boojum turned from Scott to stalk Elaine. She stared at the shape, then reached down and grabbed Alice by the front of her dress and swung her before her like a shield. Alice gasped as her broken arm was jarred by the movement.

"No, get away from me," Elaine said to the Boojum. "You're mine, and I command you to get away."

The Boojum took another step forward, and Elaine moved to keep Alice between her and the nearly invisible threat.

"No," Scott pleaded. "Let her go."

Then the Boojum lunged.

Elaine moved swiftly, interposing Alice so that the beak seemed to close on Alice's shoulder, but it did Elaine no good. Both of the women cried out, and within a few seconds, both had faded from view, leaving Scott and the others to stare at the empty stretch of lawn next to the sundial.

CHAPTER FORTY-TWO

The Road Ahead

Three weeks later

A young girl walked down a nearly deserted street in the light of early morning. The few people walking about on the sidewalk in this run down street of dusty shops couldn't help but notice her. Her clothes were dirty and worn; they had not seen soap or water for some time. Her hair was matted and oily. Her movements spoke of exhaustion and probably, given her general state, hunger.

But this was not what drew curious looks her way, because the most unusual aspect of her appearance was a cast on her left arm. And what a cast it was! Though it looked as dirty and worn as the rest of her, the girl's cast was the most artistic anyone present had ever seen. Constructed primarily of red plaster, the brace was wound through with multicolored ribbons, adorned with the feathers of some sort of tropical bird, and had no less than four LED displays showing symbols of unknown origin, or simply blinking rapidly in complex patterns.

For her part, the girl ignored everyone. But as she rounded a corner and saw a sign painted on a store window, she seemed to take heart. She quickened her pace, almost running the last several yards to the door of South Seas Surplus, and, finding the door locked this early in the day, began knocking insistently and calling out "Hello? Anyone home?" at frequent intervals.

At last, her persistence was rewarded, and a dark figure in a light tan uniform appeared at the door. On seeing the girl, he hastened forward to unlock the portal and usher her inside.

"Alice," Kirdja exclaimed, giving her a hug of welcome. "Are you really here? It has been so long since the Boojum took you and Elaine away, we had all but given up hope."

Alice, tears in her eyes, clung to Kirdja. "You know me? Thank God, I'm home then."

Kirdja lead her through the shop towards the stairs to his apartment. "Yes, yes, of course I know you. Come, you look half starved. I'll fix you something to eat, and then you can get cleaned up if you wish."

"That sounds wonderful," Alice replied. "I wouldn't say no to that cot if it's still around, either. Do you know how to find the others?"

"Hush, there's time enough for all of that. We'll have the opportunity to swap stories after you've eaten and rested. For now, just conserve your strength."

Alice followed his advice and sat quietly as he prepared her a plate of eggs in his small kitchen, which she ate and chased down with a mug of *kava*. While she ate, he went downstairs and returned with a change of clothes. The camouflage uniform wasn't her usual style, of course, but she was more than happy to don it after a quick wash-up. A few short minutes later, she was stretched out on the cot, dead to the world.

♠ ♣ ♥ ♦

Alice awoke to late afternoon sunlight filtering in around the edges of the curtains. She visited the bathroom, then made a quick sweep of the apartment's other rooms to confirm that Kirdja was not there. She decided she wasn't hungry enough to take the time for another meal, but did grab an apple from a bowl before she headed downstairs.

480

As she neared the bottom of the stairs, she could hear voices in the store, but she couldn't make out any detail through the door. She assumed they belonged to customers, and so simply pushed on through into the store when she got to the bottom. The sight that met her eyes was unexpected, but pleasantly so.

Arthur and Meredith stood with Kirdja, speaking in low tones. Samantha was next to her mother, holding her hand. Conversation cut off so abruptly when Alice pushed open the door, she still had no idea what they had been talking about, nor did she care. The icing on the cake came as Samantha squealed with delight and pulled away from Meredith to run to her and engulf her in a hug stronger than Alice would have believed the six-year-old to be capable of.

"Sam! You're back," Alice said happily, returning the hug awkwardly. "I'm so gla----", Alice halted as her parent's rush to join the girls literally knocked her breath away. "Ow, careful, Dad, the arm's still a little tender."

"Sorry," her father said as he attempted to find a way to hug her without causing pain. "We've been so worried."

"Yes," Meredith added. "All during the fight, I was trying to keep Samantha and Sarah out of harm's way, and I nearly fainted when you and that wicked woman disappeared. I thought we'd lost you for good this time."

Kirdja stepped up beside them, placing a hand on Meredith and Alice's shoulders as if bestowing a benediction. "I'll leave you for a few minutes; you all have some catching up to do. But there are others waiting to see you, Alice." He walked toward the rear of the store and let himself out into the courtyard.

"Alice, wanna ice cream cone? There's a shop just down the street," Samantha said as soon as Kirdja was gone.

Alice knelt in front of her half-sister and rubbed the top of her head affectionately. "Maybe after dinner, squirt. You're a lot better than the last time I saw you."

"She says your dollie helped her," Meredith said, the confusion evident in her voice. "She said your dollie convinced her there was too much going on out here to miss."

"So you did get a copy of my mind?" Alice asked Sam.

"Yeah, it's much more fun than Dad's. It plays games with me sometimes."

"I hope you're not spending too much time in there," Alice said, tapping the side of Sam's head with one finger lightly. "People are much more fun."

"That's just what she said," Sam replied.

"Sam is getting therapy sessions as well," Arthur told Alice. "It may take a while to fully recover, but I think she'll be just fine."

"I'm glad," Alice said.

Further discussion was curtailed when the rear door opened again and four teenagers came rushing through. Alice found herself the victim of another group hug as Scott, Sarah, and Miranda all swarmed her. Min Ki was a bit more reticent, but he wore a broad smile as he yelled, "Welcome back!"

"What happened to you?" Sarah demanded. "It's been weeks. We were starting to think the Boojum really could unmake someone."

Alice disentangled herself from the group, hanging onto Scott's hand even after the others had moved back to give her space. "I've been world hopping," she replied.

"Why?" Scott asked.

"Trying to get back home, of course. I was way out there."

Miranda scrunched her face up in confusion. "Okay, you're going to have to give us a little more detail on that one."

There was a general chorus of agreement to this sentiment, so Alice took a deep breath and ordered her thoughts. "Well, you remember what happened just before Elaine and I disappeared?"

"Yeah, you hit her with a sugar cube to disrupt her power, right?" Min Ki said.

"Not quite," Alice corrected. "I hit her with the whole bowl of sugar cubes. A single cube will cause someone's powers to go haywire and turn against its owner for a few seconds. It disrupts their mental control over the ability. But the whole bowl is a much bigger shock to the system."

"So, what, you disrupted Elaine's control for an hour or so? She's got the mirror as well, so she should be back already. She's probably trying to track us down right now." Meredith said. Obviously, the others had brought her up to speed on events while Alice had been gone.

"No, in this case, I'm pretty sure I inflicted a permanent psychic wound. It's not physical damage to her brain; her regeneration would clear that up in a second, you see? Elaine's control of the Boojum is just gone. She's on a one-way tour of the multiverse, and she won't be able to spend enough time in any one reality to be much of a threat to anyone."

"But you got back," Sarah said.

"Yeah, as long as Elaine kept a hold of me, I got dragged along through every new transition. In a way, it's a good thing, because I started to realize that different worlds have a different feel."

"What do you mean?" Scott asked.

"It's hard to describe, almost like a new sense I never knew I had," Alice said, struggling to find the right way to convey her thoughts.

The only other world I had ever visited before was Wonderland, which is very similar to Earth. It just feels a little, uh, calmer? Lower energy? When I used my looking-glass, I would...tune it?...to that frequency without realizing that was what I was doing. I guess you could think of it as the default setting."

"And Earth was your default from there," Sarah said.

"Right. Anyway, as I got dragged through world after world with Elaine, I started to realize that all sorts of other sensations are mixed up in a world's signature. There's something almost, but not quite, taste, and texture, and sound, and other things I can't even give names. They all started changing the further out we traveled. By the time Elaine released me in the world where I picked this up," she gestured with the cast, "we were into pretty weird territory."

"Weird in what way?" Arthur asked, intrigued.

"Well, people still looked more or less like people, aside from a few differences in coloration," Alice explained, "but some physical laws were starting to drift from what we know. All this decoration on the cast served a function there. I'm not sure what, exactly, because we didn't speak the same language, but when they attached the feathers, my arm stopped hurting like they had thrown a switch. Pity it didn't last more than a couple of transitions after I left."

"So why did it take you so long to get home?" Miranda asked.

"The looking-glass can only travel so far in a jump, and the more factors that need adjusting, the less I can move each time. Sometimes it took a lot of thinking to remember how one of the sensations I always took for granted was supposed to be." She sighed. "Needless to say, the return trip took a lot longer than the outward leg of the journey."

Meredith walked over and kissed Alice on the forehead. "I'm just glad you made it back so I have the chance to tell you how sorry I am about everything. I was very unhappy when you were a child, and I tried to make you hide who you are. I was wrong."

Alice smiled. "Thanks, Mom." Turning to the others, she asked, "What about Prometheus? What happened after I got hijacked?"

"Well, there was a lot of mutual glaring at first," Sarah said, "but Regis and his crowd finally started talking to us and agreed not to try to stop us from leaving anymore. So we cleared out. I think Regis was having Kasie drop the robots in Lake Mead to hide them from the authorities, because we could already hear fire trucks on the way."

"Yeah," Min Ki chimed in. "It wasn't easy, but we managed to sneak away without anyone getting a good look at us. I think Regis and his crew, which included Julianna, by the way, left too. No one wanted to try to stick around and explain what had happened."

"Then what? Did everyone just go home? Can we find them again?"

"Some went home. Julio and Hector went off to reconnect, and I think Constance decided to tag along. We all came here to try to stay off the grid, though. We weren't sure how much fallout there would be from the fight, or if Elaine would be back."

"Well, that has to change," Alice said decisively. "Elaine was only able to manipulate us the way she did because we were so afraid of public reaction and tried to stay in the shadows."

"So what do you want to do?" Arthur asked.

"Isn't it obvious? It's time for us to go public."

A Word of Thanks

The Wonderland Effect is my first full-length work of fiction. I hope you've had as much enjoyment reading it as I have experienced in writing the story. If so, please help others discover the book by leaving a review on your favorite retailer's web site.

Follow Robert Here…or Here…or…

On the web: www.DispatchesFromWonderland.com
Email: Robert@DispatchesFromWonderland.com
Mailing list: Sign up for the mythical newsletter using the MailChimp option in the right-hand menus at Dispatches from Wonderland to be notified when The Wonderland Effect #2 starts posting on the site.
Twitter: @MHatter57
Facebook: https://www.facebook.com/WonderlandWebBook
Goodreads:
https://www.goodreads.com/author/show/14026014.Robert.Arrington

About the Author

Robert Arrington spends his days posing as an unassuming computer technician for a large law firm in Raleigh, NC. But by night, he transforms into a (hmm, how to put this politely?) unassuming writer of super heroes fiction. Not exactly the wisest career choice, but we deal with reality as it is.

He lives in Raleigh with his wonderful wife of thirteen years, Lucille, who has indulged this misadventure into the realm of writing and publishing with surprising good grace. When he is not working or writing, he can generally be found at home trying to help his children (Son, age 11, and daughter, age 9) with their homework and whatever else needs some attention.

The first draft of The Wonderland Effect was published as a web serial on Robert's blog, http://www.DispatchesFromWonderland.com. Check it out if you want to see what's coming up next for Alice and her friends, find advice for writers, or check out a small sampling of random weirdness. Sign up for the mythical newsletter (the MailChimp option in the right-hand menu bar) to be notified when The Wonderland Effect #2 starts posting.

<<<<>>>>